H. L. GOLD RESURRECTED

Selected Science Fiction Stories of H. L. Gold

By H. L. Gold
Edited by Greg Fowlkes

Includes the Special Preview of
THE BLOOD RED SANDS OF MARS
A Science Fiction Novel by Greg Fowlkes

H. L. GOLD RESURRECTED

Selected Science Fiction Stories of H. L. Gold

© 2012 Resurrected Press
www.ResurrectedPress.com

Published by Resurrected Press

This classic book was handcrafted by Resurrected Press. Resurrected Press is dedicated to bringing high quality classic books back to the readers who enjoy them. These are not scanned versions of the originals, but, rather, quality checked and edited books meant to be enjoyed!

Please visit ResurrectedPress.com to view our entire catalogue!

ISBN 13: 978-1-937022-43-3

Printed in the United States of America

FOREWORD

H. L. Gold is best known today for his tenure as editor of *Galaxy Science Fiction*, a magazine that he led from it's inception in 1949 until he retired in 1961. During that period he was as much responsible for shaping the face of science fiction as John W. Campbell, the editor of *Astounding Science Fiction* had been a decade earlier. He was responsible for publishing such stories as Ray Bradbury's "The Fireman" which was later expanded int *Farenheit 451*, Robert Heinlein's *The Puppet Masters* and Alfred Bester's *The Demolished Man*.

As an editor, Gold changed the emphasis from adventure and technology to examining the sociological and psychological impacts of science and technology. He also encouraged a satirical edge to the fiction that he published. Because he was willing to pay at higher rates and offer better contract terms, Galaxy became the home for many of the most prominent science fiction authors of the day.

However, before he became an editor, and for a number of years after, Gold was also a prolific writer of science fiction and fantasy. His philosophy of writing followed the same course that he was to espouse as an editor. Rather than focusing on technology and science, his focus was on people, how they would react in a situation, and how that situation would affect them.

His characters were almost invariably one of the "common man." Rather than the scientists and spacemen that typically populated science fiction stories, his characters were more likely to be barflies, out of work actors, Jersey shore concessionaires, or race track touts. Fellow writer Anthony Boucher claimed he was "almost the only s.f. writer capable of creating lower and lower-middle class background."

At a time when characters in the genre tended to be white Anglo-Saxons, Gold, himself Jewish, used characters of a variety of ethnicities, such as the black college student who performs in a sideshow or the Mexican chili stand operator in the story "The Enormous Room," the Cherokee from Oklahoma who made a fortune from oil wells and moved to New York to bankroll musicals in "At the Post," or the Jewish operator of a hot dog stand in "Trouble With Water." He had a facility for capturing the vernacular of everyday conversation in his writing that allowed the reader to view life from the character's point of view.

While the subject matter of many of his stories was common to the genre, alien abduction, problems and paradoxes with time travel, difficulties with adapting to alien environments, he always was able to give the story an unexpected spin that emphasized the humanity of his characters.

While many fans of science fiction will be familiar with H. L. Gold the editor, H. L. Gold the writer is less well known today. For this reason, Resurrected Press is proud to bring the reader this collection of some of his best stories in *H. L. Gold Resurrected*.

About the Author

Horace Leonard Gold (April 26, 1914-February 21, 1994) was born in Montreal, Quebec and moved to the U.S. at the age of 2. He wrote science fiction for the pulp magazines and for comic books before becoming editor of Galaxy Science Fiction, a position he held from 1949 until he retired for health reasons in 1961. In addition to writing numerous short stories and a collaborating on a novel with L. Sprague de Camp, he edited a number of science fiction anthologies. In 1953 he was awarded a Hugo for best science fiction magazine editor, as well as the Westercon Lifetime Achievement Award in 1975 and the Milford Award in 1987.

Greg Fowlkes
Editor-In-Chief
Resurrected Press
www.ResurrectedPress.com

Other Resurrected Press Science Fiction

Philip K Dick Resurrected:
The Complete Works of Philip K Dick

James H. Schmitz Resurrected:
Selected Stories of James H. Schmitz

H. B. Fyfe Resurrected:
The Works of Horace Brown Fyfe

Women Resurrected:
Stories from Women Science Fiction Writers of the 50's

Robert Sheckley Resurrected:
The Early Stories of Robert Sheckley

Edmond Hamilton Resurrected:
Classic Stories of Edmond Hamilton

Raymond F. Jones Resurrected:
Selected Science Fiction Stories of Raymond F. Jones

Everett B. Cole Resurrected:
The Short Stories of Everett B. Cole

Murray Leinster Resurrected:
Science Fiction Stories from the 1950's

Alan E. Nourse Resurrected:
The Works of Alan E. Nourse

Jesse F. Bone Resurrected:
Selected Stories of Jesse Franklin Bone

Harl Vincent Resurrected:
The Astounding Stories of Harl Vincent

TABLE OF CONTENTS

A Matter of Form

Originally Published in *Astounding Science Fiction*
December 1938

A Matter of Form

Gilroy's telephone bell jangled into his slumber. With his eyes grimly shut, the reporter flopped over on his side, ground his ear into the pillow and pulled the cover over his head. But the bell jarred on.

When he blinked his eyes open and saw rain streaking the windows, he gritted his teeth against the insistent clangor and yanked off the receiver. He swore into the transmitter—not a trite blasphemy, but a poetic opinion of the sort of man who woke tired reporters at four in the morning.

"Don't blame me," his editor replied after a bitter silence. "It was your idea. You wanted the case. They found another whatsit."

Gilroy instantly snapped awake. "They found another catatonic!"

"Over on York Avenue near Ninety-first Street, about an hour ago. He's down in the observation ward at Memorial." The voice suddenly became low and confiding. "Want to know what I think, Gilroy?"

"What?" Gilroy asked in an expectant whisper.

"I think you're nuts. These catatonics are nothing but tramps. They probably drank themselves into catatonia, whatever that is. After all, be reasonable, Gilroy, they're only worth a four-line clip."

Gilroy was out of bed and getting dressed with one hand. "Not this time, chief," he said confidently. "Sure, they're only tramps, but that's part of the story. Look . . . hey! You should have been off a couple of hours ago. What's holding you up?"

The editor sounded disgruntled. "Old Man Talbot. He's seventy-six tomorrow. Had to pad out a blurb on his life."

"What! Wasting time whitewashing that murderer, racketeer—"

"Take it easy, Gilroy." The editor cautioned. "He's got a half interest in the paper. He doesn't bother us often."

"O.K. But he's still the city's one-man crime wave. Well, he'll kick off soon. Can you meet me at Memorial when you quit work?"

"In this weather?" The editor considered. "I don't know. Your news instinct is tops, and if you think this is big—Oh, hell... yes!"

Gilroy's triumphant grin soured when he ripped his foot through a sock. He hung up and explored empty drawers for another pair.

The street was cold and miserably deserted. The black snow was melting to grimy slush. Gilroy hunched into his coat and sloshed in the dirty sludge toward Greenwich Avenue. He was very tall and incredibly thin. With his head down into the driving swirl of rain, his coat flapping around his skinny shanks, his hands deep in his pockets, and his sharp elbows sticking away from his rangy body, he resembled an unhappy stork peering around for a fish.

But he was far from being unhappy. He was happy, in fact, as only a man with a pet theory can be when facts begin to fight on his side.

Splashing through the slush, he shivered when he thought of the catatonic who must have been lying in it for hours, unable to rise, until he was found and carried to the hospital, Poor devil! The first had been mistaken for a drunk, until the cop saw the bandage on his neck.

"Escaped post-brain-operatives," the hospital had reported. It sounded reasonable, except for one thing—catatonics don't walk, crawl, feed themselves or perform any voluntary muscular actions. Thus Gilroy had not been particularly surprised when no hospital or private surgeon claimed the escaped post-operatives.

A taxi driver hopefully sighted his agitated figure through the rain. Gilroy restrained an urge to hug the hackie for rescuing him from the bitter wind. He clambered in hastily.

"Nice night for a murder," the driver observed conversationally.

"Are you hinting that business is bad?"

"I mean the weather is lousy."

"Well, damned if it isn't!" Gilroy exclaimed sarcastically. "Don't let it slow you down, though. I'm in a hurry. Memorial Hospital, quick!"

The driver looked concerned. He whipped the car out into the middle of the street, scooted through a light that was just an instant too slow.

Three catatonics in a month! Gilroy shook his head. It was a real puzzler. They couldn't have escaped. In the first place, if they had, they would have been claimed; and in the second place, it was physically impossible. And how did they acquire those neat surgical wounds on the backs of their necks, closed with two professional stitches and covered with a professional bandage? New wounds, too!

Gilroy attached special significance to the fact that they were very poorly dressed and suffered from slight malnutrition. But what was the significance? He shrugged. It was an instinctive hunch.

The taxi suddenly swerved to the curb and screeched to a stop. He thrust a bill through the window and got out. The night burst abruptly. Rain smashed against him in a roaring tide. He battered upwind to the hospital entrance.

He was soaked, breathless, half-repentant for his whim in attaching importance to three impoverished catatonics. He gingerly put his hand in his clammy coat and brought out a sodden identification card.

The girl at the reception desk glanced at it. "Oh, a newspaperman! Did a big story come in tonight?"

"Nothing much," he said casually. "Some poor tramp found up on York and Ninety-first. Is he up in the screwball ward?"

She scanned the register and nodded. "Is he a friend of yours?"

"My grandson." As he moved off, both flinched at the sound of water squishing in his shoes at each step. "I must have stepped in a puddle."

When he turned around in the elevator, she was shaking her head and pursing her lips maternally. Then the ground floor dropped away.

He went through the white corridor unhesitantly. Low, horrible moans came from the main ward. He heard them with academic detachment. Near the examination room, the sound of the rising elevator stopped him. He paused, turning to see who it was.

The editor stepped out, chilled, wet, and disgusted. Gilroy reached down and caught the smaller man's arm, guiding him silently through the door and into the examination room. The editor sighed resignedly.

The resident physician glanced up briefly when they unobtrusively took places in the ring of interns about the bed. Without effort, Gilroy peered over the heads before him, inspecting the catatonic with clinical absorption.

The catatonic had been stripped of his wet clothing, toweled, and rubbed with alcohol. Passive, every muscle absolutely relaxed, his eyes were loosely closed, and his mouth hung open in idiotic slackness. The dark line of removed surgical plaster showed on his neck. Gilroy strained to one side. The hair had been clipped. He saw part of a stitch.

"Catatonia, doc?" he asked quietly.

"Who are you?" the physician snapped.

"Gilroy . . . Morning Post."

The doctor gazed back at the man on the bed. "It's catatonia, all right. No trace of alcohol or inhibiting drugs. Slight malnutrition."

Gilroy elbowed politely through the ring of interns. "Insulin shock doesn't work, eh? No reason why it should."

"Why shouldn't it?" the doctor demanded, startled. "It always works in catatonia . . . at least, temporarily."

"But it didn't in this case, did it?" Gilroy insisted brusquely.

The doctor lowered his voice defeatedly. "No."

"What's this all about," the editor asked in irritation. "What's catatonia, anyhow? Paralysis, or what?"

"It's the last stage of schizophrenia, or what used to be called dementia praecox," the physician said. "The mind revolts against responsibility and searches for a period in its existence when it was not troubled. It goes back to childhood and finds that there are childish cares; goes further and comes up against infantile worries; and finally ends up in a prenatal mental state."

"But it's a gradual degeneration," Gilroy stated. "Long before the complete mental decay, the victim is detected and put in an asylum. He goes through imbecility, idiocy, and after years of degeneration, winds up refusing to use his muscles or brain."

The editor looked baffled. "Why should insulin shock pull him out?"

"It shouldn't!" Gilroy rapped out.

"It should!" the physician replied angrily. "Catatonia is negative revolt. Insulin drops the sugar content of the blood to the point of shock. The sudden hunger jolts the catatonic out of his passivity."

"That's right," Gilroy said incisively. "But this isn't catatonia! It's mighty close to it, but you never heard of a catatonic who didn't refuse to carry on voluntary muscular actions. There's no salivary retention! My guess is that it's paralysis."

"Caused by what?" the doctor asked bitingly.

"That's for you to say. I'm not a physician. How about the wound at the base of the skull."

"Nonsense! It doesn't come within a quarter inch of the motor nerve. It's ceria flexibilitas . . . waxy flexibility." He raised the victim's arm and let go. It sagged slowly. "If it were general paralysis, it would have affected the brain. He'd have been dead."

Gilroy lifted his shoulders and lowered them. "You're on the wrong track, doc," he said quietly. "The wound has a lot to do with his condition, and catatonia can't be duplicated by surgery. Lesions can cause it, but the degeneration would still be gradual. And catatonics can't walk or crawl away. He was deliberately abandoned, same as the others."

"Looks like you're right, Gilroy," the editor conceded. "There's something fishy here. All three of them had the same wounds?"

"In exactly the same place, at the base of the skull and to the left of the spinal column. Did you ever see anything so helpless? Imagine him escaping from a hospital, or even a private surgeon."

The physician dismissed the interns and gathered up his instruments preparatory to hurried flight. "I don't see the motive. All three of them were undernourished, poorly clad; they must had been living in sub-standard conditions. Who would want to harm them?"

Gilroy bounded in front of the doctor, barring his way. "But it doesn't have to be revenge! It could be experimentation!"

"To prove what?"

Gilroy looked at him quizzically, "You don't know?"

"How should I?"

The reporter clapped his drenched hat on backward and darted to the door. "Come on, chief. We'll ask Moss for a theory."

"You won't find Dr. Moss here," the physician said. "He's off at night, and tomorrow, I think, he's leaving the hospital."

Gilroy stopped abruptly. "Moss . . . leaving the hospital!" he repeated in astonishment. "Did you hear that, chief? He's a dictator, a slave driver and a louse. But he's probably the greatest surgeon in America. Look at that, Stories breaking all around you, and you're whitewashing Old Man Talbot's murderous life!" His coat bellied out in the wash of his swift, gaunt stride. "Three catatonics found lying on the street in a month. That never happened before. They can't walk or crawl, and they have mysterious wounds at the base of their skulls. Now the greatest surgeon in the country gets kicked out of the hospital he built up in the first place. And what do you do? You sit in the office and write stories about what a swell guy Talbot is underneath his slimy exterior!"

The resident physician was relieved to hear the last of that relentlessly incisive, logical voice trail down the corridor. But he gazed down at the catatonic before leaving the room.

He felt less certain that it was catatonia. He found himself quoting the editor's remark—there definitely was something fishy there!

But what was the motive in operating on three obviously destitute men and abandoning them; and how had the operation caused a state resembling catatonia?

In a sense, he felt sorry that Dr. Moss was going to be discharged. The cold, slave-driving dictator might have given a good theory. That was the physician's scientific conscience speaking. Inside, he really felt that anything was worth getting away from that silkily mocking voice and the delicately sneering mouth.

At Fifty-fifth Street, Wood came to the last Sixth Avenue employment office. With very little hope, he read the crudely chalked signs. It was an industrial employment agency. Wood had never been inside a factory. The only job he could fill was that of apprentice upholsterer, ten dollars a week; but he was thirty-two years old and the agency would require five dollar's immediate payment.

He turned away dejectedly, fingering the three dimes in his pocket. Three dimes—the smallest thinnest, American coins—

"Anything up there, Mac?"

"Not for me," Wood replied wearily. He scarcely glanced at the man.

He took a last glance at his newspaper before dropping it to the sidewalk. That was the last paper he'd buy, he resolved; with his miserable appearance he couldn't answer advertisements. But his mind clung obstinately to Gilroy's article. Gilroy had described the horror of catatonia. A notion born of defeat made it strangely attractive to Wood. At least, the catatonics were fed and housed. He wondered if catatonia could be simulated—

But the other had been scrutinizing Wood. "College man, ain't you?" he asked as Wood trudged away from the employment office.

Wood paused and ran his hand over his stubbled face. Dirty cuffs stood away from his fringed sleeves. He knew that his hair curled long behind his ears. "Does it still show?" he asked bitterly.

"You bet. You can spot a college man a mile away."

Wood's mouth twisted. "Glad to hear that. It must be an inner light shining through the rags."

"You're a sucker, coming down here with an education. Down here they want poor slobs who don't know any better . . . guys like me, with big muscles and small brains."

Wood looked up at him sharply. He was too well dressed and alert to have prowled the agencies for any length of time. He might have just lost his job; perhaps he was looking for company. But Wood had met his kind before. He had the hard eyes of a wolf who preyed on the jobless.

"Listen," Wood said coldly. "I haven't a thing you'd want. I'm down to thirty cents. Excuse me while I sneak my books and toothbrush out of my room before the super snatches them."

The other did not recoil or protest virtuously. "I ain't blind," he said quietly. "I can see you're down and out."

"Then what do you want?" Wood snapped ill-temperedly. "Don't tell me you want a threadbare but filthy college man for company—"

His unwelcome friend made a gesture of annoyance. "Cut out the mad-dog act. I was turned down on a job today because I ain't a college man. Seventy-five a month, room and board, doctor's assistant. But I got the air because I ain't a grad."

"You've got my sympathy," Wood said, turning away.

The other caught up with him. "You're a college grad. Do you want the job? It'll cost you your first week's pay . . . my cut, you see?"

"I don't know anything about medicine I was a code expert in a stock-broker's office before people stopped having enough money for investments. Want any codes deciphered? That's the best I can do."

He grew irritated when the stranger stubbornly matched his dejected shuffle.

"You don't have to know anything about medicine. Long as you got a degree, a few muscles and a brain, that's all the doc wants."

Wood stopped short and wheeled.

"Is that on the level?"

"Sure. But I don't want to take a dead head up there and get turned down. I got to ask you the questions they asked me."

In face of a prospective job, Wood's caution ebbed away. He felt the three dimes in his pocket. They were exceedingly slim and unprotective. They meant two hamburgers and two cups of coffee, or a bed in some filthy hotel dormitory. Two thin meals and sleeping in the wet march air; or shelter for a night and no food—

"Shoot!" he said deliberately.

"Any relatives?"

"Some fifth cousins in Maine."

"Friends?"

"None who would recognize me now." He searched the stranger's face. "What's this all about? What have my friends or relatives got to do—"

"Nothing," the other said hastily. "Only you'll have to travel a little. The doc wouldn't want a wife dragging along, or have you break up your work by writing letters. See?"

Wood didn't see. It was a singularly lame explanation; but he was concentrating on the seventy-five dollars a month, room and board—food.

"Who's the doctor?" he asked.

"I ain't dumb." The other smiled humorously. "You'll go there with me and get the doc to hand over my cut."

Wood crossed to Eight Avenue with the stranger. Sitting in the subway, he kept his eyes from meeting casual, disinterested glances. He pulled his feet out of the aisle, against the base of the seat, to hide the loose, flapping right sole. His hands were cracked and scaly, with tenacious dirt deeply embedded. Bitter, defeated, with the appearance of a mature waif. What a chance there was of being hired! But at least the stranger had risked a nickel on his fare.

Wood followed him out at 103rd Street and Central Park West; they climbed the hill to Manhattan Avenue and headed several blocks downtown. The other ran briskly up the stoop of an old house. Wood climbed the steps more slowly. He checked an urge to run away, but he experienced in advance the sinking feeling of being turned away from a job. If he could only have his hair cut, his suit pressed, his shoes mended! But what was the use of thinking about that? It would cost a couple of dollars. And nothing could be done about his ragged hems.

"Come on!" the stranger called.

Wood tensed his back and stood looking at the house while the other brusquely rang the doorbell. There were three floors and no card above the bell, no doctor's white glass sign in the darkly curtained windows. From the outside it could have been a neglected boardinghouse.

The door opened. A man of his own age, about middle height, but considerably overweight, blocked the entrance. He wore a white laboratory apron. Incongruous in his pale, soft face, his nimble eyes were harsh.

"Back again?" he asked impatiently.

"It's not for me this time," Wood's persistent friend said, "I got a college grad."

Wood drew back in humiliation when the fat man's keen glance passed over his wrinkled, frayed suit and stopped distastefully at the long hair blowing wildly around his hungry, unshaven face. There—he could see it coming; "Can't use him."

But the fat man pushed back a beautiful collie with his leg and held the door wide. Astounded, Wood followed his acquaintance into the narrow hall. To give an impression of friendliness, he stoop and ruffled the dog's ear. The fat man led them into a bare front room.

"What's your name?" he asked indifferently.

Wood answer stuck in his throat. He coughed to clear it. "Wood," he replied.

"Any relatives?" Wood shook his head.

"Friends?"

"Not anymore."

"What kind of degree?"

"Science, Columbia, 1925."

The fat man's expression did not change. He reached into his left pocket and brought out a wallet. "What arrangement did you make with this man?"

"He's to get my first week's salary." Silently, Wood observed the transfer of several green bills; he looked at them hungrily, pathetically. "May I wash up and take a shave, doctor?" he asked.

"I'm not the doctor," the fat man answered. "My name is Clarence, without a mister in front of it." He turned swiftly to the sharp stranger. "What are you hanging around for?"

Wood's friend backed to the door. "Well, so long," he said. "Good break for both of us, eh, Wood?"

Wood smiled and nodded happily. The trace of irony in the stranger's hard voice escaped him entirely.

"I'll take you upstairs to your room," Clarence said when Wood's business partner had left. "I think there's a razor there."

They went out into the dark hall, the collie close behind them. An unshaded light bulb hung on a single wire above a gate-leg table. On the wall behind the table an oval, gilt mirror gave back Wood's hairy, unkempt image. A worn carpet covered the floor to a door cutting off the rear of the house, and narrow stairs climbed in a swift spiral to the next story. It was cheerless and neglected, but Wood's conception of luxury was less than exacting.

"Wait here until I make a telephone call," Clarence said.

He closed the door behind him in a room opposite the stairs. Wood fondled the friendly collie. Through the panel he heard Clarence's voice, natural and unlowered.

"Hello, Moss? . . .   Pinero brought back a man. All his answers are right . . . Columbia, 1925 . . . Not a cent, judging from his appearance . . . Call Talbot? For when? . . . O.K. . . . You'll get back as soon as you get through with the board? . . . O.K. . . . Well, what's the difference? You got all you wanted from them, anyhow."

Wood heard the receiver's click as it was replaced and taken off again.. Moss? That was the head of Memorial Hospital—the great surgeon.   But the article about the catatonics hinted something about his removal from the hospital.

"Hello, Talbot?" Clarence was saying. "Come around at noon tomorrow. Moss says everything'll be ready then . . . O.K., don't get excited. This is positively the last one! . . . Don't worry. Nothing can go wrong."

Talbot's name sounded familiar to Wood. It might have been the Talbot that the Morning Post had written about—the seventy-six-year-old philanthropist. He probably wanted Moss to operate on him. Well, it was none of his business.

When Clarence joined him in the dark hall, Wood thought only of his seventy-five a month, room and board; but more than that, he had a job! A few weeks of decent food and a chance to get some new clothes, and he would soon get rid of his defeatism.

He even forgot his wonder at the lack of shingles and waiting-room signs that a doctor's house usually had. He could only think of his neat room on the third floor, overlooking a bright back yard. And a shave—

Dr. Moss replaced the telephone with calm deliberation. Striding through the white hospital corridor to the elevator, he was conscious of curious stares. His pink, scrupulously shave, clean-scrubbed face gave no answer to their questioning eyes. In the elevator he stood with his hands thrust casually into his pockets. The operator did not dare to look at him or speak.

Moss gathered his hat and coat.   The space around the reception desk seemed more crowded than usual, with men who had the penetrating look of reporter. He walked swiftly past.

A tall, astoundingly thin man, his stare fixed predatorily on Moss, headed the wedge of reporters that swarmed after Moss.

"You can't leave without a statement to the press, doc!" he said.

"I find it easy to do," Moss taunted without stopping.

He stood on the curb with his back turned coldly on the reporters and unhurriedly flagged a taxi.

"Well, at least you can tell us whether you're still director of the hospital," the tall reporter said.

"Ask the board of trustees."

"Then how about a theory on the catatonics?"

"Ask the catatonics." The cab pulled up opposite Moss. Deliberately he opened the door and stepped in. As he rode away, he heard the thin man exclaim: "What a cold, clammy reptile!"

He did not look back to enjoy their discomfiture. In spite of his calm demeanor, he did not feel too easy himself. The man on the Morning Post, Gilroy or whatever his name was, had written a sensational article on the abandoned catatonics, and even went so far as to claim they were not catatonics. He had had all he could do to keep from being involved in the conflicting riot of theory. Talbot owned a large interest in the paper. He must be told to strangle the articles, although by now all the papers were taking up the cry.

It was a clever piece of work, detecting the fact that the victims weren't suffering from catatonia at all. But the Morning Post reporter had cut himself a man-sized job in trying to understand how three men with general paralysis could be abandoned without a trace of where they had come from, and what connection the incisions had on their condition. Only recently had Moss himself solved it.

The cab crossed to Seventh Avenue and headed uptown.

The trace of his parting smile of mockery vanished. His mobile mouth whitened, tight-lipped and grim. Where was he to get money from now? He had milked the hospital funds to a frightening debt, and it had not been enough. Like a bottomless maw, his researched could drain a dozen funds.

If he could convince Talbot, prove to him that his failures and not rally been failures, that this time he would not slip up—

But Talbot was a tough nut to crack. Not a cent was coming out of his miserly pocket until Moss completely convinced him that he was past the experimental stage. This time there would be no failure!

At Moss's street, the cab stopped and the surgeon sprang out lightly. He ran up the steps confidently, looking neither to the left or to the right, though it was a fine day with a warm yellow sun, and between the two lines of old houses Central Park could be seen budding greenly.

He opened the door and strode almost impatiently into the narrow, dark hall, ignoring the friendly collie that bounded out to greet him.

"Clarence!" he called out. "Get your new assistant down. I'm not even going to wait for a meal." He threw off his hat, coat, and jacket, hanging them up carelessly on a hook near the mirror.

"Hey, Wood!" Clarence shouted up the stairs. "Are you finished?"

They heard a light, eager step race down from the third floor.

"Clarence, my boy," Moss said in a low, impetuous voice, "I know what the trouble was. We didn't really fail at all. I'll show you . . . we'll follow exactly the same technique!"

"Then why didn't it seem to work before?"

Wood's feet came into view between the rails on the second floor. "You'll understand as soon as it's finished," Moss whispered hastily, and then Wood joined them.

Even the short time that Wood had been employed was enough to transform him. He had lost the defeatist feeling of being useless human flotsam. He was shaved and washed, but that did not account for his kindled eyes.

"Wood . . . Dr. Moss," Clarence said perfunctorily.

Wood choked out an incoherent speech that was meant to inform them that he was happy, though he didn't know anything about medicine.

"You don't have to," Moss replied silkily. "We'll teach you more about medicine than most surgeons learn in a lifetime."

It could have meant anything or nothing. Wood made no attempt to understand the meaning of the words. It was the hint of withdrawn savagery in the low voice that puzzled him. It seemed a very peculiar way of talking to a man who had been hired to move apparatus and do nothing but the most ordinary routine work.

He followed them silently into a shining, tiled operating room. He felt less comfortable than he had in his room; but when he dismissed Moss's tones as a characteristically sarcastic manner of speech, hinting more than it contained in reality, his eagerness returned. While Moss scrubbed his hands and arms in a deep basin, Wood gazed around.

In the center of the room an operating table stood, with a clean sheet clamped unwrinkled over it. Above the table five shadowless light globes branched. It was a compact room. Even Wood saw how close everything lay to the doctor's hand—trays of tampons, swabs and clamps, and a sterilizing instrument chest that gave off puffs of steam.

"We do a lot of surgical experimentation," Moss said. "Most of your work'll be handling the anesthetic. Show him how to do it, Clarence."

Wood observed intently. It appeared simple—cut-ins and shut-offs for cyclopropane, helium and oxygen; watch the dials for overrich mixture; keep your eyes on the bellows and water filter—

Trained anesthetists, he knew, tested their mixture by taking a few sniffs. At Clarence's suggestion he sniffed briefly at the whispering cone.   He didn't know cyclopropane—so lightning-fast that experienced anaesthetists are sometimes caught by it—

Wood lay on the floor with his arms and legs sticking up into the air. When he tried to straighten them, he rolled over on his side. Still they projected stiffly. He was dizzy with the anesthetic. Something that felt like surgical plaster pulled on a sensitive spot on the back of his neck.

The room was dark. Its green shades pulled down against the outer day. Somewhere above him and toward the end of the room, he heard painful breathing. Before he could raise himself to investigate, he caught the multiple tread of steps ascending and approaching the door. He drew back defensively.

The door flung open. Light flared up in the room. Wood sprang to his feet—and found he could not stand erect. He dropped back into a crawling position, facing the men who watched him with cold interest.

"He tried to stand up," the old man stated.

"What'd you think I'd do," Wood snapped. His voice was a confused, snarling growl without words. Baffled and raging he glared up at them.

"Cover him, Clarence," Moss said. "I'll look at the other one."

Wood turned his head from the threatening muzzle of the gun aimed at him, and saw the doctor lift the man on the bed. Clarence backed to the window and raised the shade. Strong moonlight roused the man. His profile was turned to Wood. His eyes fastened blankly on Moss's scrubbed pink face, never leaving it. Behind his ears curled long, wild hair.

"There you are, Talbot," Moss said to the old man. "He's sound."

"Take him out of bed and let's see him act like you said he would." The old man jittered anxiously on his cane.

Moss pulled the man's legs to the edge of the bed and raised him heavily to his feet. For a short time he stood without aid; then all at once he collapsed to his hands and knees. He stared full at Woods.

It took Woods a minute of startled bewilderment to recognize the face. He had seen it every day of his life, but never so detachedly. The eyes were blank and round, the facial muscles relaxed, idiotic.

But it was his own face—

Panic exploded in him. He gaped down at as much of himself as he could see. Two hairy legs stemmed from his shoulders, and a dog's forepaws rested firmly on the floor.

He stumbled uncertainly towards Moss. "What did you do to me?" he shouted. It came out in an animal howl. The doctor motioned the others to the door and backed away warily.

Wood felt his lips draw back tightly over his fangs. Clarence and Talbot were in the hall. Moss stood alertly in the doorway, his hand on the knob. He watched Wood closely, his eyes glacial and unmoved. When Wood sprang, he slammed the door, and Wood's shoulder crashed against it.

"He knows what happened," Moss's voice came through the panel.

It was not entirely true. Wood knew something had happened. But he refused to believe that the face of the crawling man gazing stupidly at him was his own. It was, though. And

Wood himself stood on the four legs of a dog, with a surgical plaster covering a burning wound in the back of his neck.

It was crushing, numbing, too fantastic to believe. He thought wildly of hypnosis. But just by turning his head, he could look directly at what had been his own body, braced on hands and knees as if it could not stand erect.

He was outside his own body. He could not deny that. Somehow he had been removed from it; by drugs or hypnosis, Moss had put him in the body of a dog. He had to get back into his own body again.

But how do you get back into your own body?

His mind struck blindly in all directions. He scarcely heard the three men move away from the door and enter the next room. But his mind suddenly froze with fear. His human body was complete and impenetrable, closed hermetically against his now-foreign identity.

Through his congealed terror, his animal ears brought the creak of furniture. Talbot's cane stopped its nervous, insistent tapping.

"That should have convinced even you, Talbot," he heard Moss say. "Their identities are exchanged without the slightest loss of mentality."

Wood started. It meant—No it was absurd! But it did account for the fact that his body crawled on hands and knees, unable to stand on its feet. It meant that the collie's identity was in Wood's body!

"That's O.K.," he heard Talbot say. "How about the operation part? Isn't it painful, putting their brains into different skulls?"

"You can't put them into different skulls," Moss answered with a touch of annoyance. "They don't fit. Besides, there's no need to exchange the whole brain. How do you account for the fact that people have retained their identities with parts of their brain removed?"

There was a pause. "I don't know," Talbot said doubtfully.

"Sometimes the parts of the brain that were removed contained nerve centers, and paralysis set in. But the identity was still there. Then what part of the brain contained the identity?"

Wood ignored the old man's questioning murmur. He listened intently, all his fears submerged in the straining of his sharp ears, in the overwhelming need to know what Moss had done to him.

"Figure it out," the surgeon said. "The identity must have been in some part of the brain that wasn't removed, that couldn't be touched without death. That's where it was. At the absolute base of the brain, where a scalpel couldn't get at it without having to cut through the skull, the three medullae, and the entire depth of the brain itself. There's a mysterious little body hidden away safely down there—called the pineal gland. In some way it controls the identity. Once it was a third eye."

"A third eye. And now it controls identity?" Talbot exclaimed.

"Why not? The gills of our fish ancestors became the Eustachian canal that controls the sense of balance.

"Until we developed a new technique in removing the gland—by excising from beneath the brain instead of through it—nothing at all was known about it. In the first place, trying to get at it would kill the patient; and oral or intravenous injections have no effect. But when I exchanged the pineal of a rabbit and a rat, the rabbit acted like a rat, and the rat like a rabbit—within their limitations, of course. It's empiricism—it works, but I don't know why."

"Then why did the first three act like . . . what's the word?"

"Catatonics. Well, the exchanges were really successful, Talbot; but I repeated the same mistake three times, until I figured it out. And by the way, get that reporter on something a little less dangerous. He's getting pretty warm. Excepting the salivary retention, the victims acted almost like catatonics, and for nearly the same reason. I exchanged the pineal of rats for the men's. Well, you can imagine how a rat would act with the relatively huge body of a man to control. It's beyond him. He simply gives up, goes into a passive revolt. But the difference between a dog's body and a man's isn't so great. The dog is puzzled, but at any rate he makes an attempt to control his new body."

"Is the operation painful?" Talbot asked anxiously.

"There isn't a bit of pain. The incision is very small, and heals in a short time. And as for recovery—you can see for yourself how swift it is. I operated on Wood and the dog last night."

Wood's dog brain stampeded, refusing to function intelligently. If he had been hypnotized or drugged, there might have been an eventual return. But his identity had been violently and permanently ripped from his body and forced into that of a dog. He was absolutely helpless, completely dependent on Moss to return him to his body.

"How much do you want?" Talbot was asking craftily.

"Five million!"

The old man cackled in a high, cracked voice. "I'll give you fifty thousand, cash," he offered.

"To exchange your dying body for a young, strong, healthy one?" Moss asked, emphasizing each adjective with special significance. "The price is five million."

"I'll give you seventy-five thousand," Talbot said with finality. "Raising five million is out of the question. It can't be done. All my money is tied up in my . . . uh . . . syndicates. I have to turn most of the income back into merchandise, wages, overhead and equipment. How do you expect me to have five million in cash?"

"I don't," Moss replied with faint mockery.

Talbot lost his temper. "then what are you getting at?"

"The interest on five million is exactly half your income. Briefly to use your business terminology, I'm muscling in on your rackets."

Wood heard the old man gasp indignantly. "Not a chance!" he rasped. "I'll give you eighty thousand. That's all the cash I can raise."

"Don't be a fool, Talbot," Moss said with deadly calm. "I don't want money for the sake of feeling it. I need an assured income, and plenty of it; enough to carry on my experiments without having to bleed hospitals dry and still not have enough. If this experiment didn't interest me, I wouldn't do it even for five million, much as I need it."

"Eighty thousand!" Talbot repeated.

"Hang onto your money until you rot! Let's see, with your advanced angina pectoris, that should be about six months from now, shouldn't it!"

Wood heard the old man's cane shudder nervelessly over the floor.

"You win, you cold-blooded blackmailer," the old man surrendered.

Moss laughed. Wood heard the furniture creak as they rose and set off for the stairs.

"Do you want to see Wood and the dog again, Talbot?"

"No, I'm convinced."

"Get rid of them, Clarence. No more abandoning them in the street for Talbot's clever reporters to theorize over. Put a silencer on your gun. You'll find it downstairs. Then leave them in the acid vat."

Wood's eyes flashed around the room in terror. He and his body had to escape. For him to escape alone, would mean the end of returning to his own body. Separation would make the task of forcing Moss to give him back his body impossible.

But they were on the second floor, at the rear of the house. Even if there had been a fire escape, he could not have opened the window. The only way out was through the door.

Somehow he had to turn the knob, chance meeting Clarence or Moss on the stairs or in the narrow hall, and open the heavy front door—guiding and defending himself and his body!

The collie in his body whimpered baffledly. Wood fought off the instinctive fear that froze his dog's brain. He had to be cool.

Below, he heard Clarence's ponderous steps as he went through the rooms looking for a silencer to muffle his gun.

Gilroy closed the door of the telephone booth and fished in his pocket for a coin. Of all of mankind's scientific gadgets, the telephone booth most clearly demonstrated that this is a world of five feet nine. When Gilroy pulled a coin out of his pocket, his elbow banged against the shut door; and as he dialed his number and stooped over the mouthpiece, he was forced to bend himself into the shape of a cane. But he had conditioned his lanky body to adjust itself to things scaled below his need. He did not mind the lack of room.

But he shoved his shapeless felt hat on the back of his head and whistled softly in a discouraged manner.

"Let me talk to the chief," he said. The receiver rasped in his ear. The editor greeted him abstractly; Gilroy knew he had just come on and was scattering papers over his desk, looking for the latest. "Gilroy, chief," the reporter said.

"What've you got on the catatonics?"

Gilroy sharply planed face wrinkled in earnest defeat. "Not a thing, chief," he replied hollowly.

"Where were you?"

"I was at Memorial all day, looking at the catatonics and waiting for an idea."

The editor became sympathetic. "How'd you make out?" he asked.

"Not a thing. They're absolutely dumb and motionless, and nobody around here has anything to say worth listening too. How'd you make out on the police and hospital reports?"

"I was looking at them just before you called." There was a pause. Gilroy heard the crackle of papers being shoved around. "Here they are—The fingerprint bureau has no records of them. No police department in any village, town or city recognizes their pictures."

"How about the hospitals outside New York?" Gilroy asked hopefully.

"No missing patients."

Gilroy sighed and shrugged his thin shoulders eloquently. "Well, all we have is a negative angle. They must have been picked damned carefully. All the papers around the country printed their pictures, and they don't seem to have any friends, relatives or police records."

"How about a human-interest story," the editor encouraged; "what they eat, how helpless they are, their torn, old clothes? Pad out a story about their probable lives, judging from their features and hands. How's that? Not bad, eh?"

"Aw, chief," Gilroy moaned, "I'm licked. That padding stuff isn't my line. I'm not a sob sister. We haven't anything to work on. These tramps had absolutely no connection with life. We can't find out who they were, where they came from, or what happened to them."

The editor's voice went sharp and incisive. "Listen to me, Gilroy!" he rapped out. "You stop whining, do you hear me? I'm running this paper, and as long as you don't see fit to quit, I'll send you out after birth lists if I want to.

"You thought this was a good story and you convinced me that it was. Well, I'm still convinced! I want these catatonics tracked down. I want to know all about them, and how they would up behind the eight-ball. So does the public. I'm not stopping until I do know. Get me?

"You get to work on this story and hang onto it. Don't let it throw you! And just to show you how I'm standing behind you . . . I'm giving you a blank expense account and your own discretion. Now track these catatonics down in any way you can figure out!"

Gilroy was stunned for an instant. "Well, gosh," he stammered, confused. "I'll do my best, chief. I didn't know you felt that way."

"The two of us'll crack this story wide open, Gilroy. But just come around to me with another whine about being licked, and you can start as copy boy for some other sheet. Do you get me? That's final!"

Gilroy pulled his hat down firmly. "I get you, chief," he declared manfully. "You can count on me right up to the hilt."

He slammed the receiver on its hook, yanked the door open, and strode out with a new determination. He felt like the power of the press, and the feeling was not unjustified. The might and cunning of a whole vast metropolitan newspaper was ranged solidly behind him. Few secrets could hide from its searching probe.

All he needed was patience and shrewd observation. Finding the first clue would be hardest; after that the story would unwind by itself. He marched toward the hospital exit.

He heard steps hastening behind him and felt a light, detaining touch on his arm. He wheeled and looked down at the resident physician, dressed in street clothes and coming on duty.

"You're Gilroy, aren't you?" the doctor asked. "Well, I was thinking about the incisions on the catatonics' necks—"

"What about them?" Gilroy demanded alertly, pulling out a pad.

"Quitting again?" the editor asked ten minutes later.

"Not me, chief!" Gilroy propped his stenographic pad on top of the telephone. "I'm hot on the trail. Listen to this. This resident physician over here at Memorial tipped me off to a real clue. He figured out that the incisions on the catatonics' necks aimed at some part of their brains. The incisions penetrate at a tangent a quarter of an inch off the vertebrae, so it couldn't have been to tamper with the spinal cord. You can't reach the posterior part of the brain from that angle, he says and working from the back of the neck wouldn't bring you to any important part of the neck that can't be reached better from the front or through the mouth.

"If you don't cut the spinal cord with that incision, you can't account for general paralysis, and the cords definitely weren't cut.

"So he thinks the incisions were aimed at some part of the base of the brain that can't be reached from above. He doesn't know what part or how the operation would cause general paralysis.

"Got that? O.K. Well, here's the payoff:

"To reach the exact spot of the brain you want, you ordinarily take off a good chunk of the skull, somewhere around that spot. But these incisions were predetermined to the last centimeter. And he doesn't know how. The surgeon worked entirely by measurements—like blind flying. He says only three or four surgeons in the country could have done it"

"Who are they, you cluck? Did you get their names?"

Gilroy became offended. "Of course. Moss in New York; Faber in Chicago; Crowninshield in Portland; maybe Johnson in Detroit."

"Well, what're you waiting for?" the editor shouted. "Get Moss!"

"Can't locate him. He moved from his Riverside apartment and left no forwarding address. He was peeved. The board asked for his resignation and he left with a pretty bad name for mismanagement."

The editor sprang into action. "That leaves us four men to track down. Find Moss. I'll call up the other boys you named, It looks like a good tip."

Gilroy hung up. With half a dozen vast strides, he had covered the distance to the hospital exit, moving with ungainly, predatory swiftness.

Wood was in a mind-freezing panic. He knew it hindered him, prevented him from plotting his escape, but he was powerless to control the fearful darting of his dog's brain.

It would take Clarence only a short time to find the silencer and climb the stairs to kill him and his body. Before Clarence could find the silencer, Wood and his body had to escape.

Wood lifted himself clumsily, unsteadily, to his hind legs and took the doorknob between his paws. They refused to grip. He heard Clarence stop, and the sound of scraping drawers came to his sharp ears.

He was terrified. He bit furiously at the knob. I slipped between his teeth. He bit harder. Pain stabbed his sensitive gums, but the bitter brass dented. Hanging to the knob, he lowered himself to the floor, bending his neck sharply to turn it. The tongue clicked out of the lock. He threw himself to one side, flipping back the door as he fell. It opened a crack. He thrust his snout in the opening and forced it wide.

From below, he heard the ponderous footfalls moving again. Wood stalked noiselessly into the hall and peered down the well of the stairs. Clarence was out of sight.

He drew back into the room and pulled at his body's clothing, backing down the hall again until the dog crawled voluntarily. It crept after him and down the stairs.

All at once Clarence came out of a room and made for the stairs. Wood crouched, trembling at the sound of the metallic clicking that he knew was the silencer being fitted to a gun. He barred his body. It halted, its idiot face hanging down over the step, silent and without protest.

Clarence reached the stairs and climbed confidently. Wood tensed, waiting for Clarence to turn the spiral and come into view.

Clarence sighted them and froze rigid. His mouth opened blankly, startled. The gun trembled impotently at his side and he stared up at them with his fat, white neck exposed and inviting. Then his chest heaved and his larynx tightened for a yell.

But Wood's long teeth cleared. He lunged high, directly at Clarence, and his fangs snapped together in midair.

Soft flesh ripped in his teeth. He knocked Clarence over; they fell down the stairs and crashed to the floor. Clarence thrashed around, gurgling. Wood smelled a sudden rush of blood that excited an alien lust in him. He flung himself clear and landed on his feet.

His body clumped after him, pausing to sniff Clarence. He pulled it away and darted to the front door.

From the back of the house he heard Moss running to investigate. He bit savagely at the doorknob, jerking it back awkwardly, terrified that Moss might reach him before the door opened.

But the lock clicked, and he thrust the door wide with his body. His human body flopped after him on hands and knees to the stoop. He hauled it down the steps to the sidewalk and herded it anxiously toward Central Park West, out of Moss's range.

Wood glanced over his shoulder, saw the doctor glaring at them through the curtain on the door, and, in terror, he dragged his body in a clumsy gallop to the corner where he would be protected by traffic.

He had escaped death, and he and his body were still together; but his panic grew stronger. How could he feed it, shelter it, defend it against Moss and Talbot's gangsters? And how could he force Moss to give him back his body?

But he saw that first he would have to shield his body from observation. It was hungry, and it prowled around on hands and knees, searching for food. The sight of a crawling, sniffing human body attracted disgusted attention; before long they were almost surrounded.

Wood was badly scared. With his teeth, he dragged his body into the street and guided its slow crawl to the other side, where Central Park could hide them with its trees and bushes.

Moss had been more alert. A black car sped through a red light and crowded down on them. From the other side a police car shot in and out of traffic, its siren screaming, and braked dead beside Wood and his body.

The black car checked its headlong rush.

Wood crouched defensively over his body, glowering at the two cops who charged out at them. One shoved Wood away with his foot; the other raised the body by the armpits and tried to stand it erect.

"A nut—he thinks he's a dog," he said interestedly. "The screwball ward for him, eh?"

The other nodded. Wood lost his reason. He attacked, snapping viciously. His body took up the attack, snarling horribly and biting on all sides. It was insane, hopeless; but he had no way of communicating, and he had to do something to prevent being separated from his body. The police kicked him off.

Suddenly he realized that if they had not been burdened with his body, they would have shot him. He darted wildly into traffic before they sat his body in the car.

"Want to get out and plug him before he bites somebody?" he heard.

"This nut'll take a hunk out of you," the other replied. "We'll send out an alarm from the hospital."

It drove off downtown. Wood scrambled after it. His legs pumped furiously; but it pulled away from him, and other cars came between. He lost it after a few blocks.

Then he saw the black car make a reckless turn through traffic and roar after him. It was too intently bearing down on him to have been anything but Talbot's gangsters.

His eyes and muscles coordinated with animal precision. He ran in the swift traffic, avoiding being struck, and at the same time kept watch for a footpath leading into the park.

When he found one, he sprinted into the opposite lane of traffic. Brakes screeched; a man cursed him in a loud voice. But he scurried in front of the car, gained the sidewalk, and dashed along the cement path until he came to a miniature forest of bushes.

Without hesitation, he left the path and ran through the woods. It was not a dense growth, but it covered him from sight. He scampered deep into the park.

His frightened eyes watched the carload of gangsters scour the trees on both sides of the path. Hugging the ground, he inched away from them. They beat the bushes a safe distance away from him.

While he circled behind them, creeping from cover to cover, there was small danger of being caught. But he was appalled by the loss of his body. Being near it had given him a sort of courage, even though he did not know how he was going to force Moss to give it back to him. Now, besides making the doctor operate, he had to find a way of getting near it again.

But his empty stomach was knotted with hunger. Before he could make plans he had to eat.

He crept furtively out of his shelter. The gangsters were far out of sight. Then, with infinite patience, he sneaked up on a squirrel. The alert little animal was observant and wary, It took an exhausting long time before he ambushed it and snapped its spine. The thought of eating an uncooked rodent revolted him.

He dug back into his cache of bushes with his prey. When he tried to plot a line of action, his dog's brain balked. It was terrified and maddened with helplessness.

There was good reason for its fear—Moss had Talbot's gangsters out gunning for him, and by this time the police were probably searching for him as a vicious dog.

In all his nightmares he had never imagined any so horrible. He was utterly impotent to help himself. The forces of law and crime were ranged against him; he had no way of communicating the fact that he was a man to those who could possibly help him; he was completely inarticulate; and besides, who could help him, except Moss? Suppose he did manage to evade the police, the gangsters, and sneaked past a hospital's vigilant staff, and somehow succeeded in communicating—

Even so, only Moss could perform the operation!

He had to rule out doctors and hospitals; they were too routinized to have much imagination. But, more important than that, they could not influence Moss to operate.

He scrambled to his feet and trotted cautiously though the clumps of brush in the direction of Columbus Circle. First, he had to be alert for police and gangsters. He had to find a method of communicating—but to somebody who could understand him and exert tremendous pressure on Moss.

The city's smells came to his sensitive nostrils. Like a vast blanket, covering most of them, was a sweet odor that he identified as gasoline vapor. Above it hovered the scent of vegetation, hot and moist; and below it, the musk of mankind.

To his dog's perspective, it was a different world, with a broad, distant, terrifying horizon. Smells and sounds formed scenes in his animal mind. Yet it was interesting. The pad of his paws against the soft, cushioned ground gave him an instinctive pleasure; all the clothes he needed, he carried on him; and food was not hard to find.

While he shielded himself from the police and Talbot's gangsters, he even enjoyed a sort of freedom—but it was a cowardly freedom that he did not want, that was not worth the price. As a man, he had suffered hunger, cold, lack of shelter and security, indifference. In spite of all that, his dog's body harbored a human intelligence; he belonged on his hind legs, standing erect, living the life, good or bad, of a man.

In some way he must get back to that world, out of the solitary anarchy of animaldom. Moss alone could return him. He must be forced to do it! He must be compelled to return this body he had robbed!

But how could Wood communicate, and who could help him?

Near the end of Central park, he exposed himself to overwhelming danger.

He was padding along a path that skirted the broad road. A cruising black car accelerated with deadly, predatory swiftness, sped abreast of him. He heard a muffled pop. A bullet hissed an inch over his head.

He ducked low and scurried back into the concealing bushes. He snaked nimbly from tree to tree, keeping obstacles between him and the line of fire.

The gangsters were out of the car. He heard them beating the brush for him. Their progress was slow, while his fleet legs pumped three hundred yards of safety away from them.

He burst out of the park and scampered across Columbus Circle, reckless of the traffic. On Broadway he felt more secure, hugging the buildings with dense crowds between him and the street.

When he felt certain that he had lost the gangsters, he turned west through one-way streets, alert for signs of danger.

In coping with physical danger, he discovered that his animal mind reacted instinctively, and always more cunningly than a human brain.

Impulsively, he cowered behind stoops, in doorways, behind any sort of shelter, when the traffic moved. When it stopped, packed tightly, for the light, he ran at topnotch speed. Cars skidded across his path, and several times he was almost hit; but he did not slow to a trot until he had zig-zagged downtown, going steadily away from the center of the city, and reached West Street, along North River.

He felt reasonably safe from Talbot's gangsters. But a police car approached slowly under the express highway. He crouched behind an overflowing garbage can outside a filthy restaurant. Long after it was gone he cowered there.

The shrill wind blowing over the river and across the covered docks picked a newspaper off the pile of garbage and flattened it against the restaurant window.

Through his animal mind, frozen into numbing fear, he remembered the afternoon before—standing in front of the employment agency talking to one of Talbot's gangsters—

A thought had come to him then; that it would be pleasant to be a catatonic instead of having to starve. He knew better now. But—

He reared to his hind legs and overturned the garbage can. It fell with a loud crash, rolling down toward the gutter, spilling refuse all over the sidewalk. Before a restaurant worker came out, roaring abuse, he pawed through the mess and seized a twisted newspaper in his mouth. It smelled of sour, rotting food, but he caught it up and ran.

Blocks away from the restaurant, he ran across a wide, torn lot, to cower behind a crumbling building. Sheltered from the river wind, he straightened out the paper and scanned the front page.

It was a day old, the same newspaper that he had thrown away before the employment agency. On the left column he found the catatonic story. It was signed by a reporter named Gilroy.

Then he took the edge of the sheet between his teeth and backed away with it until the newspaper opened clumsily, wrinkled, at the next page. He was disgusted by the fetid smell of putrefying food that clung to it; but he swallowed his gorge and kept turning the huge, stiff, unwieldy sheets with his inept teeth. He came to the editorial page and paused there, studying intently the copyright box.

He set off at a fast trot, wary against danger, staying close to walls of buildings, watching for cars that might contain either gangsters or policemen, darting across streets to shelter— trotting on—

The air was growing darker, and the express highway cast a long shadow. Before the sun went down, he covered almost three miles along West Street, and stopped not far from the Battery.

He gaped up at the towering Morning Post Building. It looked impregnable, its heavy doors shut against the wind.

He stood at the main entrance, waiting for somebody to hold
a door open long enough for him to lunge through it. Hopefully,
he kept his eyes on an old man. When he opened the door, Wood
was at his heels. But the old man shoved him back with gentle
firmness.

Wood bared his fangs. It was his only answer. The man
hastily pulled the door shut.

Wood tried another approach. He attached himself to a tall,
gangling man who appeared rather kindly in spite of his intent
face. Wood gazed up, wagging his tail awkwardly in friendly
greeting. The tall man stooped and scratched Wood's ears, but
he refused to take him inside. Before the door closed, Wood
launched himself savagely at the thin man and almost knocked
him down.

In the lobby, Wood darted through the legs surrounding him.
The tall man was close behind, roaring angrily. A frightened
stampede of thick-soled shoes threatened to crush Wood; but he
twisted in and out between the surging feet and gained the
stairs.

He scrambled up them swiftly. The second-floor entrance
had plate-glass doors.. It contained the executive offices.

He turned the corner and climbed up speedily. The stairs
narrowed, artificially illuminated. The third and fourth floors
were printing-plant rooms; he ran past, clambered by the
business offices, classified advertising—

At the editorial department he panted before the heavy fire
door, waiting to regain his breath. Then he gripped the knob
between his teeth and pulled it around. The door swung inward.

Thick, bitter smoke clawed his sensitive nostrils; his ears
flinched at the clattering, shouting bedlam.

Between rows of littered desks, he inched and gazed around
hopefully. He saw abstracted faces, intent on typewriters that
rattled out stories; young men racing around to gather up
batches of papers; men and women swarming in and out of the
elevators. Shrewd faces, intelligent and alert—

A few turned for an instant to look at him as he passed; then
turned back to their work, almost without having seen him.

He trembled with elation. These were the men who had the
power to influence Moss, and the acuteness to understand him!
He squatted and put his paws on the leg of a typing reporter,

staring up expectantly. The reporter stared, looked down agitatedly, and shoved him away.

"Go on, beat it!" he said angrily. "Go home!"

Wood shrank back. He did not sense danger. Worse than that, he had failed. His mind worked rapidly; suppose he had attracted interest, how would he have communicated his story intelligibly? How could he explain in the equivalent of words?

All at once the idea exploded in his mind. He had been a code translator in a stockbroker's office—

He sat back on his haunches and barked, loud, broken, long and short yelps. A girl screamed. Reporters jumped up defensively, surged away in a tightening ring. Wood barked out his message in Morse, painful, slow, straining a larynx that was foreign to him. He looked around optimistically for someone who might have understood.

Instead   he   met   hostile,   annoyed   stares—and   no comprehension.

"That's the hound that attacked me! The tall, thin man said.

"Not for food, I hope," a reporter answered.

Wood was not entirely defeated. He began to bark his message again, but a man hurried out of the glass-enclosed editor's office.

"What's all the commotion here?" he demanded. He sighted Wood among the ring of withdrawing reporters. "Get that damned dog out of here!"

"Come on—get him out of here!" the thin man shouted.

"He's a nice, friendly dog. Give him the hypnotic eye, Gilroy."

Wood stared pleadingly at Gilroy. He had not been understood, but he had found the reporter who had written the catatonic articles! Gilroy approached cautiously, repeating phrases calculated to soothe a savage dog.

Wood darted away through the rows of desks. He was so near to success—   He only needed to find a way of communicating before they caught him and put him out!

He lunged to the top of a desk and crashed a bottle of ink to the floor. It splashed into a dark puddle. Swiftly, quiveringly, he seized a piece of white paper, dipped his paw into the splotch of ink, and made a hasty attempt to write.

His surge of hope died quickly. The wrist of his forepaw was not the universal joint of a human being; it had a single upward articulation! When he brought his paw down on the paper, it flattened uselessly, and his claws worked in a unit. He could not draw back three to write with one. Instead, he made a streaked pad print—

Dejectedly, rather than antagonize Gilroy, Wood permitted himself to be driven back to an elevator. He wagged his tail clumsily. It was a difficult feat, calling into use alien muscles that he employed with intellectual deliberation. He sat down and assumed a grin that would have been friendly on a human face; but even so, it reassured Gilroy. The tall reporter patted his head. Nevertheless, he put him out firmly.

But Wood had reason to feel encouraged. He had managed to get inside the building, and had attracted attention. He knew that a newspaper was the only force powerful enough to influence Moss, but there was still the problem of communication. How could he solve it? His paw was worthless for writing, with its single articulation; and nobody in the office could understand Morse code.

He crouched against the white cement wall, his harried mind darting wildly in all directions for a solution. Without a voice or prehensile fingers, his only method of communication seemed to be barking in code. In all that throng, he was certain there would be one to interpret it.

Glances did turn to him. At least, he had no difficulty in arousing interest. But they were incomprehending looks.

For some moments he lost his reason. He ran in and out of the deep, hurrying crowd, barking his message furiously, jumping up at men who appeared more intelligent than the others, following them short distances until it was overwhelmingly apparent that they did not understand, then turning to other men, raising an ear-shattering din of appeal.

He met nothing but a timid pat or frightened rebuffs. He stopped his deafening yelps and cowered back against the wall, defeated. No one would attempt to interpret the barking of a dog in terms of code. When he was a man, he would probably have responded in the same way. The most intelligible message he could hope to convey by his barking was simply the fact that he was trying to attract interest. Nobody would search for any deeper meaning in a dog's bark.

He joined the traffic hastening toward the subway. He trotted along the curb, watchful for slowing cars, but more intent on the strewing of rubbish in the gutter. He was murderously envious of the human feet around him that walked swiftly and confidently to a known destination; smug, selfish feet, undeviating from their homeward path to help him. Their owners could convey the finest shadings and variations in emotion, commands, abstract thought by speech, writing, print, through telephone, radio, books, newspapers—

But his voice was only a piercing, inarticulate yelp that infuriated human beings; his paws were good for nothing but running; his pointed face transmitted no emotions.

He trotted along the curbs of three blocks in the business district before he found a pencil stump. He picked it up in his teeth and ran to the docks on West Street, though he had only the vague outline of a last experiment in communication.

There was plenty of paper blowing around in the river wind, some of it even clean. To the stevedores, waiting at the dock for the payoff, he appeared to be frisking. A few of them whistled at him. In reality, he chased the flying paper with deadly earnestness.

When he captured a piece, he held it firmly between his forepaws. The stub of pencil was gripped in the even space separating his sharp canine fangs.

He moved the pencil in his mouth over the sheet of paper. It was clumsy and uncertain, but he produced long, wavering block letters. He wrote: "I AM A MAN." The short message covered the whole page, leaving no space for further information.

He dropped the pencil, caught up the paper in his teeth and ran back to the newspaper building. For the first time since he had escaped from Moss, he felt assured. His attempt at writing was crude and unformed, but the message was unmistakably clear.

He joined a group of tired young legmen coming back from assignments. He stood passively until the door was opened, then lunged confidently through the little procession of cub reporters. They scattered back cautiously, permitting him to enter without a struggle.

Again he raced up the stairs to the editorial department, put the sheet of paper down on the floor, and clutched the doorknob between his powerful teeth.

He hesitated for only an instant, to find the cadaverous reporter. Gilroy was seated at a desk, typing out his article. Carrying his message in his mouth, Wood trotted directly to Gilroy. He put his paw on the reporter's sharp knee.

"What the hell!" Gilroy gasped. He pulled his leg away startledly and shoved Wood away.

But Wood came back insistently, holding his paper stretched out to Gilroy as far as possible. He trembled hopefully until the reporter snatched the message out of his mouth. Then his muscles froze, and he stared up expectantly at the angular face, scanning it for signs of growing comprehension.

Gilroy kept his eyes on the straggling letters. His face darkened angrily.

"Who's being a wise guy here?" he shouted suddenly. Most of the staff ignored him. "Who let this mutt in and gave him a crank note to bring to me? Come on—who's the genius?"

Wood jumped around him, barking hysterically, trying to explain.

"Oh, shut up!" Gilroy rapped out. "Hey copy! Take this dog down and see that he doesn't get back in! He won't bite you."

Again, Wood had failed. But he did not feel defeated. When his hysterical dread of frustration ebbed, leaving his mind clear and analytical, he realized that his failure was only one of degree. Actually, he had communicated, but lack of space had prevented him from detailed clarity. The method used was correct. He only needed to augment it.

Before the copy boy cornered him, Wood swooped up at a pencil on an empty desk.

"Should I let him keep the pencil, Mr. Gilroy?" the boy asked.

"I'll lend you mine, unless you want your arm snapped off," Gilroy snorted, turning back to his typewriter.

Wood sat back and waited beside the copy boy for the elevator to pick them up. He clenched the pencil possessively between his teeth. He was impatient to get out of the building and back to the lot on West Street, where he could plan a system of writing a more explicit message. His block letters were unmanageably huge and shaky; but, with the same logical detachment he used to employ when he was a code translator, he attacked the problem fearlessly.

He knew that he could not use the printed or written alphabet. He would have to find a substitute that his clumsy teeth could manage, and that could be compressed into less space.

Gilroy was annoyed by the collie's insistent returning. He crumpled the enigmatic, unintelligible note and tossed it in the waste-basket, but beyond considering it as a practical joke, he gave it no further thought.

His long, large-pointed fingers swiftly tapped out the last page of his story. He ended it with a short line of zeros and dashes, gathered a sheaf of papers, and brought it to the editor.

The editor studied the lead paragraph intently and skimmed hastily through the rest of the story. He appeared uncomfortable.

"Not bad, eh?" Gilroy exulted.

"Uh-what?" The editor jerked his head up blankly. "Oh. No, it's pretty good. Very good, in fact."

"I've got to hand it to you," Gilroy continued admiringly. "I'd have given up. You know—nothing to work on, just a bunch of fantastic events with no beginning and no end. Now, all of a sudden, the cops pick up a nut who acts like a dog and has an incision like the catatonics. Maybe it isn't any clearer, but at least we've got something actually happening. I don't know—I feel pretty good. We'll get to the bottom—"

The editor listened abstractly, growing more uneasy from sentence to sentence. "Did you see the latest case?" he interrupted.

"Sure. I'm in soft with the resident physician. If I hadn't been following the story right from the start, I'd have said the one they just hauled in was a genuine screwball. He goes bounding around on the floor, sniffs at things, and makes a pathetic attempt to bark. But he has an incision on the back of his neck. It's just like the others—even has two professional stitches, and it's the same number of millimeters away from the spine. He's a catatonic, or whatever we'll call it now—"

"Well, the story's shaping up faster than I thought it would," the editor said, evening the edges of Gilroy's article with ponderous care. "But—" His voice dropped huskily. "Well, I don't know how to tell you this, Gilroy."

The reporter drew his brows together and looked at him obliquely. "What's the hard word this time?" he asked mystified.

"Oh, the usual thing. You know. I've got to take you off this story. It's too bad, because it was just getting hot. I hated to tell you, Gilroy; but, after all, what the hell. That's part of the game."

"It is, huh?" Gilroy flattened his hands on the desk and leaned over resentfully. "Whose toes did we step on this time? Nobody's. The hospital has no kick coming. I couldn't mention names because I didn't know any to mention. Well, then, what's the angle?"

The editor shrugged, "I can't argue. It's a front-office order. But I've got a good lead for you to follow tomorrow—"

Savagely, Gilroy strode to the window and glared out at the darkening street. The business department wasn't behind the order, he reasoned angrily; they weren't getting ads from the hospital. And as for the big boss—Talbot never interfered with policy, except when he had to squash a revealing crime story. By eliminating the editors, who yielded an inch when public opinion demanded a mile, the business department, who fought only when advertising was at stake, Gilroy could blame no one but Talbot.

Gilroy rapped his bony knuckles impatiently against the window casement. What was the point of Talbot's order? Perhaps he had a new way of paying off traitors. Gilroy dismissed the idea immediately; he knew Talbot wouldn't go to that expense and risk possible leakage when the old way of sealing a body in a cement block and dumping it in the river was still effective and cheap.

"I give up," Gilroy said without turning around. "I can't figure out Talbot's angle."

"Neither can I," the editor admitted.

At that confession, Gilroy wheeled. "Then you know it's Talbot!"

"Of course. Who else could it be? But don't let it throw you, pal." He glanced around cautiously as he spoke. "Let this catatonic yarn take a rest. Tomorrow you can find out what's behind this bulletin that Johnson phoned in from City Hall."

Gilroy absently scanned the scribbled not.   His scowl wrinkled into puzzlement.

"What the hell is this?   All I can make out of it is the A.S.P.C.A. and the dog lovers are protesting to the mayor against organized murder of brown-and-white collies."

"That's just what it is."

"And you think Talbot's gang is behind it, naturally." When the editor nodded, Gilroy threw up his hands in despair. "This gang stuff is getting too deep for me, chief. I used to be able to call their shots. I knew why a torpedo was bumped off, or a crime was pulled; but I don't mind telling you that I can't see why a gang boss wants a catatonic yarn hushed up, or sends his mob around plugging innocent collies. I'm going home . . . get drunk—"

He stormed out of the office. Before the editor had time to shrug his shoulders, Gilroy was back again, his deep eyes blazing furiously.

"What a pair of prize dopes we are, chief!" he shouted. "Remember the collie—the one that came in with a hunk of paper in his mouth? We threw him out, remember? Well, that's the hound Talbot's gang is out gunning for. He's trying to carry messages to us!"

"Hey, you're right!" The editor heaved out of the chair and stood uncertainly. "Where is he?"

Gilroy waved his long arms expressively.

"Then come on! To hell with hats and coats!"

They dashed into the staff room. The skeleton night crew loafed around, reading papers before moping out to follow up undeveloped leads.

"Put those papers down!" the editor shouted. "Come on with me—every one of you."

He herded them, baffled and annoyed, into the elevator. At the entrance to the building, he searched up and down the street.

"He's not around, Gilroy. All right, you deadbeats, divide up and chase around the streets, whistling. When you see a brown-and-white collie, whistle to him. He'll come to you. Now beat it and do as I say."

They moved off slowly. "Whistle?" one called back anxiously.

"Yes, whistle!" Gilroy declared. "Forget your dignity. Whistle!"

They scattered, whistling piercingly the signals that war supposed to attract dogs. The few people around the business district that late were highly interested and curious, but Gilroy left the editor whistling at the newspaper building, while he whistled toward West Street. He left the shrill calls blowing away from the river, and searched along the wide highway in the growing dusk.

For an hour he pried into dark spaces between the docks, patiently covering his ground. He found nothing but occasional longshoremen unloading trucks and a light uptown traffic. There were only homeless, prowling mongrels and starving drifters; no brown-and-white collie.

He gave up when he began to feel hungry. He returned to the building hoping the others had had more luck, and angry with himself for not having followed the dog when he had had a chance.

The editor was still there, whistling more frantically than ever. He had gathered a little band of inquisitive onlookers, who waited hopefully for something to happen. The reporters were also returning.

"Find anything?" the editor paused to ask.

"Nope. He didn't show up here?"

"Not yet. Oh, he'll be back, all right. I'm not afraid of that." And he went back to his persistent whistling, disregarding stares and rude remarks. He was a man with an iron will. He sneered openly at the defeated reporters when they slunk past him into the building.

In the comparative quiet of the city, above the editor's shrills, Gilroy heard swiftly pounding feet. He gazed over the head of the pack that had gathered around the editor.

A reporter burst into view, running at top speed and doing his best to whistle attractively through dry lips at a dog streaking away from him.

"Here he comes!" Gilroy shouted. He broke through the crowd and his long legs flashed over the distance to the collie. In his excitement, empty, toneless wind blew between his teeth; but the dog shot straight for him just the same. Gilroy snatched a dirty piece of paper out of his mouth. Then the dog was gone, toward the docks; and a black car rode ominously down the street.

Gilroy half started in pursuit, paused, and stared at the slip of paper in his hand. For a moment he blamed the insufficient light, but when the editor came up to him, yelling blasphemy for letting the dog escape, Gilroy handed him the unbelievable note.

"That dog can take care of himself," Gilroy said. "Read this."

The editor drew his brows together over the message. It read:

;;;,.;.; ;,..;,.”:...;,. ;,;. ..”;., ;;:..........,;,.”..;,; ....”.”;,.. “..;
“.”.....”. ,””"”,.”.. .”,. .... “.”,;;; ..”;;,;;

"Well, I'll be damned!" the editor exclaimed. "Is it a gag?"

"Gag, my eye!"

"Well, I can't make head or tail of it!" the editor protested.

Gilroy looked around undeterminedly, as if for someone to help them, "You're not supposed to. It's a code message." He swung around, stabbing an enormously long, knobbed finger at the editor. "Know anyone who can translate code—cryptograms?"

"Uh—let's see. How about the police, or the G-men—"

Gilroy snorted. "Give it to the bulls before we know what's in it!" he carefully tucked the crudely penciled note into his breast pocket and buttoned his coat. "You stick around outside here, chief, I'll be back with the translation. Keep an eye out for the pooch."

He loped off before the editor could more than open his mouth.

In the index room of the Forty-second Street Library, Gilroy crowded into the telephone booth and dialed a number. His eyes ached and he had a dizzy headache. Close reasoning always scrambled his wits. His mind was intuitive rather than ploddingly analytical.

"Executive office, please," he told the night operator. "There must be somebody there. I don't care if it's the business manager himself. I want to speak to somebody in the executive office. I'll wait," He lolled, bent into a convenient shape, against the wall. "Hello. Who's this? . . . Oh, good. Listen, Rothbart, this is Gilroy. Do me a favor, huh? You're nearest the front entrance. You'll find the chief outside the door. Send him to the telephone, and take his place until he gets through. While you're out there, watch for a brown-and-white collie. Nab him if he shows up and bring him inside . . . Will you? . . . Thanks!"

Gilroy held the receiver to his ear, defeatedly amusing himself by identifying the sounds coming over the wire. He was no longer in a hurry, and when he had to pay another nickel before the editor finally came to the telephone, he did not mind.

"What's up, Gilroy?" the editor asked hopefully.

"Nothing, chief. That's why I called up. I went through a military code book, some kids' stuff, and a history of cryptography through the ages. I found some good codes, but nobody seems to've thought of this punctuation code. Ever see the Confederate cipher? Boy, it's a real dazzler—wasn't cracked until after the Civil War was over! The old Greeks wound strips of paper around identical sticks. When they were unrolled, the strips were gibberish; around the sticks, the words fall right into order."

"Cut it out," the editor snapped. "Did you find anything useful?"

"Sure. Everybody says the big clue is the table of frequency—the letters used more often than others. But, on the other hand, they say that in short messages, like ours, important clues like the single words 'a' and 'I,' bigrams like 'am, 'as,' and even trigrams like 'the' or 'but,' are often omitted entirely."

"Well, that's fine. What're you going to do now?"

"I don't know. Try the cops after all, I guess."

"Nothing doing," the editor said firmly. "Ask a librarian to help."

Gilroy seized the inspiration. He slammed down the receiver and strode to the reference desk.

"Where can I get hold of somebody who knows cryptograms!" he rasped.

The attendant politely consulted his colleagues. "The guard of the manuscript room is pretty good," he said, returning. "Down the hall—"

Gilroy shouted his thanks and broke into an ungainly run, ignoring the attendant's order to walk. At the manuscript room he clattered the gate until the keeper appeared and let him in.

"Take a look at this," he commanded, flinging the message on a table.

The keeper glanced curiously at it. "Oh, cryptograms, eh?"

"Yeah. Can you make anything out of it?"

"Well, it looks like a good one," the guard replied cautiously, "but I've been cracking them all for the last twenty years." They sat down at a table in the empty room. For some time the guard stared fixedly at the scrawled note. "Five symbols," he said finally. "Semicolon, period, comma, colon, quotation marks. Thirteen word units, each unit with an even number of symbols. They must be used in combinations of two."

"I figured that out already," Gilroy rapped out. "What's it say?"

The guard lifted his head, offended. "Give me a chance. Bacon's code wasn't solved for three centuries."

Gilroy groaned. He did not have as much time on his hands.

"There're only thirteen word units here," the guard went on, undaunted by the Bacon example. "Can't use frequency, bigrams or trigrams."

"I know that already," Gilroy said hoarsely.

"Then why'd you come to me if you're so smart?"

Gilroy hitched his chair away. "O.K., I won't bother you."

"Five symbols to represent twenty-six letters. Can't be. Must be something like the Russian nihilist code. They can represent only twenty-five letters. The missing one is either 'q' or 'j,' most likely, because they're not used much. Well, I'll tell you what I think."

"What's that?" Gilroy demanded, all alert.

"You'll have to reason a priori or whatever it is."

"Any way you want," Gilroy sighed. "Just get on with it."

"The square root of twenty-five is five. Whoever wrote this note must've made a square of letters, five wide and five deep. That sounds right." The guard smiled and nodded cheerfully, "Possible combinations in a square of twenty-five letters is . . . uh . . . 625. The double symbol must identify the lines down and across. Possible combinations, twenty-five. Combinations all told . . . hm-m-m . . . 15,625. Not so good. If there's a key word, we'll have to search the dictionary until we find it. Possible combinations, 15,625 multiplied by the English vocabulary— that is, if the key word is English."

Gilroy raised himself to his feet. "I can't stand it," he moaned. "I'll be back in an hour."

"No, don't go," the guard said. "You've been helping me a lot. I don't think we'll have to go through more than 625 combinations at the most. That'll take no time at all."

He spoke, of course, in relative terms. Bacon code, three centuries; Confederate code, fifteen years; war-time Russian code, unsolved. Cryptographers must look forward to eternity.

Gilroy seated himself, while the guard plotted a square:

;",.:
abcde;
fghIj"
klmno,
prstu.
vwxyz:

The first symbol combinations, two semicolons, translated to "a," by reading down the first line, from the top semicolon, and across from the side semicolon. The next, a semicolon and a comma, read "k." He went on in this fashion until he screwed up his face and pushed the half-completed translation to Gilroy. It read:

"akdd kyoiztou kp tho extzkprepd"

"Does it make sense to you?" he asked anxiously.

Gilroy strangled, unable to reply.

"It could be Polish," the guard explained, "or Japanese."

The harassed reporter fled.

When he returned an hour later, after having eaten and tramped across town, nervously chewing on cigarettes, he found the guard defended from him by a breastwork of heaped papers.

"Does it look any better?" Gilroy asked hoarsely.

The guard was too absorbed to look up or answer. By peering over his shoulder, Gilroy saw that he had plotted another square. The papers on the table were covered with discarded letter keys; at a rough guess, Gilroy estimated that the keeper had made over a hundred of them.

The one he was working with had been formed as the result of mathematical elimination. His first square, the guard had kept, changing the positions of the punctuation marks. When that had failed, he altered his alphabetic square, tried that, and reversed his punctuation marks once more.   Patient and plodding the guard had formed this square:

,.;":
zuoje,
ytnid.
xsmhc;
wrlgb"
vpkfa:

Without haste he counted down under the semicolon and across from the side semicolon, stopping at "m." Gilroy followed him, nodding at the result. He was faster than the old guard at interpreting the semicolon and comma—"o." First word: "moss."

Gilroy straightened up and took a deep breath. He bent over again and counted down and across with the guard, through the whole message, which the old man had lined off between every two symbols. Completed, it read

```
;;|;,|.;|.:|  :,|.:|:,|.”|::|..|:,|:. ;,|:.|  ..|”;|:,|
m o s s   o p e r a t e d    o n   t h e
:;|::|..|::|..|;,|;.|”.|:;|.;|  ..|::|;”|:”|;,|..|  “.|.;|
c a t a t o n i c s    t a l b o t    i s
“:|”.|;.|::|;.|:;|”.|””|  “;|”.|::|  .:|.”|:,|..|:,|:;|..|
f i  n a c i n g    h i m  p r o t e c t
      ;;|;,|  “:|.”|;,|;;|  ..|”;|:,|;;|
m e  f r o m  t h e m
```

"Hm-m-m," the guard mused. "that makes sense, if I knew what it meant."

But Gilroy had snatched the papers out of his hand.   The gate clanged shut after him.

Returning to the office in a taxi, Gilroy was not too joyful. He rapped on the inside window. "Speed it up! I've seen the sights."

He thought, if the dog's been bumped off, good-by catatonic story! The dog was his only link with the code writer.

Wood slunk along the black, narrow alleys behind the wholesale fruit markets on West Street.   Battered cans and crates of rotting fruit made welcome obstacles and shelters if Talbot's gangsters were following him.

He knew that he had to get away from the river section. The gangsters must have definitely recognized him; they would call Talbot's headquarters for greater forces. With their speedy cars they could patrol the borders of the district he was operating in, and close their lines until he was trapped.

More important was the fact that reporters had been sent out to search for him. Whether or not his simple code had been deciphered did not matter very much; the main thing was that Gilroy at last knew he was trying to communicate with him.

Wood's unerring animal sense of direction led him through the maze of densely shadowed alleys to a point nearest the newspaper office. He peered around the corner, up and down the street. The black gang car was out of sight. But he had to make an unprotected dash of a hundred yards, in the full glare of the street lights, to the building entrance.

His powerful leg muscles gathered. He sped over the hard cement sidewalk. The entrance drew nearer. His legs pumped more furiously, shortening the dangerous space more swiftly than a human being could; and for that he was grateful.

He glimpsed a man standing impatiently at the door. At the last possible moment, Wood checked his rush and flung himself toward the thick glass plate.

"There you are!" the editor cried. "Inside—quick!"

He thrust open the door. They scurried inside and commandeered an elevator, ran through the newsroom to the editor's office.

"Boy, I hope you weren't seen! It'd be curtains for both of us."

The editor squirmed uneasily behind his desk, from time to time glancing disgruntedly at his watch and cursing Gilroy's long absence. Wood stretched out on the cold floor and panted. He had expected his note to be deciphered by then, and even hoped to be recognized as a human being in a dog's body. But he realized that Gilroy probably was still engaged in decoding it.

At any rate he was secure for a while. Before long, Gilroy would return; then his story would be known. Until then he had patience.

Wood raised his head and listened. He recognized Gilroy's characteristic pace that consumed at least four feet at a step. Then the door slammed open and shut behind the reporter.

"The dog's here, huh? Wait'll you take a look at what I got!"

He threw a square of paper before the editor. Wood scanned the editor's face as he eagerly read it. He ignored the vast hamburger that Gilroy unwrapped for him. He was bewildered by Gilroy's lack of more than ordinary interest in him; but perhaps the editor would understand.

"So that's it! Moss and Talbot, eh? It's getting a lot clearer."

"I got Moss's angle," Gilroy said. "He's the only guy around here who could do an operation like that. But Talbot—I don't get his game. And who sent the note—how'd he get the dope—where is he?"

Wood almost went mad with frustration. He could explain; he knew all there was to know about Talbot's interest in Moss's experiment. The problem of communication had been solved. Moss and Talbot were exposed; but he was as far from ever from regaining his own body.

He had to write another cipher message—longer, this time, and more explicit, answering the questions Gilroy raided. But to do that—He shivered. To do that, he would have to run the gang patrol; and his enciphering square was in the corner of a lot. It would be too dark—

"We've got to get him to lead us to the one who wrote the message," Gilroy said determinedly. "That's the only way we can corner Moss and Talbot. Like this, all we have is an accusation and no legal proof."

"He must be around here somewhere."

Gilroy fastened his eyes on Wood. "That's what I think. The dog came here and barked, trying to get us to follow him. When we chased him out, he came back with a scrawled note about a half hour later. Then he brought the code message within another hour. The writer must be pretty near here. After the dog eats, we'll—" He gulped audibly and raised his bewildered gaze to the editor. Swiftly, he slipped off the edge of the desk and fumbled in the long hair of Wood's neck. "Look at this, chief—a piece of surgical plaster. When the dog bent his head to eat, the hair fell away from it."

"And you think he's a catatonic?" The editor smiled pityingly and shook his head. "You're jumpy, Gilroy."

"Maybe I am. But I'd like to see what's under the plaster."

Wood's heart pumped furiously. He knew that his incision was the precise duplicate of the catatonics', and if Gilroy could see it, he would immediately understand. When Gilroy picked at the plaster, he tried to bear the stabbing pain; but he had to squirm away. The wound was raw and new, and the deeply rooted hair was firmly glued to the plaster. He permitted Gilroy to try again. The sensation was far too fierce; he was afraid the incision would rip wide open.

"Stop it," the editor said squeamishly. "He'll bite you."

Gilroy straightened up. "I could take it off with some ether."

"You don't really think he was operated on, do you? Moss doesn't operate on dogs. He probably got into a fight, or one of Talbot's torpedoes creased him with a bullet."

The telephone bell rang insistently. "I'd still like to see what's under it," Gilroy said as the editor removed the receiver. Wood's hopes died suddenly. He felt that he was to blame for resisting Gilroy.

"What's up, Blaine?" the editor asked. He listened absorbedly, his face darkening. "O.K. Stay away if you don't want to take a chance. Phone your story in to the rewrite desk." He replaced the receiver and said to Gilroy: "Trouble, plenty of it. Talbot's gang cars are cruising around this district. Blaine was afraid to run them. I don't know how you're going to get the dog through."

Wood was alarmed. He left his meal unfinished and agitated toward the door, whimpering involuntarily.

Gilroy glanced curiously at him. "I'd swear he understood what you said. Did you see the change that came over him?"

"That's the way they react to voices," the editor said.

"Well, we've got to get him to his master," Gilroy mused, biting the inside of his cheek. "I can do it—if you're in with me."

"Of course I am. How?"

"Follow me." Wood and the editor went through the newsroom on the cadaverous reporter's swift heels. In silence they waited for an elevator, descended to the lobby. "Wait here beside the door," Gilroy said. "When I give the signal, come running."

"What signal?" the editor cried, but Gilroy had loped into the street and out of sight.

They waited tensely. In a few minutes a taxi drew up to the curb and Gilroy opened the door, sitting alertly inside. He watched the corner behind him. No one moved for a long while, then a black gang car rode slowly and vigilantly past the taxi. Gilroy waited until a moment after it turned into West Street. He waved his arms frantically.

The editor scooped Wood up in his arms, burst open the door, and darted across the sidewalk into the cab.

"Step on it!" Gilroy ordered harshly. "Up West Street!"

The taxi accelerated suddenly. Wood crouched on the floor, trembling, in despair. He had exhausted his ingenuity and he was as far as ever from regaining his body. They expected him to lead them to his master; they still did not realize that he had written the message. Where should he lead them—how could he convince them that he was the writer?

"I think this is far enough," Gilroy broke the silence. He tapped on the window. The driver stopped. Gilroy paid and waved the driver away. In the quiet isolation of the broad commercial highway, he bent his great height to Wood's level. "Come on, boy!" he urged. "Home!"

Wood was in a panic of dismay. He could think of only one place to lead them. He set off at a slow trot that did not tax them. Hugging the walls, sprinting across streets, he headed cautiously downtown.

They followed him behind the markets fronting the highway, over a hemmed-in lot. He picked his way around the deep, treacherous foundation of a building that had been torn down, up and across piles of rubbish, to a black-shadowed clearing at the lot's end. He halted passively.

Gilroy and the editor peered around into the blackness, "Come out!" Gilroy called hoarsely. "We're your friends. We want to help you."

When there was no response, they explored the lot, lighting matches to illuminate dark corners of the foundation. Wood watched them with confused emotions. By searching in the garbage heaps and the crumbling walls of the foundation they were merely wasting time.

As closely as possible in the dark, he located the site of his enciphering square. He stood near it and barked clamorously. Gilroy and the editor hastily left their futile prodding.

"He must've seen something," the editor observed in a whisper.

Gilroy cupped a match in his hand and moved the light back and forth in the triangular corner of the cleared space. He shrugged.

"Not around there," the editor said. "He's pointing at the ground."

Gilroy lowered the match. Before its light struck the ground he yelped and dropped it, waving his burned fingers in the cool air. The editor murmured sympathy and scratched another match.

"Is this what you're looking for—a lot of letters in a square?"

Wood and Gilroy crowded close. The reporter struck his own match. In its light he narrowly inspected the crudely scratched encoding square.

"Be back in a second," he said. It was too dark to see his face, but Wood heard his voice, harsh and strained. "Getting flashlight."

"What'll I do if the guy comes around?" the editor asked hastily.

"Nothing," Gilroy rasped. "He won't. Don't step on the square."

Gilroy vanished into the night. The editor struck another match and scrutinized the ground with Deerslayer thoroughness.

"What the hell did he see?" he pondered. "That guy—" He shook his head defeatedly and dropped the match.

Never in his life had Wood been so passionately excited. What had Gilroy discovered? Was it merely another circumstantial fact, like his realization that Talbot's gangsters were gunning for Wood; or was it a suspicion of Wood's identity? Gilroy had replied that the writer would not reappear, but that could mean anything or nothing. Wood frantically searched for a way of finally demonstrating who he really was. He found only a negative plan—he would follow Gilroy's lead.

With every minute that passed, the editor grew angrier, shifting his leaning position against the brick wall, pacing around. When Gilroy came back, flashing a bright cone of light before him, the editor lashed out.

"Get it over with, Gilroy. I can't waste the whole night. Even if we do find out what happened, we can't print it—"

Gilroy ignored him. He splashed the brilliant ray of his huge five-celled flashlight over the enciphering square.

"Now look at it," he said. He glanced intently at Wood, who also obeyed his order and stood at the editor's knee, searching the ground. "The guy who made that square was very cautious—he put his back to the wall and faced the lot, so he wouldn't be taken by surprise. The square is upside-down to us. No, wait!" he said sharply as the editor moved to look at the square from its base. "I don't want your footprints on it. Look at the bottom, where the writer must have stood."

The editor stared closely. "What do you see?" he asked puzzledly.

"Well, the ground is moist and fairly soft. There should be footprints. There are. Only they are not human!"

Raucously, the editor cleared his throat. "You're kidding."

"Gestalt," Gilroy said, almost to himself, "the whole is greater than the sum of its parts. You get a bunch of unconnected facts, all apparently unrelated to each other. Then suddenly one fact pops up—it doesn't seem any more important than the others— but all at once the others click into place, and you get the complete picture."

"What are you mumbling about?" the editor whispered anxiously.

Gilroy stooped his great height and picked up a yellow stump of pencil. He turned it over in his hand before passing it to the editor.

"That's the pencil this dog snatched before we threw him out. You can see his teethmarks on the sides, where he carried it. But there're teethmarks around the unsharpened end. Maybe I'm nut's—" He took the dirty code message out of his inside breast pocket and smoothed it out. "I saw these smudges the minute I looked at the note, but they didn't mean anything to me then. What do you make of them?"

The editor obediently examined the note in the glare of the flash. "They could be palmprints."

"Sure—a baby's," Gilroy said witheringly. "Only they're not. We both know they're pawprints, the same as are at the bottom of the square. You know what I'm thinking. Look at the way the dog is listening."

Without raising his voice, he half turned his head and said quite casually, "Here comes the guy who wrote the note, right behind the dog."

Involuntarily, Wood spun around to face the dark lot. Even his keen animal eyes could detect no one in the gloom. When he lifted his gaze to Gilroy, he stared full into grim, frightened eyes.

"Put that in your pipe," Gilroy said tremulously. "That's his reaction to the pitch of my voice, eh? You can't get out of it, chief. We've got a werewolf on our hands, thanks to Moss and Talbot."

Wood barked and frisked happily around Gilroy's towering legs. He had been understood!

But the editor laughed, a perfectly normal, humorous, unconvinced laugh. "You're wasting your time writing for a newspaper, Gilroy—"

"O.K., smart guy," Gilroy replied savagely. "Stop your cackling and tell me the answer to this—"

"The dog comes into the newsroom and starts barking. I thought he was just trying to get us to follow him; but I never heard a dog bark in long and short yelps before. He ran up the stairs, right past the other floors—business office, advertising department, and so on—to the newsroom, because that's where he wanted to go. We chased him out. He came back with a scrawled note, saying: 'I am a man.' Those four words took up a whole page. Even a kid learning how to write wouldn't need so much space. But if you hold the pencil in your mouth and try to connect the bars of the letters, you'd have letters something like the ones on the note.

"He needed a smaller system of letters, so he made up a simple code. But he'd lost his pencil. He stole one of ours. Then he came back, watching out for Talbot's gang cars.

"There aren't any footprints at the bottom of this square— only a dog's pawprints. And there're two smudges on the message, where he put his paws to hold down the paper while he wrote on it. All along he's been listening to every word we said.

When I said in a conversational tone that the writer was standing behind him, he whirled around. Well?"

The editor was still far from convinced. "Good job of training—"

"For a guy I used to respect, you certainly have the brain of a flea. Here—I don't know your name," he said to Wood. "What would you do if you had Moss here?"

Wood snarled.

It was Wood's moment of supreme triumph. True, he didn't have his body yet, but now it was only a matter of time. His joy at Gilroy's words was violent enough to shake even the editor's literal, unimaginative mind.

"You still don't believe it?" Gilroy accused.

"How can I?" the editor cried plaintively. "I don't even know why I'm talking to you as if it could be possible."

Gilroy probed in a pile of rubbish until he uncovered a short piece of wood. He quickly drew a single like of small alphabetical symbols. He threw the stick away, stepped back and flashed the light directly at the alphabet. "Now spell out what happened."

Wood sprang back and forth before the alphabet, stopping at the letters he required and indicating them by pointing his snout down.

"T-a-l-b-o-t w-a-n-t-e-d a y-o-u-n-g- h-e-a-l-t-h-y b-o-d-y M-o-s-s s-a-i-d h-e c-o-u-l-d g-i-v-e i-t- t-o h-i-m—"

"Well, I'll be damned!" the editor blurted.

After the exclamation there was silence. Only the almost inaudible padding of Wood's paws on the soft ground, his excited panting, and the hoarse breathing of the men could be heard. But Wood had won!

Gilroy sat at the typewriter in his apartment; Wood stood beside his chair and watched the swiftly leaping keys; but the editor stamped nervously up and down the floor.

"I've wasted half the night," he complained, "and if I print this story I'll be canned. Why, damn it, Gilroy—How do you think the public'll take it if I can't believe it myself."

"Hm-m-m," Gilroy explained.

"You're sacrificing our job. You know that, don't you?"

"It doesn't mean that much to me," Gilroy said without glancing up. "Wood has to get back his body. He can't do it unless we help him."

"Doesn't that sound ridiculous to you? 'He has to get back his body.' Imagine what the other papers'll do to that sentence!"

Gilroy shifted impatiently. "They won't see it," he stated,

"Then why the hell are you writing the story?" the editor asked, astounded. "Why don't you want me to go back to the office?"

"Quiet! I'll be through in a minute." He inserted another sheet of paper and his flying fingers covered it with black, accusing words. Wood's mouth opened in a canine grin when Gilroy smiled down at him and nodded his head confidently. "You're practically walking around on your own feet, pal. Let's go."

He flapped on his coat and carelessly dropped a battered hat on his craggy head. Wood braced himself to dart off. The editor lingered.

"Where're we going?" he asked cautiously.

"To Moss, naturally, unless you can think of a better place."

Wood could not tolerate the thought of delay. He tugged at the leg of the editor's pants.

"You bet I can think of a better place. Hey, cut it out, Wood—I'm coming along. But, hell, Gilroy! It's after ten. I haven't done a thing. Have a heart and make it short."

With Gilroy hastening him by the arm and Wood dragging at his leg, the editor had to accompany then, though he continued his protests. At the door, however, he covered Wood while Gilroy hailed a taxi. When Gilroy signaled that the street was clear, he ran across the sidewalk with Wood bundled in his arms.

Gilroy gave the address. At its sound, Wood's mouth opened in a silent snarl. He was only a short distance from Moss, with two eloquent spokesmen to articulate his demands, and, if necessary, to mobilize public opinion for him! What could Moss do against that power?

They rode up Seventh Avenue and along Central Park West. Only the editor felt they were speeding. Gilroy and Wood fretted irritably at every stop signal.

At Moss's street, Gilroy cautioned the driver to proceed slowly. The surgeon's house was guarded by two loitering black cars.

"Let us out at the corner," Gilroy said.

They scurried into the entrance to a rooming house.

"Now what?" the editor demanded. "We can't fight past them."

"How about the back way, Wood?"

Wood shook his head negatively. There was no entrance through the rear.

"Then the only way is across the roofs," Gilroy determined. He put his head out and scanned the buildings between them and Moss. "This one is six stories, the next two five, the one right next to Moss's is six, and Moss's is three. We'll have to climb up and down fire escapes and get in through Moss's roof. Ready?"

"I suppose so," the editor said fatalistically.

Gilroy tried the door. It was locked. He chose a bell at random and rang it vigorously. There was a brief pause; then the tripper buzzed. He thrust open the door and burst up the stairs, four at a leap.

"Who's there?" a woman shouted down the stair well.

They galloped past her. "Sorry, lady," Gilroy called back. "We rang your bell by mistake."

She looked disappointed and rather frightened; but Gilroy anticipated her emotion. He smiled and gayly waved his hand as he loped by.

The roof door was locked with a stout hook that had rusted into its eye. Gilroy smashed it open with the heel of his palm. They broke out onto a tarred roof, chill and black in the overcast threatening night.

Wood and Gilroy discovered the fire escape leading to the next roof. They dashed for it. Gilroy tucked Wood under his left arm and swung himself over the anchored ladder.

"This is insane!" the editor cried hoarsely. "I've never done such a crazy thing in my life. Why can't we be smart and call the cops?"

"Yeah?" Gilroy sneered without stopping. "What's your charge?"

"Against Moss? Why—"

"Think about it on the way."

Gilroy and Wood were on the next roof, waiting impatiently for the editor to descend. He came down quickly but his thoughts wandered.

"You can charge him with what he did. He made a man into a dog."

"That would sound swell in the indictment. Forget it. Just walk lightly. This damned roof creaks and lets out a note like a drum."

They advanced over the tarred sheets of metal. Beneath them, they could hear their occasionally heavy tread resounding through the hollow rooms. Wood's claws tapped a rhythmic tattoo.

They straddled over a low wall dividing the two buildings. Wood sniffed the air for enemies lurking behind chimneys, vents and doors. At instants of suspicion, Gilroy briefly flashed his light ahead. They climbed up a steel ladder to the six story building adjoining Moss's.

"How about a kidnapping charge?" the editor asked as they stared down over the wall at the roof of Moss's building.

"Please don't annoy me. Wood's body is in the observation ward at the hospital. How're you going to prove that Moss kidnapped him?"

The editor nodded in the gloom and searched for another legal charge. Gilroy splashed his light over Moss's roof. It was unguarded.

"Come on, Wood," he said, inserting the flashlight in his belt. He picked up Wood under his left arm. In order to use his left hand in climbing, he had to squeeze Wood's middle in a strangle hold.

The only think Wood was thankful for was that he could not look at the roof three stories below. Gilroy held him securely, tightly enough for his breath to struggle in whistling gasps. His throat knotted when Gilroy gashed his hand on a sharp sliver of dry paint scale.

"It's all right," Gilroy hissed reassuringly. "We're almost there."

Above them, he saw the editor clambering heavily down the insecurely bolted ladder. Between the anchoring plates it groaned and swayed away from the unclean brick wall. Rung by rung they descended warily, Gilroy clutching for each hold, Wood suspended in space and helpless—both feeling their hearts drop when the ladder jerked under their weight.

Then Gilroy lowered his foot and found the solid roof beneath it. He grinned impetuously in the dark. Wood writhed out of his hold. The editor cursed his way down to them.

He followed them to the rear fire escape. This time he offered to carry Wood down. Swinging out over the wall, Wood felt the editor's muscles quiver. Wood had nothing but a miserable animal life to lose, and yet even he was not entirely fearless in the face of the hidden dangers they were braving. He could sympathize with the editor, who had everything to lose and did not wholly believe that Wood was not a dog. Discovering a human identity in an apparently normal collie must have been a staggeringly hard fact for him to swallow.

He set Wood down on the iron bars. Gilroy quickly joined them, and yanked fiercely at the top window. It was locked.

"Need a jimmy to pry it open," Gilroy mused. He fingered the edges of the frame. "Got a knife on you?"

The editor fished absent-mindedly through his pockets. He brought out handful of keys, pencil stubs, scraps of paper, matches, and a cheap sheathed nail file. Gilroy snatched the file.

He picked at the putty in the ancient casement with the point. It chipped away easily. He loosened the tops and sides.

"Now," he breathed. "Stand back a little and get ready to catch it."

He inserted the file at the top and levered the glass out of the frame. It stuck at the bottom and sides, refusing to fall. He caught the edges and lifted it out, laying it down noiselessly out of the way.

"Let's go." He backed in through the empty casement. "Hand Wood through."

They stood in the dark room, under the same roof with Moss. Wood exultantly sensed the proximity of the one man he hated— the one man who could return his body to him. "Now!" he thought. "Now!"

"Gilroy," the editor urged, "we can charge Moss with vivisection."

"That's right," Gilroy whispered. But they heard the doorknob rattle in his hand and turn cautiously.

"Then where're you going?" the editor rasped in panic.

"We're here," Gilroy replied coolly. "So let's finish it."

The door swung back; pale weak light entered timidly. They stared down the long, narrow, dismal hall to the stairs at the center of the house. Down those stairs they would find Moss—

Wood's keen animal sense of smell detected Moss's personal odor. The surgeon had been there not long before.

He crouched around the stairhead and cautiously lowered himself from step to step. Gilroy and the editor clung to banister and wall, resting the bulk of their weight on their hands. They turned the narrow spiral where Clarence had fatally encountered the sharpness of Wood's fangs, down to the hall floor where his fat body had sprawled in blood.

Distantly Wood heard a cane tap nervously, momentarily; then it stopped at a heated, hissed command that scarcely carried even to his ears. He glanced up triumphantly at Gilroy, his deep eyes glittering, his mouth grinning savagely, baring the red tongue lolling in the white deadly trap of fangs. He had located and identified the sounds. Both Moss and Talbot were in a room at the back of the house—

He hunched his powerful shoulders and advanced slowly, stiff-legged, with the ominous air of all meat hunters stalking prey from ambush. Outside the closed door he crouched, muscles gathered for the lunge, his ears flat back along his pointed head to protect them from injury. But they heard muffled voices inaudible to men's dulled senses.

"Sit down, doc," Talbot said. "The truck'll be here soon."

"I'm not concerned with my personal safety," Moss replied tartly. "It's merely that I dislike inefficiency, especially when you claim—"

"Well, it's not Jake's fault. He's coming back from a job."

Wood could envision the faint sneer on Moss's scrubbed pink face. "You'll collapse any minute within the next six months, but the acquisitive nature is as strong as ever in you, isn't it Talbot? You couldn't resist the chance of making a profit, and at a time like this!"

"Oh, don't lose your head. The cata-whatever-you-call-it can't talk and the dog is probably robbing garbage cans. What's the lam for?"

"I'm changing my residence purely as a matter of precaution. You underestimate human ingenuity, even limited by a dog's inarticulateness."

Wood grinned up at his comrades. The editor was dough-faced, rigid with apprehension. Gilroy held a gun and his left hand snaked out at the doorknob. The editor began an involuntary motion to stop him. The door slammed inward before he completed it.

Wood and Gilroy stalked in, sinister in their grim silence. Talbot merely glanced at the gun. He had stared into too many black muzzles to be frightened by it. When his gaze traveled to Wood his jaw fell and hung open, trembling senilely. His constantly fighting lungs strangled. He screamed, a high, tortured wail, and tore frantically at his shirt, trying to release his chest from crushing pressure.

"An object lesson for you, Talbot," Moss said without emotion. "Do not underestimate an enemy."

Gilroy lost his frigid attitude. "Don't let him strangle. Help him."

"What can I do?" Moss shrugged. "It's angina pectoris. Either he pulls out of the convulsions by himself—or he doesn't. I can't help. But what do you want?"

No man answered him. Horrified, they were watching Talbot go purple in his death agony, lose the power of shrieking and tear at his chest. Gilroy's gun hand was limp; yet Moss made no attempt to escape. The air rattled through Talbot's predatory nose. He fell in a contorted heap.

"Wood felt sickened. He knew that in self-preservation doctors had to harden themselves, but only a monster of brutal callousness could have disregarded Talbot's frightful death as if it had not been going on.

"Oh, come now, it isn't as bad as all that," Moss said acidly.

Wood raised his shocked stare from the rag-doll body to Moss's hard, unfearful eyes. The surgeon had made no move to defend himself, to call for help from the squad of gangsters at the front of the house. He faced them with inhuman prepossession.

"It upsets your plans," Gilroy spat.

Moss lifted his shoulders, urbanedly, delicately disdainful. "What difference should his death make to me? I never cared for his company."

"Maybe not, but his money seemed to smell O.K. to you. He's out of the picture. He can't keep us from printing this story now." Gilroy pulled a thin folded typescript from his inside breast pocket and shoved it out at Moss.

The surgeon read it interestedly, leaning casually against a wall. He came to the end of the short article and read the lead paragraph over again. Politely, he gave it back to Gilroy.

"It's very clear," he said. "I'm accused of exchanging the identities of a man and a dog. You even describe my alleged technique."

"Alleged!" Gilroy roared savagely. "You mean you deny it?"

"Of course. Isn't it fantastic?" Moss smiled. "But that isn't the point. Even if I admitted it, how do you think I could be convicted on such evidence? The only witness seems to be the dog you call Wood. Are dogs allowed to testify in court? I don't remember, but I doubt it."

Wood was stunned. He had not expected Moss to brazen out the charge. An ordinary man would have broken down, confronted by their evidence.

Even the shrinking editor was stung into retorting: "We have proof of criminal vivisection!"

"But no proof that I was the surgeon."

"You're the only one in New York who could've done that operation."

"See how far that kind of evidence will get you."

Wood listened with growing anger. Somehow they had permitted Moss to dominate the situation, and he parried their charges with cool, sarcastic deftness. No wonder he had not tried to escape! He felt himself to be perfectly safe. Wood growled, glowered hatred at Moss. The surgeon looked down contemptuously.

"All right, we can't convict you in court," Gilroy said. He hefted his gun, tightened his finger on the trigger. "That's not what we want, anyhow. This little scientific curiosity can make you operate on Wood and transfer his identity back into his own body."

Moss's expression of disdain did not alter. He watched Gilroy's tensing trigger finger with an astonished lack of concern.

"Well, speak up," Gilroy rasped, waving the gun ominously.

"You can't force me to operate. All you can do is kill me, and I am as indifferent to my own death as I was to Talbot's." His smile broadened and twisted down at the corners, showing his teeth in a snarl that was the civilized, over-refined counterpart of Wood's. "Your alleged operation interests me, however. I'll operate for my customary fee."

The editor pushed Gilroy inside and hurriedly closed the door. "They're coming," he chattered. "Talbot's gangsters."

In two strides Gilroy put Moss between him and the door. His gun jabbed rudely into Moss's unflinching back. "Get over to the other side, you two, so the door'll hide you when it swings back," he ordered.

Wood and the editor retreated. Wood heard steps along the hall, then a pause, and a harsh voice shouted: "Hey, boss! Truck's here."

"Tell them to go away," Gilroy said in a low, suppressed tone.

Moss called, "I'm in the second room at the rear of the house."

Gilroy viciously stabbed him with the gun muzzle. "You're asking for it. I said tell them to go away!"

"You wouldn't dare to kill me until I've operated—"

"If you're not scared, why do you want them? What's the gag?"

The door flung open. A gangster started to enter. He stiffened, his keen, battle-trained eyes flashing from Talbot's twisted body to Moss, and to Gilroy, standing menacingly behind the surgeon. In a swift, smooth motion a gun leaped from his armpit holster.

"What happened to the boss?" he demanded hoarsely. "Who's he?"

"Put your gun away, Pinero. The boss died of a heart attack. That shouldn't surprise you—he was expecting it any day."

"Yeah, I know. But how'd that guy get in?"

Moss stirred impatiently. "He was here all along. Send the truck back. I'm not moving. I'll take care of Talbot."

The gangster looked uncertain, but, in lieu of another commander, he obeyed Moss's order. "Well, O.K., if you say so." He closed the door.

When Pinero had gone down the hall, Moss turned to face Gilroy.

"You're not scared—much!" Gilroy said.

Moss ignored his sarcastic outburst. "Where were we?" he asked. "Oh, yes. While you were standing there shivering, I had time to think over my offer. I'll operate for nothing."

"You bet you will!" Gilroy wagged his gun forcefully.

Moss sniffed at it. "That has nothing to do with my decision. I have no fear of death, and I'm not afraid of your evidence. If I do operate, it will because of my interest in the experiment." Wood intercepted Moss's speculative gaze. It mocked, hardened, glittered sinisterly. "But of course," Moss added smoothly," I will definitely operate. In fact, I insist on it!"

His hidden threat did not escape Wood. Once he lay under Moss's knife it would be the end. A slip of the knife—a bit of careful carelessness in the gas mixture—a deliberately caused infection—and Moss would clear himself of the accusation by claiming he could not perform the operation, and therefore was not the vivisectionist. Wood recoiled, shaking his head violently from side to side.

"Wood's right," the editor said. "He knows Moss better. He wouldn't come out of the operation alive."

Gilroy's brow creased in an uneasy frown. The gun in his hand was a futile implement of force; even Moss knew he would not use it—could not, because the surgeon was only valuable to them alive. His purpose had been to make Moss operate. Well, he thought, he had accomplished that purpose. Moss offered to operate. But all four knew that under Moss's knife, Wood was doomed. Moss had cleverly turned the victory to utter rout.

"Then what the hell'll we do?" Gilroy exploded savagely. "What do you say, Wood? Want to take the chance, or keep on in a dog's body?"

Wood snarled, backing away.

"At least, he's still alive," the editor said fatalistically.

Moss smiled, protesting with silken mockery that he would do his best to return Wood's body.

"Barring accidents," Gilroy spat. "No soap, Moss. He'll get along the way he is, and you're going to get yours."

He looked grimly at Wood, jerking his head significantly in Moss's direction.

"Come on, chief," he said, guiding the editor through the door and closing it. "These old friends want to be alone—to talk over—"

Instantly, Wood leaped before the door and crouched there menacingly, glaring at Moss with blind, vicious hatred. For the first time, the surgeon dropped his pose of indifference. He inched cautiously around the wall toward the door. He realized suddenly that this was an animal—

Wood advanced, cutting off his line of retreat. Mane bristling, head lowered ominously between blocky shoulders, bright gums showing above white curved fangs, Wood stalked over the floor, stiff-jointed, in a low, inexorably steady rhythm of approach.

Moss watched anxiously. He kept looking up at the door in an agony of longing. But Wood was there, closing the gap for the attack. He put his hands up to thrust away—

And his nerve broke. He could not talk down mad animal eyes as he could a man holding a gun. He darted to the side and ran for the door.

Wood flung himself at the swiftly pumping legs. They crashed against him, tripped. Moss sprawled face down on the floor. He crossed his arms under his head to protect his throat.

Wood slashed at an ear. It tore, streaming red. Moss screeched and clapped his hands over his face, trying to rise without dropping his guard. But Wood ripped at his fingers.

The surgeon's hands clawed out. He was kneeling, defenseless, trying to fight off the rapid, aimed lunges—and those knifelike teeth—

Wood gloated. A minute before, the scrubbed pink face had been aloof, sneering. Now it bobbed frantically at his eye level, contorted with overpowering fear, blood flowing brightly down the once scrupulously clean cheeks.

For an instant, the pale throat gleamed exposed at him. It was soft and helpless. He shot through the air. His teeth struck at an angle and snatched—The white flesh parted easily. But a bony structure snapped between his jaws as he swooped by.

Moss knelt there after Wood had struck. His pain-twisted face gasped imbecilically, hands limp at his side. Then his face drained to a ghastly lack of color and he pitched over.

He had lost, but he had also won. Wood was doomed to live out his life in a dog's body. He could not even expect to live his own life span. The average life of a dog is fifteen years. Wood could expect perhaps ten years more.

In his human body, Wood had found it difficult to find a job. He had been a code expert; but code experts, salesmen and apprentice workmen have no place in a world of shrinking markets. The employment agencies are glutted with an over-supply of normal human intelligences housed in strong, willing, expert human bodies.

The same normal human intelligence in a handsome collie's body had a greater market value. It was a rarity, a phenomenon to be gaped at after a ticket had been purchased of the privilege.

"Men've always had a fondness for freaks," Gilroy philosophized on their way to the theatre where Wood had an engagement. "Mildly amusing freaks are paid to entertain. The real funny ones are given seats of honor and power. Figure it out, Wood. I can't. Once we get rid of our love of freaks and put them where they belong, we'll have a swell world."

The taxi stopped in a side street, at the stage entrance. Lurid red-and-yellow posters, the size of cathedral murals, plastered the theatre walls; and from them smirked prettified likenesses of Wood.

"Gosh!" the driver gasped. "Wait'll my kids hear about this. I drove the Talkin' Dog! Gee, is that an honor, or ain't it?"

On all sides, pedestrians halted in awe, taxis stopped with a respectful screech of brakes, then an admiring swarm bore down on him.

"Isn't he cute?" women shrieked. "So intelligent looking!"

"Sure," Wood heard the driver boast proudly. "I drove him down here. What's he like?" His voice lowered confidentially. "Well, the guy with him—his manager, I guess—he was talkin' to him just as intelligent as I'm talkin' to you. Like he could understand ev'y word."

"Bet he could, too," a listener said definitely.

"G'on," another theorized. "He's just trained, like Rin-tin-tin, on'y better. But he's smart all right. Wisht I owned him."

The theater-district squad broke through the tangle of traffic and formed a lane to the stage door.

"Yawta be ashamed ayeshelves," a cop said. "All this over a mutt!"

Wood bared his fangs at the speaker, who retreated defensively.

"Wise guy, huh?" the mob jeered. "Think he can't understand?"

It was a piece of showmanship that Wood and Gilroy had devised. It never failed to find a feeder in the form of an officious policeman and a response from the crowd.

Even in the theater, Wood was not safe from overly enthusiastic admiration. His fellow performers persisted in scratching his unhitching back and ears, cooing and burbling in a singularly unintelligent manner.

The thriller that Wood had made in Hollywood was over, and while the opening acts went through their paces, Wood and Gilroy stood as far away from the wings as the theater construction would permit.

"Seven thousand bucks a week, pal," Gilroy mused over and over. "Just for doing something that any mug out in the audience can do twice as easily. Isn't that the payoff?"

In the year that had passed, neither was still able to accustom himself to the mounting figures in their bank book. Pictures, personal appearances, endorsements, highly fictionized articles in magazines—all at astronomical prices—

But he could never have enough money to buy back the human body he had starved in.

"O.K., Wood," Gilroy whispered. "We're on."

They were drummed onto the stage with deafening applause. Wood went through his routine perfunctorily. He identified objects that had been named by the theater manager, picking them out of a heap of piled objects.

Ushers went through the aisles, collecting questions the audience had written on slips of paper. They passed them up to Gilroy.

Wood took a long pointer firmly in his mouth and stood before a huge lettered screen. Painfully, he pointed out, letter by letter, the answers to the audience's questions. Most of them asked about the future, market tips, racing information. A few seriously probed his mind.

White light stabbed down at him. Mechanically, he spelled out the simple answers. Most of the bitterness had evaporated; in its place was a dreary defeat, and dull acceptance of his dog's life. His bank book had six figures to the left of the decimal, more than he had ever conceived or, even as a distant Utopian possibility. But no surgeon could return his body to him, or increase his life expectancy of less than ten years.

Sharply, everything was washed out of sight; Gilroy, the vast alphabet screen, the heavy pointer in his mouth, the black space smeared with pale, gaping blobs of faces, even the white light staring down—

He lay on a cot in a long ward. There was no dreamlike quality of illusion in the feel of smooth sheets beneath and above him, or in the weight of blankets resting on his outstretched¬ body.

And independently of the rest of his hand, his finger moved in response to his will. Its nail scratched at the sheet, loudly, victoriously.

An interne walking through the ward, looked around for the source of the gloating sound. He engaged Wood's eyes that were glittering avidly, deep with intelligence. Then they watched the scratching finger.

"You're coming back," the intern said at last.

"I'm coming back," Wood spoke quietly, before the scene vanished and he heard Gilroy repeat a question he had missed.

He knew then that the body-mind was a unit. Moss had been wrong; there was more to identity than that small gland, something beyond the body. The forced division Moss had created was unnatural; the transplanted tissue was being absorbed, remodeled. Somehow, he knew these returns to the natural identity would recur, more and more—till it became permanent—till he became human once more.

THE TROUBLE WITH WATER

ORIGINALLY PUBLISHED IN MARCH 1939

THE TROUBLE WITH WATER

Greenberg did not deserve his surroundings. He was the first fisherman of the season, which guaranteed him a fine catch; he sat in a dry boat—one without a single leak—far out on a lake that was ruffled only enough to agitate his artificial fly. The sun was warm, the air was cool; he sat comfortably on a cushion; he had brought a hearty lunch; and two bottles of beer hung over the stern in the cold water.

Any other man would have been soaked with joy to be fishing on such a splendid day. Normally, Greenberg himself would have been ecstatic, but instead of relaxing and waiting for a nibble, he was plagued with worries.

This short, slightly gross, definitely bald, eminently respectable businessman lived a gypsy life. During the summer he lived in a hotel with kitchen privileges in Rockaway; winters he lived in a hotel with kitchen privileges in Florida; and in both places he operated concessions. For years now, rain had fallen on schedule every week end, and there had been storms and floods on Decoration Day, July 4th and Labor Day. He did not love his life, but it was a way of making a living.

He closed his eyes and groaned. If he had only had a son instead of his Rosie! Then things might have been different—

For one thing, a son could run the hot dog and hamburger griddle, Esther could draw beer, and he would make soft drinks. There would be small difference in the profits, Greenberg admitted to himself; but at least those profits could be put aside for old age, instead of toward a dowry for his miserably ugly, dumpy, pitifully eager Rosie.

"All right—so what do I care if she don't get married?" he had cried to his wife a thousand times. "I'll support her. Other men can set up boys in candy stores with soda fountains that have only two spigots. Why should I have to give a boy a regular International Casino?"

"May your tongue rot in your head, you no-good piker!" she would scream. "It ain't right for a girl to be an old maid. If we have to die in the poor-house, I'll get my poor Rosie a husband. Every penny we don't need for living goes to her dowry!"

Greenberg did not hate his daughter, nor did he blame her for his misfortunes; yet, because of her, he was fishing with a broken rod that he had to tape together.

That morning his wife opened her eyes and saw him packing his equipment. She instantly became awake. "Go ahead!" she shrilled—speaking in a conversational tone was not one of her accomplishments—"Go fishing, you loafer! Leave me here alone. I can connect the beer pipes and the gas for the soda water. I can buy ice cream, frankfurters, rolls, syrup, and watch the gas and electric men at the same time. Go ahead—go fishing!"

"I ordered everything," he mumbled soothingly. "The gas and electric won't be turned on today. I only wanted to go fishing—it's my last chance. Tomorrow we open the concession. Tell the truth, Esther, can I go fishing after we open?"

"I don't care about that. Am I your wife or ain't I, that you should go ordering everything without asking me—"

He defended his actions. It was a tactical mistake. While she was still in bed, he should have picked up his equipment and left. By the time the argument got around to Rosie's dowry, she stood facing him.

"For myself I don't care," she yelled. "What kind of a monster are you that you can go fishing while your daughter eats her heart out? And on a day like this yet! You should only have to make supper and dress Rosie up. A lot you care that a nice boy is coming to supper tonight and maybe take Rosie out, you no-good father, you!"

From that point it was only one hot protest and a shrill curse to find himself clutching half a broken rod, with the other half being flung at his head.

Now he sat in his beautiful dry boat on an excellent game lake far out on Long Island, desperately aware that any average fish might collapse his taped rod.

What else could he expect? He had missed his train; he had had to wait for the boathouse proprietor; his favorite fly was missing; and since morning, not a fish struck at the bait. Not a single fish!

And it was getting late. He had no more patience. He ripped the cap off a bottle of beer and drank it, in order to gain courage to change his fly for a less sporting bloodworm, It hurt him, but he wanted a fish.

The hook and the squirming worm sank. Before it came to rest he felt a nibble. He sucked his breath exultantly and snapped the hook deep into the fish's mouth. Sometimes, he thought philosophically, they just won't take artificial bait. He reeled in slowly.

"Oh, Lord," he prayed, "a dollar for charity—just don't let the rod bend in half where I taped it!"

It was sagging dangerously. He looked at it unhappily and raised the ante to five dollars; even at that price it looked impossible. He dipped his rod into the water, parallel with the line to remove the strain. He was glad no one could see him do it. The line reeled in without a fight.

"Have I—God forbid!—got an eel or something not kosher?" he mumbled. "A plague on you—why don't you fight?"

He did not really care what it was—even an eel—anything at all.

He pulled in a long, pointed, brimless green hat.

For a moment he glared at it. His mouth hardened. Then, viciously, he yanked the hat off the hook, threw it on the floor and trampled on it. He rubbed his hands together in anguish.

"All day I fish," he wailed, "two dollars for train fare, a dollar for a boat, a quarter for bait, a new rod I got to buy—and a five-dollar-mortgage charity has got on me. For what? For you, you hat, you!"

Out in the water an extremely civil voice asked politely: "May I have my hat, please?"

Greenberg glowered up. He saw a little man come swimming vigorously through the water toward him; small arms crossed with enormous dignity, vast ears on a pointed face propelling him quite rapidly through the water, and, at the starboard rail, his amazing ears kept him stationary while he looked gravely at Greenberg.

"You are stamping on my hat," he pointed out without anger.

To Greenberg this was highly unimportant. "With the ears you're swimming," he grinned in a superior way, "Do you look funny!"

"How else could I swim?" the little man asked politely.

"With your arms and legs, like a regular human being, of course."

"But I am not a human being, I am a water gnome, a relative of the more common mining gnome. I cannot swim with my arms, because they must be crossed to give an appearance of dignity suitable to a water gnome; and my feet are used for writing and holding things. On the other hand, my ears are perfectly adapted for propulsion in water. Consequently, I employ them for that purpose. But please, my hat—there are several matters requiring my immediate attention, and I must not waste time."

Greenberg's unpleasant attitude toward the remarkably civil gnome is easily understandable. He had found someone he could feel superior to, and by insulting him, his depressed ego could expand. The water gnome certainly looked inoffensive enough, being only two feet tall.

"What you got that's so important to do, Big Ears?" he asked nastily.

Greenberg hoped the gnome would be offended. He was not, since his ears, to him, were perfectly normal, just as you would not be insulted if a member of a race of atrophied beings were to call you "Big Muscles," You might even feel flattered.

"I really must hurry," the gnome said, almost anxiously. "But if I have to answer your questions in order to get back my hat—we are engaged in re-stocking the Eastern waters with fish. Last year there was quite a drain. The bureau of fisheries is co-operating with us to some extent, but, of course, we can not depend too much on them. Until the population rises to normal, every fish has instructions not to nibble."

Greenberg allowed himself a smile, an annoyingly skeptical smile.

"My main work," the gnome went on resignedly, "is control of the rainfall over the Eastern seaboard. Our fact-finding committee, which is scientifically situated in the meteorological center of the continent, co-ordinates the rainfall needs of the entire continent; and when they determine the amount of rain needed in a particular spot of the East, I make it rain to that extent. Now may I have my hat, please?"

Greenberg laughed coarsely. "The first lie was big enough—about telling the fish not to bite. You make it rain like I'm The President of the United States!" He bent toward the gnome slyly, "How's about proof?"

"Certainly, if you insist." The gnome raised his patient, triangular face toward a particularly clear blue spot in the sky, a trifle to one side of Greenberg. "Watch that bit of the sky."

Greenberg looked up humorously. Even when a small dark cloud rapidly formed in the previously clear spot, his grin remained broad. It could have been coincidental. But then large drops of undeniable rain fell over a twenty-foot circle; and Greenberg's mocking grin shrank and grew sour.

He glared hatred at the gnome, finally convinced. "So you're the dirty crook who makes it rain on weekends!"

"Usually on weekends during the summer," the gnome admitted. "Ninety-two percent of the water consumption is on weekdays. Obviously we must replace that water. The weekends, of course, are the logical time."

"But you thief!" Greenberg cried hysterically, "you murderer! What do you care what you do to my concession with your rain? It ain't bad enough business would be rotten even without rain, but you got to make floods!"

"I'm sorry," the gnome replied, untouched by Greenberg's rhetoric. "We do not create rainfall for the benefit of men. We are here to protect the fish.

"Now please give me my hat. I have wasted enough time, when I should be preparing the extremely heavy rain needed for this coming weekend."

Greenberg jumped to his feet in the unsteady boat. "Rain this weekend—when I can maybe make a profit for a change! A lot you care if you ruin business. May you and your fish die a horrible, lingering death."

And he furiously ripped the green hat to pieces and hurled them at the gnome.

"I'm really sorry you did that," the little fellow said calmly, his huge ears treading water without the slightest increase of pace to indicate his anger. "We Little Folk have no tempers to lose. Nevertheless, occasionally we find it necessary to discipline certain of your people, in order to retain out dignity. I am not malignant; but, since you hate water and those who live in it, water and those who live in it will keep away from you."

With his arms still folded in great dignity, the tiny water gnome flipped his vast ears and disappeared in a neat surface dive.

Greenberg glowered at the spreading circles of waves. He did not grasp the gnome's final restraining order; he did not even attempt to interpret it. Instead he glared angrily out of the corner of his eye at the phenomenal circle of rain that fell from a perfectly clear sky. The gnome must have remembered it at length, for a moment later the rain stopped. Like a shutting faucet, Greenberg unwillingly thought.

"Good-by, weekend business," he growled. "If Esther finds out I got into an argument with the guy who makes it rain—"

He made an underhand cast, hoping for just one fish. The line flew out over the water; then the hook arched upward and came to rest several inches above the surface, hanging quite steadily and without support in the air.

"Well, go down in the water, damn you!" Greenberg said viciously, and he swished his rod back and forth to pull the hook down from its ridiculous levitation. It refused.

Muttering something incoherent about being hanged before he'd give in, Greenberg hurled his useless rod at the water. By this time he was not surprised when it hovered in the air above the lake. He merely glanced red-eyed at it, tossed out the remains of the gnome's hat, and snatched up the oars.

When he pulled back on them to row to land, they did not touch the water—naturally. Instead they flashed unimpeded through the air, and Greenberg tumbled into the bow.

"A-ha!" he grated. "Here's where the trouble begins." He bent over the side. As he suspected, the keel floated a remarkable distance above the lake.

By rowing against the air, he moved with maddening slowness toward the shore, like a medieval conception of a flying machine. His main concern was that no one should see him in this humiliating position.

At the hotel he tried to sneak past the kitchen to the bathroom, He knew that Esther waited to curse him for fishing

on the day before opening, but more especially on the very day
that a nice boy was coming to see her Rosie. If he could dress in
a hurry, she might have less to say—

"Oh, there you are, you good-for-nothing!"

He froze to a halt.

"Look at you! She screamed shrilly. "Filthy—you stink from
fish!"

"I didn't catch anything, darling," he protested timidly.

"You stink anyhow. Go take a bath, may you drown in it!
Get dressed in two minutes or less, and entertain the boy when
he gets here. Hurry!"

He locked himself in, happy to escape her voice, started the
water in the tub, and stripped from the waist up. A hot bath, he
hoped, would rid him of his depressed feeling.

First, no fish; now, rain on weekends! What would Esther
say—if she knew, of course. And, of course, he would not tell
her.

"Let myself in for a lifetime of curses!" he sneered. "Ha!"

He changed a new blade into his razor, opened the tube of
shaving cream, and stared objectively at the mirror. The
dominant feature of the soft, chubby face that stared back was
its ugly black stubble; but he set his stubborn chin and glowered.
He really looked quite fierce and indomitable. Unfortunately,
Esther never saw his face in that uncharacteristic pose,
otherwise she would speak more softly.

"Herman Greenberg never gives in!" he whispered between
savagely hardened lips. "Rain on weekends, no fish—anything
he wants; a lot I care! Believe me, he'll come crawling to me
before I go to him."

He gradually became aware that his shaving brush was not
getting wet. When he looked down and saw the water dividing
into streams that flowed around it, his determinate face slipped
and grew desperately anxious. He tried to trap the water—by
catching it in his cupped hands, by creeping up on it from
behind, as if it were some shy animal, and shoving his brush at
it—but it broke and ran away from his touch. Then he jammed
his palm against the faucet. Defeated, he heard it gurgle back
down the pipe, probably as far as the main.

"What do I do now?" he groaned. "Will Esther give it to me if
I don't take a shave! But how?...I can't shave without water."

Glumly, he shut off the bath, undressed and stepped into the tub. He lay down to soak. It took a moment of horrible stupor to realize that he was completely dry and that he lay in a waterless bathtub. The water, in one surge of revulsion had swept out onto the floor.

"Herman, stop splashing!" his wife yelled. "I just washed that floor. If I find a puddle I'll murder you!"

Greenberg surveyed the instep-deep pool over the bathroom floor. "Yes, my love," he croaked unhappily.

With an inadequate washrag he chased the elusive water, hoping to mop it all up before it could seep through to the apartment below. His washrag remained dry, however, and he knew that the ceiling underneath was dripping. The water was still on the floor.

In despair he sat on the edge of the bathtub. For some time he sat in silence. Then his wife banged on the door, urging him to come out. He started and dressed moodily.

When he sneaked out and shut the bathroom door tightly on the flood inside, he was extremely dirty and his face was raw where he had experimentally attempted to shave with a dry razor.

"Rosie!" he called in a hoarse whisper. "Sh! Where's mamma?"

His daughter sat on the studio couch and applied nail-polish to her stubby fingers. "You look terrible," she said in a conversational tone. "Aren't you going to shave?"

He recoiled at the sound of her voice, which, to him, roared out like a siren. "Quiet, Rosie! Sh!" And for further emphasis, he shoved his lips out against a warning finger. He heard his wife striding heavily around the kitchen. "I'll give you a dollar if you mop up the water I spilled in the bathroom."

"I can't papa," she stated firmly. "I'm all dressed."

"Two dollars, Rosie—all right, two and a half, you blackmailer."

He flinched when he heard her gasp in the bathroom; but, when she came out with soaked shoes, he fled downstairs. He wandered aimlessly towards the village.

Now he was in for it, he thought; screams from Esther, tears from Rosie—plus a new pair of shoes for Rosie and two and a half dollars. It would be worse, though, if he could not get rid of the whiskers—

Rubbing the tender spots where his dry razor had raked his face, he mused blankly at a drugstore window. He saw nothing to help him, but he went inside anyhow and stood hopefully at the drug counter. A face peered at him through a space scratched in the wall case mirror, and the druggist came out. A nice-looking, intelligent fellow, Greenberg saw at a glance.

"What you got for shaving that I can use without water?" he asked.

"Skin irritation, eh?" the pharmacist replied. "I got something very good for that."

"No. It's just—Well I don't like to shave with water."

The druggist seemed disappointed. "Well, I got brushless shaving cream." Then he brightened. "But I got an electric razor—much better."

"How much?" Greenberg asked cautiously.

"Only fifteen dollars, and it lasts a lifetime."

"Give me the shaving cream," Greenberg said coldly.

With the tactical science of a military expert, he walked around until some time after dark. Only then did he go back to the hotel, to wait outside. It was after seven, he was getting hungry, and the people who entered the hotel he knew as permanent summer guests. At last a stranger passed him and ran up the stairs.

Greenberg hesitated for a moment. The stranger was scarcely a boy, as Esther had definitely termed him, but Greenberg reasoned that her term was merely wish-fulfillment, and he jauntily ran up behind him.

He allowed a few minutes to pass, for the man to introduce himself and let Esther and Rosie don their company manners. Then, secure in the knowledge that there would be no scene until the guest left, he entered.

He waded through a hostile atmosphere, urbanely shook hands with Sammie Katz, who was a doctor—probably, Greenberg thought, in search of an office—and excused himself.

In the bathroom he carefully read the direction for using brushless shaving cream. He felt less confident when he realized he had to wash his face thoroughly with soap and water, but without the benefit of either, he spread the cream on, patted

it, and waited for his beard to soften. It did not, as he discovered
while shaving. He wiped his face dry. The towel was sticky and
black, with whiskers suspended in paste, and, for that, there
would be more hell to pay. He would have to spend fifteen
dollars for an electric razor after all; this foolishness was costing
him a fortune!

That they were waiting for him before beginning supper,
was, he knew, only a gesture for the sake of company. Without
changing her hard, brilliant smile, Esther whispered: "Wait! I'll
get you later—"

He smiled back, his tortured, slashed face creasing painfully.
All that could be changed by his being enormously pleasant to
Rosie's young man. If he could slip Sammie a few dollars—more
expenses, he groaned—to take Rosie out, Esther would forgive
everything.

He was too engaged in beaming and putting Sammie at ease
to think what would happen after he ate caviar canapés. Under
other circumstances Greenberg would have been repulsed by
Sammie's ultra-professional waxed mustache—an offensively
small, pointed thing—and his commercial attitude toward poor
Rosie; but Greenberg regarded him as a potential savior.

"You open an office yet, Doctor Katz?"

"Not yet. You know how things are. Anyhow, call me
Sammie."

Greenberg recognized the gambit with satisfaction, since it
seemed to please Esther so much. At one stroke Sammie had
ingratiated himself and begun bargaining negotiations.

Without another word, Greenberg lifted his spoon to attack
the soup. It would be easy to snare this eager doctor. A doctor!
No wonder Esther and Rosie were so puffed with joy.

In the proper company way, he pushed his spoon away from
him. The soup spilled onto the tablecloth.

"Not so hard, you dope," Esther hissed.

He drew the spoon toward him. The soup leaped off it like a
live thing and splashed over him—turning, just before contact to
fall on the floor. He gulped and pushed the bowl away. This
time the soup poured over the side of the plate and lay in a huge
puddle on the table.

"I didn't want any soup anyhow," he said in a horrible
attempt at levity. Lucky for him, he thought wildly, that

Sammie was there to pacify Esther with his smooth college talk—not a bad fellow, Sammie, is spite of his mustache; he'd come in handy at times.

Greenberg lapsed into a paralysis of fear. He was thirsty after having eaten the caviar, which beats herring any time as a thirst raiser. But the knowledge that he could not touch water without having it recoil and perhaps spill, made his thirst a monumental craving. He attacked the problem cunningly.

The others were talking rapidly and rather hysterically, He waited until his courage was equal to his thirst; then he leaned over the table with a glass in hand. "Sammie, do you mind—a little water, huh?"

Sammie poured from a pitcher while Esther watched for more of his tricks. It was to be expected, but still he was shocked when the water exploded out of the glass directly at Sammie's only suit.

"If you'll excuse me," Sammie said angrily, "I don't like to eat with lunatics."

And he left, though Esther cried and begged him to stay. Rosie was too stunned to move. But when the door closed, Greenberg raised his agonized eyes to watch his wife stalk thunderously towards him.

Greenberg stood on the boardwalk outside his concession and glared blearily at the peaceful, blue, highly unpleasant ocean. He wondered what would happen if he started at the edge of the water and strode out. He could probably walk right to Europe on dry land.

It was early—much too early for business—and he was tired. Neither he nor Esther had slept; and it was practically certain that the neighbors hadn't either. But above all he was incredibly thirsty.

In a spirit of experimentation, he mixed a soda. Of course its high water content made it slop onto the floor. For breakfast he had surreptitiously tried fruit juice and coffee, without success.

With his tongue dry to the point of furriness, he sat weakly on a boardwalk bench in front of his concession. It was Friday morning, which meant that the day was clear, with a promise of intense heat. Had it been Saturday, it naturally would have been raining.

"This year," he moaned, "I'll be wiped out. If I can't mix the sodas, why should beer stay in a glass for me? I thought that I could hire a boy for ten dollars a week to run the hot dog griddle; I could make sodas, and Esther could draw beer. All I can do is make hot dogs, Esther can still draw beer; but twenty or maybe twenty-five a week I got to pay a sodaman. I won't even come out square—a fortune I'll lose!"

The situation really was desperate. Concessions depend on too many factors to be anything but capriciously profitable.

His throat was fiery and his soft brown eyes held a fierce glaze when the gas and electric were turned on, the beer pipes connected, the tank of carbon dioxide hitched to the pump, and the refrigerator started.

Gradually, the beach was filling with bathers. Greenberg writhed on his bench and envied them. They could swim and drink without having liquids draw away from them as if in horror. They were not thirsty—

And then he saw his first customer approach. His business experience was that morning customers buy only soft drinks. In a mad haste he put up the shutters and fled to the hotel.

"Esther!" he cried. "I got to tell you! I can't stand it—"

Threateningly, his wife held her broom like a baseball bat. "Go back to the concession, you crazy fool. Ain't you done enough, already?"

He could not be hurt more than he had been. For once he did not cringe. "You got to help me, Esther."

"Why didn't you shave, you no-good bum? Is that any way—"

"That's what I got to tell you. Yesterday I got into an argument with a water gnome—"

"A what?" Esther looked at him suspiciously.

"A water gnome," he babbled in a rush of words. "A little man so high, with big ears that he swims with, and he makes it rain—"

"Herman!" she screamed. "Stop that nonsense. You're crazy!"

Greenberg pounded his forehead with his fist. "I ain't crazy. Look, Esther. Come with me to the kitchen."

She followed him readily enough, but her attitude made him feel more helpless and alone than ever. With her fists on her

plump hips and her feet set wide, she cautiously watched him
try to fill a glass with water.

"Don't you see? " he wailed. "It won't go in the glass. It spills
over. It runs away from me."

She was puzzled. "What happened to you?"

Brokenly, Greenberg told of his encounter with the water
gnome, leaving out no single degrading detail. "And now I can't
touch water," he ended. "I can't drink it. I can't make sodas. On
top of it all, I got such a thirst, it's killing me."

Esther's reaction was instantaneous. She threw her arms
around him, drew his head down to her shoulder, and patted
him comfortingly as if he were a child. "Herman, my poor
Herman!" she breathed tenderly. "What did we ever do to
deserve such a curse?"

"What shall I do, Esther?" he cried helplessly.

She held him at arm's length. "You got to go to a doctor," she
said firmly. "How long can you go without drinking? Without
water you'll die. Maybe sometimes I am a little hard on you, but
you know I love you—"

"I know, mamma," he sighed. "But how can a doctor help
me?"

"Am I a doctor that I should know? Go anyhow. What can
you lose?"

He hesitated. "I need fifteen dollars for an electric razor," he
said in a low, weak voice.

"So!" she replied. "If you got to, you got to. Go, darling. I'll
take care of the concession."

Greenberg no longer felt deserted and alone. He walked
almost confidently to a doctor's office. Manfully, he explained
his symptoms. The doctor listened with professional sympathy,
until Greenberg reached his description of the water gnome.

Then his eyes glittered and narrowed. "I know just the thing
for you, Mr. Greenberg," he interrupted. "Sit there until I come
back."

Greenberg sat quietly. He even permitted himself a surge of
hope. But is seemed only a moment later that he was vaguely
conscious of a siren screaming towards him; and then he was
overwhelmed by the doctor and two interns who pounced on him
and tried to squeeze him into a bag.

He resisted, of course. He was terrified enough to punch wildly. "What are you doing to me?" he shrieked. "Don't put that thing on me!"

"Easy now," the doctor soothed. "Everything will be all right."

It was on that humiliating scene that the policeman, required by law to accompany public ambulances, appeared. "What's up?" he asked.

"Don't stand there, you fathead," an intern shouted. "This man's crazy. Help us get him into this strait jacket."

But the policeman approached indecisively. "Take it easy, Mr. Greenberg. They ain't gonna hurt your while I'm here. What's it all about?"

"Mike!" Greenberg cried, and clung to his protector's sleeve. "They think I'm crazy—"

"Of course he's crazy," the doctor stated. "He came in here with a fantastic yarn about a water gnome putting a curse on him."

"What kind of a curse, Mr. Greenberg?" Mike asked cautiously.

"I got into an argument with the water gnome who makes it rain and takes care of the fish," Greenberg blurted. "I tore up his hat. Now he won't let water touch me. I can't drink, or anything—"

The doctor nodded. "There you are. Absolutely insane."

"Shut up." For a long moment Mike stared curiously at Greenberg. Then: "Did any of you scientists think of testing him? Here, Mr. Greenberg." He poured water into a paper cup and held it out.

Greenberg moved to take it. The water backed up against the cup's far lip; when he took it in his hand, the water shot out into the air.

"Crazy, is he?" Mike asked with heavy irony. "I guess you don't know there's things like gnomes and elves. Come with me, Mr. Greenberg."

They went out together and walked towards the boardwalk. Greenberg told Mike the entire story and explained how, besides being so uncomfortable to him personally, it would ruin him financially.

"Well, doctors can't help you," Mike said at length. "What do they know about the Little Folk? And I can't say I blame you for sassing the gnome. You ain't Irish or you'd have spoke with more respect to him. Anyhow, you're thirsty. Can't you drink anything?"

"Not a thing," Greenberg said mournfully.

They entered the concession. A single glance told Greenberg that business was very quiet, but even that could not lower his feelings more than they already were. Esther clutched him as soon as she saw them.

"Well?" she asked anxiously.

Greenberg shrugged in despair. "Nothing. He thought I was crazy."

Mike stared at the bar. Memory seemed to struggle behind his reflective eyes. "Sure," he said after a long pause. "Did you try beer, Mr. Greenberg?" When I was a boy my old mother told me all about elves and gnomes and the rest of the Little Folk. She knew them, all right. They don't touch alcohol, you know. Try drawing a glass of beer—"

Greenberg trudged obediently behind the bar and held a glass under the spigot. Suddenly his despondent face brightened. Beer creamed into the glass—and stayed there! Mike and Esther grinned at each other as Greenberg threw back his head and furiously drank.

"Mike!" he crowed. "I'm saved. You got to drink with me!"

"Well—" Mike protested feebly.

By late afternoon, Esther had to close the concession and take her husband and Mike to the hotel.

The following day, being Saturday, brought a flood of rain. Greenberg nursed an imposing hang-over that was constantly aggravated by his having to drink beer in order to satisfy his recurring thirst. He thought of forbidden icebags and alkaline drinks in an agony of longing.

"I can't stand it!" he groaned. "Beer for breakfast—phooey!"

"It's better than nothing," Esther said fatalistically.

"So help me, I don't know if it is. But darling, you ain't mad at me on account of Sammie, are you?"

She smiled gently," Poo! Talk dowry and he'll come back quick."

"That's what I thought. But what am I going to do about my curse?"

Cheerfully, Mike furled an umbrella and strode in with a little old woman, whom he introduced as his mother. Greenberg enviously saw evidence of the effectiveness of icebags and alkaline drinks, for Mike had been just as high as he the day before.

"Mike told me about you and the gnome," the old lady said. "Now I know the Little Folk well, and I don't hold you to blame for insulting him, seeing you never met a gnome before. But I suppose you want to get rid of your curse. Are you repentant?"

Greenberg shuddered. "Beer for breakfast! Can you ask?"

"Well, just you go to this lake and give the gnome proof."

"What kind of proof?" Greenberg asked eagerly.

"Bring him sugar. The Little Folk love the stuff—"

Greenberg beamed. "Did you hear that, Esther? I'll get a barrel—"

"They love sugar, but they can't eat it," the old lady broke in. "It melts in water. You got to figure out a way so it won't. Then the little gentleman'll know you're repentant for real."

"A-ha!" Greenberg cried. "I knew there was a catch!"

There was a sympathetic silence while his agitated mind attacked the problem from all angles. Then the old lady said in awe: "The minute I saw your place I knew Mike had told the truth. I never seen a sight like this in my life—rain coming down, like the flood, everywhere else; but all around this place, in a big circle, it's dry as a bone!"

While Greenberg scarcely heard her, Mike nodded and Esther seemed peculiarly interested in the phenomenon. When he admitted defeat and came out of his reflected stupor, he was alone in the concession, with only a vague memory of Esther's saying she would not be back for several hours.

"What am I going to do?" he muttered. "Sugar that won't melt—" He drew a glass of beer and drank it thoughtfully. "Particular they got to be yet. Ain't it good enough if I brink simple syrup?—that's sweet."

He pottered about the place, looking for something to do. He could not polish the fountain on the bar, and the few frankfurters on the griddle probably would go to waste. The floor had already been swept. So he sat uneasily and worried his problem.

"Monday, no matter what," he resolved, "I'll go to the lake. It don't pay to go tomorrow. I'll only catch a cold because of the rain."

At last Esther returned, smiling in a strange way. She was extremely gentle, tender and thoughtful; and for that he was appreciative. But that night and all day Sunday he understood the reason for her happiness.

She had spread word that, while it rained in every other place all over town, their concession was miraculously dry. So, besides a headache that made his body throb in rhythm to its vast pulse, Greenberg had to work like six men satisfying the crowd who mobbed the place to see the miracle and enjoy the dry warmth.

How much they took in will never be known. Greenberg made it a practice not to discuss such a personal matter. But it is quite definite that not even in 1929 had he done so well over a single week end.

Very early Monday morning he was dressing quietly, not to disturb his wife. Esther, however, raised herself on her elbow and looked at him doubtfully.

"Herman," she called softly, "do you really have to go?"

He turned, puzzled. "What do you mean—do I have to go?"

"Well—" She hesitated. Then: "Couldn't you wait until the end of the season, Herman, darling?"

He staggered back a step, he face working in horror. "What kind of an idea is that for my own wife to have?" he croaked. "Beer I have to drink instead of water. How can I stand it. Do you think I like beer? I can't wash myself. Already people don't like to stand near me; and how will they act at the end of the season? I go around looking like a bum because my beard is too tough for an electric razor, and I'm all the time drunk—the first Greenberg to be a drunkard. I want to be respected—"

"I know, Herman, darling," she sighed. "But I thought for the sake of our Rosie—Such a business we've never done like we did this week end. If it rains every Saturday and Sunday, but not on our concession, we'll make a fortune!"

"Esther!" Herman cried, shocked. "Doesn't my health mean anything?"

"Of course, darling. Only I thought maybe you could stand it for—"

He snatched his hat, tie and jacket, and slammed the door. Outside, though, he stood indeterminedly. He could hear his wife crying, and he realized that, if he succeeded in getting the gnome to remove the curse, he would forfeit an opportunity to make a great deal of money.

He finished dressing more slowly. Esther was right, to a certain extent. If he could tolerate his waterless condition—

"Not!" he gritted decisively. "Already my friends avoid me. It isn't right that a respectable man like me should always be drunk and not take a bath. So we make less money. Money isn't everything—"

And with great determination he went to the lake.

But that evening, before going home, Mike walked out of his way to stop in at the concession. He found Greenberg sitting on a chair, his head in his hands, and his body rocking slowly in anguish.

"What is it, Mr. Greenberg?" he asked gently.

Greenberg looked up. His eyes were dazed. "Oh, you, Mike," he said blankly. Then his gaze cleared, grew more intelligent, and he stood up and led Mike to the bar. Silently, they drank beer. "I went to the lake today," he said hollowly. "I walked all around it hollering like mad. The gnome didn't stick his head out of the water once."

"I know," Mike nodded sadly. "They're busy all the time."

Greenberg spread his hands imploringly. "So what can I do? I can't write him a letter or send him a telegram; he ain't got a door to knock on or a bell for me to ring. How do I get him to come up and talk?"

His shoulders sagged. "Here, Mike. Have a cigar. You been a real good friend, but I guess we're licked."

They stood in an awkward silence. Finally Mike blurted: "Real hot, today. A regular scorcher."

"Yeah. Esther says business was pretty good, if it keeps up."

Mike fumbled at the Cellophane wrapper. Greenberg said: "Anyhow, suppose I did talk to the gnome. What about the sugar?"

The silence dragged itself out, became tense and uncomfortable. Mike was distinctly embarrassed. His brusque nature was not adapted for comforting discouraged friends. With immense concentration he rolled the cigar between his fingers and listened for a rustle.

"Day like this's hell on cigars," he mumbled, for the sake of conversation. "Dries them like nobody's business. This one ain't, though."

"Yeah," Greenberg said abstractly. "Cellophane keeps them—"

They looked suddenly at each other, their faces clean of expression.

"Holy smoke!" Mike yelled.

"Cellophane on sugar!" Greenberg choked out.

"Yeah," Mike whispered in awe. "I'll switch my day off with Joe, an I'll go to the lake with you tomorrow. I'll call for you early."

Greenberg pressed his hand, too strangled by emotion for speech. When Esther came to relieve him, he left her at the concession with only the inexperienced griddle boy to assist her, while he searched the village for cubes of sugar wrapped in Cellophane.

The sun had scarcely risen when Mike reached the hotel, but Greenberg had long been dressed and stood on the porch waiting impatiently. Mike was genuinely anxious for his friend. Greenberg staggered along toward the station, his eyes almost crossed with the pain of a terrific hang-over.

They stopped at a cafeteria for breakfast. Mike ordered orange juice, bacon and eggs, and coffee half-and-half. When he heard the order, Greenberg had to gag down a lump in his throat.

"What'll you have?" the counterman asked.

Greenberg flushed. "Beer," he said hoarsely.

"You kidding me?" Greenberg shook his head, unable to speak. "Want anything with it? Cereal, pie, toast—"

"Just beer." And he forced himself to swallow it. "So help me," he hissed at mike, "another beer for breakfast will kill me!"

"I know how it is," Mike said around a mouthful of food.

On the train they attempted to make plans. But they were faced by a phenomenon that neither had encountered before, and so they got nowhere. They walked glumly to the lake, fully aware that they would have to employ the empirical method of discarding tactics that did not work."

"How about a boat?" Mike suggested.

"It won't stay in the water with me in it. And you can't row it."

"Well, what'll we do then?"

Greenberg bit his lip and stared at the beautiful blue lake. There the gnome lived, so near to them. "Go through the woods along the shore, and holler like hell. I'll go the opposite way. We'll pass each other and meet at the boathouse. If the gnome comes up, yell for me."

"O. K.," Mike said, not very confidently.

The lake was quite large and they walked slowly around it, pausing often to get the proper stance for particularly emphatic shouts. But two hours later, when they stood opposite each other with the full diameter of the lake between them, Greenberg heard Mike's hoarse voice: "Hey, gnome!"

"Hey, gnome!" Greenberg yelled. "Come on up!"

An hour later they crossed paths. They were tired, discouraged, and their throats burned; and only fisherman disturbed the lake's surface.

"The hell with this," Mike said. "It ain't doing any good. "Let's go back to the boathouse."

"What'll we do?" Greenberg rasped. "I can't give up!"

They trudged back around the lake, shouting half-heartedly. At the boathouse, Greenberg had to admit that he was beaten. The boathouse owner marched threateningly toward him.

"Why don't you maniacs got away from here?" he barked. "What's the idea of hollering and scaring away the fish? The guys are sore—"

"We're not going to holler any more," Greenberg said. "It's no use."

When they bought beer and Mike, on an impulse, hired a boat, the owner cooled off with amazing rapidity, and went off to unpack bait.

"What did you get a boat for?" Greenberg asked. "I can't ride in it."

"You're not going to. You're going to walk."

"Around the lake again?" Greenberg cried.

"Nope. Look, Mr. Greenberg. Maybe the gnomes can't hear us through all that water. Gnomes ain't hardhearted. If he heard us and thought you were sorry, he'd take his curse off you in a jiffy."

"Maybe." Greenberg was not convinced. "So where do I come in?"

"The way I figure it, some way or other you push water away, but the water pushes you away just as hard. Anyhow, I hope so. If it does, you can walk on the lake." As he spoke, Mike had been lifting large stones and dumping them on the bottom of the boat. "Give me a hand with these."

Any activity, however useless, was better than none, Greenberg felt. He helped Mike fill the boat until just the gunwales were above the water. The Mike got in and shoved off.

"Come on," Mike said. "Try and walk on the water."

"Greenberg hesitated. "Suppose I can't?"

"Nothing'll happen to you. You can't get wet; so you won't drown."

The logic of Mike's statement reassured Greenberg. He stepped out boldly. He experienced a peculiar sense of accomplishment when the water hastily retreated under his feet into pressure bowls, and an unseen, powerful force buoyed him upright across the lake's surface. Though his footing was not too secure, with care he was able to walk quite swiftly.

"Now what?" he asked, almost happily.

Mike had kept pace with him in the boat. He shipped his oars and passed Greenberg a rock. "We'll drop them all over the lake—make a damned noise down there and upset the place. That'll get him up."

The were hopeful now, and their comments, "Here's one that'll wake him," and "I'll hit him right on the noodle with this one," served to cheer them still further. And less than half the rocks had been dropped when Greenberg halted, a boulder in his hands. Something inside him wrapped itself tight around his heart and his jaw dropped.

Mike followed his awed, joyful gaze. To himself, Mike had to admit that the gnome, propelling himself through the water with his ears, arms folded in tremendous dignity, was a funny sight.

"Must you drop rocks and disturb us at our work?" the gnome asked.

Greenberg gulped.   "I'm sorry, Mr. Gnome," he said nervously. "I couldn't get you to come up by yelling."

The gnome looked at him. "Oh. You are the mortal who was disciplined. Why did you return?"

"To tell you that I'm sorry, and I won't insult you again."

"Have you proof of your sincerity?" the gnome asked quietly.

Greenberg fished furiously in his pocket and brought out a handful of sugar wrapped in Cellophane, which he tremblingly handed to the gnome.

"Ah, very clever, indeed," the little man said, unwrapping a cube and popping it eagerly into his mouth. "Long time since I had some."

A moment later Greenberg sputtered and floundered under the surface. Even if Mike had not caught his jacket and helped him up, he could almost have enjoyed the sensation of being able to drown.

LOVE IN THE DARK

ORIGINALLY PUBLISHED IN *SUSPENSE MAGAZINE*
FALL 1951

Love In the Dark

Being Livy Random wasn't easy. It meant having a face a little too long, a figure a little too plump, brown hair brushed and brushed yet always uncurling at the ends. It meant not being able to make herself more than passably attractive. Worse than that, being Livy Random meant being Mrs. Mark Random, the wife of that smug ;ump asleep in the other bed.

Mark wasn't snoring, he was too neat for that. He was always making even stacks of things, or putting them in alphabetical order on shelves, or straightening rugs and pictures, or breathing neatly in the other bed.

Livy closed the bedroom door with a bang. Mark didn't stir; he could fall asleep in one infuriating minute, and wake up, eight hours later to the second, in exactly the same unlovely position and disposition. Her high-heeled shoes didn't bother him when she kicked them off, and neither did the scraping chair back against the wall—he hated chair marks on the walls—when she sat down to take off her stockings. And Livy wanted, venomously to bother her husband.

Mark Random had married her because he had been sales manager of the electric battery factory, and he'd had enough of eating in restaurants while he had been a traveling salesman. Besides, it looked better for a man in his position to be married. Livy had accepted him because she was past thirty and nobody else might ask her; besides, she needed someone to support her. So she cooked for him. She cleaned for him. She even tried to keep a budget for him, though that was his idea. He gave her a meager household allowance and nothing else.

Nothing, in this case, must be understood as the complete and humiliating absence of everything. When Livy was particularly incenses about her marriage, which was generally, it was a comfort to know that she could have it easily annulled.

And Mark couldn't do a thing to stop her. He hadn't, at least, and there was no sign that he intended to, cared to, or even thought of it.

Pulling her slip over her head, Livy wondered about this. She had heard, at least as often as any other girl, that all men were beasts. Mark was, of course, a beast in a way—in his special, primly exasperating way. But he wasn't a beast in the usual sense. With Livy, anyway. Maybe some woman in a back street hovel thought he was. But that wasn't likely; he would have wedded the lady and saved the cost of this apartment.

What was wrong with Mark? It wasn't Livy, because she had known her duty and had grimly been prepared for it, though God knew this tall and pudgy person inspired nothing at all in her.

"Short and pudgy," she thought, reaching around back for the hooks. "Why doesn't somebody put hooks in front where they belong and where a body can get at them, and make a fortune? Short and pudgy is bad enough, but Mark's got to be tall and pudgy, with a stomach that pulls his shoulders down and caves in his chest. And those black-rimmed glasses—some oculist must have been stuck with those for years. That hair of his— thick, oily, wavy, and yellow. Like butter starting to melt—"

She looked at him again. What had made her think that marrying him was better than not being married at all? She could have got at least a housekeeper's job somewhere. With the possibility that some man in the household would fall in love with her.

Livy stopped. She crossed her arms over her breasts. It was the oddest sensation.

Somebody was staring at her as she undressed.

Mark? It didn't seem possible, but she held her slip in front of her and flipped the switch and looked. He was on his side, one arm under his head, and his back was to her. He never looked at her in the light, so why should he stare at her in the dark?

Livy peered under the window shades. They reached the sills; nobody could see beneath them or around them. She felt like a fool bending to glance under the beds, poking warily among the dresses and suits in the closets, and searching behind the furniture.

The light aroused Mark; that was something. He twisted around to face her blurrily.

"What's the matter?" he asked, his thin voice fuzzily peevish.

"Somebody was watching me undress," she said.

"Here?"

She tightened her lips. "I haven't undressed in the street in years," she said. "Of course it was in here!"

"You mean somebody's in the room with us?" He reached out for his glasses on the night table. "I don't see anyone."

"I know," she said flatly. "I searched the place. It's empty. Or it might as well be."

He stared at her. He wasn't, of course, looking below her face, though she still had her slip clutched in front of her. He was staring at her face as if she had a smudge on it.

"Do you often have these ideas?" he asked.

"Go on back to sleep," she said. "If you want to act like a psychiatrist, your own case would keep you busy for years."

He was still looking at her face, so she turned off the light. She held the slip until she heard him turn heavily, then grunt as he spread himself in the same position as before.

Livy hung up her slip and began peeling off her girdle. There it was again—hungry eyes peering out of the dark, touching her body with ocular caresses.

It wasn't imagination. It couldn't be. She'd been mentally undressed as often as any other not too attractive girl, and she knew the shrinking, exposed feeling too well to mistake it.

No use turning on the light again. She wouldn't find anyone in the room.

"Let's be reasonable," she thought, fighting an urge to leap into bed and scream. "I'm tired. Pooped, if you want to know. That dreary Mrs. Hall made a hash out of the bridge game. Why do I always draw town idiots as partners? Is it some curse that was put on my family back in the Middle Ages? That's all I need; it's not enough playing house with this inspecting officer searching under the furniture.

"All right. I'm exhausted and jumpy. I'm normal, or what passes for normal. If anybody mentions Freud to me, I'll start swinging this girdle like a night stick. I'm not losing my mind. I'm not having a wish-fulfillment either, if that's what you're thinking. Livy dear, it's just time I went to bed—and don't go twisting that statement around.

Her eyes did ache a bit; all that smoke. Maybe she should cut out cigarettes. Aching eyes could make you see things that weren't there. This wasn't exactly seeing, but maybe it was connected somehow.

Livy closed her eyes experimentally, and the effect was more startling than the skin sensation.

In the dark, with her eyes shut, she could ¬see who was staring at her. It gave her a shock until she realized that she could imagine it, rather; she couldn't see unless her eyes were open, could she? She tried it and the image disappeared. She closed them again and there it was.

As long as it was her imagination, she studied the imaginary owner of the imaginary eyes. She stared at him just as intently as she imagined he was staring at her.

"Stunning," was her first verdict, and then, "What a build! I must have been peering unconsciously at those physical culture magazines on the newsstands. That long blue hair and those wide blond eyes and a cute little straight nose—I always did love a man with a cleft in his chin. Heavens, did you ever see such muscles? And—wait a minute!"

She opened her eyes quickly. A girl had to have some modesty, even if her imagination didn't. And then something jarred her sense of logic.

Long blue hair and wide blond eyes? It must have been a twist of her subvocal tongue. She meant long blond hair and wide blue eyes. Of course.

She closed her eyes and rechecked. The hair was blue and the eyes were blond, or close enough to it. That wasn't all, either. It wasn't really hair. It was feathers. Long, very fine, like bird-of-paradise plumage; but feathers. As long as they were combed sort of flat, she could never have guessed. But her stunning imaginary man frowned as she stared at him, and the frown lifted his—well, feathers, into an attractive crest. Very attractive, in fact. She liked the effect much better than hair. . .

Peculiar. The dazzling creature was blushing under her stare, and turning his head away shyly. Was it possible to blush a beautiful shocking pink? And to have pointed leprechaun ears much handsomer than the regular male clam-shell variety. And since when does a mental image turn bashful?

"Who cares?" thought Livy. "You're a gorgeous thing, and any psychiatrist cures me of this particular delusion over my dead body! Now go away or I won't get a wink of sleep all night."

With her eyes shut, she saw the unearthly vision walk dutifully toward the bedroom door, open it, and close it behind him.

"That you, Livy?" asked Mark from his bed.

"Is what me?"

"Opening the door."

"I haven't budged from this spot."

She heard him roll over again and sit up. "I'm a practical man with both feet on the ground," he said. "I don't hear things unless there's something to hear. And I heard the door open and close."

Livy pulled on her nightgown over her head—warm, thick flannel because texture and sheerness didn't matter. "All right, you heard the door open and close," she said, falling back luxuriously on her soft mattress and dragging the heavy blankets up. "You can't get me to argue with you this time of night."

"Something's wrong with you," said Mark. "We'll find out what it is tomorrow."

As far as she was concerned, there was nothing wrong with her. Why shouldn't an unhappy woman imagine a handsome, thrilling man admiring her? Maybe there was some hidden and sinister significance in the blue plumage and pointed ears, but she didn't care to know about it.

She knew Mark wouldn't risk one of her tempers by waking her up to talk, so she firmly pretended to be sleeping while he dressed, made his own breakfast, and drove away. Then she got out of bed and took off the nightgown.

Sure enough, her flesh shrank. She felt as if she were being spied on.

"Look," she said testily to her subconscious, or libido, or whatever the term was, "not the first thing in the morning. Let me at least brush my teeth and have some of that black mud Mark calls coffee."

Anyway, it was ridiculous, right in broad daylight. Phantasms are for the dark. Any decent neurosis ought to know that.

Nevertheless, Livy closed her eyes to test her memory. The exciting dreamboat with the blue plumage, blond eyes, and gay ears was exactly the same—staring hungrily at her from somewhere near the vanity. Certainly she saw the vanity; she knew it was there, didn't she? She tried staring back, to see if her imaginary lover boy would blush and turn away again. He didn't, which probably meant that some quirk in her mind had grown bolder, for he grinned becomingly and his blond eyes smiled up and down her body.

"I never would have believed it," she muttered moodily, opening her eyes and proceeding to dress. "Rainy evenings I can understand, but I usually feel so nasty in the morning."

She was washing the dishes after breakfast when she felt the first physical symptoms of her delusion. It was a light, airy kiss on the back of her neck. Goosebumps bloomed. Her spine went syrupy, her knees came unhooked.

She swiftly disposed of the thrill by blaming it on a loose end of hair. But she cautiously pinned her thatch all up under a kerchief; another few ethereal kisses there, whether uncurled hair or psychological, and she would climb the wall.

Next time she felt the kiss, it started at her neck and worked down to her shoulder, six distinct and passionate touches of warm, hard lips. Weakly she realized that her hair was still tightly bound and pinned up, and that left only one conclusion to be drawn.

"All right," she said, dizzily happy, "I'm going nutty. Wonder why I never thought of it before."

There were more kisses during the day, enough to keep her glowing. Hallucinations, of course, but wonderful ones, and she resolved to hang grimly onto them. So she left Mark his dinner and a note, and went out to a movie.

In the theater, peculiarly, she felt more alone than she had at home. The picture was nothing to rave about, but she saw it three times to make sure Mark would be in bed when she returned.

He was, and breathing. She undressed in no great hurry, finally accustomed to the peeping sensation. But when she was under the covers, she screamed suddenly and scrambled out. Mark was awake by the time she turned on the light.

"Now what?" he grumbled.

She goggled at him in alarm. "It wasn't you?" she asked.

"What wasn't me?"

She sat tentatively on the edge of the bed and rubbed her arm. "Somebody—I thought it was you—I could feel his fingers on my arm just as plain—"

"Whom," Marked asked, confused, "are you talking about?"

She put her chin out. "Somebody tried to get into bed with me."

"M-mm," Mark nodded solemnly, acting not at all astonished. He put his plump, white, flat feet into slippers and wrestled into a bathrobe. He said anxiously, "Now don't get alarmed Livy. We'll see this thing through."

"Don't bother," she said. "As long as I know it wasn't you, I'm satisfied."

"I am not in the habit of slinking."

"No," she admitted, looking at him appraisingly. "You haven't the physique. Then again, if you did have, you wouldn't have to slink." She gave her head a shake, "I don't know what to think," And she began to cry.

"Now, none of that," he said. "We'll have you right in a jiffy."

She stood up, ready to run over the beds , if necessary. "Oh, no, not now, you're not."

"I don't mean what you mean," he said, and he went to the telephone extension and called Ben Dashman. He agreed with Ben that it was rather late, but added, "It's urgent, Ben, and you're the only one I can turn to. It's Livy's nerves. They've—snapped! You'll have to get your clothes on and come right over."

"Ben Dashman," Livy said scornfully. "Here's one consumer whose resistance that business psychologist can't break down. The two of you will just get to your offices all tired out tomorrow, and for what?"

"When there is a crisis, sleep is a secondary consideration," Mark said. "Ben and I are men of action. This will not be the first time we've worked through the night."

But Ben, when he arrived, sat on a chair at one side of her bed, and mark sat on his own bed and explained to Ben, over Livy's indignant body, the little he knew of what he referred to as her case. Though the information didn't amount to much, it made her just as embarrassed as the first peeping incident.

If Mark Random was pompous and oratorical, and he was, Ben Dashman could claim the doubtful credit. Mark had modeled himself after that successful expert on business psychology, who had read his way up to the vice-president-in-charge-of-sales. Ben could quote whole chapters of inspirational and analytical studies, whereas Mark had mastered no more than brief sentences and paragraphs. The voice had a lot to do with Ben's sensational rise, however, Mark had a slightly petulant voice, about Middle C, while Ben had learned to pitch his a full octave below comfort and to propel his words like strung spitballs.

Physically, Ben was even less appetizing than Mark. He had a bigger stomach, wider hips, rounder shoulders, white hair split in the center and stuck damply to his pink head, heavy lips that he loved to pucker thoughtfully, and pince-nez. Mark would have paid a lot for a pince-nez that would stay on him, but they either stopped his circulation or fell off.

"Well," said Ben when Mark was through. Livy won the bet she had made with herself that that would be his first response; it gave him time to think. "Do you have anything to add, Livy?"

"Sure. Go home, or take Mark out to a bar. I want to go to sleep."

"I mean about your—strange feeling," Ben persisted.

"I recommend it to all women," she said. "If I knew how, I'd manufacture and sell these dream admirers on the installment plan, and give them free to the needy. It's made me ten years younger. Now go way. I've got a date with my delusion."

"Listen," said Mark earnestly. "Ben got out of bed and came over here to help you. We both want to help you. Ben has read all there is to know about mental cases."

"I'm not a mental case," Livy said. "I was until now, but I'm not any more. If you both want to help me, you can develop amnesia and wander out of my life. For good. If I'm sick, it's of you."

Mark's face went purple, but Ben pacified him hastily, "Don't answer her, Mark. She doesn't know what she's saying. You know how it is with these things."

"The only reason he married me was to save money on a housekeeper," she said in a deliberate tone.

"That's right—" Ben encouraged her patronizingly.

"Are you agreeing with her?" Mark shouted.

"I mean that's right—let her get things off her chest," Ben explained. "It releases tension."

So Livy kept talking and it was wonderful. She said the most insulting true things about Mark and he didn't dare turn them into argument. She didn't know much about psychiatry, but she accused him of all the terms she could remember. It was the first time she had examined out loud the facts of her imitation marriage.

"Come to think of it," she concluded, "I don't know why I stayed here so long. As soon as I can get some money together, or a job, I'll let you know my forwarding address."

Then she went to sleep. Ben assured Mark than she seemed to have unburdened her grievances and should have no further disturbances. Her threat to leave he considered mere bravado. He advised rest and a sympathetic attitude.

Taking Ben to the door, Mark thanked him abjectly, "I don't know what I would have done without you."

"Forget it," said Ben. "If we didn't all pitch in and help each other when the footing gets rocky, there'd be no cooperation in this world."

"That's right," Mark said, brightening. "Wasn't it Emerson who pointed out that cooperation is the foundation of civilization."

"It's always safe to give Emerson the credit," Ben answered. "Now just don't worry about Livy. If she shows any alarming signs of tension, call me up, day or night, and I'll be glad to do what I can.

It was two months before Livy moved out, actually, and then only because she had no real choice. Finding a job had been harder than she had anticipated. She had no experience and the best part of the day to go job-hunting had usually been taken up by cooking, cleaning, shopping, sending out the laundry, and reading. For she had begun consuming psychology books—both normal and abnormal—searching for a parallel to her condition.

She found roughly similar cases, some of which were almost identical in unimportant respects. But the really significant symptom, which urged her on in her hunt, she found nowhere.

None of the systematically deluded women had ever had a baby by an imaginary sweetheart. And Livy, her doctor had told her after the usual tests, was indisputably pregnant.

"But that's impossible," she had protested.

"I thought so myself," the doctor, who was Mark's physician also, had confessed. "But, you see, the profession is full of surprises."

"That isn't what I mean," Livy said in a panic.

She asked for some aromatic spirits in water. She wanted a chance to rehearse her answer. It sounded absurd even to herself.

She and Mark had not changed the basis of their marriage. Mark couldn't be the father of her child. He wasn't. It was impossible. Under the circumstances, it was absolutely impossible. Yet it was also impossible for her to be pregnant. She had an alibi for every minute of their marriage.

But these days, she realized numbly, when a doctor tells a woman she is going to have a baby, she can start buying a layette.

Mark didn't bark or howl; he called Ben Dashman instead. Ben understood the situation instantly.

"Livy's conscience caused those delusions," he said. "She has obviously been having an affair."

"There was nothing obvious about it," Livy said. "It was so unobvious, in fact, that I didn't know about it myself."

This time Ben Dashman's presence didn't stop Mark from losing his temper. "Are you denying," he yelled, "that you have been having an affair?"

"Certainly," said Livy. "I'd know about it, wouldn't I?"

"Well, that's the point, Mark," Ben said ponderously. "In the condition Livy's been in lately, she might not have been responsible."

"I'm not going to be responsible, and that's for sure," Mark said. "We'll find out who the man is if we have to dig clean through her unconscious and down to her pituitary gland!"

Mark threw his glasses, the big black-rimmed ones, on the floor and trampled on them. Livy felt a little proud. She had never seen him so angry before. She had never suspected that she could have such an effect on him, or she might have tried it long ago."

"Livy," Ben said gently, "you do know who the man was, don't you?"

"Sure," she said. "It was my dreamboat, my lover boy—the one who ogled me while I was undressing, the one who tried to get in bed with me. I didn't let him until you convinced me he wasn't real. Then I didn't see any reason to be afraid."

"You mean," said Mark, terrible in his self-control, "right here in the same room with me?"

"Why not?" she asked reasonably. "It was just a delusion. Do I go around censoring your dreams? Though heaven knows they're probably about selling campaigns and how to make people battery-conscious!"

Ben waved Mark to silence. "Then am I to understand," he said, "that your only meetings with your so-called dreamboat have been here in your own bedroom, with your husband asleep in the next bed?"

"That's right," Livy said. "Exactly."

Ben stood up and pointed unpleasantly at Mark. "You," he said nastily, "are an ungrateful, inconsiderate, lying scoundrel."

"I am?" Mark asked, baffled out of his outrage. "How do you figure that, Ben?"

"Because for some obscure reason you're trying to blacken the name of your wife, when it's perfectly clear that the only man who could be the father is you."

"Oh, no! I can prove it isn't!"

"I'll bet," Livy said, "he could at that. But he doesn't have to, Ben. I'll give him an affidavit that he isn't."

"You see?" mark cried triumphantly.

Ben nodded. "I guess I do. Livy, I respect your gallantry, but it's a mistake to protect the guilty party."

"You don't catch me getting gallant at a time like this," Livy said. "I can't tell you his name, because I don't know it, but I'll be glad to tell you who he is."

She described the phantom who loved her.

"Blue feathers!" yelled Mark. "Blond eyes! She isn't crazy, Ben. Oh, no, she thinks we are!"

Ben stood up. "Mark, I think we need a conference." Mark followed him unwillingly and when Livy opened the door carefully, a few moments later, she heard Ben say, "I've read about cases like this. It's a very grave, very deep disturbance—

too deep for me to handle, though I'd love to try and believe I'd do pretty well. But the first thing she needs is protection. From herself and this unscrupulous vandal she imagines has blue plumage and blond eyes."

And Mark said, "The you think she really believes this nonsense?"

And Ben said, "Of course, poor girl. She's batty. Use your head."

And Mark said slowly, "I never thought of that. But why would she claim he's invisible?"

Livy could picture Ben lifting his fat shoulders. "It might take months or years to find out, and the important thing right now is to protect her. That wouldn't hurt you either, Mark. Nobody puts any stock in what a patient at a rest home says."

There was more discussion, but Livy didn't stay to hear it. She had climbed out the kitchen window and over the low backyard fence. Finding a taxi took a while, but she got downtown and closed out her savings account.

Now all she had to do was find a place to live. She couldn't go back to Mark, of course, and she had some bad moments imagining that her description had been broadcast and that she would be picked up and sent to an asylum. She wasn't worried for herself. But Lover Boy might not find her, and she wouldn't be able to get out and search for him.

Among the classified ads she came across a two-room furnished apartment. It turned out to be across the street from a lumber yard, far enough away from Mark to be relatively safe; and the rental was low. She could live on her savings until the baby was born. What would happen after that didn't seem to matter much right now.

When she went to bed she felt strangely alone. It wasn't Mark sleeping in the other bed that she missed. She had felt alone in the same room with him up until she thought up Dreamboat. Where was he? She squeezed her eyes shut and concentrated. No, he wasn't there. Mark's house must have been the special habitat of that particular hallucination.

She disliked facing Mark again, and perhaps Ben too, but there apparently was no other way to bring back her blue-plumed, stunning mental phantom. She dressed and called a cab.

There was a light in the bedroom, but she saved investigating that for last. She let herself in with her own key and took off her shoes, then slid through all the other rooms with her eyes firmly shut. Establishing no contact, she opened the bedroom door—and there he was.

His lips were grim, his cleft chin jutted, his blond eyes were savage, and he held his fists in uppercut position as he crouched like a boxer over Mark's raging face. He seemed to be rapping out some harsh words, but even Livy couldn't hear him.

"You stinker," she heard Mark snarl. "You hit me when I wasn't looking."

And Ben protested, "Don't be an idiot. Your unconscious is punishing you for the way you treated that sweet, troubled girl. I can show you cases just like yours—"

And Mark said, "Are you telling me I walked into something?"

Ben told him in a calm voice, "Every psychiatrists knows about the unconscious wish for punishment."

Mark yelled, "There's nothing unconscious about my wish to sock you on that fat jaw." And he did.

Lover Boy looked past the battle and saw her in the doorway. His angry face brought forth a slow, unearthly smile, and he walked carefully around the fighting fat men and took her hand. It may have been her imagination, but she felt the passionately warm, hard flesh.

She had to open her eyes outside the house and on the way back to her apartment. But she held desperately to his hand.

It was after she came home from the hospital that Ben found her. He told her he had heard of mothers radiating. But that this was the first time he had seen it. She could feel the glow in her face as she showed him the empty crib.

"I know you can't see him," she said, "but I can when I close my eyes. He's a beautiful baby. He has his father's features."

"You caused a little stir at the hospital," Ben said soberly. "That's how I found you."

She laughed. "Oh, you mean the doctor? I thought he'd order himself a straightjacket."

"Well, delivering an invisible baby is no joke, especially when you're called away from a stag party," Ben said soberly. "He was finally convinced that it was only the liquor, but he hasn't touched a drop since. They never did discover the baby, did they?"

"I had it in my room all the time. They were afraid I'd sue and give them a lot of bad publicity. But I said it was all right." She turned away from the crib. "I don't suppose Mark minded the Reno divorce, did he?"

"He knows he was getting off lucky. These kissless-marriage annulments can drive a man to changing his name and moving to another state. But tell me, Livy, how did you arrange the second marriage?"

"By telephone," she said. "I guess you've heard the groom's name and birthplace."

Ben hissed on his glasses, wiped them meticulously. "There was some mention in the newspapers."

"Clrkxsdyl 93J16," she said gaily. "I call him Clark for short. And he comes from Alpha Centauri somewhere. I wouldn't have known that, except he learned to use a typewriter—we don't hear the same frequencies, he says."

Ben's eyes slid away from hers and looked around the shabby apartment. "Well, you do seem happy, I must say."

"There's only one thing that bothers me," she said. "Clark could have picked any woman on Earth. I'm about as average as you can get without being a freak. Why did he want me?"

"There's no explaining love," Ben evaded uneasily. He put his pudgy had in his inside pocket and looked directly at her. "Let's not have any false pride," he said. "You haven't asked Mark for a cent, but you have no income and I'd be glad—"

"Oh, we're doing fine," said Livy, shaking her hair, which she had let grow long and straight with no sign of a permanent. "We're getting a raise soon."

"A raise?" Ben was surprised. "From where? For doing what?"

"I'm supposed to be working for Grant's Detective Agency. But it's really Clark who's the operative—private eye, he calls it now, after reading all those mystery stories—and he types up the reports. All I have to do is correct his English now and then. Imagine, he's even learning slang. Grant can't figure out how we get information that's so hard to uncover, but it's easier than pie for Clark."

"Sure," said Ben, going to the door. "But what are you laughing at?"

"Those blue feathers. They tickle!"

Although Ben could have dropped the situation there, there was one thing you could say for him; he was conscientious. He made one more investigation.

"What do you want to know about her for?" Mr. Grant asked coldly and suspiciously.

"I'm a friend of hers," Ben explained, handing Grant his business card. "I just want to make sure she's earning a good living. She divorced a—well, somebody I used to know, and she wouldn't take any alimony. I offered to help her out, but she said she's doing all right working for you."

Grant's professionally slitted eyes developed a glint of smug possession. "Oh, I was afraid you might want to hire her away from me," he said. "That girl is the best operative I've ever had. She could shadow a nervous sparrow. Why, she's got methods—"

"Good, huh?"

"Good?" repeated Grant. "You'd think she was invisible!"

And Three to Get Ready . . .

Originally Published in *Fantastic*
Summer 1952

AND THREE TO GET READY . . .

Usually, people get committed to the psycho ward by their families or courts, but this guy came alone and said he wanted to be put away because he was deadly dangerous. Miss Nelson, the dragon at the reception desk, put in a call for Dr. Schatz and he took me along just in case. I'm a psycho-ward orderly, which means I'm big and know gentle judo to put these poor characters into pretzel shapes that don't hurt them, but keep them from hurting themselves or somebody else.

He was sitting there, hunched together as if he was afraid that he'd make a move that might kill anyone nearby, and about as dangerous looking as a wilted carnation. Not much bigger than one, either. Maybe five four, one hundred and twenty-five pounds, slender shoulders, slender hands, little feet, the kind of delicate face no guy would ever pick for himself, but a complexion you'd switch with if you've got a beard of Brillo like mine that needs shaving every damned day.

"Do you have this gentleman's history, Miss Nelson?" asked Dr. Schatz, before talking to the patient.

Her prim lips got even tighter. "I'm afraid not, doctor. He . . . says it would be like committing suicide to give it to me."

The little fellow nodded miserably.

"But we must have at least your name—" Dr. Schatz began.

He skittered clear over to the end of the bench and huddled there, shaking. "But that's exactly what I can't give you! Not only mine—anybody's!

One thing you've got to say for these psychiatrists; they may feel surprised, but they never show it. Tell them you can't eat soup with anything except an egg-beater and they'll even manage to look as if they do that, too. I guess it's something you learn. I'm getting pretty good at it myself, but not when I come up against something as new as this twitch's line. I couldn't keep my eyebrows down.

Dr. Schatz, though, nodded and gave him a little smile and suggested going up to the mental hygiene office, where there wouldn't be so many people around. The little guy got up and came right along. They went into Schatz's office and I went to the room adjoining, with just a thin door I could hear through and open in a hurry if anything happened. You'd be surprised how seldom anything does happen, but it doesn't pay to take chances.

"Now, suppose you tell me what's bothering you," I heard Dr. Schatz say quietly. "Or isn't that possible, either?"

"Oh, I can tell you that," the little guy said. "I just can't tell you—my name. Or yours, if I knew it. Or anyone else's."

"Why?"

The little guy was silent for a minute. I could hear him breathing hard and I knew he was pushing the words up to his mouth, trying to make them come out.

"When I say somebody's name three times," he whispered, "the person dies."

"I see." You can't throw Dr. Schatz that easy. "Only persons?"

"Well . . ." The little guy hitched his chair closer; I heard it shriek and grate on the cement floor. "Look, I'm here because it's driving me nuts, doc. You think I am already, so I've got to convince you I'm not. I have to give you proof that I'm right."

The doctor waited. They always do at times like that; it kind of forces the patients to say things they maybe didn't want to.

"The first one was Willard Greenwood," said the little guy in a slow, tense voice. "You remember him—the undersecretary down in Washington. A healthy man, right? Good career ahead of him. I see his name in the papers. Willard Greenwood. It has a . . . a round sound to it. I find myself saying it. I say it three times. Right out loud while I'm looking at his picture. So what happens?"

"Greenwood committed suicide last week," Dr. Schatz said. "He'd evidently had psychological difficulties for some time."

"Yes. I didn't think much about it. A coincidence, like. But then I see a newsreel of this submarine launching a few days ago. The Barnacle. I say the name out loud three times, same as anybody else might. You've done that yourself sometimes, haven't you? Haven't you?"

"Of course. Names occasionally have a fascination."

"Sure, So The Barnacle runs into something and sinks. I began to suspect what was going on so, like an experiment you might say, I picked another name out of the papers. I figured it ought to be somebody who isn't psycho, like Greenwood turned out to be, or old and sick, or a submarine which might be expected to run into danger. It had to be somebody young and healthy. I picked the name out of the school news. A girl named Clara Newland. Graduating from Emanuel High. Seventeen."

"She died?"

The little guy gives a kind of sob. "Automobile crash. She was the only one who was killed. The others only got hurt. Last Sunday."

"Those could be coincidences, you know," Dr. Schatz said very gently. "Perhaps you said other names aloud and nothing happened, but you remember those because something did."

The guy kicked his chair back; I could hear it slide. He probably got up and leaned over the desk; they do that when they're all excited. I put my hand on the knob and got ready.

"As soon as I knew what was going on," he said. "I stopped saying names three times. I didn't dare say them even once, because they might make me say them again and then again— and you know what the payoff would be. But then last night . . ."

"Yes?" Dr Schatz said, prompting him when he halted.

"A bar got held up. It was when the customers had left and the bartender was getting ready to lock the place. Two guys. There was a scuffle and the bartender was killed. The cops came. One of the crooks was shot; the other got away. The crook who was shot was—"

I opened the door a slit and looked in. he was showing a clipping to Schatz, with his finger pointing shakily at one place.

"Paul Michaels," said the doctor.

"Don't say it!" the little guy yelled. I was ready to race in, but Dr. Schatz made a warning motion that the guy wouldn't notice that told me I wasn't needed. "I don't want to say it! If I do, it'll be three times and he'll die!"

"I think I understand," Schatz said. "You're afraid to mention names three times because of the result, and—well what do you want us to do?"

"Keep me here. Stop me from saying names three times. Save God knows how many people from me. Because I'm deadly!"

Schatz said we'd do our best, and he got the guy committed for observation. It wasn't easy, because he still wouldn't give his name, and Dr. Merriman, the head of the psychiatric department, almost had another heart attack fighting about it.

We got together, Dr. Schatz and I, after the little guy had his pajamas and stuff issued and a bed assigned to him.

"That's a hell of a thing to carry around," I said, "thinking people die when you say their names three times. It would drive anybody batty."

"A vestige of childhood," he told me, and explained how kids unconsciously believe their wishes can do anything. I could remember some of that from my own childhood—my old man was a holy terror with his strap and many's the time I wished he was dead—and then got scared that maybe he would die and it would all be my fault. But I outgrew it, which Schatz said most people do. Only there are some who don't like our little nameless friend, and they often get themselves twisted up like this.

"But that Paul Michaels," I said. "The crook who got shot. He's in the critical ward right here in this hospital."

"It's a city hospital," he answered, lighting a butt and looking tired. "Everything the private hospitals won't touch, we get. That's why we have this patient, too."

"Any special instructions?" I asked.

"I don't think so. This kind of case is seldom either suicidal or homicidal, unless the guilt feelings get out of hand. Keep him calm, that's all. Sedation if he needs it."

I had plenty to do around the mental hygiene ward without the little guy to worry about, but he wasn't much trouble. Until about an hour or two after supper, that is. I had some beds to move around and a tough customer to get into the hydrotherapy room, so I didn't pay much attention to the little guy and his restless eyes.

He came up to me, twitchy as hell, and grabbed my arm with both his hands.

"I keep thinking about that—that name," he babbled. "I keep wanting to say it. Do something! Don't let me say it!"

"Who?" I asked, blank for a minute, and then I remembered. "You mean this crook Paul Michaels—"

He got white and jumped up and tried to stop my mouth, but I'd already said it. I tried to calm him down and finally had the nurse give him some phenobarb, all the time explaining that the name had slipped out and I was sorry. You know, soothing him.

He was trembling, "Now I know I'm going to say it. I just know I will." And he shuffled over to the window and sat there holding his head, looking sick.

I got to bed about midnight, still wondering about the poor little guy who thought he could kill people with that easy. I had the next morning off, but I didn't take it. There were cops all over the place and Dr. Schatz looked real worried.

"I don't know how our new patient is going to take this," he said shaking his head. "That Paul Michaels we had here—"

"Had?" I repeated. "What do you mean, had? He transferred to a prison hospital or something?"

"He's dead," Schatz said.

I closed my mouth after a few seconds. "Aw, nuts," I grumbled, disgusted with myself. "I was almost believing the little guy did it. Michaels was shot up bad. Hell, he was on the critical list."

"That's right. There'd be nothing remarkable if he died . . . from a bullet wound. But his throat was slit."

"And the little guy?"

"We had him full of Nembutal. He was shouting that he had said Michael's name three times and that Michaels would have to die and he would be responsible."

"You haven't told him yet," I said.

"Naturally not. It would really put him into a spin."

It was a solid mess from top floor to basement, so I had to give up my morning off. The patients, except the little guy who was in isolation, all found out about Michaels somehow—you can't stop things like that from spreading—and I had a time handling them. In between, though, I learned how the case was developing.

There was this old cop Slattery we generally have for cases like Michaels sitting outside the critical ward, watching who went in and out. There had been somebody with Michaels on the stickup, see, who made it while Michaels was plugged, and the cops don't take chances that maybe the accomplice or someone from the underworld might want to get at the patient when he's helpless. They always put a guard on.

Well, Slattery is all right, but he maybe isn't so alert anymore, and somebody slipped past him late at night, cut Michael's neck with probably a razor blade, and then got out again without Slattery noticing. The other patients were all doped up or asleep, so they were no help. Slattery, though, swore nobody except nurses on duty in the ward or on the floor went past him. He claimed he didn't fall asleep once during the night, and the funny thing is the nurses said the same. Or maybe it's not so funny, they like the old man and might do a little lying to help him off a rough spot.

Well, that put the girls on an even worse spot. If they were telling the truth, that Slattery had been awake the whole night, then one of them must have done it. Because Slattery had said that only the nurses went in and out of the ward. Captain Warren, the homicide man, jumped on that fast and got the girls to line up in front of Slattery.

"Well, Slattery?" Warren said. "One of these nurses must have been the killer. Do you recognize one who went in there with no business to? Or did one of them act suspicious, and which was it?"

Slattery looked unhappy as he went down the line and stared at the girl's faces. He shook his head figuring, I guess, that he was in for some real trouble now.

"It was pretty dim in the ward," he mumbled. "All they keep on is a little night light—just enough so the girls can find their way around without tripping, but not bright enough to keep the patients awake. I can't even be sure which nurses went in and out."

"Nothing suspicious?" Warren demanded.

"Search me. They were nurses and my job is to keep anybody else out. As long as they were nurses and it was so dim in there, one of them could have had an Army rifle under her uniform and I wouldn't know."

Captain Warren questioned the girls, got nowhere, and had them all checked to see if one didn't know Michaels well enough to want to knock him off.

I got all that from Sally Norton, one of the homely babes in the mental hygiene ward, when she came back from the grilling to go on duty. She went to her locker to change and then ran back, yipping, and grabbed Dr. Schatz. She had her uniform up in front of her, like a shield, kind of, and she was shaking angrily.

"Just take a look at this, doctor!" she said. "Came back clean from the laundry yesterday and I haven't even worn it yet, and look at it now!"

"If there's anything wrong with the laundry, take it up with them," he said, annoyed. "I'm having enough trouble keeping my patients quiet with all this racket going on over Michaels."

"But that's just it. I wouldn't be surprised if it has something to do with Michaels." And she showed him the sleeve, where there were red spots down near the wrist.

Schatz called in Captain Warren and Dr. Merriman, the head of the mental hygiene department. Merriman looked sicker than usual; he kept his hand inside his jacket over his heart. All this excitement wasn't doing him any more good than it was doing the patients.

Warren was interested, all right. Being there in the hospital, it was easy to run a test and prove the spots were blood, human, type B—which happened to be Michaels's blood type. He wasn't the only one in the hospital with that type, of course, but it wasn't so common that Captain Warren could disregard it.

Warren started to give Sally a bad time, but Dr. Merriman cut in and told him about the little guy and the story about saying names three times.

"What in hell kind of nonsense is this?" Warren asked. "I'm looking for evidence, not a screwball fairy tale some nut thought up."

"Exactly," Dr. Schatz said fast; he'd been trying to head off Dr. Merriman, but hadn't dared to interrupt. "It's a fairly typical delusion with no more basis in fact than witches or goblins. I can't sanction questioning a disturbed patient because of it."

"You don't have to bother," said Warren. "I've got more important things—"

"The point," Dr. Merriman went on, "is that this man claimed he was afraid to mention—specifically, mind you—the name of

Paul Michaels. That was why he wanted to be committed in fact."

Warren looked baffled. "You mean you think he said Michaels's name three times and Michaels died because of that?"

"Certainly not," Merriman said stiffly. "It's a remarkable coincidence that deserves investigation, that's all. Or perhaps my idea of police work differs from yours."

I don't know how Schatz managed it, but he let Captain Warren know that Dr, Merriman was getting on in years and ought to be humored. So I went along with them to the little guy's bed, where he was just coming out of the sedative. He was still groggy, but he saw us coming and ducked his left hand under the blanket.

Well, that's all you have to do to get a cop suspicious, make a sudden move like running out of a bank at high noon or duck one hand under a blanket. Warren hauled it out, with the little guy resisting and trying to hide his pinky in his palm. The cop straightened out the pinky. It was colored red under the fingernail.

"Blood?" I asked, confused, and then got busy because the little guy was trying to pull away while Captain Warren took some scrapings.

It wasn't blood. It was lipstick, according to the lab test.

"There," said Dr. Schatz, satisfied, "you see? You've upset my patient, and for what?"

"Plenty," Warren said between his teeth, "and I'm going to upset him some more."

H e had me hold the little buy down—I didn't want to until Dr. Merriman overrode Schatz's objections and ordered me to— while two cops put the little guy into Sally Norton's stained uniform and painted his mouth with lipstick.

You know, with that slender build of his and the cap on, he didn't look bad. Better than Sally, if you want to know, but who doesn't?

"All right," Schatz said, "he could have gotten past Slattery in that dim light. Admitted. But what makes you think he did? And why should he have done so?"

"The lipstick on the pinky," said Warren. "If you want to do a decent job, you don't just slap it on—you shape it with your little finger. Why? That depends. If the guy is psycho, he could have done Michaels in just because. But suppose he's the guy who was with Michaels on the job—Michaels was the only one who could have identified him. But Michaels was in a coma. So this character had to get into the hospital somehow and slit Michaels throat to keep him from talking. Either way, it figures."

Dr. Merriman nodded. "That was my own opinion, captain."

"You're lying! You're lying!" the little guy screamed. "I said his name three times and he died! They always die! It's the curse I have to bear!"

"We'll see," said Dr, Merriman. "Say my name three times."

The little guy cowered away. "I—I can't. I have enough deaths on my conscious now."

"You heard me!" Dr. Merriman shouted, turning a dangerous red in the face. "Say my name three times!"

The little guy looked appealingly at Dr. Schatz, who said soothingly, "Go ahead. I know you're convinced it works, but it's completely contrary to logic. Wishes can't kill. This may prove it to you."

The little guy said Dr, Merriman's name three times, pale and shaking and looking ready to throw up with fear.

Warren put Slattery—and another guard—on the psycho ward, and started a check on the little guy's fingerprints.

When I got to work the next day, the ward was a tomb. It might as well have been. Sally Norton was crying and Dr. Schatz was all pinch-faced and the little guy was practically running around the room yelling that he shouldn't have been forced to do it.

"Do what?" I wanted to know.

"Dr. Merriman died last night," Schatz said.

I looked at the little guy in horror. "Him?"

"No, no, of course not," said Schatz. But it was in a flat voice, not the impatient way he would have told me a day ago. "Dr. Merriman had a cardiac lesion. He could have gone at any time. There may even have been a deep unconscious wish to escape the pain and fear, and this patient's delusion could have given Dr. Morrison a psychological escape. It's the principle behind voodooism. The victim wills himself to death; the hexer merely supplied the suggestion."

It was pretty bad for a while, until Captain Warren showed up with a big grin on his face. It soured when he heard that Dr,

Merriman had died, but he threw out the idea that the little guy had done it.

Matter of fact, he had the cops put the arm on him and said, "Arnold Roach, I arrest you for complicity in the murder—" And so forth and so on.

The little guy, whose name turned out to be what Warren said, had been unlucky enough to leave some fingerprints around. They had him, sure enough, except that he stuck to this whammy story and hired a good psychiatrist, who got him and insanity plea. So we have him back in the ward here. And if you think he's given up and started mentioning people's names even once, let alone three times, you're battier than he is. He screams whenever somebody mentions any name. It's a hell of a job remembering not to call patients by name when he's around. "Look, what do you think?" I asked Dr. Schatz. "Is the guy psychotic or did he cop a lucky plea?"

Dr. Schatz ran his hand across his mouth and talked through his fingers. "I think he's psychotic. There's never any proof of that, of course, but his behavior bears me out. It's definitely psychotic."

"And what about this story of his about saying names three times? All right, maybe he made up those items before he showed up here—after all, they were dead already and nobody could say he had or hadn't said their names three times before they died. And Michaels—the little guy helped him shuffle out with a razor across the throat. But what about Dr. Merriman?"

"I've already told you," Schatz said tiredly. "Cardiac lesion and hypothetical death wish triggered by suggestion."

I put the mop back in the bucket and began wringing it after a fast swab at the floor. I didn't feel happy and I showed it.

"That's just a guess," I answered. "What if the little guy is right and people do die when he says their names three times?"

"Why don't you try it and see?" he asked.

I almost upset the pail. "Me? You're the psychiatrist. Why don't you?"

"Because I know it's purely a childish delusion. I don't need any proof."

"That," I said, leaning on the mop, "is not a scientific attitude, doctor."

"The devil with it," he grunted in annoyance. "If it's bothering you that much, I'll do it."

But he always seems to have something else to do whenever I remind him.

THE OLD DIE RICH

ILLUSTRATED BY WILLIAM ASHMAN
ORIGINALLY PUBLISHED IN *GALAXY*
MARCH 1953

It is the kind of news item you read at least a dozen times a year, wonder about briefly, and then promptly forget—but the real story is the one that the reporters are unable to cover!

THE OLD DIE RICH

"You again, Weldon," the Medical Examiner said wearily.

I nodded pleasantly and looked around the shabby room with a feeling of hopeful eagerness. Maybe *this* time, I thought, I'd get the answer. I had the same sensation I always had in these places—the quavery senile despair at being closed in a room with the single shaky chair, tottering bureau, dim bulb hanging from the ceiling, the flaking metal bed.

There was a woman on the bed, an old woman with white hair thin enough to show the tight-drawn scalp, her face and body so emaciated that the flesh between the bones formed parchment pockets. The M.E. was going over her as if she were a side of beef that he had to put a federal grade stamp on, grumbling meanwhile about me and Sergeant Lou Pape, who had brought me here.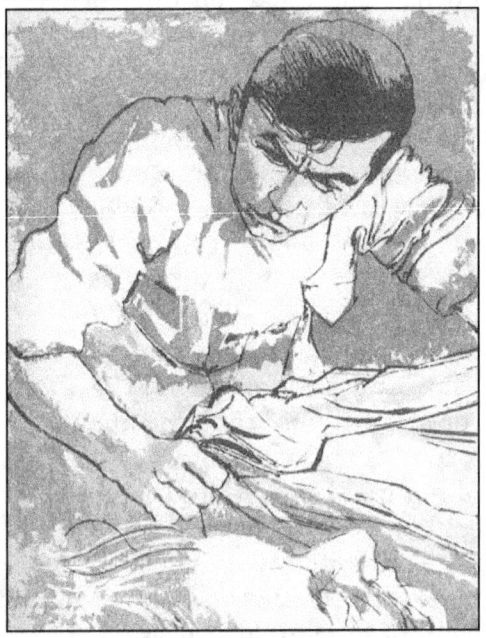

"When are you going to stop taking Weldon around to these cases, Sergeant?" the M.E. demanded in annoyance. "Damned actor and his morbid curiosity!"

For the first time, Lou was stung into defending me. "Mr. Weldon is a friend of mine—I used to be an actor, too, before I joined the force—and he's a follower of Stanislavsky."

The beat cop who'd reported the D.O.A. whipped around at the door. "A Red?"

*   *   *   *   *

I let Lou Pape explain what the Stanislavsky method of acting was, while I sat down on the one chair and tried to apply it. Stanislavsky was the great pre-Revolution Russian stage director whose idea was that actors had to think and feel like the characters they portrayed so they could *be* them. A Stanislavskian works out everything about a character right up to the point where a play starts—where he was born, when, his relationship with his parents, education, childhood, adolescence, maturity, attitudes toward men, women, sex, money, success, including incidents. The play itself is just an extension of the life history created by the actor.

How does that tie in with the old woman who had died? Well, I'd had the cockeyed kind of luck to go bald at 25 and I'd been playing old men ever since. I had them down pretty well—it's not just a matter of shuffling around all hunched over and talking in a high cracked voice, which is cornball acting, but learning what old people are like inside—and these cases I talked Lou Pape into taking me on were studies in senility. I wanted to understand them, know what made them do what they did, *feel* the compulsion that drove them to it.

The old woman on the bed, for instance, had $32,000 in five bank accounts ... and she'd died of starvation.

You've come across such cases in the news, at least a dozen a year, and wondered who they were and why they did it. But you read the items, thought about them for a little while, and then forgot them. My interest was professional; I made my living playing old people and I had to know as much about them as I could.

That's how it started off, at any rate. But the more cases I investigated, the less sense they made to me, until finally they were practically an obsession.

Look, they almost always have around $30,000 pinned to their underwear, hidden in mattresses, or parked in the bank, yet they starve themselves to death. If I could understand them, I could write a play or have one written; I might really make a name for myself, even get a Hollywood contract, maybe, if I could act them as they should be acted.

So I sat there in the lone chair, trying to reconstruct the character of the old woman who had died rather than spend a single cent of her $32,000 for food.

*   *   *   *   *

"Malnutrition induced by senile psychosis," the M.E. said, writing out the death certificate. He turned to me. "There's no mystery to it, Weldon. They starve because they're less afraid of death than digging into their savings."

I'd been imagining myself growing weak from hunger and trying to decide that I ought to eat even if it cost me something. I came out of it and said, "That's what you keep telling me."

"I keep hoping it'll convince you so you won't come around any more. What are the chances, Weldon?"

"Depends. I will when I'm sure you're right. I'm not."

He shrugged disgustedly, ordered the wicker basket from the meat wagon and had the old woman carried out. He and the beat cop left with the basket team. He could at least have said good-by. He never did, though.

A fat lot I cared about his attitude or dogmatic medical opinion. Getting inside this character was more important. The setting should have helped; it was depressing, rank with the feel of solitary desperation and needless death.

Lou Pape stood looking out the one dirty window, waiting patiently for me. I let my joints stiffen as if they were thirty years older and more worn out than they were, and empathized myself into a dilemma between getting still weaker from hunger and drawing a little money out of the bank.

I worked at it for half an hour or so with the deep concentration you acquire when you use the Stanislavsky method. Then I gave up.

"The M.E. is wrong, Lou," I said. "It doesn't feel right."

Lou turned around from the window. He'd stood there all that time without once coughing or scratching or doing anything else that might have distracted me. "He knows his business, Mark."

"But he doesn't know old people."

"What is it you don't get?" he prompted, helping me dig my way through a characterization like the trained Stanislavskian he was—and still would have been if he hadn't gotten so sick of the insecurity of acting that he'd become a cop. "Can't money be more important to a psychotic than eating?"

"Sure," I agreed. "Up to a point. Undereating, yes. Actual starvation, no."

"Why not?"

"You and the M.E. think it's easy to starve to death. It isn't. Not when you can buy day-old bread at the bakeries, soup bones for about a nickel a pound, wilted vegetables that groceries are glad to get rid of. Anybody who's willing to eat that stuff can stay alive on nearly nothing a day. Nearly nothing, Lou, and hunger is a damned potent instinct. I can understand hating to spend even those few cents. I can't see going without food altogether."

*   *   *   *   *

He took out a cigarette; he hadn't until then because he didn't want to interrupt my concentration. "Maybe they get too weak to go out after old bread and meat bones and wilted vegetables."

"It still doesn't figure." I got up off the shaky chair, my joints now really stiff from sitting in it. "Do you know how long it takes to die of starvation?"

"That depends on age, health, amount of activity—"

"Nuts!" I said. "It would take weeks!"

"So it takes weeks. Where's the problem—if there is one?"

I lit the pipe I'd learned to smoke instead of cigarettes—old men seem to use pipes more than anything else, though maybe it'll be different in the next generation. More cigarette smokers now, you see, and they'd stick to the habit unless the doctor ordered them to cut it out.

"Did you ever try starving for weeks, Lou?" I asked.

"No. Did you?"

"In a way. All these cases you've been taking me on for the last couple of years—I've tried to be them. But let's say it's possible to die of starvation when you have thousands of dollars put away. Let's say you don't think of scrounging off food stores or working out a way of freeloading or hitting soup lines. Let's say you stay in your room and slowly starve to death."

He slowly picked a fleck of tobacco off his lip and flicked it away, his sharp black eyes poking holes in the situation I'd built up for him. But he wasn't ready to say anything yet.

"There's charity," I went on, "relief—except for those who have their dough in banks, where it can be checked on—old age pension, panhandling, cadging off neighbors."

He said, "We know these cases are hermits. They don't make contact with anybody."

"Even when they're starting to get real hungry?"

"You've got something, Mark, but that's the wrong tack," he said thoughtfully. "The point is that *they* don't have to make contact; other people know them or about them. Somebody would check after a few days or a week—the janitor, the landlord, someone in the house or the neighborhood."

"So they'd be found before they died."

"You'd think so, wouldn't you?" he agreed reluctantly. "They don't generally have friends, and the relatives are usually so distant, they hardly know these old people and whether they're alive or not. Maybe that's what threw us off. But you don't need friends and relatives to start wondering, and investigate when you haven't shown up for a while." He lifted his head and looked at me. "What does that prove, Mark?"

"That there's something wrong with these cases. I want to find out what."

*　　*　　*　　*　　*

I got Lou to take me down to Headquarters, where he let me see the bankbooks the old woman had left.

"She took damned good care of them," I said. "They look almost new."

"Wouldn't you take damned good care of the most important thing in the world to you?" he asked. "You've seen the hoards of money the others leave. Same thing."

I peered closely at the earliest entry, April 23, 1907, $150. My eyes aren't that bad; I was peering at the ink. It was dark, unfaded. I pointed it out to Lou.

"From not being exposed to daylight much," he said. "They don't haul out the bankbooks or money very often, I guess."

"And that adds up for you? I can see them being psychotics all their lives ... but not *senile* psychotics."

"They hoarded, Mark. That adds up for me."

"Funny," I said, watching him maneuver his cigarette as if he loved the feel of it, drawing the smoke down and letting it out in plumes of different shapes, from rings to slender streams. What a living he could make doing cigarette commercials on TV! "I can see *you* turn into one of these cases, Lou."

He looked startled for a second, but then crushed out the butt carefully so he could watch it instead of me. "Yeah? How so?"

"You've been too scared by poverty to take a chance. You know you could do all right acting, but you don't dare giving up this crummy job. Carry that far enough and you try to stop spending money, then cut out eating, and finally wind up dead of starvation in a cheap room."

"Me? I'd never get that scared of being broke!"

"At the age of 70 or 80?"

"Especially then! I'd probably tear loose for a while and then buy into a home for the aged."

I wanted to grin, but I didn't. He'd proved my point. He'd also shown that he was as bothered by these old people as I was.

"Tell me, Lou. If somebody kept you from dying, would you give him any dough for it, even if you were a senile psychotic?"

I could see him using the Stanislavsky method to feel his way to the answer. He shook his head. "Not while I was alive. Will it, maybe, not give it."

"How would that be as a motive?"

*   *   *   *   *

He leaned against a metal filing cabinet. "No good, Mark. You know what a hell of a time we have tracking down relatives to give the money to, because these people don't leave wills. The few relatives we find are always surprised when they get their inheritance—most of them hardly remember dear old who-ever-it-was that died and left it to them. All the other estates eventually go to the State treasury, unclaimed."

"Well, it was an idea." I opened the oldest bankbook again. "Anybody ever think of testing the ink, Lou?"

"What for? The banks' records always check. These aren't forgeries, if that's what you're thinking."

"I don't know what I'm thinking," I admitted. "But I'd like to turn a chemist loose on this for a little while."

"Look, Mark, there's a lot I'm willing to do for you, and I think I've done plenty, but there's a limit—"

I let him explain why he couldn't let me borrow the book and then waited while he figured out how it could be done and did it. He was still grumbling when he helped me pick a chemist out of the telephone directory and went along to the lab with me.

"But don't get any wrong notions," he said on the way. "I have to protect State property, that's all, because I signed for it and I'm responsible."

"Sure, sure," I agreed, to humor him. "If you're not curious, why not just wait outside for me?"

He gave me one of those white-tooth grins that he had no right to deprive women audiences of. "I could do that, but I'd rather see you make a sap of yourself."

I turned the bankbook over to the chemist and we waited for the report. When it came, it had to be translated.

*   *   *   *   *

The ink was typical of those used 50 years ago. Lou Pape gave me a jab in the ribs at that. But then the chemist said that, according to the amount of oxidation, it seemed fresh enough to be only a few months or years old, and it was Lou's turn to get jabbed. Lou pushed him about the aging, asking if it couldn't be the result of unusually good care. The chemist couldn't say—that depended on the kind of care; an airtight compartment, perhaps, filled with one of the inert gases, or a vacuum. They hadn't been kept that way, of course, so Lou looked as baffled as I felt.

He took the bankbook and we went out to the street.

"See what I mean?" I asked quietly, not wanting to rub it in.

"I see something, but I don't know what. Do you?"

"I wish I could say yes. It doesn't make any more sense than anything else about these cases."

"What do you do next?"

"Damned if I know. There are thousands of old people in the city. Only a few of them take this way out. I have to try to find them before they do."

"If they're loaded, they won't say so, Mark, and there's no way of telling them from those who are down and out."

I rubbed my pipe disgruntledly against the side of my nose to oil it. "Ain't this a beaut of a problem? I wish I liked problems. I hate them."

Lou had to get back on duty. I had nowhere to go and nothing to do except worry my way through this tangle. He headed back to Headquarters and I went over to the park and sat in the sun, warming myself and trying to think like a senile psychotic who would rather die of starvation than spend a few cents for food.

I didn't get anywhere, naturally. There are too many ways of beating starvation, too many chances of being found before it's too late.

And the fresh ink, over half a century old....

$$* \quad * \quad * \quad * \quad *$$

I took to hanging around banks, hoping I'd see someone come in with an old bankbook that had fresh ink from 50 years before. Lou was some help there—he convinced the guards and tellers that I wasn't an old-looking guy casing the place for a gang, and even got the tellers to watch out for particularly dark ink in ancient bankbooks.

I stuck at it for a month, although there were a few stage calls that didn't turn out right, and one radio and two TV parts, which did and kept me going. I was almost glad the stage parts hadn't been given to me; they'd have interrupted my outside work.

After a month without a thing turning up at the banks, though, I went back to my two rooms in the theatrical hotel one night, tired and discouraged, and I found Lou there. I expected him to give me another talk on dropping the whole thing; he'd been doing that for a couple of weeks now, every time we got together. I felt too low to put up an argument. But Lou was holding back his excitement—acting like a cop, you know, instead of projecting his feelings—and he couldn't haul me out to his car as fast as he probably wanted me to go.

"Been trying to get in touch with you all day, Mark. Some old guy was found wandering around, dazed and suffering from malnutrition, with $17,000 in cash inside the lining of his jacket."

"*Alive?*" I asked, shocked right into eagerness again.

"Just barely. They're trying intravenous feeding to pull him through. I don't think he'll make it."

"For God's sake, let's get there before he conks out!"

Lou raced me to the City Hospital and up to the ward. There was a scrawny old man in a bed, nothing but a papery skin stretched thin over a face like a skull and a body like a Halloween skeleton, shivering as if he was cold. I knew it wasn't the cold. The medics were injecting a heart stimulant into him and he was vibrating like a rattletrap car racing over a gravel road.

"Who are you?" I practically yelled, grabbing his skinny arm. "What happened to you?"

He went on shaking with his eyes closed and his mouth open.

"Ah, hell!" I said, disgusted. "He's in a coma."

"He might start talking," Lou told me. "I fixed it up so you can sit here and listen in case he does."

"So I can listen to delirious ravings, you mean."

Lou got me a chair and put it next to the bed. "What are you kicking about? This is the first live one you've seen, isn't it? That ought to be good enough for you." He looked as annoyed as a director. "Besides, you can get biographical data out of delirium that you'd never get if he was conscious."

*   *   *   *   *

He was right, of course. Not only data, but attitudes, wishes, resentments that would normally be repressed. I wasn't thinking of acting at the moment, though. Here was somebody who could tell me what I wanted to know ... only he couldn't talk.

Lou went to the door. "Good luck," he said, and went out.

I sat down and stared at the old man, *willing* him to talk. I don't have to ask if you've ever done that; everybody has. You keep thinking over and over, getting more and more tense, "Talk, damn you, *talk!*" until you find that every muscle in your body is a fist and your jaws are aching because you've been clenching your teeth so hard. You might just as well not bother, but once in a while a coincidence makes you think you've done it. Like now.

The old man sort of came to. That is, he opened his eyes and looked around without seeing anything, or it was so far away and long ago that nobody else could see what he saw.

I hunched forward on the chair and willed harder than ever. Nothing happened. He stared at the ceiling and through and beyond me. Then he closed his eyes again and I slumped back, defeated and bitter—but that was when he began talking.

There were a couple of women, though they might have been little girls in his childhood, and he had his troubles with them. He was praying for a toy train, a roadster, to pass his tests, to keep from being fired, to be less lonely, and back to toys again. He hated his father, and his mother was too busy with church bazaars and such to pay much attention to him. There was a sister: she died when he was a kid. He was glad she died, hoping maybe now his mother would notice him, but he was also filled with guilt because he was glad. Then somebody, he felt, was trying to shove him out of his job.

The intravenous feeding kept dripping into his vein and he went on rambling. After ten or fifteen minutes of it, he fell asleep. I felt so disappointed that I could have slapped him awake, only it wouldn't have done any good. Smoking would have helped me relax, but it wasn't allowed, and I didn't dare go outside for one, for fear he might revive again and this time come up to the present.

*   *   *   *   *

"Broke!" he suddenly shrieked, trying to sit up.

I pushed him down gently, and he went on in frightful terror, "Old and poor, nowhere to go, nobody wants me, can't make a living, read the ads every day, no jobs for old men."

He blurted through weeks, months, years—I don't know—of fear and despair. And finally he came to something that made his face glow like a radium dial.

"An ad. No experience needed. Good salary." His face got dark and awful. All he added was, "El Greco," or something that sounded like it, and then he went into terminal breathing.

I rang for the nurse and she went for the doctor. I couldn't stand the long moments when the old man's chest stopped moving, the abrupt frantic gulps of air followed by no breath at all. I wanted to get away from it, but I had to wait for whatever more he might say.

It didn't come. His eyes fogged and rolled up and he stopped taking those spasmodic strangling breaths. The nurse came back with the doctor, who felt his pulse and shook his head. She pulled the blanket over the old man's face.

I left, feeling sick. I'd learned things I already knew about hate and love and fear and hope and frustration. There was an ad in it somewhere, but I had no way of telling if it had been years ago or recently. And a name that sounded like "El Greco." That was a Spanish painter of four-five hundred years ago. Had the old guy been remembering a picture he'd seen?

No, he'd come up at least close to the present. The ad seemed to solve his problem about being broke. But what about the $17,000 that had been found in the lining of his jacket? He hadn't mentioned that. Of course, being a senile psychotic, he could have considered himself broke even with that amount of money. None coming in, you see.

That didn't add up, either. His was the terror of being old and jobless. If he'd had money, he would have figured how to make it last, and that would have come through in one way or another.

There was the ad, there was his hope, and there was this El Greco. A Greek restaurant, maybe, where he might have been bumming his meals.

But where did the $17,000 fit in?

*   *   *   *   *

Lou Pape was too fed up with the whole thing to discuss it with me. He just gave me the weary eye and said, "You're riding this too hard, Mark. The guy was talking from fever. How do I know what figures and what doesn't when I'm dealing with insanity or delirium?"

"But you admit there's plenty about these cases that doesn't figure?"

"Sure. Did you take a look at the condition the world is in lately? Why should these old people be any exception?"

I couldn't blame him. He'd pulled me in on the cases with plenty of trouble to himself, just to do me a favor. Now he was fed up. I guess it wasn't even that—he thought I was ruining myself, at least financially and maybe worse, by trying to run down the problem. He said he'd be glad to see me any time and gas about anything or help me with whatever might be bothering me, if he could, but not these cases any more. He told me to lay off them, and then he left me on my own.

I don't know what he could have done, actually. I didn't need him to go through the want ads with me, which I was doing every day, figuring there might be something in the ravings about an ad. I spent more time than I liked checking those slanted at old people, only to find they were supposed to become messengers and such.

One brought me to an old brownstone five-story house in the East 80s. I got on line with the rest of the applicants—there were men and women, all decrepit, all looking badly in need of money—and waited my turn. My face was lined with collodion wrinkles and I wore an antique shiny suit and rundown shoes. I didn't look more prosperous or any younger than they did.

I finally came up to the woman who was doing the interviewing. She sat behind a plain office desk down in the main floor hall, with a pile of application cards in front of her and a ballpoint pen in one strong, slender hand. She had red hair with gold lights in it and eyes so pale blue that they would have seemed the same color as the whites if she'd been on the stage. Her face would have been beautiful except for her rigid control of expression; she smiled abruptly, shut it off just like that, looked me over with all the impersonality and penetration of an X-ray from the soles to the bald head, exactly as she'd done with the others. But that skin! If it was as perfect as that all over her slim, stiffly erect, proudly shaped body, she had no business off the stage!

"Name, address, previous occupation, social security number?" she asked in a voice with good clarity, resonance and diction. She wrote it all down while I gave the information to her. Then she asked me for references, and I mentioned

Sergeant Lou Pape. "Fine," she said. "We'll get in touch with you if anything comes up. Don't call us—we'll call you."

I hung around to see who'd be picked. There was only one, an old man, two ahead of me in the line, who had no social security number, no references, not even any relatives or friends she could have checked up on him with.

Damn! *Of course* that was what she wanted! Hadn't all the starvation cases been people without social security, references, either no friends and relatives or those they'd lost track of?

I'd pulled a blooper, but how was I to know until too late?

Well, there was a way of making it right.

*   *   *   *   *

When it was good and dark that evening, I stood on the corner and watched the lights in the brownstone house. The ones on the first two floors went out, leaving only those on the third and fourth. Closed for the day ... or open for business?

I got into a building a few doors down by pushing a button and waiting until the buzzer answered, then racing up to the roof while some man yelled down the stairs to find out who was there. I crossed the tops of the two houses between and went down the fire escape.

It wasn't easy, though not as tough as you might imagine. The fact is that I'm a whole year younger than Lou Pape, even if I could play his grandpa professionally. I still have muscles left and I used them to get down the fire escape at the rear of the house.

The fourth floor room I looked into had some kind of wire mesh cage and some hooded machinery. Nobody there.

The third floor room was the redhead's. She was coming out of the bathroom with a terrycloth bathrobe and a towel turban on when I looked in. She slid the robe off and began dusting herself with powder. That skin *did* cover her.

She turned and moved toward a vanity against the wall that I was on the other side of. The next thing I knew, the window was flung up and she had a gun on me.

"Come right in— Mr. Weldon, isn't it?" she said in that completely controlled voice of hers. One day her control would crack, I thought irrelevantly, and the pieces would be found from Dallas to North Carolina. "I had an idea you seemed more curious than was justified by a help-wanted ad."

"A man my age doesn't get to see many pretty girls," I told her, making my own voice crack pathetically in a senile whinny.

She motioned me into the room. When I was inside, I saw a light over the window blinking red. It stopped the moment I was in the room. A silent burglar alarm.

She let her pale blue eyes wash insolently over me. "A man your age can see all the pretty girls he wants to. You're not old."

"And you use a rinse," I retorted.

She ignored it. "I specifically advertised for old people. Why did you apply?"

It had happened so abruptly that I hadn't had a chance to use the Stanislavsky method to *feel* old in the presence of a beautiful nude woman. I don't even know if it would have worked. Nothing's perfect.

"I needed a job awful bad," I answered sullenly, knowing it sounded like an ad lib.

*   *   *   *   *

She smiled with more contempt than humor. "You had a job, Mr. Weldon. You were very busy trying to find out why senile psychotics starve themselves to death."

"How did you know that?" I asked, startled.

"A little investigation of my own. I also happen to know you didn't tell your friend Sergeant Pape that you were going to be here tonight."

That was a fact, too. I hadn't felt sure enough that I'd found the answer to call him about it. Looking at the gun in her steady hand, I was sorry I hadn't.

"But you did find out I own this building, that my name is May Roberts, and that I'm the daughter of the late Dr. Anthony Roberts, the physicist," she continued. "Is there anything else you want me to tell you about yourself?"

"I know enough already. I'm more interested in you and the starvation cases. If you weren't connected with them, you wouldn't have known I was investigating them."

"That's obvious, isn't it?" She reached for a cigarette on the vanity and used a lighter with her free hand. The big mirror gave me another view of her lovely body, but that was beginning to interest me less than the gun. I thought of making a grab for it. There was too much distance between us, though, and she knew better than to take her eyes off me while she was lighting up. "I'm not afraid of professional detectives, Mr. Weldon. They deal only with facts and every one of them will draw the same conclusions from a given set of circumstances. I don't like amateurs. They guess too much. They don't stick to reality. The result—" her pale eyes chilled and her shapely mouth went hard—"is that they are likely to get too close to the truth."

I wanted a smoke myself, but I wasn't willing to make a move toward the pipe in my jacket. "I may be close to the truth, Miss Roberts, but I don't know what the devil it is. I still don't know how you're tied in with the senile psychotics or why they starve with all that money. You could let me go and I wouldn't have a thing on you."

She glanced down at herself and laughed for real for the first time. "You wouldn't, would you? On the other hand, you know where I'm working from and could nag Sergeant Pape into getting a search warrant. It wouldn't incriminate me, but it would be inconvenient. I don't care to be inconvenienced."

"Which means what?"

"You want to find out my connection with senile psychotics. I intend to show you."

"How?"

She gestured dangerously with the gun. "Turn your face to the wall and stay that way while I get dressed. Make one attempt to turn around before I tell you to and I'll shoot you. You're guilty of housebreaking, you know. It would be a little inconvenient for me to have an investigation ... but not as inconvenient as for you."

*   *   *   *   *

I faced the wall, feeling my stomach braid itself into a tight, painful knot of fear. Of what, I didn't know yet, only that old people who had something to do with her died of starvation. I wasn't old, but that didn't seem very comforting. She was the most frigid, calculating, *deadly* woman I'd ever met. That alone was enough to scare hell out of me. And there was the problem of what she was capable of.

Hearing the sounds of her dressing behind me, I wanted to lunge around and rush her, taking a chance that she might be too busy pulling on a girdle or reaching back to fasten a bra to have the gun in her hand. It was a suicidal impulse and I gave it up instantly. Other women might compulsively finish concealing themselves before snatching up the gun. Not her.

"All right," she said at last.

I faced her. She was wearing coveralls that, if anything, emphasized the curves of her figure. She had a sort of babushka that covered her red hair and kept it in place—the kind of thing women workers used to wear in factories during the war. She had looked lethal with nothing on but a gun and a hard expression. She looked like a sentence of execution now.

"Open that door, turn to the right and go upstairs," she told me, indicating directions with the gun.

I went. It was the longest, most anxious short walk I've ever taken. She ordered me to open a door on the fourth floor, and we were inside the room I'd seen from the fire escape. The mesh cage seemed like a torture chamber to me, the hooded motors designed to shoot an agonizing current through my emaciating body.

"You're going to do to me what you did to the old man you hired today?" I probed, hoping for an answer that would really answer.

She flipped on the switch that started the motors and there was a shrill, menacing whine. The wire mesh of the cage began blurring oddly, as if vibrating like the tines of a tuning fork.

"You've been an unexpected nuisance, Weldon," she said above the motors. "I never thought you'd get this far. But as long as you have, we might as well both benefit by it."

"Benefit?" I repeated. "*Both* of us?"

She opened the drawer of a work table and pulled out a stack of envelopes held with a rubber band. She put the stack at the other edge of the table.

"Would you rather have all cash or bank accounts or both?"

My heart began to beat. *She was where the money came from!*

*   *   *   *   *

"You trying to tell me you're a philanthropist?" I demanded.

"Business is philanthropy, in a way," she answered calmly. "You need money and I need your services. To that extent, we're doing each other a favor. I think you'll find that the favor I'm going to do for you is a pretty considerable one. Would you mind picking up the envelopes on the table?"

I took the stack and stared at the top envelope. "May 15, 1931," I read aloud, and looked suspiciously at her. "What's this for?"

"I don't think it's something that can be explained. At least it's never been possible before and I doubt if it would be now. I'm assuming you want both cash and bank accounts. Is that right?"

"Well, yes. Only—"

"We'll discuss it later." She looked along a row of shelves against one wall, searching the labels on the stacks of bundles there. She drew one out and pushed it toward me. "Please open that and put on the things you'll find inside."

I tore open the bundle. It contained a very plain business suit, black shoes, shirt, tie and a hat with a narrow brim.

"Are these supposed to be my burial clothes?"

"I asked you to put them on," she said. "If you want me to make that a command, I'll do it."

I looked at the gun and I looked at the clothes and then for some shelter I could change behind. There wasn't any.

She smiled. "You didn't seem concerned about my modesty. I don't see why your own should bother you. Get dressed!"

I obeyed, my mind anxiously chasing one possibility after another, all of them ending up with my death. I got into the other things and felt even more uncomfortable. They were all only an approximate fit: the shoes a little too tight and pointed, the collar of the shirt too stiffly starched and too high under my chin, the gray suit too narrow at the shoulders and the ankles. I wished I had a mirror to see myself in. I felt like an ultra-conservative Wall Street broker and I was sure I resembled one.

"All right," she said. "Put the envelopes in your inside pocket. You'll find instructions on each. Follow them carefully."

"I don't get it!" I protested.

"You will. Now step into the mesh cage. Use the envelopes in the order they're arranged in."

"But what's this all about?"

"I can tell you just one thing, Mr. Weldon—don't try to escape. It can't be done. Your other questions will answer themselves if you follow the instructions on the envelopes."

She had the gun in her hand. I went into the mesh cage, not knowing what to expect and yet too afraid of her to refuse. I didn't want to wind up dead of starvation, no matter how much money she might have given me—but I didn't want to get shot, either.

She closed the mesh gate and pushed the switch as far as it would go. The motors screamed as they picked up speed; the mesh cage vibrated more swiftly; I could see her through it as if there were nothing between us.

And then I couldn't see her at all.

I was outside a bank on a sunny day in spring.

*   *   *   *   *

My fear evaporated instantly—I'd escaped somehow!

But then a couple of realizations slapped me from each side. It was day instead of night. I was out on the street and not in her brownstone house.

Even the season had changed!

Dazed, I stared at the people passing by. They looked like characters in a TV movie, the women wearing long dresses and flowerpot hats, their faces made up with petulant rosebud mouths and bright blotches of rouge; the men in hard straw hats, suits with narrow shoulders, plain black or brown shoes— the same kind of clothes I was wearing.

The rumble of traffic in the street caught me next. Cars with square bodies, tubular radiators....

For a moment, I let terror soak through me. Then I remembered the mesh cage and the motors. May Roberts could have given me electro-shock, kept me under long enough for the season to change, or taken me South and left me on a street in daylight.

But this was a street in New York. I recognized it, though some of the buildings seemed changed, the people dressed more shabbily.

Shrewd stagesetting? Hypnosis?

That was it, of course! She'd hypnotized me....

Except that a subject under hypnosis doesn't know he's been hypnotized.

Completely confused, I took out the stack of envelopes I'd put in my pocket. I was supposed to have both cash and a bank account, and I was outside a bank. She obviously wanted me to go in, so I did. I handed the top envelope to the teller.

He hauled $150 out of it and looked at me as if that was enough to buy and sell the bank. He asked me if I had an account there. I didn't. He took me over to an officer of the bank, a fellow with a Hoover collar and a John Gilbert mustache, who signed me up more cordially than I'd been treated in years.

I walked out to the street, gaping at the entry in the bankbook he'd handed me. My pulse was jumping lumpily, my lungs refusing to work right, my head doing a Hopi rain dance.

The date he'd stamped was May 15, 1931.

* * * * *

I didn't know which I was more afraid of—being stranded, middle-aged, in the worst of the depression, or being yanked back to that brownstone house. I had only an instant to realize that I was a kid in high school uptown right at that moment. Then the whole scene vanished as fast as blinking and I was outside another bank somewhere else in the city.

The date on the envelope was May 29th and it was still 1931. I made a $75 deposit there, then $100 in another place a few days later, and so forth, spending only a few minutes each time and going forward anywhere from a couple of days to almost a month.

Every now and then, I had a stamped, addressed envelope to mail at a corner box. They were addressed to different stock brokers and when I got one open before mailing it and took a look inside, it turned out to be an order to buy a few hundred shares of stock in a soft drink company in the name of Dr. Anthony Roberts. I hadn't remembered the price of the shares being that low. The last time I'd seen the quotation, it was more than five times as much as it was then. I was making dough myself, but I was doing even better for May Roberts.

A few times I had to stay around for an hour or so. There was the night I found myself in a flashy speakeasy with two envelopes that I was to bet the contents of, according to the instructions on the outside. It was June 21, 1932, and I had to bet on Jack Sharkey to take the heavyweight title away from Max Schmeling.

The place was serious and quiet—no more than three women, a couple of bartenders, and the rest male customers, including two cops, huddling up close to the radio. An affable character was taking bets. He gave me a wise little smile when I put the money down on Sharkey.

"Well, it's a pleasure to do business with a man who wants an American to win," he said, "and the hell with the smart dough, eh?"

"Yeah," I said, and tried to smile back, but so much of the smart money was going on Schmeling that I wondered if May Roberts hadn't made a mistake. I couldn't remember who had won. "You know what J. P. Morgan said—don't sell America short."

"I'll take a buck for my share," said a sour guy who barely managed to stand. "Lousy grass growing in the lousy streets, nobody working, no future, nothing!"

"We'll come out of it okay," I told him confidently.

He snorted into his gin. "Not in our lifetime, Mac. It'd take a miracle to put this country on its feet again. I don't believe in miracles." He put his scowling face up close to mine and breathed blearily and belligerently at me. "Do you?"

"Shut up, Gus," one of the bartenders said. "The fight's starting."

*   *   *   *   *

I had some tough moments and a lot of bad Scotch, listening. It went the whole 15 rounds, Sharkey won, and I was in almost as bad shape as Gus, who'd passed out halfway through the battle. All I can recall is the affable character handing over a big roll and saying, "Lucky for me more guys don't sell America short," and trying to separate the money into the right amounts and put them into the right envelopes, while stumbling out the door, when everything changed and I was outside a bank again.

I thought, "My God, what a hangover cure!" I was as sober as if I hadn't had a drink, when I made that deposit.

There were more envelopes to mail and more deposits to make and bets to put down on Singing Wood in 1933 at Belmont Park and Max Baer over Primo Carnera, and then Cavalcade at Churchill Downs in 1934, and James Braddock over Baer in 1935, and a big daily double payoff, Wanoah-Arakay at Tropical Park, and so on, skipping through the years like a flat stone over water, touching here and there for a few minutes to an hour at a time. I kept the envelopes for May Roberts and myself in different pockets and the bankbooks in another. The envelopes were beginning to bulge and the deposits and accrued interest were something to watch grow.

The whole thing, in fact, was so exciting that it was early October of 1938—a total of maybe four or five hours subjectively—before I realized what she had me doing. I wasn't thinking much about the fact that I was time traveling or how she did it; I accepted that, though the sensation in some ways was creepy, like raising the dead. My father and mother, for instance, were still alive in 1938. If I could break away from whatever it was that kept pulling me jumpily through time, I could go and see them.

The thought attracted me enough to make me shake badly with intent, yet pump dread through me. I wanted so damned badly to see them again and I didn't dare. I couldn't....

Why couldn't I?

Maybe the machine covered only the area around the various banks, speakeasies, bars and horse parlors. If I could get out of the area, whatever it might be, I could avoid coming back to whatever May Roberts had lined up for me.

Because, naturally, I knew now what I was doing: I was making deposits and winning sure bets just as the "senile psychotics" had done. The ink on their bankbooks and bills was fresh because it *was* fresh; it wasn't given a chance to oxidize— at the rate I was going, I'd be back to my own time in another few hours or so, with $15,000 or better in deposits, compound interest and cash.

If I'd been around 70, you see, she could have sent me back to the beginning of the century with the same amount of money, which would have accumulated to something like $30,000.

Get it now?

I did.

And I felt sick and frightened.

The old people had died of starvation somehow with all that dough in cash or banks. I didn't give a hang if the time travel was responsible, or something else was. I wasn't going to be found dead in my hotel and have Lou Pape curse my corpse because I'd been borrowing from him when, since 1931, I'd had a little fortune put away. He'd call me a premature senile psychotic and he'd be right, from his point of view, not knowing the truth.

*   *   *   *   *

Rather than make the deposit in October, 1938, I grabbed a battered old cab and told the driver to step on it. When I showed him the $10 bill that was in it for him, he squashed down the gas pedal. In 1938, $10 was real money.

We got a mile away from the bank and the driver looked at me in the rear-view mirror.

"How far you want to go, mister?"

My teeth were together so hard that I had to unclench them before I could answer, "As far away as we can get."

"Cops after you?"

"No, but somebody is. Don't be surprised at anything that happens, no matter what it is."

"You mean like getting shot at?" he asked worriedly, slowing down.

"You're not in any danger, friend. I am. Relax and step on it again."

I wondered if she could still reach me, this far from the bank, and handed the guy the bill. No justice sticking him for the ride in case she should. He pushed the pedal down even harder than he had been doing before.

We must have been close to three miles away when I blinked and was standing outside the first bank I'd seen in 1931.

I don't know what the cab driver thought when I vanished out of his hack. He probably figured I'd opened the door and jumped while he wasn't looking. Maybe he even went back and searched for a body splashed all over the street.

Well, it would have been a hopeless hunt. I was a week ahead.

I gave up and drearily made my deposit. The one from early October that I'd missed I put in with this one.

There was no way to escape the babe with the beautiful hard face, gorgeous warm body and plans for me that all seemed to add up to death. I didn't try any more. I went on making deposits, mailing orders to her stock brokers, and putting down bets that couldn't miss because they were all past history.

I don't even remember what the last one was, a fight or a race. I hung around the bar that had long ago replaced the speakeasy, until the inevitable payoff, got myself a hamburger and headed out the door. All the envelopes I was supposed to use were gone and I felt shaky, knowing that the next place I'd see was the room with the wire mesh cage and the hooded motors.

It was.

*   *   *   *   *

She was on the other side of the cage, and I had five bankbooks and envelopes filled with cash amounting to more than $15,000, but all I could think of was that I was hungry and something had happened to the hamburger while I was traveling through time. I must have fallen and dropped it, because my hand was covered with dust or dirt. I brushed it off and quickly felt my face and pulled up my sleeves to look at my arms.

"Very smart," I said, "but I'm nowhere near emaciation."

"What made you think you would be?" she asked.

"Because the others always were."

She cut the motors to idling speed and the vibrating mesh slowed down. I glared at her through it. God, she was lovely—as lovely as an ice sculpture! The kind of face you'd love to kiss and slap, kiss and slap....

"You came here with a preconceived notion, Mr. Weldon. I'm a businesswoman, not a monster. I like to think there's even a good deal of the altruist in me. I could hire only young people, but the old ones have more trouble finding work. And you've seen for yourself how I provide nest eggs for them they'd otherwise never have."

"And take care of yourself at the same time."

"That's the businesswoman in me. I need money to operate."

"So do the old people. Only they die and you don't."

She opened the gate and invited me out. "I make mistakes occasionally. I sometimes pick men and women who prove to be too old to stand the strain. I try not to let it happen, but they need money and work so badly that they don't always tell the truth about their age and state of health."

"You could take those who have social security cards and references."

"But those who don't have any are in worse need!" She paused. "You probably think I want only the money you and they bring back, that it's merely some sort of profit-making scheme. It isn't."

"You mean the idea is not just to build up a fortune for you with a cut for whoever helps you do it?"

"I said I need money to operate, Mr. Weldon, and this method serves. But there are other purposes, much more important. What you have gone through is—basic training, you might say.

You know now that it's possible to travel through time, and what it's like. The initial shock, in other words, is gone and you're better equipped to do something for me in another era."

"Something else?" I stared at her puzzledly. "What else could you want?"

"Let's have dinner first. You must be hungry."

*　　*　　*　　*　　*

I was, and that reminded me: "I bought a hamburger just before you brought me back. I don't know what happened to it. My hand was dirty and the hamburger was gone, as if I'd fallen somehow and dropped it and got dirt on my hand."

She looked worriedly at the hand, probably afraid I'd cut it and disqualified myself. I could understand that; you never know what kind of diseases can be picked up in different times, because I remember reading somewhere that germs keep changing according to conditions. Right now, for instance, strains of bacteria are becoming resistant to antibiotics. I knew her concern wasn't really for me, but it was pleasant all the same.

"That could be the explanation, I suppose," she said. "The truth is that I've never taken a time voyage—somebody has to operate the controls in the present—so I can't say it's possible or impossible to fall. It must be, since you did. Perhaps the wrench back from the past was too violent and you slipped just before you returned."

She led me down to an ornate dining room, where the table had been set for two. The food was waiting on the table, steaming and smelling tasty. Nobody was around to serve us. She pointed out a chair to me and we sat down and began eating. I was a little nervous at first, afraid there might be something in the food, but it tasted fine and nothing happened after I swallowed a little and waited for some effect.

"You did try to escape the time tractor beam, didn't you, Mr. Weldon?" she asked. I didn't have to answer; she knew. "That's a mistaken notion of how it functions. The control beam doesn't cover *area*; it covers *era*. You could have flown to any part of the world and the beam would still have brought you back. Do I make myself clear?"

She did. Too bloody clear. I waited for the rest.

"I assume you've already formed an opinion of me," she went on. "A rather unflattering one, I imagine."

"'Bitch' is the cleanest word I can find. But a clever one. Anybody who can invent a time machine would have to be a genius."

"I didn't invent it. My father did—Dr. Anthony Roberts— using the funds you and others helped me provide him with." Her face grew soft and tender. "My father was a wonderful man, a great man, but he was called a crackpot. He was kept from teaching or working anywhere. It was just as well, I suppose, though he was too hurt to think so; he had more leisure to develop the time machine. He could have used it to extort repayment from mankind for his humiliation, but he didn't. He used it to help mankind."

"Like how?" I goaded.

"It doesn't matter, Mr. Weldon. You're determined to hate me and consider me a liar. Nothing I tell you can change that."

*   *   *   *   *

She was right about the first part—I hadn't dared let myself do anything except hate and fear her—but she was wrong about the second. I remembered thinking how Lou Pape would have felt if I had died of starvation with over $15,000, after borrowing from him all the time between jobs. Not knowing how I got it, he'd have been sore, thinking I'd played him for a patsy. What I'm trying to say is that Lou wouldn't have had enough information to judge me. I didn't have enough information yet, either, to judge her.

"What do you want me to do?" I asked warily.

"Everybody but one person was sent into the past on specific errands—to save art treasures and relics that would otherwise have been lost to humanity."

"Not because the things might be worth a lot of dough?" I said nastily.

"You've already seen that I can get all the money I want. There were upheavals in the past—great fires, wars, revolutions, vandalism—and I had my associates save things that would have been destroyed. Oh, beautiful things, Mr. Weldon! The world would have been so much poorer without them!"

"El Greco, for instance?" I asked, remembering the raving old man who had been found wandering with $17,000 in his coat lining.

"El Greco, too. Several paintings that had been lost for centuries." She became more brisk and efficient-seeming. "Except for the one man I mentioned, I concentrated on the past—the future is too completely unknown to us. And there's an additional reason why I tentatively explored it only once. But the one person who went there discovered something that would be of immense value to the world."

"What happened to *him*?"

She looked regretful. "He was too old. He survived just long enough to tell me that the future has something we need. It's a metal box, small enough to carry, that could supply this whole city with power to run its industries and light its homes and streets!"

"Sounds good. Who'd you say benefits if I get it?"

"We share the profits equally, of course. But it must be understood that we sell the power so cheaply that everybody can afford it."

"I'm not arguing. What's the other reason you didn't bother with the future?"

"You can't bring anything from the future to the present that doesn't exist right now. I won't go into the theory, but it should be obvious that nothing can exist before it exists. You can't bring the box I want, only the technical data to build one."

"Technical data? I'm an actor, not a scientist."

"You'll have pens and weatherproof notebooks to copy it down in."

*   *   *   *   *

I couldn't make up my mind about her. I've already said she was beautiful, which always prejudices a man in a woman's favor, but I couldn't forget the starvation cases. They hadn't shared anything but malnutrition, useless money and death. Then again, maybe her explanation was a good one, that she wanted to help those who needed help most and some of them lied about their age and physical condition because they wanted the jobs so badly. All I knew about were those who had died. How did I know there weren't others—a lot more of them than the fatal cases, perhaps—who came through all right and were able to enjoy their little fortunes?

And there was her story about saving the treasures of the past and wanting to provide power at really low cost. She was right about one thing: she didn't need any of that to make money with; her method was plenty good enough, using the actual records of the past to invest in stocks, bet on sports—all sure gambles.

But those starvation cases....

"Do I get any guarantees?" I demanded.

She looked annoyed. "I'll need you for the data. You'll need me to turn it into manufacture. Is that enough of a guarantee?"

"No. Do I come out of this alive?"

"Mr. Weldon, please use some logic. I'm the one who's taking the risk. I've already given you more money than you've ever had at one time in your life. Part of my motive was to pay for services about to be rendered. Mostly, it was to give you experience in traveling through time."

"And to prove to me that I can't run out," I added.

"That happens to be a necessary attribute of the machine. I couldn't very well move you about through time unless it worked that way. If you'd look at my point of view, you'd see that I lose my investment if you don't bring back the data. I can't withdraw your money, you realize."

"I don't know what to think," I said, dissatisfied with myself because I couldn't find out what, if anything, was wrong with the deal. "I'll get you the data for the power box if it's at all possible and then we'll see what happens."

Finished eating, we went upstairs and I got into the cage.

She closed the circuit. The motors screamed. The mesh blurred.

And I was in a world I never knew.

*   *   *   *   *

You'd call it a city, I suppose; there were enough buildings to make it one. But no city ever had so much greenery. It wasn't just tree-lined streets, like Unter den Linden in Berlin, or islands covered with shrubbery, like Park Avenue in New York. The grass and trees and shrubs grew around every building, separating them from each other by wide lawns. The buildings were more glass—or what looked like glass—than anything else. A few of the windows were opaque against the sun, but I couldn't see any shades or blinds. Some kind of polarizing glass or plastic?

I felt uneasy being there, but it was a thrill just the same, to be alive in the future when I and everybody who lived in my day was supposed to be dead.

The air smelled like the country. There was no foul gas boiling from the teardrop cars on the glass-level road. They were made of transparent plastic clear around and from top to bottom, and they moved along at a fair clip, but more smoothly than swiftly. If I hadn't seen the airship overhead, I wouldn't have known it was there. It flew silently, a graceful ball without wings, seeming to be borne by the wind from one horizon to the other, except that no wind ever moved that fast.

One car stopped nearby and someone shouted, "Here we are!" Several people leaped out and headed for me.

I didn't think. I ran. I crossed the lawn and ducked into the nearest building and dodged through long, smoothly walled, shadowlessly lit corridors until I found a door that would open. I slammed it shut and locked it. Then, panting, I fell into a soft chair that seemed to form itself around my body, and felt like kicking myself for the bloody idiot I was.

What in hell had I run for? They couldn't have known who I was. If I'd arrived in a time when people wore togas or bathing suits, there would have been some reason for singling me out, but they had all had clothes just like ours—suits and shirts and ties for the men, a dress and high heels for the one woman with them. I felt somewhat disappointed that clothes hadn't changed any, but it worked out to my advantage; I wouldn't be so conspicuous.

Yet why should anyone have yelled "Here we are!" unless.... No, they must have thought I was somebody else. It didn't figure any other way. I had run because it was my first startled reaction and probably because I knew I was there on what might be considered illegal business; if I succeeded, some poor inventor would be done out of his royalties.

I wished I hadn't run. Besides making me feel like a scared fool, I was sweaty and out of breath. Playing old men doesn't make climbing down fire escapes much tougher than it should be, but it doesn't exactly make a sprinter out of you—not by several lungfuls.

*   *   *   *   *

I sat there, breathing hard and trying to guess what next. I had no more idea of where to go for what I wanted than an ancient Egyptian set down in the middle of Times Square with instructions to sneak a mummy out of the Metropolitan Museum. I didn't even have that much information. I didn't know any part of the city, how it was laid out, or where to get the data that May Roberts had sent me for.

I opened the door quietly and looked both ways before going out. After losing myself in the cross-connecting corridors a few times, I finally came to an outside door. I stopped, tense, trying to get my courage. My inclination was to slip, sneak or dart out, but I made myself walk away like a decent, innocent citizen. That was one disguise they'd never be able to crack. All I had to do was act as if I belonged to that time and place and who would know the difference?

There were other people walking as if they were in no hurry to get anywhere. I slowed down to their speed, but I wished wistfully that there was a crowd to dive into and get lost.

A man dropped into step and said politely, "I beg your pardon. Are you a stranger in town?"

I almost halted in alarm, but that might have been a giveaway. "What makes you think so?" I asked, forcing myself to keep at the same easy pace.

"I—didn't recognize your face and I thought—"

"It's a big city," I said coldly. "You can't know everyone."

"If there's anything I can do to help—"

I told him there wasn't and left him standing there. It was plain common sense, I had decided quickly while he was talking to me, not to take any risks by admitting anything. I might have been dumped into a police state or the country could have been at war without my knowing it, or maybe they were suspicious of strangers. For one reason or another, ranging from vagrancy to espionage, I could be pulled in, tortured, executed, God knows what. The place looked peaceful enough, but that didn't prove a thing.

I went on walking, looking for something I couldn't be sure existed, in a city I was completely unfamiliar with, in a time when I had no right to be alive. It wasn't just a matter of getting the information she wanted. I'd have been satisfied to hang around until she pulled me back without the data....

But then what would happen? Maybe the starvation cases were people who had failed her! For that matter, she could shoot me and send the remains anywhere in time to get rid of the evidence.

Damn it, I didn't know if she was better or worse than I'd supposed, but I wasn't going to take any chances. I had to bring her what she wanted.

*   *   *   *   *

There was a sign up ahead. It read: TO SHOPPING CENTER. The arrow pointed along the road. When I came to a fork and wondered which way to go, there was another sign, then another pointing to still more farther on.

I followed them to the middle of the city, a big square with a park in the center and shops of all kinds rimming it. The only shop I was interested in said: ELECTRICAL APPLIANCES.

I went in.

A neat young salesman came up and politely asked me if he could do anything for me. I sounded stupid even to myself, but I said, "No, thanks, I'd just like to do a little browsing," and gave a silly nervous laugh. Me, an actor, behaving like a frightened yokel! I felt ashamed of myself.

He tried not to look surprised, but he didn't really succeed. Somebody else came in, though, for which I was grateful, and he left me alone to look around.

I don't know if I can get my feelings across to you. It's a situation that nobody would ever expect to find himself in, so it isn't easy to tell what it's like. But I've got to try.

Let's stick with the ancient Egyptian I mentioned a while back, the one ordered to sneak a mummy out of the Metropolitan Museum. Maybe that'll make it clearer.

The poor guy has no money he can use, naturally, and no idea of what New York's transportation system is like, where the museum is, how to get there, what visitors to a museum do and say, the regulations he might unwittingly break, how much an ordinary citizen is supposed to know about which customs and such. Now add the possible danger that he might be slapped into jail or an insane asylum if he makes a mistake and you've got a rough notion of the spot I felt I was in. Being able to speak English doesn't make much difference; not knowing what's regarded as right and wrong, and the unknown consequences, are enough to panic anybody.

That doesn't make it clear enough.

Well, look, take the electrical appliances in that store; that might give you an idea of the situation and the way it affected me.

The appliances must have been as familiar to the people of that time as toasters and TV sets and lamps are to us. But the things didn't make a bit of sense to me ... any more than our appliances would to the ancient Egyptian. Can you imagine him trying to figure out what those items are for and how they work?

*   *   *   *   *

Here are some gadgets you can puzzle over:

There was a light fixture that you put against any part of a wall—no screws, no cement, no wires, even—and it held there and lit up, and it stayed lit no matter where you moved it on the wall. Talk about pin-up lamps ... this was really it!

Then I came across something that looked like an ashtray with a blue electric shimmer obscuring the bottom of the bowl. I lit my pipe—others I'd passed had been smoking, so I knew it was safe to do the same—and flicked in the match. It disappeared. I don't mean it was swirled into some hidden compartment. *It vanished.* I emptied the pipe into the ashtray and that went, too. Looking around to make sure nobody was watching, I dredged some coins out of my pocket and let them drop into the tray. They were gone. Not a particle of them was left. A disintegrator? I haven't got the slightest idea.

There were little mirror boxes with three tiny dials on the front of each. I turned the dials on one—it was like using three dial telephones at the same time—and a pretty girl's face popped onto the mirror surface and looked expectantly at me.

"Yes?" she said, and waited for me to answer.

"I—uh—wrong number, I guess," I answered, putting the box down in a hurry and going to the other side of the shop because I didn't have even a dim notion how to turn it off.

The thing I was looking for was on a counter—a tinted metal box no bigger than a suitcase, with a lipped hole on top and small undisguised verniers in front. I didn't know I'd found it, actually, until I twisted a vernier and every light in the store suddenly glared and the salesman came rushing over and politely moved me aside to shut it off.

"We don't want to burn out every appliance in the place, do we?" he asked quietly.

"I just wanted to see if it worked all right," I said, still shaking slightly. It could have blown up or electrocuted me, for all I knew.

"But they always work," he said.

"Ah—always?"

"Of course. The principle is simple and there are no parts to get worn out, so they last indefinitely." He suddenly smiled as if he'd just caught the gist. "Oh, you were joking! Naturally—

everybody learns about the Dynapack in primary education. You were interested in acquiring one?"

"No, no. The—the old one is good enough. I was just—well, you know, interested in knowing if the new models are much different or better than the old ones."

"But there haven't been any new models since 2073," he said. "Can you think of any reason why there should be?"

"I—guess not," I stammered. "But you never can tell."

"You can with Dynapacks," he said, and he would have gone on if I hadn't lost my nerve and mumbled my way out of the store as fast as I could.

*   *   *   *   *

You want to know why? He'd asked me if I wanted to "acquire" a Dynapack, not *buy* one. I didn't know what "acquire" meant in that society. It could be anything from saving up coupons to winning whatever you wanted at some kind of lottery, or maybe working up the right number of labor units on the job—in which case he'd want to know where I was employed and the equivalent of social security and similar information, which I naturally didn't have—or it could just be fancy sales talk for buying.

I couldn't guess, and I didn't care to expose myself any more than I had already. And my blunder about the Dynapack working and the new models was nothing to make me feel at all easier.

Lord, the uncertainties and hazards of being in a world you don't know anything about! Daydreaming about visiting another age may be pleasant, but the reality is something else again.

"Wait a minute, friend!" I heard the salesman call out behind me.

*   *   *   *   *

I looked back as casually, I hoped, as the pedestrians who heard him. He was walking quickly toward me with a very worried expression on his face. I stepped up my own pace as unobtrusively as possible, trying to keep a lot of people between us, meanwhile praying that they'd think I was just somebody who was late for an appointment. The salesman didn't break into a run or yell for the cops, but I couldn't be sure he wouldn't.

As soon as I came to a corner, I turned it and ran like hell. There was a sort of alley down the block. I jumped into it, found a basement door and stayed inside, pressed against the wall, quivering with tension and sucking air like a swimmer who'd stayed underwater too long.

Even after I got my wind back, I wasn't anxious to go out. The place could have been cordoned off, with the police, the army and the navy all cooperating to nab me.

What made me think so? Not a thing except remembering how puzzled our ancient Egyptian would have been if he got arrested in the subway for something everybody did casually and without punishment in his own time—spitting! I could have done something just as innocent, as far as you and I are concerned, that this era would consider a misdemeanor or a major crime. And in what age was ignorance of the law ever an excuse?

Instead of going back out, I prowled carefully into the building. It was strangely silent and deserted. I couldn't understand why until I came to a lavatory. There were little commodes and wash basins that came up to barely above my knees. The place was a school. Naturally it was deserted—the kids were through for the day.

I could feel the tension dissolve in me like a ramrod of ice melting, no longer keeping my back and neck stiff and taut. There probably wasn't a better place in the city for me to hide.

A primary school!

The salesman had said to me, "Everybody learns about the Dynapack in primary education."

*   *   *   *   *

Going through the school was eerie, like visiting a familiar childhood scene that had been distorted by time into something almost totally unrecognizable.

There were no blackboards, teacher's big desk, children's little desks, inkwells, pointers, globes or books. Yet it was a school. The small fixtures in the lavatory downstairs had told me that, and so did the miniature chairs drawn neatly under the low, vividly painted tables in the various schoolrooms. A large comfortable chair was evidently where the teacher sat when not wandering around among the pupils.

In front of each chair, firmly attached to the table, was a box with a screen, and both sides of the box held spools of wire on blunt little spindles. The spools had large, clear numbers on them. Near the teacher's chair was a compact case with more spools on spindles, and there was a large screen on the inside wall, opposite the enormous windows.

I went into one of the rooms and sat down in the teacher's chair, wondering how I was going to find out about the Dynapack. I felt like an archaeologist guessing at the functions of strange relics he'd found in a dead city.

Sitting in the chair was like sitting on a column of air that let me sit upright or slump as I chose. One of the arms had a row of buttons. I pressed one and waited nervously to find out if I'd done something that would get me into trouble.

Concealed lights in the ceiling and walls began glowing, getting brighter, while the room gradually turned dark. I glanced around bewilderedly to see why, because it was still daylight.

The windows seemed to be sliding slightly, very slowly, and as they slid, the sunlight was damped out. I grinned, thinking of what my ancient Egyptian would make of that. I knew there were two sheets of polarizing glass, probably with a vacuum between to keep out the cold and the heat, and the lights in the room were beautifully synchronized with the polarized sliding glass.

I wasn't doing so badly. The rest of the objects might not be too hard to figure out.

The spools in the case alongside the teacher's chair could be wire recordings. I looked for something to play them with, but there was no sign of a playback machine. I tried to lift a spool off a spindle. It wouldn't come off.

Hah! The wire led down the spindle to the base of the box, holding the spool in place. That meant the spools could be played right in that position. But what started them playing?

*   *   *   *   *

I hunted over the box minutely. Every part of it was featureless—no dials, switches or any unfamiliar counterparts. I even tried moving my hands over it, figuring it might be like a theramin, and spoke to it in different shades of command, because it could have been built to respond to vocal orders. Nothing happened.

Remember the Poe story that shows the best place to hide something is right out in the open, which is the last place anyone would look? Well, these things weren't manufactured to baffle people, any more than our devices generally are. But it's only by trying everything that somebody who didn't know what a switch is would start up a vacuum cleaner, say, or light a big chandelier from a wall clear across the room.

I'd pressed every inch of the box, hoping some part of it might act as a switch, and I finally touched one of the spindles. The spool immediately began spinning at a very low speed and the screen on the wall opposite the window glowed into life.

"The history of the exploration of the Solar System," said an announcer's deep voice, "is one of the most adventuresome in mankind's long list of achievements. Beginning with the crude rockets developed during World War II...."

There were newsreel shots of V-1 and V-2 being blasted from their takeoff ramps and a montage of later experimental models. I wished I could see how it all turned out, but I was afraid to waste the time watching. At any moment, I might hear the footsteps of a guard or janitor or whoever tended buildings then.

I pushed the spindle again. It checked the spool, which rewound swiftly and silently, and stopped itself when the rewinding was finished. I tried another. A nightmare underwater scene appeared.

"With the aid of energy screens," said another voice, "the oceans of the world were completely charted by the year 2027...."

I turned it off, then another on developments in medicine, one on architecture, one on history, the geography of such places as the interior of South America and Africa that were—or are— unknown today, and I was getting frantic, starting the wonderful wire films that held full-frequency sound and pictures in absolutely faithful color, and shutting them off hastily when I discovered they didn't have what I was looking for.

They were courses for children, but they all contained information that our scientists are still groping for ... and I couldn't chance watching one all the way through!

I was frustratedly switching off a film on psychology when a female voice said from the door, "May I help you?"

*   *   *   *   *

I snapped around to face her in sudden fright. She was young and slim and slight, but she could scream loud enough to get help. Judging by the way she was looking at me, outwardly polite and yet visibly nervous, that scream would be coming at any second.

"I must have wandered in here by mistake," I said, and pushed past her to the corridor, where I began running back the way I had come.

"But you don't understand!" she cried after me. "I really want to help—"

Yeah, help, I thought, pounding toward the street door. A gag right out of that psychology film, probably—get the patient to hold still, humor him, until you can get somebody to put him where he belongs. That's what one of our teachers would do, provided she wasn't too scared to think straight, if she found an old-looking guy thumbing frenziedly through the textbooks in a grammar school classroom.

When I came to the outside door, I stopped. I had no way of knowing whether she'd given out an alarm, or how she might have done it, but the obvious place to find me would be out on the street, dodging for cover somewhere.

I pushed the door open and let it slam shut, hoping she'd hear it upstairs. Then I found a door, sneaked it open and went silently down the steps.

In the basement, I looked for a furnace or a coal bin or a fuel tank to hide behind, but there weren't any. I don't know how they got their heat in the winter or cooled the building in the summer. Probably some central atomic plant that took care of the whole city, piping in the heat or coolant in underground conduits that were led up through the walls, because there weren't even any pipes visible.

I hunched into the darkest corner I could find and hoped they wouldn't look for me there.

*   *   *   *   *

By the time night came, hunger drove me out of the school, but I did it warily, making sure nobody was in sight.

The streets of the shopping center were more or less deserted. There was no sign of a restaurant. I was so empty that I felt dizzy as I hunted for one. But then a shocking realization made me halt on the sidewalk and sweat with horror.

Even if there had been a restaurant, what would I have used for money?

Now I got the whole foul picture. She had sent old people back through time on errands like mine ... and they'd starved to death because they couldn't buy food!

No, that wasn't right. I remembered what I had told Lou Pape: anybody who gets hungry enough can always find a truck garden or a food store to rob.

Only ... I hadn't seen a truck garden or food store anywhere in this city.

And ... I thought about people in the past having their hands cut off for stealing a loaf of bread.

This civilization didn't look as if it went in for such drastic punishments, assuming I could find a loaf of bread to steal. But neither did most of the civilizations that practiced those barbarisms.

I was more tired, hungry and scared than I'd ever believed a human being could get. Lost, completely lost in a totally alien world, but one in which I could still be killed or starve to death

... and God knew what was waiting for me in my own time in case I came back without the information she wanted.

Or maybe even if I came back with it!

That suspicion made up my mind for me. Whatever happened to me now couldn't be worse than what she might do. At least I didn't have to starve.

I stopped a man in the street. I let several others go by before picking him deliberately because he was middle-aged, had a kindly face, and was smaller than me, so I could slug him and run if he raised a row.

"Look, friend," I told him, "I'm just passing through town—"

"Ah?" he said pleasantly.

"—And I seem to have mislaid—" No, that was dangerous. I'd been about to say I'd mislaid my wallet, but I still didn't know whether they used money in this era. He waited with a patient, friendly smile while I decided just how to put it. "The fact is that I haven't eaten all day and I wonder if you could help me get a meal."

He said in the most neighborly voice imaginable, "I'll be glad to do anything I can, Mr. Weldon."

*   *   *   *   *

My entire face seemed to drop open. "You—you called me—"

"Mr. Weldon," he repeated, still looking up at me with that neighborly smile. "Mark Weldon, isn't it? From the 20th Century?"

I tried to answer, but my throat had tightened up worse than on any opening night I'd ever had to live through. I nodded, wondering terrifiedly what was going on.

"Please relax," he said persuasively. "You're not in any danger whatever. We offer you our utmost hospitality. Our time, you might say, is your time."

"You know who I am," I managed to get out through my constricted glottis. "I've been doing all this running and ducking and hiding for nothing."

He shrugged sympathetically. "Everyone in the city was instructed to help you, but you were so nervous that we were afraid to alarm you with a direct approach. Every time we tried to, as a matter of fact, you vanished into one place or another.

We didn't follow for fear of the effect on you. We had to wait until you came voluntarily to us."

My brain was racing again and getting nowhere. Part of it was dizziness from hunger, but only part. The rest was plain frightened confusion.

They knew who I was. They'd been expecting me. They probably even knew what I was after.

And they wanted to help!

"Let's not go into explanations now," he said, "although I'd like to smooth away the bewilderment and fear on your face. But you need to be fed first. Then we'll call in the others and—"

I pulled back. "What others? How do I know you're not setting up something for me that I'll wish I hadn't gotten into?"

"Before you approached me, Mr. Weldon, you first had to decide that we represented no greater menace than May Roberts. Please believe me, we don't."

So he knew about that, too!

"All right, I'll take my chances," I gave in resignedly. "Where does a guy find a place to eat in this city?"

* * * * *

It was a handsome restaurant with soft light coming from three-dimensional, full-color nature murals that I might mistakenly have walked into if I'd been alone, they looked so much like gardens and forests and plains. It was no wonder I couldn't find a restaurant or food store or truck garden anywhere—food came up through pneumatic chutes in each building, I'd been told on the way over, grown in hydroponic tanks in cities that specialized in agriculture, and those who wanted to eat "out" could drop into the restaurant each building had. Every city had its own function. This one was for people in the arts. I liked that.

There was a glowing menu on the table with buttons alongside the various selections. I looked starvingly at the items, trying to decide which I wanted most. I picked oysters, onion soup, breast of guinea hen under Plexiglas and was hunting for the tastiest and most recognizable dessert when the pleasant little guy shook his head regretfully and emphatically.

"I'm afraid you can't eat any of those foods, Mr. Weldon," he said in a sad voice. "We'll explain why in a moment."

A waiter and the manager came over. They obviously didn't want to stare at me, but they couldn't help it. I couldn't blame them, I'd have stared at somebody from George Washington's time, which is about what I must have represented to them.

"Will you please arrange to have the special food for Mr. Weldon delivered here immediately?" the little guy asked.

"Every restaurant has been standing by for this, Mr. Carr," said the manager. "It's on its way. Prepared, of course—it's been ready since he first arrived."

"Fine," said the little guy, Carr. "It can't be too soon. He's very hungry."

I glanced around and noticed for the first time that there was nobody else in the restaurant. It was past the dinner hour, but, even so, there are always late diners. We had the place all to ourselves and it bothered me. They could have ganged up on me....

But they didn't. A light gong sounded, and the waiter and manager hurried over to a slot of a door and brought out a couple of trays loaded with covered dishes.

"Your dinner, Mr. Weldon," the manager said, putting the plates in front of me and removing the lids.

I stared down at the food.

"This," I told them angrily, "is a hell of a trick to play on a starving man!"

*   *   *   *   *

They all looked unhappy.

"Mashed dehydrated potatoes, canned meat and canned vegetables," Carr replied. "Not very appetizing. I know, but I'm afraid it's all we can allow you to eat."

I took the cover off the dessert dish.

"Dried fruits!" I said in disgust.

"Rather excessively dried, I'm sorry to say," the manager agreed mournfully.

I sipped the blue stuff in a glass and almost spat it out. "Powdered milk! Are these things what you people have to live on?"

"No, our diet is quite varied," Carr said in embarrassment. "But we unfortunately can't give you any of the foods we normally eat ourselves."

"And why in blazes not?"

"Please eat, Mr. Weldon," Carr begged with frantic earnestness. "There's so much to explain—this is part of it, of course—and it would be best if you heard it on a full stomach."

I was famished enough to get the stuff down, which wasn't easy; uninviting as it looked, it tasted still worse.

When I was through, Carr pushed several buttons on the glowing menu. Dishes came up from an opening in the center of the table and he showed me the luscious foods they contained.

"Given your choice," he said, "you'd have preferred them to what you have eaten. Isn't that so, Mr. Weldon?"

"You bet I would!" I answered, sore because I hadn't been given that choice.

"And you would have died like the pathetic old people you were investigating," said a voice behind me.

I turned around, startled. Several men and women had come in while I'd been eating, their footsteps as silent as cats on a rug. I looked blankly from them to Carr and back again.

"These are the clothes we ordinarily wear," Carr said. "An 18th Century motif, as you can see—updated knee breeches and shirt waists, a modified stock for the men, the daring low bodices of that era, the full skirts treated in a modern way by using sheer materials for the women, bright colors and sheens, buckled shoes of spun synthetics. Very gay, very ornamental, very comfortable, and thoroughly suitable to our time."

"But everybody I saw was dressed like me!" I protested.

"Only to keep you from feeling more conspicuous and anxious than you already were. It was quite a project, I can tell you— your styles varied so greatly from decade to decade, especially those for women—and the materials were a genuine problem; they'd gone out of existence long ago. We had the textile and tailoring cities working a full six months to clothe the inhabitants of this city, including, of course, the children. Everybody had to be clad as your contemporaries were, because we knew only that you would arrive in this vicinity, not where you might wander through the city."

"There was one small difference you didn't notice," added a handsome mature woman. "You were the only man in a gray suit. We had a full description of what you were wearing, you see, and we made sure nobody else was dressed that way. Naturally, everyone knew who you were, and so we were kept informed of your movements."

"What for?" I demanded in alarm. "What's this all about?"

*   *   *   *   *

Pulling up chairs, they sat down, looking to me like a witchcraft jury from some old painting.

"I'm Leo Blundell," said a tall man in plum-and-gold clothes. "As chairman of—of the Mark Weldon Committee, it's my responsibility to handle this project correctly."

"Project?"

"To make certain that history is fulfilled, I have to tell you as much as you must know."

"I wish *somebody* would!"

"Very well, let me begin by telling you much of what you undoubtedly know already. In a sense, you are more a victim of Dr. Anthony Roberts than his daughter. Roberts was a brilliant physicist, but because of his eccentric behavior, he was ridiculed for his theories and hated for his arrogance. He was an almost perfect example of self-defeat, the way in which a man will hamper his career and wreck his happiness, and then blame the world for his failure and misery. To get back to his connection with you, however, he invented a time machine—unfortunately, its secret has since been lost and never re-discovered—and used it for anti-social purposes. When he died, his daughter May carried on his work. It was she who sent you to this time to learn the principle by which the Dynapack operates. She was a thoroughly ruthless woman."

"Are you sure?" I asked uneasily.

"Quite sure."

"I know a number of old people died after she sent them on errands through time, but she said they'd lied about their age and health."

"One would expect her to say that," a woman put in cuttingly.

Blundell turned to her and shook his head. "Let Mr. Weldon clarify his feelings about her, Rhoda. They are obviously very mixed."

"They are," I admitted. "She seemed hard, the first time I saw her, when I answered her ad, but she could have been just acting businesslike. I mean she had a lot of people to pick from and she had to be impersonal and make certain she had the right one. The next time—I hope you don't know about that—it was really my fault for breaking into her room. I really had a lot of admiration for the way she handled the situation."

"Go on," Carr encouraged me.

"And I can't complain about the deal she gave me. Sure, she came out ahead on the money I bet and invested for her. But I did all right myself—I was richer than I'd ever been in my life— and she gave that money to me before I even did anything to earn it!"

"Besides which," somebody else said, "she offered you half of the profits on the Dynapack."

*   *   *   *   *

I looked around at the faces for signs of hostility. I saw none. That was surprising. I'd come from the past to steal something from them and they weren't at all angry. Well, no, it wasn't really stealing. I wouldn't be depriving them of the Dynapack. It just would have been invented before it was supposed to be.

"She did," I said. "Though I wouldn't call that part of it philanthropy. She needed me for the data and I needed her to manufacture the things."

"And she was a very beautiful woman," Blundell added.

I squirmed a bit. "Yes."

"Mr. Weldon, we know a good deal about her from notes that have come down to us among her private papers. She had a safety deposit box under a false name. I won't tell you the name; it was not discovered until many years later, and we will not voluntarily meddle with the past."

I sat up and listened sharply. "So that's how you knew who I was and what I'd be wearing and what I came for! You even knew when and where I'd arrive!"

"Correct," Blundell said.

"What else do you know?"

"That you suspected her of being responsible for the deaths of many old people by starvation. Your suspicion was justified, except that her father had caused all those that occurred before 1947, when she took over after his own death. All but two people were sent into the past. Roberts was curious about the future, of course, but he did not want to waste a victim on a trip that would probably be fruitless. In the past, you understand, he knew precisely what he was after. The future was completely unknown territory."

"But she took the chance," I said.

"If you can call deliberate murder taking a chance, yes. One man arrived in 2094, over fifty years ago. The other was yourself. The first one, as you know, died of malnutrition when he was brought back to your era."

"And what happened to me?" I asked, jittering.

"You will not die. We intend to make sure of that. All the other victims—I presume you're interested in their errands?"

"I think I know, but I'd like to find out just the same."

"They were sent to the past to buy or steal treasures of various sorts—art, sculpture, jewelry, fabulously valuable manuscripts and books, anything that had great scarcity value."

"That's not possible," I objected. "She had all the money she wanted. Any time she needed more, all she had to do was send somebody back to put down bets and buy stocks that she knew were winners. She had the records, didn't she? There was no way she or her father could lose!"

* * * * *

He moved his shoulders in a plum-and-gold shrug. "Most of the treasures they accumulated were for acquisition's sake—and for the sake of vengeance for the way they believed Dr. Roberts had been treated. When there were unusual expenses, such as replacing the very costly parts of the time machine, that required more than they could produce in ready cash, both Roberts and his daughter 'discovered' these treasures."

He waited while I digested the miserable meal and the disturbing information he had given me. I thought I'd found a loophole in his explanation: "You said people were sent back to the past to *buy* treasures, besides stealing them."

"I did," he agreed. "They were provided with currency of whatever era they were to visit."

I felt my forehead wrinkle up as my theory fell apart. "Then they could buy food. Why should they have died of malnutrition?"

"Because, as May Roberts herself told you, nothing can exist before it exists. Neither can anything exist after it is out of existence. If you returned with a Dynapack, for example, it would revert to a lump of various metals, because that was what it was in your period. But let me give you a more personal instance. Do you remember coming back from your first trip with dust on your hand?"

"Yes. I must have fallen."

"On one hand? No, Mr. Weldon. May Roberts was greatly upset by the incident; she was afraid you would realize why the hamburger had turned to dust—and why the old people died of starvation. *All* of them, not just a few."

He paused, giving me a chance to understand what he had just said. I did, with a sick shock.

"If I ate your food," I said shakily, "I'd feel satisfied until I was returned to my own time. *But the food wouldn't go along with me!*"

* * * * *

Blundell nodded gravely. "And so you, too, would die of malnutrition. The foods we have given you existed in your era. We were very careful of that, so careful that many of them probably were stored years before you left your time. We regret that they are not very palatable, but at least we are positive they will go back with you. You will be as healthy when you arrive in the past as when you left.

"Incidentally, she made you change your clothes for the same reason—they had been made in 1930. She had clothing from every era she wanted visited and chose old people who would fit them best. Otherwise, you see, they'd have arrived naked."

I began to shake as if I were as old as I'd pretended to be on the stage. "She's going to pull me back! If I don't bring her the information about the Dynapack, she'll shoot me!"

"That, Mr. Weldon, is our problem," Blundell said, putting his hand comfortingly on my arm to calm me.

"Your problem? I'm the one who'll get shot, not you!"

"But we know in complete detail what will happen when you are returned to the 20th Century."

I pulled my arm away and grabbed his. "You know that? Tell me!"

"I'm sorry, Mr. Weldon. If we tell you what you did, you might think of some alternate action, and there is no knowing what the result would be."

"But I didn't get shot or die of malnutrition?"

"That much we can tell you. Neither."

They all stood up, so bright and attractive in their colorful clothes that I felt like a shirt-sleeved stage hand who'd wandered in on a costume play.

"You will be returned in a month, according to the notes May Roberts left. She gave you plenty of time to get the data, you see. We propose to make that month an enjoyable one for you. The resources of our city—and any others you care to visit—are at your disposal. We wish you to take full advantage of them."

"And the Dynapack?"

"Let us worry about that. We want you to have a good time while you are our guest."

I did.

It was the most wonderful month of my life.

*   *   *   *   *

The mesh cage blurred around me. I could see May Roberts through it, her hand just leaving the switch. She was as beautiful as ever, but I saw beneath her beauty the vengeful, vicious creature her father's bitterness had turned her into; Blundell and Carr had let me read some of her notes, and I knew. I wished I could have spent the rest of my years in the future, instead of having to come back to this.

She came over and opened the gate, smiling like an angel welcoming a bright new soul. Then her eyes traveled startledly over me and her smile almost dropped off. But she held it firmly in place.

She had to, while she asked, "Do you have the notes I sent you for?"

"Right here," I said.

I reached into my breast pocket and brought out a stubby automatic and shot her through the right arm. Her closed hand opened and a little derringer clanked on the floor. She gaped at me with an expression of horrified surprise that should have been recorded permanently; it would have served as a model for generations of actors and actresses.

"You—brought back a weapon!" she gasped. "You shot me!" She stared vacantly at her bleeding arm and then at my automatic. "But you can't—bring anything back from the future. And you aren't—dying of malnutrition."

She said it all in a voice shocked into toneless wonder.

"The food I ate and this gun are from the present," I said. "The people of the future knew I was coming. They gave me food that wouldn't vanish from my cells when I returned. They also gave me the gun instead of the plans for the Dynapack."

"And you took it?" she screamed at me. "You idiot! I'd have shared the profits honestly with you. You'd have been worth millions!"

"With acute malnutrition," I amended. "I like it better this way, thanks—poor, but alive. Or relatively poor, I should say, because you've been very generous and I appreciate it."

"By shooting me!"

"I hated to puncture that lovely arm, but it wasn't as painful as starving or getting shot myself. Now if you don't mind—or even if you do—it's your turn to get into the cage, Miss Roberts."

She tried to grab for the derringer on the floor with her left hand.

"Don't bother," I said quietly. "You can't reach it before a bullet reaches you."

*   *   *   *   *

She straightened up, staring at me for the first time with terror in her eyes.

"What are you going to do to me?" she whispered.

"I could kill you as easily as you could have killed me. Kill you and send your body into some other era. How many dozens of deaths were you responsible for? The law couldn't convict you of them, but I can. And I couldn't be convicted, either."

She put her hand on the wound. Blood seeped through her fingers as she lifted her chin at me.

"I won't beg for my life, Weldon, if that's what you want. I could offer you a partnership, but I'm not really in a position to offer it, am I?"

She was magnificent, terrifyingly intelligent, brave clear through ... and deadlier than a plague. I had to remember that.

"Into the cage," I said. "I have some friends in the future who have plans for you. I won't tell you what they are, of course; you didn't tell me what I'd go through, did you? Give my friends my fondest regards. If I can manage it, I'll visit them—and you."

She backed warily into the cage. It would have been pleasant to kiss those wonderful lips good-by. I'd thought about them for a whole month, wanting them and loathing them at the same time.

It would have been like kissing a coral snake. I knew it and I concentrated on shutting the gate on her.

"You'd like to be rich, wouldn't you, Weldon?" she asked through the mesh.

"I can be," I said. "I have the machine. I can send people into the past or future and make myself a pile of dough. Only I'd give them food to take along. I wouldn't kill them off to keep the secret to myself. Anything else on your mind?"

"You want me," she stated.

I didn't argue.

"You could have me."

"Just long enough to get my throat slit or brains blown out. I don't want anything that much."

I rammed the switch closed.

The mesh cage blurred and she was gone. Her blood was on the floor, but she was gone into the future I had just come from.

That was when the reaction hit me. I'd escaped starvation and her gun, but I wasn't a hero and the release of tension flipped my stomach over and unhinged my knees.

Shaking badly, I stumbled through the big, empty house until I found a phone.

*   *   *   *   *

Lou Pape got there so quickly that I still hadn't gotten over the tremors, in spite of a bottle of brandy I dug out of a credenza, maybe because the date on the label, 1763, gave me a new case of the shivers.

I could see the worry on Lou's face vanish when he assured himself that I was all right. It came back again, though, when I told him what had happened. He didn't believe any of it, naturally. I guess I hadn't really expected him to.

"If I didn't know you, Mark," he said, shaking his big, dark head unhappily, "I'd send you over to Bellevue for observation. Even knowing you, maybe that's what I ought to do."

"All right, let's see if there's any proof," I suggested tiredly. "From what I was told, there ought to be plenty."

We searched the house clear down to the basement, where he stood with his face slack.

"Christ!" he breathed. "The annex to the Metropolitan Museum!"

The basement ran the length and breadth of the house and was twice as high as an average room, and the whole glittering place was crammed with paintings in rich, heavy frames, statuettes, books, manuscripts, goblets and ewers and jewelry made of gold and huge gems, and tapestries in brilliant color ... and everything was as bright and sparkling and new as the day it was made, which was almost true of a lot of it.

"The dame was loaded and she was an art collector, that's all," Lou said. "You can't sell me that screwy story of yours. She was a collector and she knew where to find things."

"She certainly did," I agreed.

"What did you do with her?"

"I told you. I shot her through the arm before she could shoot me and I sent her into the future."

He took me by the front of the jacket. "You killed her, Mark. You wanted all this stuff for yourself, so you knocked her off and got rid of her body somehow."

"Why don't you go back to acting, where you belong, Lou, and leave sleuthing to people who know how?" I asked, too worn to pull his hands loose. "Would I kill her and call you up to get right over here? Wouldn't I have sneaked these things out first? Or more likely I'd have sneaked them out, hidden them and nobody—including you—would know I'd ever been here. Come on, use your head."

"That's easy. You lost your nerve."

"I'm not even losing my patience."

*   *   *   *   *

He pushed me away savagely. "If you killed her for this stuff or because of that crazy yarn you gave me, I'm a cop and you're no friend. You're just a plain killer I happened to have known once, and I'll make sure you fry."

"You always did have a taste for that kind of dialogue. Go ahead and wrap me up in an airtight case, have them throw the book at me, send me up the river, put me in the hot squat. But you'll have to do the proving, not me."

He headed for the stairs. "I will. And don't try to make a break or I'll plug you as if I never saw you before."

He put in a call at the phone upstairs. I didn't give a particular damn who it was he'd called. I was too relieved that I hadn't killed May Roberts; destroying anything that beautiful, however evil, would have stayed with me the rest of my life. There was another reason for my relief—if I'd killed her and left the evidence for Lou to find, he'd never help me. No, that's not quite so; he'd probably have tried to get me to plead insanity on the basis of my unbelievable explanation.

But most of all, I couldn't get rid of the look on her face when I'd shot her through the arm, the arm that was so wonderful to look at and that had held a murderous little gun to greet me with.

She was in the future now. She wouldn't be executed by them; they regarded crime as an illness, and they'd treat her with their marvelously advanced therapy and she'd become a useful, contented citizen, living out her existence in an era that had given me more happiness than I'd ever had.

I sat and tried to stupefy myself with brandy that should long ago have dried to brick-hardness, while Lou Pape stood at the door with his hand near his holster and glared at me. He didn't take his eyes off me until somebody named Prof. Jeremiah

Aaronson came in and was introduced briefly and flatly to me. Then Lou took him upstairs.

It was minutes before I realized what they were going to do. I ran up after them.

I was just in time to see Aaronson carefully take the housing off the hooded motors, and leap back suddenly from the fury of lightning sparks.

*　　*　　*　　*　　*

The whole machine fused while we watched helplessly—motors, switches, panel and mesh cage. They flashed blindingly and blew apart and melted together in a charred and molten pile.

"Rigged," Aaronson said in the tone of a bitter curse. "Set to short if it was tampered with. I wouldn't be surprised if there were incendiaries placed at strategic spots. Nothing else could have made a mess like this."

He finally glanced down at his hand and saw it was scorched. He hissed with the realization of pain, blew on the burn, shook it in the air to cool it, and pulled a handkerchief out of his back pocket by reaching all the way around the rear for it with his left hand.

Lou looked helplessly at the heap of cooling slag. "Can you make any sense of it, Prof?" he asked.

"Can you?" Aaronson retorted. "Melt down a microtome or any other piece of machinery you're unfamiliar with, and see if you can identify it when it looks like this."

He went out, wrapping his hand in the handkerchief.

Lou kicked glumly at a piece of twisted tubing. "Aaronson is a top physicist, Mark. I was hoping he'd make enough out of the machine to—ah, hell, I wanted to believe you! I couldn't. I still can't. Now we'll have to dig through the house to find her body."

"You won't find it or the secret of the machine," I answered miserably. "I told you they said the secret would be lost. This is how. Now I'll never be able to visit the future again. I'll never see them or May Roberts. They'll straighten her out, get rid of her hate and vindictiveness, and it won't do me a damned bit of good because the machine is gone and she's generations ahead of me."

He turned to me puzzledly. "You're not afraid to have us dig for her body, Mark?"

"Tear the place apart if you want."

"We'll have to," he said. "I'm calling Homicide."

"Call in the Marines. Call in anybody you like."

"You'll have to stay in my custody until we're through."

I shrugged. "As long as you leave me alone while you're doing your digging, I don't give a hang if I'm under arrest for suspicion of murder. I've got to do some straightening out. I wish the people in the future could take on the job—they could do it faster and better than I can—but some nice, peaceful quiet would help."

*   *   *   *   *

He didn't touch me or say a word to me as we waited for the squad to arrive. I sat in the chair and shut out first him and then the men with their sounding hammers and crowbars and all the rest.

She'd been ruthless and callous, and she'd murdered old people with no more pity than a wolf among a herd of helpless sheep.

But Blundell and Carr had told me that she was as much a victim as the oldsters who'd died of starvation with the riches she'd given them still untouched, on deposit in the banks or stuffed into hiding places or pinned to their shabby clothes. She needed treatment for the illness her father had inflicted on her. But even he, they'd said, had been suffering from a severe emotional disturbance and proper care could have made a great and honored scientist out of him.

They'd told me the truth and made me hate her, and they'd told me their viewpoint and made that hatred impossible.

I was here, in the present, without her. The machine was gone. Yearning over something I couldn't change would destroy me. I had no right to destroy myself. Nobody did, they'd told me, and nobody who reconciles himself to the fact that some situations just are impossible to work out ever could.

I'd realized that when the squad packed up and left and Lou Pape came over to where I was sitting.

"You knew we wouldn't find her," he said.

"That's what I kept telling you."

"Where is she?"

"In Port Said, exotic hellhole of the world, where she's dancing in veils for the depraved—"

"Cut out the kidding! Where is she?"

"What's the difference, Lou? She's not here, is she?"

"That doesn't mean she can't be somewhere else, dead."

"She's not dead. You don't have to believe me about anything else, just that."

He hauled me out of the chair and stared hard at my face. "You aren't lying," he said. "I know you well enough to know you're not."

"All right, then."

"But you're a damned fool to think a dish like that would have any part of you. I don't mean you're nothing a woman would go for, but she's more fang than female. You'd have to be richer and better-looking than her, for one thing—"

"Not after my friends get through with her. She'll know a good man when she sees one and I'd be what she wants." I slid my hand over my naked scalp. "With a head of hair, I'd look my real age, which happens to be a year younger than you, if you remember. She'd go for me—they checked our emotional quotients and we'd be a natural together. The only thing was that I was bald. They could have grown hair on my head, which would have taken care of that, and then we'd have gotten together like gin and tonic."

*   *   *   *   *

Lou arched his black eyebrows at me. "They really could grow hair on you?"

"Sure. Now you want to know why I didn't let them." I glanced out the window at the smoky city. "That's why. They couldn't tell me if I'd ever get back to the future. I wasn't taking any chances. As long as there was a possibility that I'd be stranded in my own time, I wasn't going to lose my livelihood. Which reminds me, you have anything else to do here?"

"There'll be a guard stationed around the house and all her holdings and art will be taken over until she comes back—"

"She won't."

"—or is declared legally dead."

"And me?" I broke in.

"We can't hold you without proof of murder."

"Good enough. Then let's get out of here."

"I have to go back on duty," he objected.

"Not any more. I've got over $15,000 in cash and deposits—enough to finance you and me."

"Enough to kill her for."

"Enough to finance you and me," I repeated doggedly. "I told you I had the money before she sent me into the future—"

"All right, all right," he interrupted. "Let's not go into that again. We couldn't find a body, so you're free. Now what's this about financing the two of us?"

I put my fingers around his arm and steered him out to the street.

"This city has never had a worse cop than you," I said. "Why? Because you're an actor, not a cop. You're going back to acting, Lou. This money will keep us both going until we get a break."

He gave me the slit-eyed look he'd picked up in line of duty. "That wouldn't be a bribe, would it?"

"Call it a kind of memorial to a lot of poor, innocent old people and a sick, tormented woman."

We walked along in silence out in the clean sunshine. It was our silence; the sleek cars and burly trucks made their noise and the pedestrians added their gabble, but a good Stanislavsky actor like Lou wouldn't notice that. Neither would I, ordinarily, but I was giving him a chance to work his way through this situation.

"I won't hand you a lie, Mark," he said finally. "I never stopped wanting to act. I'll take your deal on two considerations."

"All right, what are they?"

"That whatever I take off you is strictly a loan."

"No argument. What's the other?"

He had an unlit cigarette almost to his lips. He held it there while he said: "That any time you come across a case of an old person who died of starvation with $30,000 stashed away somewhere, you turn fast to the theatrical page and not tell me or even think about it."

"I don't have to agree to that."

*   *   *   *   *

He lowered the cigarette, stopped and turned to me. "You mean it's no deal?"

"Not that," I said. "I mean there won't be any more of those cases. Between knowing that and both of us back acting again, I'm satisfied. You don't have to believe me. Nobody does."

He lit up and blew out a pretty plume, fine and slow and straight, which would have televised like a million in the bank. Then he grinned. "You wouldn't want to bet on that, would you?"

"Not with a friend. I do all my sure-thing betting with bookies."

"Then make it a token bet," he said. "One buck that somebody dies of starvation with a big poke within a year."

I took the bet.

I took the dollar a year later.

No Charge for Alterations

ILLUSTRATED BY H. SHARP
ORIGINALLY PUBLISHED IN *AMAZING STORIES*,
APRIL-MAY 1953

"Wanta know what's wrong with women these days? Spoiled! The whole kit and kaboodle of 'em. They want to sing in nightclubs and hookup with some millionaire and wear beautiful clothes. Housework is something for gadgets to take care of, with maids to run the gadgets. Afraid to get a few calluses on their dainty hands!

"We got a way to handle that on Deneb. A girl gets highfalutin up there, the Doc puts her in the Ego Alter room. Thicken up her ankles a little, take some of the sparkle out of her eyes and hair, and you get a woman fit to pull a plow!"

Hold it, Madam! H. L. Gold said that; not us. Personally, we like girls—not Percherons!

No Charge For Alterations

If there was one thing Dr. Kalmar hated, and there were many, it was having a new assistant fresh from a medical school on Earth. They always wanted to change things. They never realized that a planet develops its own techniques to meet its own requirements, which are seldom similar to those of any other world. Dr. Kalmar never got along with his assistants and he didn't expect to get along with this young Dr. Hoyt who was coming in on the transfer ship from Vega.

Dr. Kalmar had been trained on Earth himself, of course, but he wistfully remembered how he had revered Dr. Lowell when he had been Lowell's assistant. He'd known that his own green learning was no match for Dr. Lowell's wisdom and experience after 30 years on Deneb, and he had avidly accepted his lessons.

Why, he grumbled to himself on his way to the spaceport to meet the unknown whippersnapper, why didn't Earth turn out young doctors the way it used to? They ought to have the arrogance knocked out of them before they left medical school. That's what must have happened to him, because his attitude had certainly been humble when he landed.

The spaceport was jammed, naturally. Ship arrivals were infrequent enough to bring everybody from all over the planet who was not on duty at the farms, mines, factories, freight and passenger jets and all the rest of the busy activities of this comparatively new colony. They brought their lunches and families and stood around to watch. Dr. Kalmar went to the platform.

The ship sat down on a mushroom of fire that swiftly became a flaming pancake and then was squashed out of existence.

"I'm waiting for a shipment of livestock," enthused the man standing next to Dr. Kalmar.

"You're lucky," the doctor said. "They can't talk back."

The man looked at him sympathetically. "Meeting a female?"

"Gabbier and more annoying," said Dr. Kalmar, but he didn't elaborate and the man, with the courtesy of the frontier, did not pry for an explanation.

Livestock and freight came down on one elevator and passengers came down another. Slidewalks carried the cargo to Sterilization and travelers to the greeting platform. Dr. Kalmar felt his shoulders droop. The man with the medical bag had to be Dr. Hoyt and he was even more brisk, erect and muscular than Dr. Kalmar had expected, with a superior and inquisitive look that made the last assistant, unbearable as he'd been, seem as tractable as one of the arriving cows.

Dr. Hoyt spotted him instantly and came striding over to grab his hand in a grip like an ore-crusher. "You're Dr. Kalmar. Glad to know you. I'm sure we'll get along fine together. Miserable trip. Had to change ships four times to get here. Hope the food's better than shipboard slop. Got a nice hospital to work in? Do I live in or out?"

Dr. Kalmar was grudgingly forced to say rapidly, "Right. Likewise. I hope so. Too bad. Suits us. I think so. In."

He got Dr. Hoyt into a jetcab and told the driver to make time back to the hospital. Appointments were piling up while he had to make the courtesy trip out to the spaceport, which was another nuisance. Now he'd have all of those and a talkative assistant who'd want to know the reasons for everything.

"Pretty barren," said Dr. Hoyt, looking out the window at the vegetationless ground below. "Why's that?"

He'd known he was going to Deneb, Dr. Kalmar thought angrily. The least he could have done was read up on the place. *He* had.

"It's an Earth-type planet," Dr. Kalmar said in a blunt voice, "except that life never developed on it. We had to bring everything—benign germ cultures, seed, animals, fish, insects— a whole ecology. Our farms are close to the cities. Too wasteful of freight to move them out very far. Another few centuries and we'll have a *real* population, millions of people instead of the 20,000 we have now in a couple of dozen settlements around this world. Then we'll have the whole place a nice shade of green."

"City boy myself," said Dr. Hoyt. "Hate the country. Hydroponics and synthetic meat—that's the answer."

"For Earth. It'll be a long time before we get that crowded here on Deneb."

"Deneb," the young doctor repeated, dissatisfied. "That's the name of the star. You mean to tell me the planet has the same name?"

"Most solar systems have only one Earth-type planet. It saves a lot of trouble to just call that planet Deneb, Vega or whatever."

"Is *that* clutch of shacks the *city*?" exclaimed Dr. Hoyt.

"Denebia," said Dr. Kalmar, beginning to enjoy himself finally.

"Why, you could lose it in a suburb or Bosyorkdelphia!"

"That monstrosity that used to be New York, Pennsylvania, Connecticut, Rhode Island and Massachusetts? I wouldn't want to."

He was pleased when Dr. Hoyt sank into stunned silence. If luck was with him, that stupefaction might last the whole day. It seemed as though it might, for the sight of the modest little hospital was too much for the youngster who had just come from the mammoth health factories of Earth.

Dr. Hoyt revived somewhat when he saw the patients waiting in the scantily furnished outer room, but Dr. Kalmar said, "Better get yourself settled," and opened a door for his immature colleague.

"But there's only one bed in this room," Dr. Hoyt objected. "You must have made a mistake."

Dr. Kalmar, recalling the crowded cubicles of Earth, gave out a proud little dry laugh. "You're on Deneb now, boy. Here you'll have to get used to spaciousness. We like elbow room."

The young doctor went in hesitantly, leaving the door open for a fast escape in case an error had been made. Dr. Kalmar had done the same when he'd arrived nine years ago. Judging by his own experience, it would take Dr. Hoyt a full six months to get used to having a room all to himself. There would be plenty of time to start showing him the ropes tomorrow, and in the meantime there were the backed-up appointments to be taken care of.

Dr. Kalmar went to his office and had his nurse, Miss Dupont, send in the first patient.

It was a girl of 17, Avis Emery, who had been brought by her parents. She sat sullenly, dark-haired, too daintily pretty and delicately shapely for a frontier world like this, while Mr. Emery put the file from Social Control on the doctor's desk.

"We're farmers—" the man began.

Dr. Kalmar interrupted, "The information is in the summary. Avis is to be assigned her mate next year, but she wants to go to Earth and become a nightclub singer. She refuses to marry a boy who'd be able to help around the farm, and she won't work on it herself."

He looked up severely at the parents. "This is your own fault, you know. You pampered her. Farm labor is too valuable for pampering. We can't afford it."

"You can blame me, Doc," said Mr. Emery miserably. "She's such a pretty little thing—I couldn't work her the way Sue and I work ourselves."

"And then she started getting notions," Mrs. Emery added, giving her husband a vicious glare. Dr. Kalmar could imagine the nights of argument and accusation before they were at last forced to go for medical help to solve their self-created problem. "Singing in nightclubs back on Earth, marrying a billionaire, living in a sky yacht!"

"Avis," said Dr. Kalmar gently. "You know it's not that easy, don't you? There are lots and lots of pretty girls on Earth and very few billionaires. If you did get a job singing in a nightclub, you know you'd have to do some unpleasant things because there's so much competition for customers. Things like stripteasing, drinking at the tables and going out with whoever the owner tells you to."

The girl's face grew animated for the first time. "Well, sure! Why do you think I want to go?"

"And you don't love Deneb and your farm?"

"I hate both of them!"

"But you realize that we must have food. Doesn't it make you feel important to grow more food so we can increase our population?"

"No! Why should I care? I want to go to Earth!"

Dr. Kalmar shook his head regretfully. He pushed a button on his desk. It was connected to a gravity generator directly under the girl's chair. Four gravities suddenly pushed her down into it and a hypodermic needle jabbed her swiftly with a hypnotic drug. She slumped. He released the button and the artificial gravity abated, but she remained dazed and relaxed.

"You're not going to hurt her, are you, Doc?" Mr. Emery begged.

"Certainly not. But I suppose you know Social Control's orders."

They nodded, the husband gloomily, the wife with a single sharp jerk of her head.

"You go right ahead and do it," she said. "I'm sick of working my fingers to the bone while she primps and preens and talks all the time about going to Earth."

"Come, Avis," Dr. Kalmar said in a low, commanding voice.

She stood up, blank-faced, and followed him out to the Ego Alter room. He closed the door, sat her down in the insulated seat next to the control console, put the wired plastic helmet on her and adjusted it to fit her skull snugly.

Running his finger down the treatment sheet of her Social Control file, he set the dials according to its instructions. The psychic areas to be reduced were sex drive, competitiveness and imagination, while the areas of reproductive urge and cooperation were to be intensified. He regulated the individual timers and sent the varying charge through her brain.

There was no reaction, no convulsion, no distortion of features. She sat there as if nothing had happened, but her personality had changed as completely as though she had been retrained from birth.

Miss Dupont came in without knocking. She knew, of course, that any patient in the Ego Alter room would be incapable of being disturbed.

"Rephysical, Dr. Kalmar?" she asked.

"I'm afraid so. Will you prepare her, please?"

The nurse removed the girl's clothes. There was no resistance.

"Such a lovely body," she said. "It's a shame."

He shrugged. "Until we have enough people and farms and industries, Miss Dupont, we'll just have to get used to altering people to fit the needs of our society. I'm sure you understand that."

"Yes, but it still seems a shame. Bodies like that don't grow on trees."

He gently moved the girl into the Rephysical Chamber. "They grow in this machine, though. As soon as we can afford it, which ought to be only a few hundred years from now, we can make any woman look like this, or even better."

"And don't forget the men," Miss Dupont said as he started the mitogenetic generator. "We could use some Adonises around here."

"We'll have them," he assured her.

"Somebody will. None of us'll live that long."

Working like a sculptor with a cathode in one hand and an anode in the other, Dr. Kalmar began reshaping the girl who stood fixedly in the boxlike chamber. The flesh fled from the cathode and chased after the anode as he broadened the fine nose, thickened the mobile lips, squared the slender jaw and drew out carefully the delicately arched orbital ridges.

"I'll leave the curl in her hair," he said. "Every woman needs at least one feature she can be proud of."

"You're telling me," Miss Dupont replied.

"Synthetic tissue, please."

She drew out a tube with a variable nozzle and started working just ahead of him. A spray of high-velocity cells shot through the girl's smooth skin at the neck, shoulders, breasts, hips and legs, forming shapeless lumps that he guided into cords and muscles. The slim figure quickly broadened, grew brawny and competent-looking, the body of a woman who could breed phenomenally while farming alongside her man.

Dr. Kalmar racked up the instruments and helped Miss Dupont dress the girl in coveralls and sandals. He felt the pride of craftsmanship when he found that the clothing supplied for her by Social Control exactly fitted her. He injected an antidote to the hypnotic and gave her the standard test for emotional response as her expressionless face cleared to placidity.

"Do you know where you are, Avis?"

"Yes. Ego Alter and Rephysical."

"What have we done to you?"

"Changed me to fit my environment."

"Do you resent being changed?"

Illustrator: H. Sharp

"No." She paused and looked worried. "Who's taking care of the crops while I'm here?"

"They can wait till you and your parents get back, Avis. Let's show them the change, shall we?"

"All right," she said. "I think they'll be proud of me. This is how they always wanted me to be."

"And you?"

"Oh, I feel much better. As if I don't have to try so hard."

"I'm glad, Avis. Miss Dupont, better have a sedative ready when her father sees her. I think he'll need it."

"And her mother?" asked the nurse practically.

"She'll probably want a drink to celebrate. Give her one."

*   *   *   *   *

Dr. Kalmar's prognosis was correct, only it didn't go far enough. His young assistant from Earth had come scooting out of his disquietingly large quarters and was jittering in the office when they entered.

"Is *that* the pretty girl who was waiting when we came in?" he yelped in outrage. "What have you done to her?"

Dr. Kalmar gave the sedative to him instead of Mr. Emery, who was shocked, but had known in advance what to expect. Miss Dupont prepared another sedative quickly, gave Mrs. Emery a celebration drink and moved the family toward the door.

"She looks fine, Doctor," the mother said happily. "Avis ought to be a big help around the house and farm from now on."

"I'm sure she will," he said.

"But she was so lovely!" wept Mr. Emery, though in a rapidly becalming voice as the sedative took effect.

The door closed behind them.

"You ought to be reported to the Medical Association back on Earth!" Dr. Hoyt said angrily. "Ruining a girl's looks like that!"

Dr. Kalmar sighed. He had hoped to be able to put off this orientation lecture until the following day, when there wouldn't be so many patients jamming his appointment book.

"All right, let's get it over with. First, I was also trained on Earth and know how Ego Alter and Rephysical are used there: Ego Alter to remove psychic blocks so people can compete better, and Rephysical so they'll be more attractive. Second, we're not under the jurisdiction of Earth's Medical Association. Third, we'd damn well better not be, because our problems and solutions aren't the same at all."

"You'd have been jailed for spoiling that girl's chances of a good marriage!"

"I didn't," Dr. Kalmar said quietly. "I improved them."

"You did nothing of the—" Dr. Hoyt stopped. "Improved? How?"

"I keep telling you this is a frontier world and you keep acting as if you understand, but you don't. Look, a family is an economic liability on Earth; it consumes without producing. That's why girls have so much trouble finding husbands there. Out here it's different. A family is an asset—if every member in it is willing to work."

"But a pretty girl like that can always get by."

"No Denebian can afford to marry a pretty girl. It's too risky. She can't work as hard as we do and still take care of her looks. And he'd worry about her constantly, which would cut into his efficiency. By having me make her a merely attractive girl in a wholesome, hearty way, Social Control guarantees more than just a marriage for her—it guarantees a contented married life."

"Sweating away on a farm," Dr. Hoyt said.

"Now that her anti-social strivings are gone, she'll realize that Deneb needs farmers instead of nightclub singers. She'll take pride in being a good worker, she'll raise as many children as she'll be capable of bearing, and she'll have a good husband and a prosperous farm. That wouldn't have satisfied her before. It will now. And she's better for it and so is Deneb."

Dr. Hoyt shook his head. "It's all upside down."

"You'll get used to it. Why not take today off and explore Denebia? You need a rest after all those months in space."

"Maybe I will," said Dr. Hoyt vaguely, slightly anesthetized.

"Good." Dr. Kalmar buzzed for Miss Dupont. "Send in the next patient, please. Oh, and Dr. Hoyt is taking the day off."

*   *   *   *   *

But the young assistant was stunned into staying by the huge size of the Social Control file that was carried by the next patient, Mr. Fallon, and his wife.

"I know just what you're thinking, Dr. Kalmar!" cried Mrs. Fallon distractedly, but with a nervously bright smile. "Those awful Fallons again! I don't blame you a bit, but—"

As a matter of fact, that was exactly what Dr. Kalmar was thinking, plus the defeated feeling that they were all he needed to make the day complete.

"Good Lord, what's in all those files?" Dr. Hoyt exclaimed.

Dr. Kalmar could have explained, but he didn't feel up to it.

Mr. Fallon, a wispy, shyly affable, poetic-looking chap, did it for him. "Papers," he said.

"I know that, but why so many?" Dr. Hoyt asked impatiently.

Miss Dupont seemed wryly amused as she watched his consternation.

"I guess you might say it's because I can't make my mind up," confessed Mrs. Fallon with an uneasy giggle. She was a big woman who might have gurgled over a collection of toy dogs on Earth, but here she was a freight checker and her husband was a statistician in the Department of Supply, though on Earth he might have been anything from a composer to a social worker. "No matter how often we rephysical Harry, I always get tired of his looks in a few months."

"And how often has that been done?" Dr. Hoyt demanded.

"I think it's eleven times. Isn't that right, dear?"

"No, sweet," said Mr. Fallon. "Thirteen."

Dr. Kalmar could have interrupted, but he considered it wiser to let his assistant learn the hard way. Miss Dupont was enjoying it too much to interfere.

"We've made him tall and we've made him short, skinny, fat, bulging with muscle, red hair, black hair, blond hair, gray hair— I don't know, just about everything in the book," said Mrs. Fallon, "and I simply can't seem to find one I'd like for keeps."

"Then why the devil don't you get another husband?"

Mrs. Fallon looked shocked. "Why, he was assigned to me!"

"Dr. Hoyt just came from Earth," Dr. Kalmar cut in at last, before a brawl could start. "He's not familiar with our methods."

"Let's hear the cockeyed reason," Dr. Hoyt said resignedly.

"We keep our population balanced," said Dr. Kalmar. "Too many of either sex creates tension, hostility, loss of efficiency; look at Earth if you want proof. We can't risk even a little of that, so we use prenatal sex control to keep them exactly equal."

"There's a wife for every man," Mr. Fallon put in genially, "and a husband for every woman. Works out fine."

"With no surplus," Dr. Kalmar added. "There are no floaters to allow the kind of marital moving day you have on Earth, where so many just up and shift over to new mates. We get ours for life. That's where Ego Alter and Rephysical come in."

"You mean people bring in their mates to have them done over?"

"If they're not satisfied and if the mates agree to be changed."

"I don't mind," said Mr. Fallon virtuously. "I figure Mabel will decide what she wants one of these changes, and then we can settle down and be happy with each other."

"But what about you?" asked Dr. Hoyt, bewildered. "Don't you want her changed?"

"Oh, no. I like her fine just as she is."

"You see now how it works?" Dr. Kalmar asked. "We can't have a variety of mates, but we can have all the variety we want in one mate. It comes to the same thing, as far as I can see, and causes much less confusion, especially since we need stable relationships."

Dr. Hoyt was striving heroically to stay indignant in spite of the sedative. "And do many ask to have their mates changed?"

"I guess we're a sort of record, aren't we?" Mr. Fallon boasted.

"I guess you are," agreed Dr. Kalmar. "And now, Dr. Hoyt, if there aren't any more questions, I'd like to proceed with this couple."

Dr. Hoyt stretched his eyes wide to keep them open. "It's all screwy to me, but it's none of my business. As soon as I finish my internship, I'm heading back to Earth, where things make sense, so I don't have to understand this mishmash you call a planet. Need help?"

"If you'd find out what Mrs. Fallon has in mind this time, it would let me run the patients through a lot faster."

"How would they feel about it?" Dr. Hoyt asked.

"It's all right with me," Mr. Fallon said amiably. "I'm pretty used to this, you know."

"But what are we going to make you look like, Harry?" his wife fretted. "I felt very jealous of other women when you were handsome and I didn't like you just ordinary-looking."

"Why not go through the model book with Dr. Hoyt?" suggested Dr. Kalmar. "There are still some types you haven't tried."

"There *are*?" she asked in gratified astonishment. "Would you mind very much, Dr. Hoyt?"

"Glad to," he said.

Miss Dupont brought out the model book for him, and he and Mrs. Fallon studied the facial and physical types that were very explicitly illustrated there in three-dimensional full color. Mr. Fallon, contentedly working out math problems on a sheet of paper, left the choice entirely to her.

*   *   *   *   *

Meanwhile, Dr. Kalmar and Miss Dupont swiftly took care of a succession of other patients, raising the tolerance level of frustration in a watchmaker, replating the acne-pitted skin of a sensitive youth, restoring a finger lost in a machine-shop accident, and building up good-natured aggression in an ore miner whose productivity had slumped.

Mrs. Fallon still hadn't decided when the last patient had been taken care of. She said unhappily, "I don't know. I simply absolutely don't know. Couldn't you suggest *something*, Dr. Hoyt?"

"Wouldn't be ethical," he told her bluntly. "Not allowed to."

Dr. Kalmar, checking the Social Control papers with Miss Dupont, wondered if he should interfere. It would lower confidence in Dr. Hoyt, which meant that people would insist on Dr. Kalmar's treating them. Then, instead of having an assistant to remove some of the load, he'd have to do the work of two men. He decided to let the young doctor handle it.

But Dr. Hoyt stood up in exasperation, slammed the book shut, and said, "Mrs. Fallon, if you know what you want, I'll be glad to oblige. But I'm not a telepathy—"

"Is there anything I can do?" Dr. Kalmar interrupted quickly, before his assistant could create any more damage.

"He doesn't have to get huffy," Mrs. Fallon said indignantly. "All I asked for was a suggestion or two."

"Insult my wife, will he?" Mr. Fallon belligerently added.

"It's my fault," Dr. Kalmar said. "Dr. Hoyt just got in today from Earth and he's tired and he naturally doesn't understand all our ways yet—"

"*Yet?*" Dr. Hoyt repeated in disgust. "What makes you think I'll ever—"

"And I shouldn't have burdened him with this problem until he's had a chance to rest up and look around," Dr. Kalmar continued in a slightly louder voice. "Now, let's see if we can't settle this problem before closing time, eh?"

The Fallons subsided, Dr. Hoyt watched with a sarcastic eye, though he kept silent as Dr. Kalmar and Miss Dupont, working as a shrewd team, gave them the suggestion they had been looking for. It was all done very smoothly, so smoothly that Dr. Kalmar felt professional pride because even his stiff-necked assistant was unable to detect the fact that it *was* a suggestion.

Dr. Kalmar got Mrs. Fallon to reminisce about the alterations her husband had undergone, and Miss Dupont promptly agreed with her when she explained why each had been unsatisfactory. It took some time, but he eventually brought her back to what Mr. Fallon had looked like when she'd first married him.

"Now, isn't that the strangest thing?" she said, puzzled. "I can't remember. Can you, dear?"

"It's a little mixed up," Mr. Fallon admitted. "Let's see, I know I was taller and I think I had a long, thin face—"

"Oh, we don't have to guess," Dr. Kalmar said. "Nurse, we have the information on file, don't we?"

"Yes, Doctor," she said, and instantly produced a photograph. They evidently thought it was merely filing efficiency; they hadn't noticed her searching for the picture quietly while Dr. Kalmar had been leading them on. He had, in fact, delayed asking her until she'd nodded to indicate that she had found it.

Mr. Fallon frowned as if he'd recognized the face but couldn't remember the name. His wife gave a little shriek of admiration.

"Why, Harry, you looked perfectly wonderful!"

"Those deep dimples made shaving pretty hard," he recalled.

"But they're *darling*! Why did you ever let me change you?"

"Because I wanted you to be happy, sweet."

It was as simple as that—a bit of practical psychology based on knowledge of the patients. Dr. Kalmar wished wistfully that old Dr. Lowell had been there to observe. He would have approved, which might have made up for Dr. Hoyt's unpleasant expression.

"I hope this is the one you want," Dr. Kalmar said as he took them to the front door after the rephysical.

"Goodness, I hope so!" Mrs. Fallon exclaimed. She looked fondly at her husband, and this time had to look up to see his face. "I'm almost *positive* this is what I want Harry to be."

"Well, if it isn't, sweet," Mr. Fallon said, "we'll try something else. I don't mind as long as it makes you happy."

They closed the door behind them, leaving the hospital empty of all but the small staff.

"They're crazy!" Dr. Hoyt exploded. "He's not the one we should be changing. That idiotic female needs a good Ego Alter!"

"He hasn't asked for it," Dr. Kalmar pointed out patiently.

"Then he ought to!"

"That's his decision, isn't it? There's such a thing as ethics, you know."

"I've never seen anything more insane than the way you work," snapped Dr. Hoyt. "I can't wait to finish my stretch here and go home."

He stamped out, weaving slightly because of the sedative.

"Well, what do you think of our assistant?" asked Dr. Kalmar.

"He's cute," Miss Dupont said irrationally.

Dr. Kalmar glowered at her. He'd forgotten that she was due to have a mate assigned to her this year.

$$*\qquad*\qquad*\qquad*\qquad*$$

Routine at the hospital was anything but routine. Dr. Hoyt barely kept from yelping each time someone was treated, and his help was given so unwillingly that Dr. Kalmar, sweating under a double load and with Dr. Hoyt to argue with at the same time, was all for putting him on the ship and asking Earth for another intern. But Miss Dupont talked him out of it.

For no discernible reason other than loneliness, Dr. Hoyt was taking her out. She was pleased, even though he crabbed constantly about the shabby-looking clothes she wore, which were typical of Deneb, and the way they fitted her.

Either the two of them didn't talk shop, or she had no influence with him—his criticism and impatience grew sharper each week.

It bothered Dr. Kalmar more than he thought it should, and much more than Mrs. Kalmar wanted it to. She was a pleasant little woman who liked things as they were, which was why Dr. Kalmar had hesitated all this while to ask her to undergo a slight rephysical; he would have preferred her a little taller, more filled out, her slight wrinkles deleted and, while he was thinking about it, he wished she'd let him give her space-black hair instead of her indeterminately blondish mop. But he'd rather have her as she was than peevish, so he had never mentioned it.

"Don't let the boy upset you, she said. "It's only that he's so young and inexperienced. You can't expect him to adjust quickly to a new environment and a whole new medical orientation."

"But that's just what annoys me! Why, I used to hang onto every word of Dr. Lowell's when I came here! I never thought I knew better than he did."

"Well, dear, you're you and Dr. Lowell is Dr. Lowell and Dr. Hoyt is Dr. Hoyt."

He tried to think of an answer and couldn't. "I suppose so."

"Maybe you'd feel better if you spoke to Dr. Lowell about it."

"What could he do? This is really an internal problem that I should work out with Dr. Hoyt. I can't involve Dr. Lowell in it."

But it became intolerable when there was a young girl who wanted to be a boy and Dr. Kalmar and Dr. Hoyt got into the worst battle yet. Naturally, she had to be given an Ego Alter to make her happy about being a girl, whereas Dr. Hoyt argued that she should be allowed to be a boy if that was what she wanted. Dr. Kalmar explained angrily once more that the sexes were exactly balanced and Dr. Hoyt quoted the rule of personal choice. It was applicable on Earth, but not on Deneb, Dr. Kalmar retorted, to which Dr. Hoyt snorted something about playing God.

Dr. Kalmar confessed harshly to his wife that she was right. He had to bring old Dr. Lowell into the situation; it was out of Dr. Kalmar's control and was keeping the hospital in a turmoil. It was time for Dr. Lowell to inspect the hospital, the job he had taken in place of actual retirement. Dr. Kalmar needed help from Miss Dupont to bring the problem out into the open. But she became unexpectedly obstinate.

"I won't hurt Leo's career," she explained flatly.

Dr. Kalmar gave her a vacant look. "Leo?"

She blushed. "Dr. Hoyt. He's honestly trying to understand, but he finds it so different from Earth. Practically everything we do here is in reverse."

"But so is our environment, Miss Dupont. Earth is over-crowded and Deneb is under-populated, so of course our methods would be the opposite of Earth's. He has to be made to see that we must solve our problems our own way."

She studied his face suspiciously. "That's all you want?"

"Certainly. Damn it, do you think I want him fired and sent back to Earth before his internship's up? I know it would hurt his record. Besides, I need an assistant—but not one I have to bicker with every time I make a move."

"Well, in that case—"

"Good girl. All you have to do is help me hold off the cases he'd argue about until Dr. Lowell gets here." He stared down glumly at his hands, which were gripping each other tightly. "God knows I'm no diplomat. Dr. Lowell is. He convinced me easily enough when I came here. Maybe he can do the same with Dr. Hoyt."

"Oh, I hope he can," Miss Dupont said earnestly. "I want so much to have you and Leo work together in harmony."

He glanced up, curious. "Why?"

"Because I'm in love with him."

He found himself nodding bitterly. Having Dr. Hoyt go back to Earth wouldn't be a fraction as bad as Miss Dupont leaving with him. So now there was something else to worry about.

*   *   *   *   *

Dr. Lowell came bouncing out of the jetcab a few days later. "The hospital better be spotless!" he called out jovially, paying off the hackie. "I'm in a mean mood. Liable to suspend everybody."

There was a strange lift to Dr. Kalmar's spirits as the old man entered the office. He wished without hope that he could inspire the same sort of reverence and respect. Impossible, of course. Dr. Lowell was great; he himself was nothing more than competent.

Dr. Kalmar introduced his young assistant to the old man.

"Young and strong," Dr. Lowell approved. "That's what we need on Deneb. Skill is important, but health and youth even more so."

"For those who stay," said Dr. Hoyt frostily. "I'm not."

Dr. Kalmar felt himself quiver with rage. The wet-nosed pup couldn't talk to Dr. Lowell like that!

But Dr. Lowell was saying cheerily, "You seem to have made up your mind to go back. No matter. Some decisions are like egg-shells—made only to be broken. I hope that's what you'll do with yours."

"Not a chance," Dr. Hoyt said. He didn't take the arrogant expression off his face even when Miss Dupont looked at him pleadingly.

"Then I say let's signal the next ship—" Dr. Kalmar began.

Dr. Lowell cut in quickly, "You two have patients to attend to, I see. Don't worry about me. I know my way around this poor little wretch of a building. Not much like Earth hospitals, is it?" He headed for the medical supply room, adding just before he went in, "A lot can be said for small installations. The personal touch, you know."

Dr. Kalmar enviously realized how deftly the old man had put the youngster in his place, whereas he would have stood there and slugged it out verbally. Lord, if he could only acquire that awesome wisdom!

"Well, back to work," he said, trying to imitate the cheeriness at least.

"Sure, let's ruin some more lives," Dr. Hoyt almost snarled.

"Leo, *please!*" whispered Miss Dupont imploringly.

Five minutes later the two doctors were furiously arguing over a very old man who had been sent by Social Control to have his eyesight strengthened.

"You have no right to let anybody dodder around like this!" Dr. Hoyt yelled. "What in hell is Rephysical for if not for such cases?"

"You probably think we ought to make him look like 25 again," Dr. Kalmar yelled back. "If that's all you've learned working here—"

"Now, now," said Dr. Lowell soothingly. He'd come in unnoticed by either of the men. "Dr. Hoyt is right, of course. We *would* like to make old people young and some day we'll be able to afford it. But not for some time to come."

"Why not?" Dr. Hoyt demanded in a lower tone, visibly flattered by Dr. Lowell's seemingly taking his side.

"Rephysical can't actually make anyone young. It can only give the outward appearance of youth and replace obviously diseased parts. But an old body is an old organism; it has to break down eventually. If we give it more vigor than it can endure, it breaks down too soon, much sooner than if we let it age normally. That represents economic loss as well as a humanitarian one."

"I don't follow you," Dr. Hoyt said bewilderedly.

"Well, our patient used to be a machinist. A good one. Now he's only able to be an oiler. A good one, too, when you improve his eyesight. He can go on doing that for years, performing a useful function. But he'd wear himself out in no time as a machinist again if you de-aged him."

"Is that supposed to make sense?"

"It does," said Dr. Lowell, "for Deneb."

Dr. Hoyt wanted to continue the discussion, but Dr. Lowell was already on his way to inspect another part of the hospital. Grumbling, the young man helped chart the optical nerves that had to be replaced and measure the new curve of the retinas ordered by Social Control.

But he fought just as strenuously over other cases, especially a retired freight-jet pilot who had to have his reflexes slowed down so he could become a contented meteorologist. Whenever there was a loud disagreement of this sort, Dr. Lowell was there to mediate calmly.

* * * * *

At the end of the day, Dr. Kalmar was emotionally exhausted. He said as he and Dr. Lowell were washing up, "The kid's hopeless. I thought you could straighten him out—God knows I couldn't—but he'll never see why we have to work the way we do."

"What do you suggest?" Dr. Lowell asked through a towel.

"Send him back to Earth. Get an intern who's more malleable."

Dr. Lowell tossed the towel into the sterilizer. "Can't be done. We're expanding so fast all over the Galaxy that Earth can't train and ship out enough doctors for the new colonies. If we sent him back, I don't know when we'd get another."

Dr. Kalmar swallowed. "You mean it's him or nobody?"

"Afraid so."

"But he'll never fit in on Deneb!"

"You did," Dr. Lowell said.

Dr. Kalmar tried to smile modestly. "I realized immediately how little I knew and how much more experience you had. I was willing to learn. Why, I used to listen to you and watch you work and try to see your reasons for doing things—"

"You think so?" asked Dr. Lowell.

Dr. Kalmar glanced at him in astonishment. "You know I did. I still do, for that matter."

"When you landed on Deneb," said Dr. Lowell, "you were the most stubborn, opinionated young ass I'd ever met."

Dr. Kalmar's smile became an appreciative grin. "Damn, I wish I had that light touch of yours!"

"You were so dogmatic and argumentative that Dr. Hoyt is a suggestible schoolboy in comparison."

"Well, you don't have to go that far," Dr. Kalmar said. "I get what you're driving at—every intern needs orientation and I should be more patient and understanding."

"Then you don't follow me at all," stated Dr. Lowell. "Invite Dr. Hoyt, Miss Dupont and me to your house for dinner tonight and maybe you'll get a better idea of what I mean."

"Anything for a free meal, eh?"

"And to keep a doctor here on Deneb that we'd lose otherwise."

"Implying that I can't do it."

"Isn't that the decision you'd come to?"

"Yes, I guess it is," Dr. Kalmar confessed. "All right, how about dinner at my house tonight? I'll round up the other two and call Harriet so she'll expect us."

"Delighted to come," said Dr. Lowell. "Nice of you to ask me."

Miss Dupont was elated at the invitation and Dr. Hoyt said he had nothing else to do anyway. On the videophone Mrs. Kalmar was dismayed for a moment, until Dr. Lowell told her to put through an emergency order to Central Commissary and he'd verify it.

That was when Dr. Kalmar realized how serious the old man was. On a raw planet where crises were everyday routine, a situation had to be catastrophic before it could be called an emergency.

*   *   *   *   *

Dinner on Deneb was the same as anywhere else in the Galaxy. To free women for other work, food was delivered weekly in cooked form. A special messenger from Central Commissary had brought the emergency rations and Mrs. Kalmar had simply punctured the self-heat cartridges and put the servings in front of each guest; the containers were disposable plates and came with single-use plastic utensils. No garbage, no preparation, no cleaning up afterward, except to toss them all into the converter furnace. Dr. Hoyt was still not accustomed to wholly grown foods; he'd been raised on synthetics, of course, which were the staples on Earth.

"Well, that was good," said Dr. Lowell, getting up from the table with his round little belly comfortably expanded. "Now, let's have a few drinks before we start a professional bull session. Where do you keep your liquor? I'd like to mix my special so Dr. Hoyt can see we colonials are not so provincial."

"Good Lord, I haven't had your special for years!" exclaimed Dr. Kalmar. "Since about the time I came to Deneb, in fact."

"That's why it's a special. Reserved for state occasions, such as arrivals of colleagues from our dear old home planet."

"Oh, you don't have to go to all that bother," said Dr. Hoyt. "You'd have to make it twice—once now and once when I leave."

"That won't be for quite a while, will it?" Miss Dupont asked anxiously.

"As soon as I finish my internship. No more alien worlds for me. I like Earth."

Mrs. Kalmar got him to talk about it, which was much easier than getting him to stop, while Dr. Kalmar showed the old man where the liquor stock and fixings were kept. Watching him mix the ingredients with a chemist's care, Dr. Kalmar felt a glow of nostalgia. He recalled the celebration at Dr. Lowell's house, several months after he had come from Earth, when he'd enjoyed himself so much that he'd passed out. It was one of the pleasanter memories of his start on Deneb.

"Can't mix them all in a single batch," Dr. Lowell explained, bringing the drinks over one at a time as he finished preparing them. "Mrs. Kalmar ... Miss Dupont ... our gracious host, Dr. Kalmar ... and now Dr. Hoyt and myself." He lifted his glass at Dr. Hoyt. "Welcome to our latest associate—product, like ourselves, of the great medical schools of Earth. It's a forlorn hope, but may he learn as much from us about our peculiar methods as we learn from him about the latest terrestrial advances."

Dr. Hoyt, smiling as if he didn't think it possible, stood up when they'd downed their toast to him. "To Earth," he said. "May I get back in record time." He gulped it, said, "Delicious—for a colonial drink," and froze with his smile as fixed as if it had been painted on.

"Leo!" Miss Dupont cried, and shook him, but he stayed frozen.

"The man's allergic to alcohol!" said Dr. Kalmar, astonished.

"Do something!" Mrs. Kalmar begged. "Don't let him stand there like that! He—he looks like a petrified man!"

"Don't get panicky," said Dr. Lowell in a quiet, confident voice. "That's when you passed out, Dr. Kalmar. Right after your first taste of my special."

"But *we* haven't," Dr. Kalmar objected.

"Naturally. Your drinks weren't drugged."

"Drugged?" shrieked Miss Dupont. "You doped him?"

"That's rather obvious, isn't it?"

"But—what for?" Dr. Kalmar stammered.

"Same reason I slipped you a mickey not long after you got here. We can't take any chances that he'll ship back to Earth. You see?"

"I don't," raged Miss Dupont. "I think it's a cheap, dirty, foul trick and it won't work, either. You can't *keep* him drugged."

"I don't like you talking to Dr. Lowell like that," said Dr. Kalmar indignantly.

"You should be the last one to object," Mrs. Kalmar pointed out. "He said he drugged you, too."

"I know," Dr. Kalmar said blankly. "I don't understand—"

"You will," promised Dr. Lowell. "Just come along and don't interfere. Better give him the order; it'll keep things straighter."

Mrs. Kalmar was grimly disapproving and Miss Dupont was close to hysteria. Only Dr. Kalmar retained his awed respect for Dr. Lowell. If the old man said it was all right, it was, even if he couldn't see the reason.

"Go ahead," urged Dr. Lowell.

"Dr. Hoyt!"

"Yes, Dr. Kalmar?"

"You will come with us!"

"Yes, Dr. Kalmar."

Dr. Lowell took them back to the hospital.

"Now what?" asked Dr. Kalmar.

"You actually don't know?" Miss Dupont demanded. "He wants to put Leo through the Ego Alter."

"That's absurd," Dr. Kalmar said angrily, "and an outright slander. Dr. Lowell wouldn't consider such a thing—the boy didn't ask for it and it wasn't authorized by Social Control."

Dr. Lowell smiled genially and opened the door to the Ego Alter room. "I hate to disillusion you, Dr. Kalmar. That's exactly what I have in mind—the same thing I did to you."

"That's absurd," Dr. Kalmar repeated, but with less conviction and more confusion than before.

"It worked. Tell him to sit down."

Dr. Kalmar did, and automatically fitted the wired plastic helmet to Dr. Hoyt's head.

"You can't!" cried Miss Dupont as he reached for the dials on the control console. "It's not fair!"

"Let's not get involved in a discussion on ethics," Dr. Lowell said. "Deneb can't afford to lose him; we need every doctor we have. If he goes back to Earth it may be years before we get a replacement."

"But you can't do it without his consent!"

"There's time for that later," the old man grinned. "Keep his eyes on you, Dr. Kalmar, while you build up his father image. Cut down on hostility, aggression and power drive. Boost social responsibility and adventurousness. But make sure he's looking at you constantly."

"I won't allow it," said Mrs. Kalmar flatly. "You won't make my husband violate his oath."

"I did it to him, didn't I?" Dr. Lowell replied jovially. "It got you a husband."

Miss Dupont grabbed at Dr. Kalmar's hand, but he had already turned on the current.

"Anything else?" he asked.

"Well, he has to get married, of course," Dr. Lowell said. "Let him look at Miss Dupont—she's scheduled for this year, isn't she?—while you give him a shot of mating urge. Now, wipe out the memory of this incident and put him on a joy jag. We can validate that by liquoring him up afterward. When you're finished, bring him to."

Dr. Hoyt came out of it almost with a whoop. He lurched out of the insulated seat, stared at Miss Dupont for a moment with eyes that almost glittered, and seized and kissed her.

"My goodness!" she gasped.

"Now, what were you saying about ethics?" Dr. Lowell asked.

There was no answer. Both Miss Dupont and Mrs. Kalmar had frozen.

"You drugged them, too?" Dr. Kalmar weakly wanted to know.

"A bit slower-acting," admitted the old man. "All you have to do with them is wipe out the last half hour. Don't want any witnesses to an unethical act, you know. Oh, and put them on a jag also."

Dr. Kalmar followed instructions.

Finished, they left the three uproariously drunk in the waiting room and went to wash up. Dr. Kalmar went along bewilderedly. The old man was as unconcerned as if he did this sort of thing daily.

"I was as arrogant and belligerent as this squirt was?"

"Worse," Dr. Lowell said. "He was willing to finish out his internship. You weren't. Still worried about the ethics?"

"Yes. Naturally."

"All right, apply some logic, then. Are you happier on Deneb than you'd have been on Earth?"

"Well, certainly. I'd have been lucky to get a job doctoring in a summer camp. I wouldn't trade a roomy planet like this for the jammed cubicles of Earth. And I like our methods better than terrestrial dogma. But those are my preferences. I can't inflict them on anybody else."

"The hell they were your preferences. You bickered more about our methods and longed more loudly for the tenements of Earth than this lad ever did. All it took was a slight Ego Alter and you have a happier life than you would have had. Right?"

Dr. Kalmar felt his tension ease. If the old man said it was right, it was. He became momentarily resentful when he realized that that reaction had been installed by Dr. Lowell, but then he smiled. It really was right. A bit arbitrary, perhaps, but for the good of Dr. Hoyt and Deneb in the long run, just as it had been for himself.

"Look," he said, drying his arms. "I've been wanting my wife to go through a slight rephysical."

"Why don't you ask her?"

"The fact is that I'm afraid she'll think I'm dissatisfied and I don't want her to get resentful."

"Maybe she'd like you to do some changing, too."

"What for? I'm all right."

"She probably feels the same way about herself."

"But all I want are a few changes in her. She's as high as a space pilot now. It would be a cinch to—"

Dr. Lowell flung down the towel and gave him an outraged glare. "There's such a thing as professional ethics, Dr. Kalmar!"

"But you—"

"That's different. It was a social decision, not a selfish one. If you ask her and she agrees, that's up to her. But you can't take advantage of her in an egocentric, arbitrary way. You just try it and I'll have you sent back to Earth."

Dr. Kalmar felt his knees grow weak in alarm. "No, no. It's not that important. Just an insignificant kind of wish."

And it was, he discovered when they went out to the waiting room. Unused to jags, Mrs. Kalmar was more affectionate than she'd been since they were first married; he'd have to remember to go on them periodically with her. Miss Dupont, unwilling to budge out of Dr. Hoyt's tight arms, had glassily joyous eyes. Dr. Hoyt didn't let her go until he caught sight of Dr. Kalmar.

"Greatest doctor I ever met," he said enthusiastically. "Won'ful planet, Deneb. Just wanna marry Miss Dupont, stay here and learn at your feet. Okay?"

Dr. Kalmar's glance at the old man was no less worshipful. "It couldn't be okayer," he said.

At the Post

AT THE POST

By H. L. GOLD

ILLUSTRATED BY VIDMER
ORIGINALLY PUBLISHED IN *GALAXY SCIENCE FICTION*
OCTOBER 1953

How does a person come to be scratched from the human race?
Psychiatry did not have the answer—
perhaps Clocker's turf science did!

AT THE POST

When Clocker Locke came into the Blue Ribbon, on 49th Street west of Broadway, he saw that nobody had told Doc Hawkins about his misfortune. Doc, a pub-crawling, non-practicing general practitioner who wrote a daily medical column for a local tabloid, was celebrating his release from the alcoholic ward, but his guests at the rear table of the restaurant weren't in any mood for celebration.

"What's the matter with you—have you suddenly become immune to liquor?" Clocker heard Doc ask irritably, while Clocker was passing the gem merchants, who, because they needed natural daylight to do business, were traditionally accorded the tables nearest the windows. "I said the drinks were on me, didn't I?" Doc insisted. "Now let us have some bright laughter and sparkling wit, or must we wait until Clocker shows up before there is levity in the house?"

Seeing the others glance toward the door, Doc turned and looked at Clocker. His mouth fell open silently, for the first time in Clocker's memory.

"Good Lord!" he said after a moment. "Clocker's become a *character!*"

Clocker felt embarrassed. He still wasn't used to wearing a business suit of subdued gray, and black oxfords, instead of his usual brilliant sports jacket, slacks and two-tone suede shoes; a tie with timid little figures, whereas he had formerly been an authority on hand-painted cravats; and a plain wristwatch in place of his spectacular chronograph.

By all Broadway standards, he knew, Doc was correct—he'd become strange and eccentric, a character.

*   *   *   *   *

"It was Zelda's idea," Clocker explained somberly, sitting down and shaking his head at the waiter who ambled over. "She wanted to make a gentleman out of me."

"*Wanted to?*" Doc repeated, bewildered. "You two kids got married just before they took my snakes away. Don't tell me you phhtt already!"

Clocker looked appealingly at the others. They became busy with drinks and paper napkins.

Naturally, Doc Hawkins knew the background: That Clocker was a race handicapper—publisher, if you could call it that, of a tiny tip sheet—for Doc, in need of drinking money, had often consulted him professionally. Also that Clocker had married Zelda, the noted 52nd Street stripteuse, who had social aspirations. What remained to be told had occurred during Doc's inevitably temporary cure.

"Isn't anybody going to tell me?" Doc demanded.

"It was right after you tried to take the warts off a fire hydrant and they came and got you," said Clocker, "that Zelda started hearing voices. It got real bad."

"How bad?"

"She's at Glendale Center in an upholstered room. I just came back from visiting her."

Doc gulped his entire drink, a positive sign that he was upset, or happy, or not feeling anything in particular. Now, however, he was noticeably upset.

"Did the psychiatrists give you a diagnosis?" he asked.

"I got it memorized. Catatonia. Dementia praecox, what they used to call, one of the brain vets told me, and he said it's hopeless."

"Rough," said Doc. "Very rough. The outlook is never good in such cases."

"Maybe they can't help her," Clocker said harshly, "but I will."

"People are not horses," Doc reminded him.

"I've noticed that," said Handy Sam, the armless wonder at the flea circus, drinking beer because he had an ingrown toenail and couldn't hold a shot glass. Now that Clocker had told the grim story, he felt free to talk, which he did enthusiastically. "Clocker's got a giant brain, Doc. Who was it said Warlock'd turn into a dog in his third year? Clocker, the only dopester in the racket. And that's just one—"

"Zelda was my best flesh act," interrupted Arnold Wilson Wyle, a ten-percenter whom video had saved from alimony jail. "A solid boffola in the bop basements. Nobody regrets her sad condition more than me, Clocker, but it's a sure flop, what you got in mind. Think of your public. For instance, what's good at Hialeah? My bar bill is about to be foreclosed and I can use a long shot."

Clocker bounced his fist on the moist table. "Those couch artists don't know what's wrong with Zelda. I do."

"You do?" Doc asked, startled.

"Well, almost. I'm so close, I can hear the finish-line camera clicking."

Buttonhole grasped Doc's lapel and hung on with characteristic avidity; he was perhaps Clocker's most pious subscriber. "Doping races is a science. Clocker maybe never doped the human race, but I got nine to five he can do it. Go on, tell him, Clocker."

*   *   *   *   *

Doc Hawkins ran together the rings he had been making with the wet bottom of his tumbler. "I shall be most interested," he said with tabloid irony, clearly feeling that immediate disillusionment was the most humane thing for Clocker. "Perhaps we can collaborate on an article for the psychiatric journals."

"All right, look." Clocker pulled out charts resembling those he worked with when making turf selections. "Zelda's got catatonia, which is the last heat in the schizophrenia parlay. She used to be a hoofer before she started undressing for dough, and now she does time-steps all day."

Doc nodded into a fresh glass that the waiter had put before him. "Stereotyped movements are typical of catatonia. They derive from thwarted or repressed instinctual drive; in most instances, the residue of childhood frustrations."

"She dance all day, huh, Clocker?" asked Oil Pocket, the Oklahoma Cherokee who, with the income of several wells, was famed for angeling bareback shows. He had a glass of tequila in one hand, the salted half of a lemon in the other. "She dance good?"

"That's just it," Clocker said. "She does these time-steps, the first thing you learn in hoofing, over and over, ten-fifteen hours a day. And she keeps talking like she's giving lessons to some jerk kid who can't get it straight. And she was the kid with the hot routines, remember."

"The hottest," agreed Arnold Wilson Wyle. "Zelda doing time-steps is like Heifetz fiddling at weddings."

"I still like to put her in show," Oil Pocket grunted. "She stacked like brick tepee. Don't have to dance good."

"You'll have a long wait," observed Doc sympathetically, "in spite of what our young friend here says. Continue, young friend."

Clocker spread his charts. He needed the whole table. The others removed their drinks, Handy Sam putting his on the floor so he could reach it more easily.

"This is what I got out of checking all the screwball factories I could reach personal and by mail," Clocker said. "I went around and talked to the doctors and watched the patients in the places near here, and wrote to the places I couldn't get to. Then I broke everything down like it was a stud and track record."

Buttonhole tugged Doc's lapel. "That ain't scientific, I suppose," he challenged.

"Duplication of effort," Doc replied, patiently allowing Buttonhole to retain his grip. "It was all done in an organized fashion over a period of more than half a century. But let us hear the rest."

*   *   *   *   *

"First," said Clocker, "there are more male bats than fillies."

"Females are inherently more stable, perhaps because they have a more balanced chromosome arrangement."

"There are more nuts in the brain rackets than labor chumps."

"Intellectual activity increases the area of conflict."

"There are less in the sticks than in the cities, and practically none among the savages. I mean real savages," Clocker told Handy Sam, "not marks for con merchants."

"I was wondering," Handy Sam admitted.

"Complex civilization creates psychic insecurity," said Doc.

"When these catatonics pull out, they don't remember much or maybe nothing," Clocker went on, referring to his charts.

Doc nodded his shaggy white head. "Protective amnesia."

"I seen hundreds of these mental gimps. They work harder and longer at what they're doing, even just laying down and doing nothing, than they ever did when they were regular citizens."

"Concentration of psychic energy, of course."

"And they don't get a damn cent for it."

*   *   *   *   *

Doc hesitated, put down his half-filled tumbler. "I beg your pardon?"

"I say they're getting stiffed," Clocker stated. "Anybody who works that hard ought to get paid. I don't mean it's got to be money, although that's the only kind of pay Zelda'd work for. Right, Arnold?"

"Well, sure," said Arnold Wilson Wyle wonderingly. "I never thought of it like that. Zelda doing time-steps for nothing ten-fifteen hours a day—that ain't Zelda."

"If you ask me, she *likes* her job," Clocker said. "Same with the other catatonics I seen. But for no pay?"

Doc surprisingly pushed his drink away, something that only a serious medical puzzle could ever accomplish. "I don't understand what you're getting at."

"I don't know these other cata-characters, but I do know Zelda," said Arnold Wilson Wyle. "She's got to get something out of all that work. Clocker says it's the same with the others and I take his word. What are they knocking theirself out for if it's for free?"

"They gain some obscure form of emotional release or repetitive gratification," Doc explained.

"Zelda?" exploded Clocker. "You offer her a deal like that for a club date and she'd get ruptured laughing."

"I tell her top billing," Oil Pocket agreed, "plenty ads, plenty publicity, whole show built around her. Wampum, she says; save money on ads and publicity, give it to her. Zelda don't count coups."

Doc Hawkins called over the waiter, ordered five fingers instead of his customary three. "Let us not bicker," he told Clocker. "Continue."

*   *   *   *   *

Clocker looked at his charts again. "There ain't a line that ain't represented, even the heavy rackets and short grifts. It's a regular human steeplechase. And these sour apples do mostly whatever they did for a living—draw pictures, sell shoes, do lab experiments, sew clothes, Zelda with her time-steps. By the hour! In the air!"

"In the air?" Handy Sam repeated. "Flying?"

"Imaginary functioning," Doc elaborated for him. "They have nothing in their hands. Pure hallucination. Systematic delusion."

"Sign language?" Oil Pocket suggested.

"That," said Clocker, before Doc Hawkins could reject the notion, "is on the schnoz, Injun. Buttonhole says I'm like doping races. He's right. I'm working out what some numbers-runner tells me is probabilities. I got it all here," he rapped the charts, "and it's the same thing all these flop-ears got in common. Not their age, not their jobs, not their—you should pardon the expression—sex. They're *teaching*."

Buttonhole looked baffled. He almost let go of Doc's lapel.

Handy Sam scratched the back of his neck thoughtfully with a big toe. "Teaching, Clocker? Who? You said they're kept in solitary."

"They are. I don't know who. I'm working on that now."

Doc shoved the charts aside belligerently to make room for his beefy elbows. He leaned forward and glowered at Clocker. "Your theory belongs in the Sunday supplement of the alleged newspaper I write for. Not all catatonics work, as you call it. What about those who stand rigid and those who lie in bed all the time?"

"I guess you think that's easy," Clocker retorted. "You try it sometime. I did. It's work, I tell you." He folded his charts and put them back into the inside pocket of his conservative jacket.

He looked sick with longing and loneliness. "Damn, I miss that mouse. I got to save her, Doc! Don't you get that?"

Doc Hawkins put a chunky hand gently on Clocker's arm. "Of course, boy. But how can you succeed when trained men can't?"

"Well, take Zelda. She did time-steps when she was maybe five and going to dancing school—"

"Time-steps have some symbolic significance to her," Doc said with more than his usual tact. "My theory is that she was compelled to go against her will, and this is a form of unconscious rebellion."

"They don't have no significance to her," Clocker argued doggedly. "She can do time-steps blindfolded and on her knees with both ankles tied behind her back." He pried Buttonhole's hand off Doc's lapel, and took hold of both of them himself. "I tell you she's teaching, explaining, breaking in some dummy who can't get the hang of it!"

"But who?" Doc objected. "Psychiatrists? Nurses? You? Admit it, Clocker—she goes on doing time-steps whether she's alone or not. In fact, she never knows if anybody is with her. Isn't that so?"

"Yeah," Clocker said grudgingly. "That's what has me boxed."

*   *   *   *   *

Oil Pocket grunted tentatively, "White men not believe in spirits. Injuns do. Maybe Zelda talk to spirits."

"I been thinking of that," confessed Clocker, looking at the red angel unhappily. "Spirits is all I can figure. Ghosts. Spooks. But if Zelda and these other catatonics are teaching ghosts, these ghosts are the dumbest jerks anywhere. They make her and the rest go through time-steps or sewing or selling shoes again and again. If they had half a brain, they'd get it in no time."

"Maybe spirits not hear good," Oil Pocket offered, encouraged by Clocker's willingness to consider the hypothesis.

"Could be," Clocker said with partial conviction. "If we can't see them, it may be just as hard for them to see or hear us."

Oil Pocket anxiously hitched his chair closer. "Old squaw name Dry Ground Never Rainy Season—what you call old maid—hear spirits all the time. She keep telling us what they say. Nobody listen."

"How come?" asked Clocker interestedly.

"She deaf, blind. Not hear thunder. Walk into cactus, yell like hell. She hardly see us, not hear us at all, how come she see and hear spirits? Just talk, talk, talk all the time."

Clocker frowned, thinking. "These catatonics don't see or hear us, but they sure as Citation hear and see *something*."

Doc Hawkins stood up with dignity, hardly weaving, and handed a bill to the waiter. "I was hoping to get a private racing tip from you, Clocker. Freshly sprung from the alcoholic ward, I can use some money. But I see that your objectivity is impaired by emotional considerations. I wouldn't risk a dime on your advice even after a race is run."

"I didn't expect you to believe me," said Clocker despairingly. "None of you pill-pushers ever do."

"I can't say about your psycho-doping," declared Arnold Wilson Wyle, also rising. "But I got faith in your handicapping. I'd still like a long shot at Hialeah if you happen to have one."

"I been too busy trying to help Zelda," Clocker said in apology.

They left, Doc Hawkins pausing at the bar to pick up a credit bottle to see him through his overdue medical column.

Handy Sam slipped on his shoes to go. "Stick with it, Clocker. I said you was a scientist—"

"*I* said it," contradicted Buttonhole, lifting himself out of the chair on Handy Sam's lapels. "If anybody can lick this caper, Clocker can."

Oil Pocket glumly watched them leave. "Doctors not think spirits real," he said. "I get sick, go to Reservation doctor. He give me medicine. I get sicker. Medicine man see evil spirits make me sick. Shakes rattle. Dances. Evil spirits go. I get better."

"I don't know what in hell to think," confided Clocker, miserable and confused. "If it would help Zelda, I'd cut my throat from head to foot so I could become a spirit and get the others to lay off her."

"Then you spirit, she alive. Making love not very practical."

"Then what do I do—hire a medium?"

"Get medicine man from Reservation. He drive out evil spirits."

Clocker pushed away from the table. "So help me, I'll do it if I can't come up with something cheaper than paying freight from Oklahoma."

"Get Zelda out, I pay and put her in show."

"Then if I haul the guy here and it don't work, I'm in hock to you. Thanks, Oil Pocket, but I'll try my way first."

*   *   *   *   *

Back in his hotel room, waiting for the next day so he could visit Zelda, Clocker was like an addict at the track with every cent on a hunch. After weeks of neglecting his tip sheet to study catatonia, he felt close to the payoff.

He spent most of the night smoking and walking around the room, trying not to look at the jars and hairbrushes on the bureau. He missed the bobbypins on the floor, the nylons drying across the shower rack, the toothpaste tubes squeezed from the top. He'd put her perfumes in a drawer, but the smell was so pervasively haunting that it was like having her stand invisibly behind him.

As soon as the sun came up, he hurried out and took a cab. He'd have to wait until visiting hours, but he couldn't stand the slowness of the train. Just being in the same building with her would—almost—be enough.

When he finally was allowed into Zelda's room, he spent all his time watching her silently, taking in every intently mumbled word and movement. Her movements, in spite of their gratingly basic monotony, were particularly something to watch, for Zelda had blue-black hair down to her shapely shoulders, wide-apart blue eyes, sulky mouth, and an astonishing body. She used all her physical equipment with unconscious provocativeness, except her eyes, which were blankly distant.

Clocker stood it as long as he could and then burst out, "Damn it, Zelda, how long can they take to learn a time-step?"

She didn't answer. She didn't see him, hear him, or feel him. Even when he kissed her on the back of the neck, her special place, she did not twist her shoulder up with the sudden thrill.

He took out the portable phonograph he'd had permission to bring in, and hopefully played three of her old numbers—a ballet tap, a soft shoe, and, most potent of all, her favorite slinky strip tune. Ordinarily, the beat would have thrown her off, but not any more.

"Dead to this world," muttered Clocker dejectedly.

He shook Zelda. Even when she was off-balance, her feet tapped out the elementary routine.

"Look, kid," he said, his voice tense and angry, "I don't know who these squares are that you're working for, but tell them if they got you, they got to take me, too."

Whatever he expected—ghostly figures to materialize or a chill wind from nowhere—nothing happened. She went on tapping.

He sat down on her bed. *They* picked people the way he picked horses, except he picked to win and they picked to show. To show? Of course. Zelda was showing them how to dance and also, probably, teaching them about the entertainment business. The others had obviously been selected for what they knew, which they went about doing as singlemindedly as she did.

*   *   *   *   *

He had a scheme that he hadn't told Doc because he knew it was crazy. At any rate, he hoped it was. The weeks without her had been a hell of loneliness—for him, not for her; she wasn't even aware of the awful loss. He'd settle for that, but even better would be freeing her somehow. The only way he could do it would be to find out who controlled her and what they were after. Even with that information, he couldn't be sure of succeeding, and there was a good chance that he might also be caught, but that didn't matter.

The idea was to interest *them* in what he knew so *they* would want to have him explain all he knew about racing. After that— well, he'd make his plans when he knew the setup.

Clocker came close to the automatic time-step machine that had been his wife. He began talking to her, very loudly, about the detailed knowledge needed to select winners, based on stud records, past performances of mounts and jockeys, condition of track and the influence of the weather—always, however, leaving out the data that would make sense of the whole complicated industry. It was like roping a patsy and holding back the buzzer until the dough was down. He knew he risked being cold-decked, but it was worth the gamble. His only worry was that hoarseness would stop him before he hooked *their* interest.

An orderly, passing in the corridor, heard his voice, opened the door and asked with ponderous humor, "What you doing, Clocker—trying to take out a membership card in this country club?"

Clocker leaped slightly. "Uh, working on a private theory," he said, collected his things with a little more haste than he would have liked to show, kissed Zelda without getting any response whatever, and left for the day.

But he kept coming back every morning. He was about to give up when the first feelings of unreality dazed and dazzled him. He carefully suppressed his excitement and talked more loudly about racing. The world seemed to be slipping away from him. He could have hung onto it if he had wanted. He didn't. He let the voices come, vague and far away, distorted, not quite meaningless, but not adding up to much, either.

And then, one day, he didn't notice the orderly come in to tell him that visiting hours were over. Clocker was explaining the fundamentals of horse racing ... meticulously, with immense patience, over and over and over ... and didn't hear him.

*　　*　　*　　*　　*

It had been so easy that Clocker was disappointed. The first voices had argued gently and reasonably over him, each claiming priority for one reason or another, until one either was assigned or pulled rank. That was the voice that Clocker eventually kept hearing—a quiet, calm voice that constantly faded and grew stronger, as if it came from a great distance and had trouble with static. Clocker remembered the crystal set his father had bought when radio was still a toy. It was like that.

Then the unreality vanished and was replaced by a dramatic new reality. He was somewhere far away. He knew it wasn't on Earth, for this was like nothing except, perhaps, a World's Fair. The buildings were low and attractively designed, impressive in spite of their softly blended spectrum of pastel colors. He was in a huge square that was grass-covered and tree-shaded and decorated with classical sculpture. Hundreds of people stood with him, and they all looked shaken and scared. Clocker felt nothing but elation; he'd arrived. It made no difference that he didn't know where he was or anything about the setup. He was where Zelda was.

"How did I get here?" asked a little man with bifocals and a vest that had pins and threaded needles stuck in it. "I can't take time for pleasure trips. Mrs. Jacobs is coming in for her fitting tomorrow and she'll positively murder me if her dress ain't ready."

"She can't," Clocker said. "Not any more."

"You mean we're dead?" someone else asked, awed. It was a softly pudgy woman with excessively blonde hair, a greasily red-lipped smile and a flowered housecoat. She looked around with great approval. "Hey, this ain't bad! Like I always said, either I'm no worse than anybody else or they're no better'n me. How about that, dearie?"

"Don't ask me," Clocker evaded. "I think somebody's going to get an earful, but you ain't dead. That much I can tell you."

The woman looked disappointed.

Some people in the crowd were complaining that they had families to take care of while others were worried about leaving their businesses. They all grew silent, however, when a man climbed up on a sort of marble rostrum in front of them. He was very tall and dignified and wore formal clothes and had a white beard parted in the center.

"Please feel at ease," he said in a big, deep, soothing voice, like a radio announcer for a symphony broadcast. "You are not in any danger. No harm will come to you."

"You *sure* we ain't dead, sweetie?" the woman in the flowered housecoat asked Clocker. "Isn't that—"

"No," said Clocker. "He'd have a halo, wouldn't he?"

"Yeah, I guess so," she agreed doubtfully.

The white-bearded man went on, "If you will listen carefully to this orientation lecture, you will know where you are and why. May I introduce Gerald W. Harding? Dr. Harding is in charge of this reception center. Ladies and gentlemen, Dr. Harding."

*   *   *   *   *

A number of people applauded out of habit ... probably lecture fans or semi-pro TV studio audiences. The rest, including Clocker, waited as an aging man in a white lab smock, heavy-rimmed eyeglasses and smooth pink cheeks, looking like a benevolent doctor in a mouthwash ad, stood up and faced the crowd. He put his hands behind his back, rocked on his toes a few times, and smiled benevolently.

"Thank you, Mr. Calhoun," he said to the bearded man who was seating himself on a marble bench. "Friends—and I trust you will soon regard us *as* your friends—I know you are puzzled at all this." He waved a white hand at the buildings around them. "Let me explain. You have been chosen—yes, carefully screened and selected—to help us in undoubtedly the greatest cause of all history. I can see that you are asking yourselves *why* you were selected and what this cause is. I shall describe it briefly. You'll learn more about it as we work together in this vast and noble experiment."

The woman in the flowered housecoat looked enormously flattered. The little tailor was nodding to show he understood the points covered thus far. Glancing at the rest of the crowd, Crocker realized that he was the only one who had this speech pegged. It was a pitch. These men were out for something.

He wished Doc Hawkins and Oil Pocket were there. Doc doubtless would have searched his unconscious for symbols of childhood traumas to explain the whole thing; he would never have accepted it as *some* kind of reality. Oil Pocket, on the other hand, would somehow have tried to equate the substantial Mr. Calhoun and Dr. Harding with tribal spirits. Of the two, Clocker felt that Oil Pocket would have been closer.

Or maybe he was in his own corner of psychosis, while Oil Pocket would have been in another, more suited to Indians. Spirits or figments? Whatever they were, they looked as real as anybody he'd ever known, but perhaps that was the naturalness of the supernatural or the logic of insanity.

Clocker shivered, aware that he had to wait for the answer. The one thing he did know, as an authority on cons, was that this had the smell of one, supernatural or otherwise. He watched and listened like a detective shadowing an escape artist.

"This may be something of a shock," Dr. Harding continued with a humorous, sympathetic smile. "I hope it will not be for long. Let me state it in its simplest terms. You know that there are billions of stars in the Universe, and that stars have planets as naturally as cats have kittens. A good many of these planets are inhabited. Some life-forms are intelligent, very much so, while others are not. In almost all instances, the dominant form of life is quite different from—yours."

Unable to see the direction of the con, Clocker felt irritated.

"Why do I say *yours*, not *ours*?" asked Dr. Harding. "Because, dear friends, Mr. Calhoun and I are not of your planet or solar system. No commotion, please!" he urged, raising his hands as the crowd stirred bewilderedly. "Our names are not Calhoun and Harding; we adopted those because our own are so alien that you would be unable to pronounce them. We are not formed as you see us, but this is how we *might* look if we were human beings, which, of course, we are not. Our true appearance seems to be—ah—rather confusing to human eyes."

*   *   *   *   *

Nuts, Clocker thought irreverently. Get to the point.

"I don't think this is the time for detailed explanations," Dr. Harding hurried on before there were any questions. "We are friendly, even altruistic inhabitants of a planet 10,000 light-years from Earth. Quite a distance, you are thinking; how did we get here? The truth is that we are not 'here' and neither are you. 'Here' is a projection of thought, a hypothetical point in space, a place that exists only by mental force. Our physical appearances and yours are telepathic representations. Actually, our bodies are on our own respective planets."

"Very confusing," complained a man who looked like a banker. "Do you have any idea of what he's trying to tell us?"

"Not yet," Clocker replied with patient cynicism. "He'll give us the convincer after the buildup."

The man who looked like a banker stared sharply at Clocker and moved away. Clocker shrugged. He was more concerned with why he didn't feel tired or bored just standing there and listening. There was not even an overpowering sense of urgency and annoyance, although he wanted to find Zelda and this lecture was keeping him from looking for her. It was as if his emotions were somehow being reduced in intensity. They existed, but lacked the strength they should have had.

So he stood almost patiently and listened to Dr. Harding say, "Our civilization is considerably older than yours. For many of your centuries, we have explored the Universe, both physically and telepathically. During this exploration, we discovered your planet. We tried to establish communication, but there were grave difficulties. It was the time of your Dark Ages, and I'm sorry to report that those people we made contact with were generally burned at the stake." He shook his head regretfully. "Although your civilization has made many advances in some ways, communication is still hampered—as much by false knowledge as by real ignorance. You'll see in a moment why it is very unfortunate."

"Here it comes," Clocker said to those around him. "He's getting ready finally to slip us the sting."

The woman in the housecoat looked indignant. "The nerve of a crumb like you making a crack about such a fine, decent gentleman!"

"A blind man could see he's sincere," argued the tailor. "Just think of it—*me*, in a big experiment! Will Molly be surprised when she finds out!"

"She won't find out and I'll bet she's surprised right now," Clocker assured him.

"The human body is an unbelievably complicated organism," Dr. Harding was saying. The statement halted the private discussion and seemed to please his listeners for some reason. "We learned that when we tried to assume control of individuals for the purpose of communication. Billions of neural relays, thousands of unvolitional functions—it is no exaggeration to compare our efforts with those of a monkey in a power plant. At our direction, for example, several writers produced books that were fearfully garbled. Our attempts with artists were no more successful. The static of interstellar space was partly responsible, but mostly it was the fact that we simply couldn't work our way through the maze that is the human mind and body."

*   *   *   *   *

The crowd was sympathetic. Clocker was neither weary nor bored, merely longing for Zelda and, as a student of grifts, dimly irritated. Why hold back when the chumps were set up?

"I don't want to make a long story of our problems," smiled Dr. Harding. "If we could visit your planet in person, there would be no difficulty. But 10,000 light-years is an impossible barrier to all except thought waves, which, of course, travel at infinite speed. And this, as I said before, is very unfortunate, because the human race is doomed."

The tailor stiffened. "Doomed? Molly? My kids? All my customers?"

"*Your* customers?" yelped the woman in the housecoat. "How about mine? What's gonna happen, the world should be doomed?"

Clocker found admiration for Dr. Harding's approach. It was a line tried habitually by politicians, but they didn't have the same kind of captive audience, the control, the contrived background. A cosmic pitch like this could bring a galactic payoff, whatever it might be. But it didn't take his mind off Zelda.

"I see you are somewhat aghast," Dr. Harding observed. "But is my statement *really* so unexpected? You know the history of your own race—a record of incessant war, each more devastating than the last. Now, finally, Man has achieved the power of worldwide destruction. The next war, or the one after that, will unquestionably be the end not only of civilization, but of humanity—perhaps even your entire planet. Our peaceful, altruistic civilization might help avert catastrophe, but that would require our physical landing on Earth, which is not possible. Even if it were, there is not enough time. Armageddon draws near.

"Then why have we brought you here?" asked Dr. Harding. "Because Man, in spite of his suicidal blunders, is a magnificent race. He must not vanish without leaving *a complete record* of his achievements."

The crowd nodded soberly. Clocker wished he had a cigarette and his wife. In her right mind, Zelda was unswervingly practical and she would have had some noteworthy comments to make.

"This is the task we must work together on," said Dr. Harding forcefully. "Each of you has a skill, a talent, a special knowledge we need for the immense record we are compiling. Every area of human society must be covered. We need you— urgently! Your data will become part of an imperishable social document that shall exist untold eons after mankind has perished."

*   *   *   *   *

Visibly, the woman in the housecoat was stunned. "They want to put down what *I* can tell them?"

"And tailoring?" asked the little man with the pin-cushion vest. "How to make buttonholes and press clothes?"

The man who looked like a banker had his chin up and a pleased expression on his pudgy face.

"I always knew I'd be appreciated some day," he stated smugly. "I can tell them things about finance that those idiots in the main office can't even guess at."

Mr. Calhoun stood up beside Dr. Harding on the rostrum. He seemed infinitely benign as he raised his hands and his deep voice.

"Friends, we need *your* help, *your* knowledge. I *know* you don't want the human race to vanish without a *trace*, as though it had never existed. I'm *sure* it thrills you to realize that some researcher, *far* in the *future*, will one day use the very knowledge that *you* gave. Think what it means to leave *your* personal imprint indelibly on cosmic history!" He paused and leaned forward. "Will you help us?"

The faces glowed, the hands went up, the voices cried that they would.

Dazzled by the success of the sell, Clocker watched the people happily and flatteredly follow their frock-coated guides toward the various buildings, which appeared to have been laid out according to very broad categories of human occupation.

He found himself impelled along with the chattering, excited woman in the housecoat toward a cerise structure marked SPORTS AND RACKETS. It seemed that she had been angry at not having been interviewed for a recent epic survey, and this was her chance to decant the experiences of twenty years.

Clocker stopped listening to her gabble and looked for the building that Zelda would probably be in. He saw ARTS AND ENTERTAINMENT, but when he tried to go there, he felt some compulsion keep him heading toward his own destination.

Looking back helplessly, he went inside.

*   *   *   *   *

He found that he was in a cubicle with a fatherly kind of man who had thin gray hair, kindly eyes and a firm jaw, and who introduced himself as Eric Barnes. He took Clocker's name, age, specific trade, and gave him a serial number which, he explained, would go on file at the central archives on his home planet, cross-indexed in multiple ways for instant reference.

"Now," said Barnes, "here is our problem, Mr. Locke. We are making two kinds of perpetual records. One is written; more precisely, microscribed. The other is a wonderfully exact duplicate of your cerebral pattern—in more durable material than brain matter, of course."

"Of course," Clocker said, nodding like an obedient patsy.

"The verbal record is difficult enough, since much of the data you give us must be, by its nature, foreign to us. The duplication of your cerebral pattern, however, is even more troublesome. Besides the inevitable distortion caused by a distance of 10,000 light-years and the fields of gravitation and radiation of all types intervening, the substance we use in place of brain cells absorbs memory quite slowly." Barnes smiled reassuringly. "But you'll be happy to know that the impression, once made, can *never* be lost or erased!"

"Delighted," Clocker said flatly. "Tickled to pieces."

"I knew you would be. Well, let us proceed. First, a basic description of horse racing."

Clocker began to give it. Barnes held him down to a single sentence—"To check reception and retention," he said.

The communication box on the desk lit up when Clocker repeated the sentence a few times, and a voice from the box said, "Increase output. Initial impression weak. Also wave distortion. Correct and continue."

Barnes carefully adjusted the dials and Clocker went on repeating the sentence, slowing down to the speed Barnes requested. He did it automatically after a while, which gave him a chance to think.

He had no plan to get Zelda out of here; he was improvising and he didn't like it. The setup still had him puzzled. He knew he wasn't dreaming all this, for there were details his imagination could never have supplied, and the notion of spirits with scientific devices would baffle even Oil Pocket.

Everybody else appeared to accept these men as the aliens they claimed to be, but Clocker, fearing a con he couldn't understand, refused to. He had no other explanation, though, no evidence of any kind except deep suspicion of any noble-sounding enterprise. In his harsh experience, they always had a profit angle hidden somewhere.

Until he knew more, he had to go along with the routine, hoping he would eventually find a way out for Zelda and himself. While he was repeating his monotonous sentence, he wondered what his body was doing back on Earth. Lying in a bed, probably, since he wasn't being asked to perform any physical jobs like Zelda's endless time-step.

That reminded him of Doc Hawkins and the psychiatrists. There must be some here; he wished vengefully that he could meet them and see what they thought of their theories now.

*   *   *   *   *

Then came the end of what was apparently the work day.

"We're making splendid progress," Barnes told him. "I know how tiresome it is to keep saying the same thing over and over, but the distance is *such* a great obstacle. I think it's amazing that we can even *bridge* it, don't you? Just imagine—the light that's reaching Earth at this very minute left our star when mammoths were roaming your western states and mankind lived in caves! And yet, with our thought-wave boosters, we are in instantaneous communication!"

The soap, Clocker thought, to make him feel he was doing something important.

"Well, you are doing something important," Barnes said, as though Clocker had spoken.

Clocker would have turned red if he had been able to. As it was, he felt dismay and embarrassment.

"Do you realize the size and value of this project?" Barnes went on. "We have a more detailed record of human society than Man himself ever had! There will be not even the most insignificant corner of your civilization left unrecorded! Your life, my life—the life of this Zelda whom you came here to rescue—all are trivial, for we must die eventually, but the project will last eternally!"

Clocker stood up, his eyes hard and worried. "You're telling me you know what I'm here for?"

"To secure the return of your wife. I would naturally be aware that you had submitted yourself to our control voluntarily. It was in your file, which was sent to me by Admissions."

"Then why did you let me in?"

"Because, my dear friend—"

"Leave out the 'friend' pitch. I'm here on business."

Barnes shrugged. "As you wish. We let you in, as you express it, because you have knowledge that we should include in our archives. We hoped you would recognize the merit and scope of out undertaking. Most people do, once they are told."

"Zelda, too?"

"Oh, yes," Barnes said emphatically. "I had that checked by Statistics. She is extremely cooperative, quite convinced—"

"Don't hand me that!"

*   *   *   *   *

Barnes rose. Straightening the papers on his desk, he said, "You want to speak to her and see for yourself? Fair enough."

He led Clocker out of the building. They crossed the great square to a vast, low structure that Barnes referred to as the Education and Recreation Center.

"Unless there are special problems," Barnes said, "our human associates work twelve or fourteen of your hours, and the rest of the time is their own. Sleep isn't necessary to the psychic projection, of course, though it is to the body on Earth. And what, Mr. Locke, would you imagine they choose as their main amusements?"

"Pinball machines?" Clocker suggested ironically. "Crap games?"

"Lectures," said Barnes with pride. "They are eager to learn everything possible about our project. We've actually had the director himself address them! Oh, it was inspiring, Mr. Locke— color films in three dimensions, showing the great extent of our archives, the many millions of synthetic brains, each with indestructible memories of skills and crafts and professions and experiences that soon will be no more—"

"Save it. Find Zelda for me and then blow. I want to talk to her alone."

Barnes checked with the equivalent of a box office at the Center, where, he told Clocker, members of the audience and staff were required to report before entering, in case of emergency.

"Like what?" Clocker asked.

"You have a suspicious mind," said Barnes patiently. "Faulty neuron circuit in a synthetic duplicate brain, for example. Photon storms interfering with reception. Things of that sort."

"So where's the emergency?"

"We have so little time. We ask the human associate in question to record again whatever was not received. The percentage of refusal is actually *zero*! Isn't that splendid?"

"Best third degree I ever heard of," Clocker admitted through clamped teeth. "The cops on Earth would sell out every guy they get graft from to buy a thing like this."

*   *   *   *   *

They found Zelda in a small lecture hall, where a matronly woman from the other planet was urging her listeners to conceal nothing, however intimate, while recording—"Because," she said, "this must be a psychological as well as a cultural and sociological history."

Seeing Zelda, Clocker rushed to her chair, hauled her upright, kissed her, squeezed her.

"Baby!" he said, more choked up than he thought his control would allow. "Let's get out of here!"

She looked at him without surprise. "Oh, hello, Clocker. Later. I want to hear the rest of this lecture."

"Ain't you glad to see me?" he asked, hurt. "I spend months and shoot every dime I got just to find you—"

"Sure I'm glad to see you, hon," she said, trying to look past him at the speaker. "But this is so important—"

Barnes came up, bowed politely. "If you don't mind, Miss Zelda, I think you ought to talk to your husband."

"But what about the lecture?" asked Zelda anxiously.

"I can get a transcription for you to study later."

"Well, all right," she agreed reluctantly.

Barnes left them on a strangely warm stone bench in the great square, after asking them to report back to work at the usual time. Zelda, instead of looking at Clocker, watched Barnes walk away. Her eyes were bright; she almost radiated.

"Isn't he wonderful, Clocker?" she said. "Aren't they all wonderful? Regular scientists, every one of them, devoting their whole life to this terrific cause!"

"What's so wonderful about that?" he all but snarled.

She turned and gazed at him in mild astonishment. "They could let the Earth go boom. It wouldn't mean a thing to them. Everybody wiped out just like there never were any people. Not even as much record of us as the dinosaurs! Wouldn't that make you feel simply awful?"

"I wouldn't feel a thing." He took her unresponsive hand. "All I'm worried about is us, baby. Who cares about the rest of the world doing a disappearing act?"

"I do. And so do they. They aren't selfish like some people I could mention."

"Selfish? You're damned right I am!"

*   *   *   *   *

He pulled her to him, kissed her neck in her favorite place. It got a reaction—restrained annoyance.

"I'm selfish," he said, "because I got a wife I'm nuts about and I want her back. They got you wrapped, baby. Can't you see that? You belong with me in some fancy apartment, the minute I can afford it, like one I saw over on Riverside Drive—seven big rooms, three baths, one of them with a stall shower like you always wanted, the Hudson River and Jersey for our front lawn—"

"That's all in the past, hon," she said with quiet dignity. "I have to help out on this project. It's the least I can do for history."

"The hell with history! What did history ever do for us?" He put his mouth near her ear, breathing gently in the way that once used to make her squirm in his arms like a tickled doe. "Go turn in your time-card, baby. Tell them you got a date with me back on Earth."

She pulled away and jumped up. "No! This is my job as much as theirs. More, even. They don't keep anybody here against their will. I'm staying because I want to, Clocker."

Furious, he snatched her off her feet. "I say you're coming back with me! If you don't want to, I'll drag you, see?"

"How?" she asked calmly.

He put her down again slowly, frustratedly. "Ask them to let you go, baby. Oil Pocket said he'd put you in a musical. You always did want to hit the big time—"

"Not any more." She smoothed down her dress and patted up her hair. "Well, I want to catch the rest of that lecture, hon. See you around if you decide to stay."

He sat down morosely and watched her snake-hip toward the Center, realizing that her seductive walk was no more than professional conditioning. She had grown in some mysterious way, become more serene—at peace.

He had wondered what catatonics got for their work. He knew now—the slickest job of hypnotic flattery ever invented. That was *their* pay.

But what did the pitchmen get in return?

*   *   *   *   *

Clocker put in a call for Barnes at the box office of the Center. Barnes left a lecture for researchers from his planet and joined Clocker with no more than polite curiosity on his paternal face. Clocker told him briefly and bitterly about his talk with Zelda, and asked bluntly what was in it for the aliens.

"I think you can answer that," said Barnes. "You're a scientist of a sort. You determine the probable performance of a group of horses by their heredity, previous races and other factors. A very laborious computation, calling for considerable aptitude and skill. With that same expenditure of energy, couldn't you earn more in other fields?"

"I guess so," Clocker said. "But I like the track."

"Well, there you are. The only human form of gain we share is desire for knowledge. You devote your skill to predicting a race that is about to be run; we devote ours to recording a race that is about to destroy itself."

Clocker grabbed the alien's coat, pushed his face grimly close. "There, that's the hook! Take away the doom push and this racket folds."

Barnes looked bewildered. "I don't comprehend—"

"Listen, suppose everything's square. Let's say you guys really are leveling, these marks aren't being roped, you're knocking yourself out because your guess is that we're going to commit suicide."

"Oh." Barnes nodded somberly. "Is there any doubt of it? Do you honestly believe the holocaust can be averted?"

"I think it can be stopped, yeah. But you birds act like you don't want it to be. You're just laying back, letting us bunch up, collecting the insurance before the spill happens."

"What else can we do? We're scientists, not politicians. Besides, we've tried repeatedly to spread the warning and never once succeeded in transmitting it."

Clocker released his grip on the front of Barnes's jacket. "You take me to the president or commissioner or whoever runs this club. Maybe we can work something out."

"We have a board of directors," Barnes said doubtfully. "But I can't see—"

"Don't rupture yourself trying. Just take me there and let me do the talking."

Barnes moved his shoulders resignedly. He led Clocker to the Administration Building and inside to a large room with paneled walls, a long, solid table and heavy, carved chairs. The men who sat around the table appeared as solid and respectable as the furniture. Clocker's guess was that they had been chosen deliberately, along with the decorations, to inspire confidence in the customer. He had been in rigged horse parlors and bond stores and he knew the approach.

*   *   *   *   *

Mr. Calhoun, the character with the white beard, was chairman of the board. He looked unhappily at Clocker.

"I was afraid there would be trouble," he said. "I voted against accepting you, you know. My colleagues, however, thought that you, as our first voluntary associate, might indicate new methods, but I fear my judgment has been vindicated."

"Still, if he knows how extinction can be prevented—" began Dr. Harding, the one who had given the orientation lecture.

"He knows no such thing," a man with several chins said in an emphatic basso voice. "Man is the most destructive dominant race we have ever encountered. He despoiled his own planet, exterminated lower species that were important to his own existence, oppressed, suppressed, brutalized, corrupted—it's the saddest chronicle in the Universe."

"Therefore his achievements," said Dr. Harding, "deserve all the more recognition!"

Clocker broke in: "If you'll lay off the gab, I'd like to get my bet down."

"Sorry," said Mr. Calhoun. "Please proceed, Mr. Locke."

Clocker rested his knuckles on the table and leaned over them. "I have to take your word you ain't human, but you don't have to take mine. I never worried about anybody but Zelda and myself; that makes me human. All I want is to get along and not hurt anybody if I can help it; that makes me what some people call the common man. Some of my best friends are common men. Come to think of it, they all are. They wouldn't want to get extinct. If we do, it won't be our fault."

Several of the men nodded sympathetic agreement.

"I don't read much except the sport sheets, but I got an idea what's coming up," Clocker continued, "and it's a long shot that any country can finish in the money. We'd like to stop war for good, all of us. Little guys who do the fighting and the dying. Yeah, and lots of big guys, too. But we can't do it alone."

"That's precisely our point," said Calhoun.

"I mean us back on Earth. People are afraid, but they just don't know for sure that we can knock ourself off. Between these catatonics and me, we could tell them what it's all about. I notice you got people from all over the world here, all getting along fine because they have a job to do and no time to hate each other. Well, it could be like that on Earth. You let us go back and you'll see a selling job on making it like up here like you never saw before."

Mr. Calhoun and Dr. Harding looked at each other and around the table. Nobody seemed willing to answer.

Mr. Calhoun finally sighed and got out of his big chair. "Mr. Locke, besides striving for international understanding, we have experimented in the manner you suggest. We released many of our human associates to tell what our science predicts on the basis of probability. A human psychological mechanism defeated us."

"Yeah?" Clocker asked warily. "What was that?"

"Protective amnesia. They completely and absolutely forgot everything they had learned here."

*　*　*　*　*

Clocker slumped a bit. "I know. I talked to some of these 'cured' catatonics—people you probably sprung because you got all you wanted from them. They didn't remember anything." He braced again. "Look, there has to be a way out. Maybe if you snatch these politicians in all the countries, yank them up here, they couldn't stumble us into a war."

"Examine your history," said Dr. Harding sadly, "and you will find that we have done this experimentally. It doesn't work. There are always others, often more unthinking, ignorant, stupid or vicious, ready to take their places."

Clocker looked challengingly at every member of the board of directors before demanding, "What are the odds on me remembering?"

"You are our first volunteer," said a little man at the side of the table. "Any answer we give would be a guess."

"All right, guess."

"We have a theory that your psychic censor might not operate. Of course, you realize that's only a theory—"

"That ain't all I don't realize. What's it mean?"

"Our control, regrettably, is a wrench to the mind. Lifting it results in amnesia, which is a psychological defense against disturbing memories."

"I walked into this, don't forget," Clocker reminded him. "I didn't know what I was getting into, but I was ready to take anything."

"That," said the little man, "is the unknown factor. Yes, you did submit voluntarily and you were ready to take anything— but were you psychologically prepared for this? We don't know. We *think* there may be no characteristic wrench—"

"Meaning I won't have amnesia?"

"Meaning that you *may* not. We cannot be certain until a test has been made."

"Then," said Clocker, "I want a deal. It's Zelda I want; you know that, at any rate. You say you're after a record of us in case we bump ourself off, but you also say you'd like us not to. I'll buy that. I don't want us to, either, and there's a chance that we can stop it together."

"An extremely remote one," Mr. Calhoun stated.

"Maybe, but a chance. Now if you let me out and I'm the first case that don't get amnesia, I can tell the world about all this. I might be able to steer other guys, scientists and decent politicians, into coming here to get the dope straighter than I could. Maybe that'd give Earth a chance to cop a pardon on getting extinct. Even if it don't work, it's better than hanging around the radio waiting for the results."

$$* \quad * \quad * \quad * \quad *$$

Dr. Harding hissed on his glasses and wiped them thoughtfully, an adopted mannerism, obviously, because he seemed to see as well without them. "You have a point, Mr. Locke, but it would mean losing your contribution to our archives."

"Well, which is more important?" Clocker argued. "Would you rather have my record than have us save ourself?"

"Both," said Mr. Calhoun. "We see very little hope of your success, while we regard your knowledge as having important sociological significance. A very desirable contribution."

The others agreed.

"Look, I'll come back if I lame out," Clocker desperately offered. "You can pick me up any time you want. But if I make headway, you got to let Zelda go, too."

"A reasonable proposition," said Dr. Harding. "I call for a vote."

They took one. The best Clocker could get was a compromise.

"We will lift our control," Mr. Calhoun said, "for a suitable time. If you can arouse a measurable opposition to racial suicide—*measurable*, mind you; we're not requiring that you reverse the lemming march alone—we agree to release your wife and revise our policy completely. If, on the other hand, as seems more likely—"

"I come back here and go on giving you the inside on racing," Clocker finished for him. "How much time do I get?"

Dr. Harding turned his hands palm up on the table. "We do not wish to be arbitrary. We earnestly hope you gain your objective and we shall give you every opportunity to do so. If you fail, you will know it. So shall we."

"You're pretty sure I'll get scratched, aren't you?" Clocker asked angrily. "It's like me telling a jockey he don't stand a chance—he's whammied before he even gets to the paddock. Anybody'd think do-gooders like you claim you are would wish me luck."

"But we do!" exclaimed Mr. Calhoun. He shook Clocker's hand warmly and sincerely. "Haven't we consented to release you? Doesn't this prove our honest concern? If releasing *all* our human associates would save humanity, we would do so instantly. But we have tried again and again. And so, to use your own professional terminology, we are hedging our bets by continuing to make our anthropological record until you demonstrate another method ... if you do."

"Good enough," approved Clocker. "Thanks for the kind word."

The other board members followed and shook Clocker's hand and wished him well.

Barnes, being last, did the same and added, "You may see your wife, if you care to, before you leave."

"If I care to?" Clocker repeated. "What in hell do you think I came here for in the first place?"

*   *   *   *   *

Zelda was brought to him and they were left alone in a pleasant reading room. Soft music came from the walls, which glowed with enough light to read by. Zelda's lovely face was warm with emotion when she sat down beside him and put her hands in his.

"They tell me you're leaving, hon," she said.

"I made a deal, baby. If it works— well, it'll be like it was before, only better."

"I hate to see you leave. Not just for me," she added as he lit up hopefully. "I still love you, hon, but it's different now. I used to want you near me every minute. Now it's loving you without starving for you. You know what I mean?"

"That's just the control they got on you. It's like that with me, too, only I know what it is and you don't."

"But the big thing is the project. Why, we're footnotes in history! Stay here, hon. I'd feel so much better knowing you were here, making your contribution like they say."

He kissed her lips. They were soft and warm and clinging, and so were her arms around his neck. This was more like the Zelda he had been missing.

"They gave you a hypo, sweetheart," he told her. "You're hooked; I'm not. Maybe being a footnote is more important than doing something to save our skin, but I don't think so. If I can do anything about it, I want to do it."

"Like what?"

"I don't know," he admitted. "I'm hoping I get an idea when I'm paroled."

She nuzzled under his chin. "Hon, I want you and me to be footnotes. I want it awful bad."

"That's not what really counts, baby. Don't you see that? It's having you and stopping us humans from being just a bunch of old footnotes. Once we do that, we can always come back here and make the record, if it means that much to you."

"Oh, it does!"

He stood and drew her up so he could hold her more tightly. "You do want to go on being my wife, don't you, baby?"

"Of course! Only I was hoping it could be here."

"Well, it can't. But that's all I wanted to know. The rest is just details."

He kissed her again, including the side of her neck, which produced a subdued wriggle of pleasure, and then he went back to the Administration Building for his release.

*   *   *   *   *

Awakening was no more complicated than opening his eyes, except for a bit of fogginess and fatigue that wore off quickly, and Clocker saw he was in a white room with a doctor, a nurse and an orderly around his bed.

"Reflexes normal," the doctor said. He told Clocker, "You see and hear us. You know what I'm saying."

"Sure," Clocker replied. "Why shouldn't I?"

"That's right," the doctor evaded. "How do you feel?"

Clocker thought about it. He was a little thirsty and the idea of a steak interested him, but otherwise he felt no pain or confusion. He remembered that he had not been hungry or thirsty for a long time, and that made him recall going over the border after Zelda.

There were no gaps in his recollection.

He didn't have protective amnesia.

"You know what it's like there?" he asked the doctor eagerly. "A big place where everybody from all over the world tell these aliens about their job or racket." He frowned. "I just remembered something funny. Wonder why I didn't notice it at the time. Everybody talks the same language. Maybe that's because there's only one language for thinking." He shrugged off the problem. "The guys who run the shop take it all down as a record for whoever wants to know about us a zillion years from now. That's on account of us humans are about to close down the track and go home."

The doctor bent close intently. "Is that what you believe *now* or—while you were—disturbed?"

Clocker's impulse to blurt the whole story was stopped at the gate. The doctor was staring too studiously at him. He didn't have his story set yet; he needed time to think, and that meant getting out of this hospital and talking it over with himself.

"You kidding?" he asked, using the same grin that he met complainers with when his turf predictions went sour. "While my head was out of the stirrups, of course."

The doctor, the nurse and the orderly relaxed.

* * * * *

"I ought to write a book," Clocker went on, being doggedly humorous. "What screwball ideas I got! How'd I act?"

"Not bad," said the orderly. "When I found you yakking in your wife's room, I thought maybe it was catching and I'd better go find another job. But Doc here told me I was too stable to go psychotic."

"I wasn't any trouble?"

"Nah. All you did was talk about how to handicap races. I got quite a few pointers. Hell, you went over them often enough for anybody to get them straight!"

"I'm glad somebody made a profit," said Clocker. He asked the doctor, "When do I get out of here?"

"We'll have to give you a few tests first."

"Bring them on," Clocker said confidently.

They were clever tests, designed to trip him into revealing whether he still believed in his delusions. But once he realized that, he meticulously joked about them.

"Well?" he asked when the tests were finished.

"You're all right," said the doctor. "Just try not to worry about your wife, avoid overworking, get plenty of rest—"

Before Clocker left, he went to see Zelda. She had evidently recorded the time-step satisfactorily, because she was on a soft-shoe routine that she must have known cold by the time she'd been ten.

He kissed her unresponsive mouth, knowing that she was far away in space and could not feel, see or hear him. But that didn't matter. He felt his own good, honest, genuine longing for her, unchecked by the aliens' control of emotions.

"I'll spring you yet, baby," he said. "And what I told you about that big apartment on Riverside Drive still goes. We'll have a time together that ought to be a footnote in history all by itself. I'll see you ... after I get the real job done."

He heard the soft-shoe rhythm all the way down the corridor, out of the hospital, and clear back to the city.

*　　*　　*　　*　　*

Clocker's bank balance was sick, the circulation of his tip sheet gone. But he didn't worry about it; there were bigger problems.

He studied the newspapers before even giving himself time to think. The news was as bad as usual. He could feel the heat of fission, close his eyes and see all the cities and farms in the world going up in a blinding cloud. As far as he was concerned, Barnes and Harding and the rest weren't working fast enough; he could see doom sprinting in half a field ahead of the completion of the record.

The first thing he should have done was recapture the circulation of the tip sheet. The first thing he actually did do was write the story of his experience just as it had happened, and send it to a magazine.

When he finally went to work on his sheet, it was to cut down the racing data to a few columns and fill the rest of it with warnings.

"This is what you want?" the typesetter asked, staring at the copy Clocker turned in. "You *sure* this is what you want?"

"Sure I'm sure. Set it and let's get the edition out early. I'm doubling the print order."

"Doubling?"

"You heard me."

When the issue was out, Clocker waited around the main newsstands on Broadway. He watched the customers buy, study unbelievingly, and wander off looking as if all the tracks in the country had burned down simultaneously.

Doc Hawkins found him there.

"Clocker, my boy! You have no idea how anxious we were about you. But you're looking fit, I'm glad to say."

"Thanks," Clocker said abstractedly. "I wish I could say the same about you and the rest of the world."

Doc laughed. "No need to worry about us. We'll muddle along somehow."

"You think so, huh?"

"Well, if the end is approaching, let us greet it at the Blue Ribbon. I believe we can still find the lads there."

They were, and they greeted Clocker with gladness and drinks. Diplomatically, they made only the most delicate references to the revamping job Clocker had done on his tip sheet.

"It's just like opening night, that's all," comforted Arnold Wilson Wyle. "You'll get back into your routine pretty soon."

"I don't want to," said Clocker pugnaciously. "Handicapping is only a way to get people to read what I *really* want to tell them."

"Took me many minutes to find horses," Oil Pocket put in. "See one I want to bet on, but rest of paper make me too worried to bother betting. Okay with Injun, though—horse lost. And soon you get happy again, stick to handicapping, let others worry about world."

Buttonhole tightened his grip on Clocker's lapel. "Sure, boy. As long as the bobtails run, who cares what happens to anything else?"

"Maybe I went too easy," said Clocker tensely. "I didn't print the whole thing, just a little part of it. Here's the rest."

*   *   *   *   *

They were silent while he talked, seeming stunned with the terrible significance of his story.

"Did you explain all this to the doctors?" Doc Hawkins asked.

"You think I'm crazy?" Clocker retorted. "They'd have kept me packed away and I'd never get a crack at telling anybody."

"Don't let it trouble you," said Doc. "Some vestiges of delusion can be expected to persist for a while, but you'll get rid of them. I have faith in your ability to distinguish between the real and unreal."

"But it all *happened*! If you guys don't believe me, who will? And you've *got* to so I can get Zelda back!"

"Of course, of course," said Doc hastily. "We'll discuss it further some other time. Right now I really must start putting my medical column together for the paper."

"What about you, Handy Sam?" Clocker challenged.

Handy Sam, with one foot up on the table and a pencil between his toes, was doodling self-consciously on a paper napkin. "We all get these ideas, Clocker. I used to dream about having arms and I'd wake up still thinking so, till I didn't know if I did or didn't. But like Doc says, then you figure out what's real and it don't mix you up any more."

"All right," Clocker said belligerently to Oil Pocket. "You think my story's batty, too?"

"Can savvy evil spirits, good spirits," Oil Pocket replied with stolid tact. "Injun spirits, though, not white ones."

"But I keep telling you they ain't spirits. They ain't even human. They're from some world way across the Universe—"

Oil Pocket shook his head. "Can savvy Injun spirits, Clocker. No spirits, no savvy."

"Look, you see the mess we're all in, don't you?" Clocker appealed to the whole group. "Do you mean to tell me you can't feel we're getting set to blow the joint? Wouldn't you want to stop it?"

"If we could, my boy, gladly," Doc said. "However, there's not much that any individual or group of individuals can do."

"But how in hell does anything get started? With one guy, two guys—before you know it, you got a crowd, a political party, a country—"

"What about the other countries, though?" asked Buttonhole. "So we're sold on your story in America, let's say. What do we do—let the rest of the world walk in and take us over?"

"We educate them," Clocker explained despairingly. "We start it here and it spreads to there. It doesn't have to be everybody. Mr. Calhoun said I just have to convince a few people and that'll show them it can be done and then I get Zelda back."

Doc stood up and glanced around the table. "I believe I speak for all of us, Clocker, when I state that we shall do all within our power to aid you."

"Like telling other people?" Clocker asked eagerly.

"Well, that's going pretty—"

"Forget it, then. Go write your column. I'll see you chumps around—around ten miles up, shaped like a mushroom."

He stamped out, so angry that he untypically let the others settle his bill.

*   *   *   *   *

Clocker's experiment with the newspaper failed so badly that it was not worth the expense of putting it out; people refused to buy. Clocker had three-sheets printed and hired sandwich men to parade them through the city. He made violent speeches in Columbus Circle, where he lost his audience to revivalist orators; Union Square, where he was told heatedly to bring his message to Wall Street; and Times Square, where the police made him move along so he wouldn't block traffic. He obeyed, shouting his message as he walked, until he remembered how amusedly he used to listen to those who cried that Doomsday was near. He wondered if they were catatonics under imperfect control. It didn't matter; nobody paid serious attention to his or their warnings.

The next step, logically, was a barrage of letters to the heads of nations, to the U.N., to editors of newspapers. Only a few of his letters were printed. The ones in Doc's tabloid did best, drawing such comments as:

"Who does this jerk think he is, telling us everybody's going to get killed off? Maybe they will, but not in Brooklyn!"

"When I was a young girl, some fifty years ago, I had a similar experience to Mr. Locke's. But my explanation is quite simple. The persons I saw proved to be my ancestors. Mr. Locke's new-found friends will, I am sure, prove to be the same. The World Beyond knows all and tells all, and my Control, with whom I am in daily communication Over There, assures me that mankind is in no danger whatever, except from the evil effects of tobacco and alcohol and the disrespect of youth for their elders."

"The guy's nuts! He ought to go back to Russia. He's nothing but a nut or a Communist and in my book that's the same thing."

"He isn't telling us anything new. We all know who the enemy is. The only way to protect ourselves is to build TWO GUNS FOR ONE!"

"Is this Locke character selling us the idea that we all ought to go batty to save the world?"

Saddened and defeated, Clocker went through his accumulated mail. There were politely non-committal acknowledgments from embassies and the U.N. There was also a check for his article from the magazine he'd sent it to; the amount was astonishingly large.

He used part of it to buy radio time, the balance for ads in rural newspapers and magazines. City people, he figured, were hardened by publicity gags, and he might stir up the less suspicious and sophisticated hinterland. The replies he received, though, advised him to buy some farmland and let the metropolises be destroyed, which, he was assured, would be a mighty good thing all around.

The magazine came out the same day he tried to get into the U.N. to shout a speech from the balcony. He was quietly surrounded by a uniformed guard and moved, rather than forced, outside.

*   *   *   *   *

He went dejectedly to his hotel. He stayed there for several days, dialing numbers he selected randomly from the telephone book, and getting the brushoff from business offices, housewives and maids. They were all very busy or the boss wasn't in or they expected important calls.

That was when he was warmly invited by letter to see the editor of the magazine that had bought his article.

Elated for actually the first time since his discharge from the hospital, Clocker took a cab to a handsome building, showed his invitation to a pretty and courteous receptionist, and was escorted into an elaborate office where a smiling man came around a wide bleached-mahogany desk and shook hands with him.

"Mr. Locke," said the editor, "I'm happy to tell you that we've had a wonderful response to your story."

"Article," Clocker corrected.

The editor smiled. "Do you produce so much that you can't remember what you sold us? It was about—"

"I know," Clocker cut in. "But it wasn't a story. It was an article. It really—"

"Now, now. The first thing a writer must learn is not to take his ideas too seriously. Very dangerous, especially in a piece of fiction like yours."

"But the whole thing is true!"

"Certainly—while you were writing it." The editor shoved a pile of mail across the desk toward him. "Here are some of the comments that have come in. I think you'll enjoy seeing the reaction."

Clocker went through them, hoping anxiously for no more than a single note that would show his message had come through to somebody. He finished and looked up blankly.

"You see?" the editor asked proudly. "You're a find."

"The new Mark Twain or Jonathan Swift. A comic."

"A satirist," the editor amended. He leaned across the desk on his crossed forearms. "A mail response like this indicates a talent worth developing. We would like to discuss a series of stories—"

"Articles."

"Whatever you choose to call them. We're prepared to—"

"You ever been off your rocker?" Clocker asked abruptly.

*   *   *   *   *

The editor sat back, smiling with polite puzzlement. "Why, no."

"You ought to try it some time." Clocker lifted himself out of the chair and went to the door. "That's what I want, what I was trying to sell in my article. We all ought to go to hospitals and get ourself let in and have these aliens take over and show us where we're going."

"You think that would be an improvement?"

"What wouldn't?" asked Clocker, opening the door.

"But about the series—"

"I've got your name and address. I'll let you know if anything turns up. Don't call me; I'll call you."

Clocker closed the door behind him, went out of the handsome building and called a taxi. All through the long ride, he stared at the thinning out of the city, the huddled suburban communities, the stretches of grass and well-behaved woods that were permitted to survive.

He climbed out at Glendale Center Hospital, paid the hackie, and went to the admitting desk. The nurse gave him a smile.

"We were wondering when you'd come visit your wife," she said. "Been away?"

"Sort of," he answered, with as little emotion as he had felt while he was being controlled. "I'll be seeing plenty of her from now on. I want my old room back."

"But you're perfectly normal!"

"That depends on how you look at it. Give me ten minutes alone and any brain vet will be glad to give me a cushioned room."

Hands in his pockets, Clocker went into the elevator, walked down the corridor to his old room without pausing to visit Zelda. It was the live Zelda he wanted to see, not the tapping automaton.

He went in and shut the door.

*   *   *   *   *

"Okay, you were right and I was wrong," Clocker told the board of directors. "Turn me over to Barnes and I'll give him the rest of the dope on racing. Just let me see Zelda once in a while and you won't have any trouble with me."

"Then you are convinced that you have failed," said Mr. Calhoun.

"I'm no dummy. I know when I'm licked. I also pay anything I owe."

Mr. Calhoun leaned back. "And so do we, Mr. Locke. Naturally, you have no way of detecting the effect you've had. We do. The result is that, because of your experiment, we are gladly revising our policy."

"Huh?" Clocker looked around at the comfortable aliens in their comfortable chairs. Solid and respectable, every one of them. "Is this a rib?"

"Visits to catatonics have increased considerably," explained Dr. Harding. "When the visitors are alone with our human associates, they tentatively follow the directions you gave in your article. Not all do, to be sure; only those who feel as strongly about being with their loved ones as you do about your wife."

"We have accepted four voluntary applicants," said Mr. Calhoun.

Clocker's mouth seemed to be filled with cracker crumbs that wouldn't go down and allow him to speak.

"And now," Dr. Harding went on, "we are setting up an Information Section to teach the applicants what you have learned and make the same arrangement we made with you. We are certain that we shall, before long, have to increase our staff as the number of voluntary applicants increases geometrically, after we release the first few to continue the work you have so admirably begun."

"You mean I *made* it?" Clocker croaked unbelievingly.

"Perhaps this will prove it to you," said Mr. Calhoun.

He motioned and the door opened and Zelda came in.

"Hello, hon," she said. "I'm glad you're back. I missed you."

"Not like I missed you, baby! There wasn't anybody controlling *my* feelings."

Mr. Calhoun put his hands on their shoulders. "Whenever you care to, Mr. Locke, you and your wife are free to leave."

Clocker held Zelda's hands and her calmly fond gaze. "We owe these guys plenty, baby," he said to her. "We'll help make the record before we take off. Ain't that what you want?"

"Oh, it is, hon! And then I want you."

"Then let's get started," he said. "The quicker we do, the quicker we get back."

THE ENORMOUS ROOM

BY H. L. GOLD & ROBERT KREPPS
ORIGINALLY PUBLISHED IN *AMAZING STORIES*,
OCT.-NOV. 1953

One big name per story is usually considered to be sufficient. So when two of them appear in one by-line, it can certainly be called a scoop; so that's what we'll call it. H. L. Gold and science-fiction go together like a blonde and a henna rinse. Robert Krepps is also big time. You may know him also under his other label—Geoff St. Reynard, but a Krepps by any name can write as well.

THE ENORMOUS ROOM

The roller coaster's string of cars, looking shopworn in their flaky blue and orange paint, crept toward the top of the incline, the ratcheted lift chain clanking with weary patience. In the front seat, a young couple held hands and prepared to scream. Two cars back, a heavy, round-shouldered, black-mustached man with a swarthy skin clenched his hands on the rail before him. A thin blond fellow with a briefcase on his lap glanced back and down at the receding platform, as though trying to spot a friend he had left behind. Behind him was a Negro youth, sitting relaxed with one lean foot on the seat; he looked as bored as someone who'd taken a thousand coaster rides in a summer and expected to take ten thousand more.

In the last car, a tall broad man put his elbows on the backboard and stared at the sky without any particular expression on his lined face.

The chain carried its load to the peak and relinquished it to the force of gravity. The riders had a glimpse of the sprawling amusement park spread out below them like a collection of gaudy toys on the floor of a playroom; then the coaster was roaring and thundering down into the hollow of the first big dip.

Everyone but the Negro boy and the tall man yelled. These two looked detached—without emotion—as though they wouldn't have cared if the train of cars went off the tracks.

The cars didn't go off the tracks. The people did.

The orange-blue rolling stock hit the bottom, slammed around a turn and shot upward again, the wind of its passage

whistling boisterously. But by then there were none to hear the
wind, to feel the gust of it in watered eyes or open shouting
mouths. The cars were empty.

*   *   *   *   *

"Is this what happens to *everybody* who takes a ride on the
coaster?" asked a bewildered voice with a slight Mexican accent.
"*Santos*," it continued, "to think I have waited so many years for
this!"

"What is it?" said a woman. "Was there an accident? Where
are we?"

"I don't know, dear. Maybe we jumped the tracks. But it
certainly doesn't look like a hospital."

John Summersby opened his eyes. The last voice had told the
truth: the room didn't look like a hospital. It didn't look like
anything that he could think of offhand.

It was about living-room size, with flat yellow walls and a
gray ceiling. There was a quantity of musty-smelling straw on
the floor. Four tree trunks from which the branches had been
lopped were planted solidly in that floor, which felt hard and a
little warm on Summersby's back. Near the roof was a round
silver rod, running from wall to wall; over in a corner was a large
shallow box filled with something, he saw as he slowly stood up,
that might have been sand. An old automobile tire lay in the
straw nearby, and a green bird-bath sort of thing held water that
splashed from a tiny fountain in its center. Five other people,
four men and a woman, were standing or sitting on the floor.

"If it was a hospital, we'd be hurt," said a thin yellow-haired
man with a briefcase under one arm. "I'm all right. Feel as good
as I ever did."

Several men prodded themselves experimentally, and one
began to take his own pulse. Summersby stretched and blinked
his eyes; they felt gummy, as though he'd been asleep a long
time, but his mouth wasn't cottony, so he figured the blacked-out
interval must have been fairly short.

"Where's the door?" asked the woman.

Everyone stared around the room except Summersby, who
went to the fountain, scooped up a palmful of water, and drank
it. It was rather warm, with no chemical taste.

"There isn't any door," said a Negro boy. "Hey, there isn't a door at all!"

"There must be a door," said the heavy man with the accent.

Several of them ran to the walls. "Here's something," said the blond man, pushing with his fingertips. "Looks like a sliding panel, but it won't budge. We never came in through anything *that* small, anyway." He looked over at Summersby. "You didn't, at least. I guess they could have slid me through it."

"They?" said the woman in a piercing voice. "Who are they?"

"Yes," said the heavy man, looking at the blond man accusingly, "who put us here?"

"Don't ask me," said the blond man. He looked at a watch, held it to his ear, and Summersby saw him actually go pale, as at a terrible shock. "My God," he gasped, "what day is this?"

"Tuesday," said the Negro.

"That's right. We got on the coaster about eleven Tuesday morning. It's three o'clock Thursday!" His voice was flat and astonished as he held up the watch. "Two days," he said, winding it. "This thing's almost run down."

"How do you know it's Thursday?" asked Summersby.

"This is a chronograph, High-pockets," said the blond man.

"Calvin, we've been kidnapped!" the woman said shrilly, clutching at a man who must be her husband or boy friend.

"No, no, dear. How could they do it on a roller coaster?"

"*Maria y Jose!*" said the Mexican. "Then for two days that idiot relief man has had charge of my chili stand! It'll go to hell!"

"Our things at the hotel," the woman said, "all my new clothes and the marriage license."

"They'll be all right, dear."

"And where's my bag?"

The blond man stooped and picked up a leather handbag from the straw. "This it?" She took it and rummaged inside before she said, "Thank you."

"I don't like all this," said the Negro boy. "Where are we? I got to get back to my job. Where's the door?"

*   *   *   *   *

"Come on," said the man with the briefcase shortly, "let's get out of here and find out what's what." He was going along the wall, pushing and rapping it. "How did they cop us, that's what I'd like to know. All I remember is hitting the bottom of that big dip, and then I was waking up in here." He stopped, then said sharply, "I hear something moving. My God! It sounds as big as an elephant."

Then the wall began to glide noiselessly and smoothly to the left, and he scuttled back to the knot of them, looking over his shoulder.

The entire wall slid sideways and vanished, leaving an open end to the room through which Summersby could see a number of large structures that seemed to be machinery, painted various colors. There was no sign of movement. He wondered, in a quiet, detached way, what sort of people might be out there.

"It sounded big," said the blond man again, and looked up at Summersby.

"I am six feet five," said Summersby bleakly. "Whoever it is will have to go some to top me."

*   *   *   *   *

Illustrator: Tom O'Sullivan

An unknown thing moved beyond the room with a brief shuffling sound and then a hand came in through the open end. It was on an arm with a wrist the thickness of Summersby's biceps, an arm two yards long with no indication that it might not be even longer. The hand itself was a foot and a half broad, with a prehensile thumb at either side. Summersby did not notice how many fingers it had. The backs of the fingers and the whole great arm were covered with a thick gray-black thatch of coarse hair, and the naked palm was gun-metal gray. Between one thumb and finger it held a long green rod that was tipped by an ivory-colored ball.

There was no sign of anyone looking in, only the incredible arm and hand.

The others cried out and drew together. Summersby stood still, watching the hand. It poked the stick forward in short jabs, once just missing his head. Then it made a wide sweep and the stick collided with the fat Mexican. He squealed, and at once the hand shot forward, exposing still more of the thick arm, and prodded him away from the group. He skipped toward a far corner, but the stick had him now and was tapping him relentlessly toward the open end.

"*Amigos!*" he yelled, his voice full of anguish. "*Por favor*, save me!"

"Go along with it peaceably," advised the Negro youth frightenedly. "Don't get it annoyed." He was shaking and his glasses kept sliding down his sweaty nose so that he had to push them up continually.

"What is it?" the woman was asking, over and over.

The Mexican was driven to the edge of the room. The place beyond seemed to be much larger than their prison. He waved his hands despairingly.

"Now, quick, you have only a *momentito* to save me! Don't *stand* there!"

The stick touched him and he jumped as if he had been shocked. The wall began to slide into place again.

"Let's rush it," said the man with the briefcase suddenly.

"Why?" asked Summersby. The wall closed and they were alone, staring at one another.

*　　*　　*　　*　　*

"There wasn't anything we could do," the Negro said. "It happened too quick. But if it comes in again we better fight it." He looked around, plainly expecting to be contradicted. "We can't get split up like this."

"Possibly one of us can suggest something," said the husband. He was a sober-looking man of about twenty-eight or thirty, with a face veneered by stubborn patience. "We should make a real try at escape."

"We know where the door is, at least," said the blond man. He went to the sliding wall and threw his weight obliquely against it. "Give me a hand here, will you, big fellow?"

"You won't move it that way," said Summersby. He sat down on the automobile tire, which seemed to have been chewed on by some large animal. "It's probably electrically operated."

"We can try, can't we?"

Summersby did not answer. In one corner, six feet off the floor, was a thing he had not noticed before, a network of silver strands like an enormous spider's web or a cat's cradle. He stared at it, but after the first moment he did not actually see it. He was thinking of the forest, and wishing dully that he might have died there.

The woman spoke sharply, intruding on his detachment; he hoped someone would sit on her. "Will you please *do* something, Calvin! We must get out of this place."

"Where are we, anyway?" asked the Negro boy, who looked about nineteen, a tall, well-built youth with beautiful hands. "How'd they get us here? And what was that thing that took the Mex?"

"It doesn't matter where we are," snapped the woman.

"Yes, it does, ma'am," said the youth. "We got to know how they brought us here before we can escape."

"The hell we do," said the blond man. "We can't guess our location until we get out. I think you're right about the door," he told Summersby. "There isn't any lock to it you could reach from inside. The mechanism for sliding and locking must be inside the wall itself. Nothing short of a torch will get through to it." He came over to Summersby. "We'll have to gimmick it next time it opens."

"With what?" asked the woman's husband.

"Something small, so it won't be noticed."

"Your briefcase?" suggested the husband, who had a hard New England twang.

"No, chum," said the blond man, "not my briefcase."

"Hey, look," said the Negro. "What happened, anyway? I remember the coaster hitting the dip and then nothing, no wind or motion, until I woke up here. And it's two days later."

"I lost consciousness at the same place," said the New Englander.

"Something was done to knock us out," said the blond man. "Then we must have been taken off the cars at the end of the ride, and brought here." He rubbed his chin, which was stubbled with almost invisible whiskers. "That's impossible, on the face of it," he went on, "but it must be the truth." He grinned; it was the first time Summersby had seen any of them smile. "Unless I'm in a hatch," he said.

"Are we in South America? Or Africa?" asked the Negro.

"Why?"

"That hand!"

"Yeah," said the blond man, "that never grew on anything American." The colored boy looked at him, ready to take offence. "Could it be a freak gorilla?"

"That size and with two thumbs?" asked the boy. "And what would it be doing roaming around loose?"

"Could it be a machine?" asked the husband. "A robot?" His wife screamed, and Summersby got up and went over to the door, getting as far as possible from them. His stomach was a hard ball of hunger, and he wished he were a thousand miles away. Anywhere.

"That hand was alive," said the Negro. "I never saw anything like it in biology, but I'd sure love to dissect it. Did you see those two thumbs? I don't know any animal that has two thumbs."

"Would you come over, sir?" called the New Englander. Summersby realized he was talking to him. "We must plan a course of action." Reluctantly Summersby joined them. "My name is Calvin Full, sir, and this is Mrs. Full."

Summersby took his hand; it was dry and had a preciseness about its grip that irritated him. "John Summersby."

"I'm a milk inspector. My wife and I were on our honeymoon," said Full. "I work through the southern portions of Vermont; that's in the New York milk shed, you know."

"I didn't know. I'm a forest ranger," said Summersby. Retired, he thought bitterly, pensioned off to die with a rotten heart. They couldn't even let a man die on the job, in the woods.

"My work," said Calvin Full, "consists of watching for unsanitary and unsterile practices, making tuberculin tests, and so forth. I'm afraid I'm not much good at this sort of emergency."

His wife, who had been looking as if she would scream again, turned to him. Her almost-pretty face, cleared of fright, was swept by pride. "You're as brave as the next man, Calvin, and as clever. You'll get us home."

"I hope so, dear. But Mr. Summersby must be a great deal more used to problems of this sort."

They all gaped up at him expectantly. Because of his size, of course; he was the big born leader! "Sir" in trouble, "High-pockets" when things were clear again. The hell with them. He kept his mouth shut.

The blond man said, "I'm Tom Watkins."

"Adam Pierce," said the Negro.

"What do you do, Adam?"

The boy pushed his glasses up on his nose again, frowning. "I go to C.C.N.Y. Summers, I'm the Wild Man from Zululand in the sideshow, and I shill for the coaster when I'm not on duty. It helps out my family some, for me to be making money in the summers."

"Are you taking subjects that might help us?" asked Full.

"I major in English. I'm going to teach it when I graduate. Then I take psych, biology, the usual courses."

"Hmm," said Watkins, looking at the end of the room through which the Mexican had been taken. "Psych and biology. Could be some use here."

"What we need is a locksmith," said Summersby. He felt himself unwillingly drawn into the group, sharing their problems that were not his, and it angered him. He fished out a bent pack of cigarettes, lit one and was about to put the rest away.

"Nothing but a torch would help. I know a little about locks myself." Watkins grinned genially. "I'm out of smokes," he said, and Summersby gave him the pack. He took one and passed it to Full, who declined. Adam took one. The boy reached up and pushed at his glasses again; a look of irritation appeared on his face. "Say," he muttered, "is this room a little wobbly, or is it my eyes?"

"Wobbly?"

"Wavy. See how those tree trunks are blurred?"

"You need your glasses changed, Adam," said Watkins.

"No, sir." Adam took them off and started to polish them on a handkerchief; then his brown eyes opened wide. "I can see!" he said. The others stared at him. "My astigmatism's gone! My glasses make everything blur, but I can see plain as noon without 'em. Look, I've had astigmatism since I was a kid!"

"What happened?" asked the woman, addressing her husband. "How could that be, Calvin?"

"Don't know, dear."

"My headache is gone," she said. "I never realized it till this boy mentioned his eyes."

"Mrs. Full has suffered from an almost constant headache for years," said Calvin, and sniffed twice. "My post-nasal drip is missing, too. Do you suppose my sinus trouble is cleared up?"

"That's what must have been happening those two days we were out," said Watkins, knocking ash from his cigarette. "We were put through a hospital or something. I feel good, even if I'm damned hungry."

Summersby looked from one to another, detesting them; against his will, against sanity and decency that fought for recognition, he detested them. He had a heart for which there was no help, a heart no two-day period of miraculous cures could touch. Their puny ailments had been relieved, but he was still at the slow, listless task of dying.

"Listen," said Watkins jubilantly, "whoever or whatever brought us here, it's a cinch they don't mean to harm us. They wouldn't mend us if they were going to hurt us, would they?"

"In two days," said Adam, nodding hard. "Two days! How could they do it?"

There was an air of near-gaiety about them that repelled Summersby. In a desperate rebellion against these boons handed out to everyone but himself, he tried to hurt them. "What do you do to a duck before you cook it? Clean it. Think that over."

Adam Pierce looked at him levelly. "No, sir. If that duck has sinus trouble or bad eyes, you don't have to fix that up before you eat it. No, sir."

"What about the Mexican?" Summersby asked. "What's happened to him?"

Then the wall slid open again and they all started forward; Summersby looked after them bitterly, feeling the resentment drain out and leave only the old hopelessness, the apathetic disregard of everything but death.

II

Porfirio Villa had known from the first that this adventure of his was a mistake. His wife had told him to stay off the roller coaster, but he had sneered. What could happen? The people always got off again, laughing and wiping their brows. He had the bad burn on his left hand, caused by an accidental smacking of the steam table in a rage at his fool of a helper;—that idiot who now had had charge of the stand for two days! *lodo feo!*—and so, enforced to a vacation, he must step into the cars and go crawling up that terrible incline, giggling nervously, and then rush madly down the other side. Dreaming is better than doing; he should have stayed in his chili stand and dreamed of the ride.

Por Dios! What a terror the rising, what a discomfort the drop, what a fearful thing the disappearance of the park and the awakening in this place ... this place a man could not believe in, though he stood upon its floor and gazed round-eyed, with sweating lips and shaking hands, upon its size, its devices for unknown purposes, its impossible inhabitant!

The thing was twelve feet tall. Was it a machine? He had seen machines in the *revistas* and the cinema, looking much like this one, a clumsy copy of a man moving, speaking, tearing people to pieces. There was also King Kong, who resembled this thing.

If it was not alive, it moved very creditably. The gray-furred legs were long and thin, placed on the sides of the body at the waist; the arms, much thicker than the legs, swung very low, and must be fully eight feet long. It was backing from him slowly, holding out one hand—six fingers and two thumbs, *demonio!*—with the green stick. That stick stung like a bee when it touched you.

The monster was already a good distance away. Porfirio cast his eyes slyly to one side, the other. There was a complication of machinery so great that even a teacher of mechanics would be dismayed.

There! A hole between two pink walls. He glanced once at the thing, standing now with its impossible face turned down to him, and then he ran for the hole.

It was after him with a short cry, but he reached the hole and scuttled through. Four paths faced him. What a time for decisions! He took the left-hand path, went round several turns, came to two more openings. The pink walls were smooth and featureless, well over his head so that he could not tell where he was. He ran like the mouse in the game next to his chili stand, the game in which suckers bet on which escape—the red, green, blue or white—the mouse would choose. Paths opened and Porfirio plunged on, losing his sense of direction, becoming more terrified as he went. His famished guts dragged him down, made him a weak frightened mouse indeed.

He panted past two doorways and abruptly, like the flashing of a pigeon's wing, the greenstick shot down before him, held in that monstrous gray hand!

The stick appeared and disappeared, herding him, chivvying him from place to place, all places looking alike, till finally the great room lay again before his eyes. Whimpering, he stepped out of the pink maze and leaned against the wall, his chest and belly heaving. He was done. Let it murder him. A man could not run forever.

The brute stood over him. Cautiously it brought its face down to peer. Its eyes were set in deep pits, there was a hole between them, and far below in the watermelon-shaped head, a mouth like a man's with lips the color of rust on iron.

Panting, he gazed at it, then flung up one arm in a futile blow that fell short by two feet. The thing was angering him. Let it watch out for itself!

A hand, unnoticed, had crept round behind him and now took him by the back of the shirt, belt, and trousers, and lifted him off the floor. He regretted the useless punch. Now he would be dead.

The monster inspected him, prodding aside his bedraggled collar points and digging gently at his belly with the rod, which did not sting him this time. It made a sound from its mouth like the last weak bellow of a dying *toro*—"Mmwaa gnaa!" then set him down once more with a thump that jolted his teeth, nearly fractured his ankles.

Maria y Jose, but it moved as fast as a lizard's tongue! Escape was beyond hope.

It backed away from him, stood by a huge box and gestured with the green stick. It wanted him to come. He walked toward it. The box was enormous, oblong, like a huge shoe box. Only when he had come to it did he realize it was the room in which he had awakened earlier.

In this hall it was lost. Untouched by the monster, he looked at the hall with seeing eyes for the first time. It had yellow walls and a gray roof, like the box. He clapped a hand to his head. Like a theater without seats! Over ten varas high, thirty broad and forty long: or he should say, being a man of the States now for many years, roughly thirty feet by seventy-five by a hundred. Scattered here and there in staggering confusion were the machines, the gadgets, the unknown things. All colors he had ever seen were there. It was gaudy as the amusement park, but slicker and more fresh-looking.

The creature laid a hand on the box, and the wall began to slide open. He looked up, and it gestured, telling him as plainly as words to go in. He was to enter again. It seemed as happy a thing to him as the breaking of a Christmas pinata.

He braced himself now. *He* had emerged, while *they* had cowered behind, refusing him aid. Worms that they were, he would show them the bearing of a hero, one who had braved mysterious dangers while all others trembled. He sucked in his belly, threw forward his chest, placed his fists carefully on his hips and strutted into the strawed room, turning his head proudly from side to side. He heard the wall close behind him.

The worms came crowding to him.

"What is it? What happened?"

Porfirio Villa, adventurer, laughed. The relief that washed through him was making him shake, his empty stomach still heaved after the panic, but from somewhere in his soul he dredged up the casual laugh. "Very little happened," he said. "Truly very little of interest."

III

Mrs. Full sat on the straw, twisting her hands together. She did not know she was doing it until she had to disentangle them to pull her skirt lower on her folded legs, and then she deliberately put one hand flat on the floor so that she would not appear to be nervous. She wanted Calvin to be as proud of her in this terrible crisis as she was of him.

But Calvin was calm, at any rate; so she was impatiently proud of him.

"We've got to slam something into that opening next time the wall slides back," said Watkins. She nodded at him approvingly. There was a man who might be of some help.

"What do you think these creatures are, Mr. Watkins?" she asked quietly, though she felt like screeching the question.

"I haven't the least idea, ma'am."

"Freak gorillas," said Calvin.

"No, sir," said Adam. "I've been thinking. Wasn't the Java Ape Man about nine feet tall?"

"Five and a half's more like it," said Watkins. "At least that's how I remember it."

"Well, *some* fossil man was nine feet tall," said Adam dogmatically. "Couldn't that thing be one of them? There's plenty of places in the world where a race of people or animals could have developed without Homo sapiens being any the wiser. Now suppose they got hold of us?"

"How?" asked Calvin.

"Through people working for 'em. We might all have been doped and put on a plane and we might be on an island somewhere now, or in the middle of a jungle, with these whatcha-may-call-'ems."

"How were we doped?" persisted Calvin.

"Gosh, I don't know that!"

"And what the devil do they want with us?" asked Watkins.

*   *   *   *   *

Mrs. Full did not hear what Adam said. She was wondering, with a cold horror, if the creatures were near enough human to desire white girls as—as mates. "Calvin, we've got to get home!" she cried.

"We will, dear." He patted her shoulder. "Don't you worry."

"Someone has to worry."

"We all are, ma'am," said the pleasant Watkins. "Except you, I guess, Summersby," he added accusingly.

Summersby stared at him, seemed about to speak, then looked away. She was afraid of this great man. He might be a lunatic, with that lined, tormented face.

"We might be in the East Indies somewhere," said Adam thoughtfully. "A plane could get us there from New York in a lot less than two days."

"Where are these East Indies?" asked Villa. Mrs. Full wished he would stop rubbing his stomach that way. It reminded her that she was very hungry.

"Someplace near Siam," said Adam vaguely. "Question is, if we're there, or anyplace else for that matter, *why* are we?"

A number of reasons shot through Mrs. Full's mind, all of them too fantastic to suggest aloud. They might be potential mates for these incredible animals, or slaves, or food, or.... She was surprised at herself for thinking of such things; one would suppose she had been reared on a diet of sensational thrillers.

She rose and walked aside, ostensibly studying the green fountain (which augmented her suffering with its tinkling splash). "Oh, Calvin," she said.

He came over to her. "Yes, dear?"

"Calvin, I—" she halted unable to phrase her question. But he did it for her.

"I've been thinking: if there are—certain basic needs—I mean, if you find it necessary to—"

"I do, Calvin," she said gratefully.

"Oh. Well, there is the, hmm, sand box. I believe it's meant for such, ah, purposes."

"Calvin! In front of you, in front of these strangers?" She was shocked, and put up one hand to push nervously at her hair, which felt untidy.

"We'll ask them to turn their backs. After all, such things must be attended to."

"I'd rather die," she said, but not at all certainly.

"There are sacrifices to be made in this predicament, and modesty is one," he clipped out. "Er, gentlemen."

Watkins said, "I know, it just hit me too."

"What?"

"I've got to go to the john."

"Yes," said Calvin stiffly. "I suggest we retire to the farther end from the sand box, while one by one—"

"We could rig a screen or something, but there isn't anything to do it with," said Watkins. He walked away; despite his outspoken manner, he seemed to have the proper instincts.

Adam followed him. Summersby turned his back. Calvin looked at the Mexican. "Come along."

"Why?" asked Villa, raising his black brows. "What is there in a simple relieving of—"

Calvin strode to him, catching him by the nape, lifted him bodily from the floor, and sent him reeling after the others. He half-turned, then walked on, muttering, "Crazy *gringos*!" Calvin went and stood a little behind the others, his back to her.

The minutes following were interminable, horribly embarrassing. At last she touched his shoulder. "All right, Calvin," she whispered.

One by one the others used the sand box. By the time they were through with the unspeakably primitive ritual, she had become almost inured to it, and considered herself to be admirably calm. There were unsuspected resources in her nature, she thought.

"When do you suppose they feed us?" asked Watkins. He was holding his tan briefcase under his left arm; he hadn't once laid it down. "I'm so empty I rattle."

"Soon," said Calvin firmly, and she felt reassured.

Summersby was standing by the door-wall, his great hands working along the seams of his trouser legs. A violent temper, held in check, thought Mrs. Full. He was the worst of the problems facing them, except for the unknown animals.

Even as she looked at him, the wall opened again. This time no one jumped or shrieked, though she felt her breath hiss back over her tongue. Watkins said, "Well, Viva, here's your pal again."

The Mexican glared. Evidently the joke was a stale one to him. "My name is Villa, not Viva. I hope you get a good taste of that green stick, you little man!"

"Viva Villa," said Watkins. "Lead on. You know the way."

The awful arm came in like a hairy python, groping blindly with the rod.

Summersby, standing near the opening, was the first to be touched. It tapped him lightly, and he walked out of the room, really very bravely, she thought. The rod discovered Adam. The boy backed up, too frightened to put on a show of boldness. The rod slapped him impatiently, and he yelled and darted forward into the other room. He and Summersby stood together, staring up at something that could not be seen from inside the prison box.

"It's electrical," said Calvin. "Like a bull prod."

"Yes, dear," she said automatically.

"We may as well go out. I don't want you shocked."

"All right, Calvin." She took his arm. Watkins had been caught and herded out. As they stepped forward after him, she glanced sideways at her husband. She would have liked to tell him she loved him, but it would have been too melodramatic. She pressed his arm tightly, affectionately. They walked out into the great hall.

*   *   *   *   *

Villa's cursory description had not prepared Calvin Full for the reality of the huge beings.

There were three of them. They stood absolutely motionless, grotesquely humanoid figures with smallish, sunken eyes fixed rigidly on the people some yards away. Then, as Calvin watched, two of them thrust out their hands holding the ball-tipped rods. The gestures were almost too swift to follow.

He stared at the central figure, and it gazed back with its withdrawn, pupilless, rust-red eyes. Its head was, as Villa had told them, the shape of a watermelon, with the eyes wide-set on either side of a gently agitating orifice that was probably a nostril. The mouth, very human in shape, with full lips the color of the eyeballs, was quite low in the face. There was a rough growth of gray-black hair on the crown of the big head and a fuzz of it, less dark, on the face itself. There seemed to be no ears.

Its body, long and thick, was dwarfed by the tremendous arms. Its feet were large, toeless, and flat; its legs joined smoothly to the trunk about halfway up. It wore clothing of a sort, which surprised Calvin Full, perhaps more than anything else about the being. There was a kind of short sleeveless jacket of amber color caught at the front by a long silver bar, and a white skirt worn under the legs, reaching from just below the hip joints to the bottom of the torso.

Its companions were almost identical with it, except for clothing of different hues and varying cut.

The thing in the middle now opened its mouth and made a noise that reminded Full of an off-key clarinet.

"Gpwk?" it said, with a rising inflection. "Hummr gpwk?"

Abruptly it came forward, its motions flowing and yet a bit jerky, its long legs carrying it rhythmically, but with a hint of gawkiness; Calvin thought of a galloping giraffe he and his wife had seen in a travelogue some nights before. It towered over them, bending at the hip joints.

"Steady, dear," he said.

"I'm all right," his wife said shakily, seeming just on the verge of screaming.

"Wish I could say the same," said Adam Pierce, the Negro boy. "What a specimen!"

"Look like anything to you?" asked Watkins.

"Hell, no. Unless it's something from Mars."

"Maybe we're on Mars," said Watkins conversationally, but no one responded.

*   *   *   *   *

It's as sensible a suggestion as the East Indian one, thought Calvin. He had not the slightest idea where they were, and he saw no sense in worrying over it until they had more information to build theories on.

The beast making no further move, his wife at last leaned toward him and said in his ear, "Calvin, can you tell what—I mean whether it's male or female?"

He studied it carefully. He couldn't even make a guess. He shook his head.

Then it reached forward its stick and thrust it directly at Calvin's face. He backed off, startled and somewhat frightened. At once the thing touched Mrs. Full with the ivory ball, as if to separate her from the knot of men.

She cried out in pain, and Calvin leaped forward; he had a flash of the great paw coming at him with the prod aimed for his face again. It touched his forehead, he felt an intense shock, and then he was powerless to move.

His mind screamed, he could feel tiny muscles try sluggishly to crawl deep under his skin, but he was paralyzed where he stood in an attitude of charging; he knew his face must be twisted in horror and rage, but he could feel nothing. Only his mind and eyesight seemed wholly clear.

He saw his wife taken off, stumbling unwillingly and looking back at him over her shoulder. Watkins said, (Calvin could hear plainly, he found), "Watch it, he's falling!" Then the paralysis left him and he slumped as though all his bones had been extracted. Someone caught him under the arms, holding him up. He tried to move, but aside from rolling his eyes and lolling his tongue out, he was helpless.

Summersby, behind him, said, "Are his eyes open?"

"Yeah." Watkin's face appeared before him. "Poor guy looks half dead."

Calvin blinked and made a try at speech, but nothing came out but a flop-tongued drooling sound.

The two creatures remaining near them squatted down and observed them, making fragmentary noises to each other. Watkins started to walk after the third, which had escorted Mrs. Full across the wide room and was on the point of making her get onto a low platform on which were a number of structures of purple tubing and crimson boxes and varicolored small contrivances. One of the pair flicked its goad across his path.

Villa said, "Come back, you foolish, do you think you can take that stick?" He sounded furious, probably because he was afraid of the beasts becoming enraged.

Calvin made a wracking effort to say, "Let him go," for surely they couldn't stand callously by and see his wife undergo the Lord knew what tortures; but the sound he made was unintelligible.

Watkins said, "Blast it, Viva, we don't know what the thing might do to her."

"Come on back," said Summersby. "Do you want to get this?" He hefted the limp Full.

Calvin writhed and managed to move his hands up and down.

"He's gaining," said Watkins, coming back.

"Those rods pack a wallop," said Adam. "What sort of power can they have in 'em? Seems to me they're away beyond our science."

"They're not hitched to batteries," said Watkins. "Say, look at all this machinery. If these animals built it, they're a pretty advanced race."

*   *   *   *   *

Mrs. Full was seated now on a large thing like a chrome-and-rubber chair, one of those modern abominations which she and Calvin so cordially detested. He could not see her face. The twelve-foot brute was moving its fingers before her, evidently telling her to do something. Calvin heard her say plaintively, "But what *is* it?"

Summersby hoisted him up and about then feeling began to come back to him with a sharp, unpleasant tingling of the skin. He said, "Help her!" quite distinctly.

"Nothing's happening to her," said Watkins. "Take it easy."

Mrs. Full was apparently pulling levers and moving blocks of vividly colored material back and forth on rods; like an abacus, thought her husband.

Suddenly one of the other pair of creatures gave a cry, "Brrm hmmr!" and pointed to the left. From a muddle of gear rose a small airship, orange, with a nose like a spaceship and streamlined fins, and a square box on its tail. It made no noise, but rose straight toward the ceiling, moving slowly, jerkily.

His wife had her back to it. He heard her give an exasperated, bewildered cry. "What on earth ... what are you *doing*?" She spoke to the creature as if it understood. "I don't see why you—"

Calvin pushed free of Summersby. He could stand now, shakily. The beast indicated a blue block on a vertical bar; Mrs. Full moved it down, the airship halted and began to sail toward them. "Do you see the toy ship?" called Calvin. "You're flying the ship!"

"Oh, my," she said helplessly. "What shall I do now?"

"This is crazy," said Watkins. "Absolutely crazy."

"Go on moving things," Calvin called to his wife. "Experiment. It wants you to fly it." It occurred to him that this was too obvious to bother stating. He must be distracted by weakness. He rubbed his tingling arms and hands, hoping she wouldn't crash the ship. Villa and Adam Pierce were calling encouragement to her as the orange thing drifted up and down and sideways.

Now the twelve-foot being gestured briefly at a portion of the apparatus, Mrs. Full caught his meaning and moved something, and the ship tilted and flew along the wall without touching it. All three of the creatures uttered sounds that might be taken for words of pleasure.

"Good girl!" yelled Watkins. "Keep it up!"

She turned to them and Calvin saw she was smiling. "There's really nothing to it," she said. The airship bumped into the wall and fell. The animal above her squawked and pressed down a lever, which evidently sent out a beam or impulse that caught the ship in midair and held it suspended. Then it grasped Mrs. Full and carried her, flailing her limbs, over to the corner.

Calvin started forward, apprehensive.

"Hold it, Cal, you don't want another shock." Watkins took his arm.

The creature kicked aside a mound of small gadgets, sending them helter-skelter, picked up what looked like a big five-legged stool and set it on its feet. It was perhaps ten feet high. Then he deposited Mrs. Full on its smooth round top and turned her bodily so that she faced the wall.

"Help her!" snapped Calvin.

"We can't do a damn thing."

"Just wait a minute, sir," said Adam. "He's leaving her alone. I don't think he'll hurt her."

She twisted her head around, looking frightened. Her legs hung over the edge. The being strode back with its curious gawky-graceful walk, and firmly turned her face to the wall again, using one big rubbery finger. "Oh!" she said, in a small voice, and remained staring at the wall, like a naughty child on a dunce's stool. The beast came over to the group.

*   *   *   *   *

The three talked among themselves, glancing at the men. The airship hung on its invisible beam of energy, ignored. Mrs. Full patted up her hair. She must be terrified, thought Calvin.

The three came to them, their skirts swishing like taffeta. They knelt—it was an odd movement, their high-hipped legs angling to the sides, their bodies slanting forward as their heads dropped toward the humans—and stared at one and then another. The one who was evidently the leader put out his green goad, but slowly, as if showing no harm was intended, and pushed at Calvin's jacket. The ivory ball touched his chest but no shock followed. The thing made noises, perhaps comparing his clothing with its own.

"Take it off, Cal," said Watkins.

"Why?"

"He'd like to see it. Be friendly."

"That's it," agreed Adam, "be friendly."

He removed his jacket and handed it to the brute, who received it dubiously, fingered it, exhibited it to the other two, and dropped it. Calvin bent to pick it up; the goad barred his way. Two large fingers plucked at his trousers. He felt himself flush with outrage.

"No!"

Watkins chuckled. "I'll bet you will."

"Don't make it mad," said Adam.

"I won't take my trousers off."

"If we took them off, it might soothe this monster," suggested Villa. "Let us throw him down and take off his pants."

"Try it," said Calvin. The Mexican started toward him. Then the creature had lifted him high in the air, peering closely at the trousers. It tugged at them. "Ouch!" said Calvin. The beast would tear them off; the humiliation of that would be worse than removing them himself. It might rip them to shreds. He loosened his belt and unbuttoned and unzipped just in time; they came off over his shoes and were held up in front of the sunken red eyes. Calvin was set down, carefully enough, and the garment was handed to the other monstrosities. Calvin cast a look at the stool. He was glad his wife was not witnessing his shame.

"Nice shorts," said Villa.

Full whirled on him, angry enough to bark out an insult, even an oath, but the man was evidently sincere in his praise.

"Thank you," he said stiffly.

His trousers were thrown to him and he shoved his feet into them and secured them once more. He put on his jacket.

One of the beasts which had not taken an active part in the business now walked to Mrs. Full and picked her up by the back of the waist, as though she had been a cat, and brought her over. For one ghastly moment Calvin thought it was going to divest her of her skirt, but after scrutinizing her a while, it set her down among them.

He took her hand. "Are you all right, dear?"

She was amazingly calm. "I am, Calvin, I am. I don't believe they mean us any harm, after all."

The first great animal pointed at the box, waving his prod.

"We're supposed to go in again, I guess," said Watkins.

"Let's go, then," said Adam. "No sense in getting shocked."

They trooped in, and the wall closed behind them.

IV

Adam Pierce had an idea. It had begun to grow in his mind while the woman was running the miniature spaceship, but he had thought it over until he was certain it wasn't so silly as to make them laugh at him. Now he felt sure he'd hit on the truth; too many evidences for it, and nothing much that he could see against it.

"I have an idea," he said.

"To get out?" asked the woman.

"No, ma'am. I think I know where we are."

"Where?" asked everyone, except the big man, Summersby, who was sitting on the tire looking away from them.

"In a lab! This is a laboratory, and those big things are some kind of scientists!"

"You could be right," said Watkins reluctantly. "My God, what a spot, if you're right!"

"Sure. That's why we were snatched off the coaster, however it happened. They wanted to experiment on us, and study us. They got this lab someplace where it's secret, and they make tests—"

"There was a contrivance like a milking machine," said Full.

"You don't know *what* it's used for," said Adam darkly. He imagined it might be an especially nasty way of picking over a man's brains or body. "Look, it all fits. That stool, that's a funny way to punish a person, but all their stuff is a little cockeyed."

"By our standards," added Watkins.

"That's what I meant. Look, you punish a guinea pig when it does something wrong, if you're trying to teach it some trick or other; I mean, suppose you want to determine its intelligence, you give it a problem, and if it does the thing wrong it gets a shock, maybe, or a bat on the nose. That stool was punishment. If you hadn't crashed the rocket," he said to Mrs. Full, "it might have given you a reward."

"Maybe some food," said Villa.

"Here's another angle," said Watkins, who obviously knew something about lab work. "They may be trying to give us neuroses. Scientists induce neuroses in all kinds of critters, by punishment and complex problems and—"

"What is that?" asked Villa.

"Neuroses?" Watkins rubbed his chin. "Well, say they want to make an animal nervous, anxious, worried." Villa nodded.

"You mean they might be trying to drive us mad?" said the woman in a high scared voice.

"I doubt it," said Calvin Full.

"They might be," said Watkins.

"Then let's get out of here," said his wife. She went trotting to the wall. "Didn't anyone shove a barrier into this?"

"I forgot," said Full. She gave him a dirty look.

"Anyway," Adam went on, "that could explain why we were fixed up before they woke us—it was like quarantine. They wouldn't want sick animals."

"Who was fixed up how?" asked the Mexican suspiciously.

"My astigmatism," he said to Villa, "and this gentleman's sinus trouble, and his wife's headache."

"And they pulled a rotten wisdom tooth for me," said Watkins. "I just discovered it a minute ago. Hole's healed up neatly."

Villa was peeling away the bandage on his hand. Now he gave a glad shout. "*Madre de Dios!* Look, the burn has gone!" He showed them his hand. "Tuesday, a terrible scorched place; today, behold, it is well!"

The woman said, "You know, this *might* be a laboratory. When I taught kindergarten we had simple tests for the children that were somewhat like that remote control apparatus."

*   *   *   *   *

Watkins pushed the big man, Summersby, on the shoulder. "I wish you'd get into this," he said irritably. "We need all the brains we have to get out."

Summersby looked at him. "You think we'll get out?" he asked.

"Why not?"

"Why?" Summersby sounded tired, and as if his mind was a long way off. "If these are scientists, they'll keep a fairly close watch on their lab animals."

"You're a forest ranger, man. Don't you have to meet emergencies all the time?" Watkins was exasperated. Adam thought, I wouldn't talk to the big fellow that way; he looks as wild as a panther.

"I'm sorry," said Summersby, turning away again. "I don't think we can escape, or plan to, until we have more information."

"You needn't inflict your morbidity on us," said Full. "Because you're a defeatist is no reason for us to be."

Summersby stood up. He looked as tall to Adam as one of the monsters. "If we're guinea pigs, we'll end up as guinea pigs," he said. "And what do experimenters do with guinea pigs, finally? They infect or dissect them. Now leave me alone!" He walked to the farthest corner and sat down on the straw, staring at his feet.

Adam reached up automatically to push at his glasses, found them missing, and was confused for an instant. Then he said, "There's a thought. We better bust out as quick as we can."

"Summersby won't help," said Watkins. "Anybody else feel fatalistic about this mess?"

"I must get back to my chili stand," said Villa. "And my wife," he added.

"Adam, you're nearer to college courses than I am," said Watkins. Adam nodded. "How many places in the world are there, big enough and unexplored enough to hide a race of giants like these?"

"I guess parts of Africa and South America, maybe the Arctic, some islands. I don't really know."

"Neither do I."

"Perhaps we aren't on the earth at all," said Mrs. Full. They all looked at her. "I read a book once in which a party of people discovered a land beneath the earth's surface," she went on, actually blushing a little. "It was a trashy sort of book, but—but I thought possibly there might be something in the idea."

"There might," said her husband.

"Wherever we are, we've got to get out of this box before we do anything else," said Adam. He felt panicky, as the realization sank into him of what they might be in for, in this alien lab, under the care of scientists that looked more like apes than anything.

"Look!" shouted Villa. Adam whirled and saw the small panel, that Watkins had discovered earlier, just sliding open. A large platter came through, heaped with what looked like a collection of junk. The huge hand which had pushed it in withdrew, the panel slipping shut after it. Villa was the first to reach the platter. "*Santos*," he muttered. "*Santos y santas!*"

*   *   *   *   *

The platter was two feet square, of sky-blue plastic, and on it lay seven pies, several dozen cupcakes, a double handful of macaroon cookies, and a quantity of glass shards. Some of the pies were upside down.

"What on earth...." said Mrs. Full.

"Looks like the contents of a bakery window," said Watkins, leaning over with his briefcase clamped to his thin chest. "Window and all, I might add."

Villa picked up a custard pie. It had been smeared up by rough handling but it looked good to Adam. He chose one for himself, and Watkins handed Mrs. Full an apple pie. She thanked him. They all took tentative bites.

"What do you make of this?" Watkins asked Summersby, still trying to drag him into their group. The big man shrugged. "The glass," went on the blond fellow, "that doesn't make sense. Do they think we eat glass?"

"Possibly," said Calvin Full.

Among the six of them, they consumed all the eatable contents of the tray. Almost immediately Adam felt his eyelids drooping. "I'm sleepy," he said, yawning.

"So am I," said Villa. He lay prone and closed his eyes at once.

Adam sat down, more heavily than he had meant to. He was vaguely disturbed by the sudden tiredness.

"Someone ought to stand guard," said Mrs. Full.

"I will," said Summersby unexpectedly.

"I'll do it," said Watkins. He started to pace up and down. "I'm a little groggy myself, but I'll take first trick."

V

When they were let out of their prison box next morning—nine o'clock Friday, by the chronograph, and they had slept another fifteen hours—there were five of the gigantic beast-creatures waiting for them. Any hopes that Tom Watkins had had of rooting around the big hall for a way of escape died with a dejected grunt. There must be well over a ton of enemies there, with their caverned red eyes peering down at the humans. No chance to explore under those gazes.

The boss of the alien scientists—Watkins recognized it, or him (or was it her?), by the clothing and by certain differences in facial structure—came and bent over them. Watkins was smoking a cigarette he had bummed from Villa, Summersby's having given out the day before. He took a hearty drag and blew out the smoke, which unfortunately lifted right into the creature's eyes. It shook its head and made a squawking sound, "Hwrak!" and flipped its green prodder into his belly. He abruptly sat down, with the sensation of having stuck his finger into a lamp socket. "My God!" he said. Cal helped him up.

Summersby walked off toward a twenty-foot-high door. None of the beings tried to stop him. The boss motioned Watkins to go with it, so he rather shakily followed it across the room.

Before him was a gadget that resembled a five-manual organ console. The banks of keys were broad and there was a kind of chair, or stool, fixed on a horizontal bar in front of them. The giant indicated that he was to get onto it.

"Now what?" he said, when he had been stopped directly in front of the apparatus. "Expect me to play this? Look, Buster, I'm tone deaf, I haven't had my coffee yet, and I'd just as soon dance a polka as play you a tune."

The thing pressed down two of the keys—they were of an amethyst color, longer and more tapered than those of an organ—and looked at Watkins.

"Drop dead," he said to it. He was always bitterly antagonistic to everything and everybody if he didn't have three cups of coffee before he got out of bed. "Go on, you big ape, make me play."

It hit him on the head with a couple of its big rubbery fingers. He felt as if a cop had sloshed him with a blackjack, and all the hostility went out of him. He leaned forward and pushed down half a dozen keys at random.

There was no sound, at least none that he could hear, though he remembered the whistle he had at home to call his dog, and wondered if the notes of this organ were sub- or supersonic. Certainly there was no reason to suppose this race of creatures was limited to the same range of hearing that humans were.

The thing went down the hall some yards and folded itself into a sitting position before a large white space on the wall. When Watkins did nothing, it gestured angrily with its goad. He pressed more keys. It jerked its head around and stared at the white space.

Accidentally he discovered that by pressing with his calves on certain pedals below the stool he could maneuver the seat to either side. The gadget began to intrigue him.

He had never played any musical instrument, but had always had a quiet desire to produce music. He couldn't hear this organ's sounds, but he could go through the motions with fervor. He did.

The boss scientist gazed raptly at the wall screen; was it concentrating on what he played? Did his random selection of keys indicate something to it, something about his mental powers or emotions or—what?

Or was it possible that the playing produced images or colors on the blank space? He craned his neck, but could distinguish nothing. Pounding on, he called over his shoulder, "Come here, somebody!"

No one answered. Pushing keys at random, he turned to look for them. Each of them was doing something under the supervision of a twelve-foot beast, except for Summersby, who was still examining the door. "Hey, High-pockets!" he yelled, knowing the big man hated the nickname, but not giving a damn. "Summersby! Come here!"

"What is it?" said Summersby in a moment, standing below his seat.

"Take a squint at that screen the old boy's gaping at. I want to know what the devil I'm doing."

Summersby walked over and stood beside the scientist.

"What's happening?"

"Nothing."

"Nothing at all?"

"Well, the screen's mottled gray and white, and the pattern's swirling slowly; but that's all."

"Is it particularly beautiful?" asked Watkins.

"No. It's hardly distinguishable."

*   *   *   *   *

Sliding right and left on the bar, striking first one and then another of the manuals, Watkins said to Summersby, "What do you figure these scientists are, anyway?"

"Mammals," said the big man.

"I suppose so—"

"They have navels. They weren't hatched."

"Oh." Watkins hadn't noticed that. "Where are we, then?" .

"I don't know."

Another scientist wandered over and sat down beside the first. Shortly they seemed to get in each other's way, and there was a lot of shoving and squawking. At last one of them hit the other in the face with an open hand. Then they were rolling on the floor, snatching at one another's hair and pummeling the big bodies and heads with those gargantuan fists. It sounded like a brawl between elephants. Watkins swiveled round to watch. Mrs. Full said to someone—Watkins heard her distinctly in a lull in the ruckus—"If these are scientists, what are the common people like?" For the first time that day he grinned. He had stopped playing the organ. The other scientists had gathered around the fight and were uttering strange cries, like wild geese honking. Cheering them on? he wondered.

Adam came over. "Mr. Watkins," he said, "could we have been wrong about them? Do you think a scientist would act like that?"

"They sure seem to be a quarrelsome race, Adam," he said, "they're not noticing what we do. Suppose you go look for a way out."

"We want to get away as soon as we can," nodded the boy. "Dangerous around here!" He ran down the hall.

The giants arose and straightened their clothing. They had patched up their argument in the midst of fighting over it. The leader walked toward a tall device of pipes and boards and steps, motioning Mrs. Full to follow.

Apparently Watkins had been forgotten. He took his briefcase off his lap, where he had held it all the time he played, and dropped it to the floor. Then he hung by his hands and let go. He picked up the case and went to investigate the room.

Before he had done more than glimpse the enormous door, he was picked up kitten-fashion by a scientist, who carried him off, dangling and swearing, to another infernal machine.

For a couple of hours they were put through paces, all of them; sometimes one man would be working a gadget while all the scientists and humans watched him, at other periods they would each be hard at work doing something the result of which they had no conception of.

*   *   *   *   *

Several of the machines could be figured: the pink maze, one or two others; and Watkins had at least a theory on the organ. The sleek modernistic machinery which directed the airship was plain enough. There were certain designs and arrangements to follow that flew it up and down the room. They were hard to memorize but Mrs. Full and the somber ranger, Summersby, became adept at them.

Then there were the others....

There was a remote control device that played "music," weird haunting all-but-harmonies that sounded worst when the creatures appeared most pleased, and earned the punishment stool or a brutal cuffing for the operator when he did manage to produce something resembling a tune. Evidently bearing a relation to this was the sharp slap Adam got when he started to sing "The Whiffenpoof Song" while idling around a pile of outsize blocks like a child's building bricks. What the human ear relished, the giant ear flinched from.

There was a sort of vertical maze that verged on the four-dimensional, for when they thought they were finding a way out the top they would come abruptly to the side, or even the bottom, and have to begin anew. This one was obviously impossible to figure out, thought Watkins. It must be one of the ways in which the scientists induced neuroses in their experimental subjects. He had a quick mind for puzzles and intricacies of any kind, but this one stumped him cold.

"You think it's calculated to drive you crazy?" he asked Cal.

The New Englander considered for a minute. Then he nodded. "Possibly," he said.

"You think it might work?"

This time Cal pondered longer. At last he said, "Not if we don't let it."

"I could develop a first-class neurosis," said Watkins to Mrs. Full, "if I let myself really go."

"We must all keep our heads, Mr. Watkins," she told him. "Those of us who have not given up—" She glanced at Summersby with a frown—"must hold a tight rein on ourselves."

"That's right, ma'am," he said. They all called her "ma'am" or "Mrs. Full." Nobody knew her first name. He wondered if she'd be insulted if he asked her, and decided that she would.

Capriciously, then, on the heels of a series of punishments, the head scientist went out of the room and came back with food for them. It flung the food—three chickens—on the floor. Villa snatched one of them up with a happy shout, but at once his dark face soured. "Raw? How can we cook them?" His hand with the fowl dropped limply to his side.

"We can make a fire," said Calvin. Watkins was a little surprised that it was Cal who made the suggestion first, but the Vermont man added, "I've made enough campfires to know something about it."

"Mr. Full is an enthusiastic hunter," said his wife.

"A fire of what?" asked Villa, managing to look starved, helpless, and wistful, all at once.

Summersby said, "There are plates of plastic over there, and plenty of short rods. I don't know what these beasts use them for, but if they're fireproof, we can construct a grill with them." He went without further talk to a stack of the multicolored slabs and dowels, which lay beside a neat array of what looked like conduit pipes, electromagnets, and coiled cable. He picked up an armload. One of the giants put a hand down before him. He pushed it aside and strode back to the group. Gutty, thought Watkins, or just hungry? Or is it his sense of kismet?

"I'll cut some kindling from the trees in our room," said Calvin. "Who has a knife?"

Summersby handed him a large pocket knife, and set about making a grill over two of the plastic slabs. It was a workmanlike job when he had finished. He held his lighter under one of the rods, which was apparently impervious to fire. He nodded to himself. Looks more human, thought Watkins, than he has yet.

Villa was plucking one of the chickens, humming to himself. Mrs. Full was working on another, Adam on the third. Watkins felt useless, and sat down, running his fingers along the smooth side of his briefcase.

Cal made a heap of chips and pieces of wood and bark under the grill. Summersby lit it. The giants, who were grouped around them at a few yards' distance, mumbled among themselves as the shavings took flame. The plucked and drawn fowls were laid on the grill. Watkins' mouth began to water.

"Now if we only had some coffee," he said to Adam. "One lousy pot of greasy-spoon coffee!"

VI

"I have seen you," said Villa to Adam, who was gnawing on a drumstick. "You wear the wig and a bone in the nose, and a tigerskin around you."

"Sure," said Adam. "I'm the Wild Man from Zululand. It's one job where my color's an advantage."

"A fine job!" said Villa. "You should have come down to my stand. The best chili in New York."

"I had a bowl there last week. Without my make-up, I mean."

"I will give you a bowl free when we go home. With tacos," added Villa generously.

"It's good stuff," said the boy.

Calvin Full wiped his fingers and his lips on a handkerchief. He looked about at the hall, through which the giants had now scattered; some of them were tinkering with the machines, others were simply loitering, as if bored by the whole matter of scientific research. They had lost their early wariness of the humans, and did not carry the green goads, but kept them tucked into holsters at the back of their swishing skirts.

One of them removed the blond man, Watkins, and set him to doing something with a pipe-and-block apparatus. The processes they went through with their strange mechanical and electrical gadgets, the end results they achieved, were a mystery to Calvin. And as the afternoon wore on, their conduct as a whole became even more mysterious. It was, from human standards, totally irrational. One would begin a test, analysis, or whatever it might be; he would follow it through its devious windings to its ambiguous result, or to no result, and suddenly leave it to begin something else, or come to watch the humans perform.

*   *   *   *   *

The longer he observed their conduct, the more worried he became. Finally, after a good bit of hiding and spying, he found out something which he had been trying to figure for hours; and then it seemed time for him to talk to someone about their escape.

The blond man had been peering into his briefcase. He zipped it shut quickly as Calvin approached, with a kind of guilty movement. What does he have in there? Calvin wondered.

"Mr. Watkins," he said, rubbing his chin and wishing he had a razor, "did you ever see a scientist, or laboratory assistant, skip from one thing to another as these creatures do?"

"I never did."

"Nor did I. They don't take care of their equipment, either; several times one or another has kicked down a neat pile of gear, and once I distinctly heard something break."

"It might be junked machinery," suggested Watkins.

"I doubt it."

One of the giants made a raucous noise—*Brangg!*

"And how irritable they are, in addition to their capriciousness and sloppiness! I can't imagine a race of emotional misfits producing equipment of such complexity. Their science is beyond ours in many ways, yet look at this place." He made a broad gesture. "When we were let out this morning, it was clean and well ordered. I've inspected dairies that were far dirtier. Now it's a hodge-podge of scattered materials, upset stacks of gear, tipped-over instruments. What sort of mind can bear such confusion?"

Watkins smiled. "The minds that conceived—well, that vertical maze, for instance—must be orderly after a fashion, even though it isn't the human fashion."

"This is far from what I wanted to say, though. Have you been noticing the door?"

"There isn't much to notice. It's a sliding panel like our wall."

"When one of the creatures leaves, he passes his right hand across what is evidently an electric eye beam, as nearly as I can place it about ten or eleven feet off the floor. That opens the door."

"Good going, Cal!" said Watkins. "I hadn't seen 'em do it."

"Our try for escape should be made as soon as possible," went on Calvin in a low voice. "As we've talked about, the object of these tests and experiments may be to infect us with neuroses—" Watkins grinned again—"I know my phrasing isn't right," said Calvin stiffly, "but I never looked into such matters. There's also Summersby's suggestion about the fate of guinea pigs. So I think we'd better try to get out right away."

"With five of them here?"

"If we have any luck, we may find an opportunity, yes. Occasionally they get absorbed in something, and that door makes no noise."

Watkins looked at his briefcase uncertainly. "Okay," he said finally. "May as well try it. Though God knows where we are when we do get out of the lab."

Calvin congratulated himself on his choice of an ally. "Good man," he said.

In the next hour they managed to build a crude platform beside the door, of various boxlike things, nondescript plastic blocks and impedimenta. The giants didn't even look at them. They were, indeed, a strange race. Now the platform was high enough so that Calvin felt he could reach the opening ray.

Summersby wandered over. "What are you doing?" he asked, seeming to force out the question from politeness, not curiosity.

"We're going to make a break, High-pockets," said Watkins. "Want to help?"

"They won't let you," said the big man.

"We can try, can't we?" asked Watkins hotly.

"It's your neck."

"Listen, you may be the size of a water buffalo, but if Cal and Adam and I piled on you, you'd go down all right. Why don't you cooperate?"

Summersby stared at him a moment and Calvin thought he was going to say something, something that would be important; but he shrugged and went across the hall and into the prison box.

"What's eating that big bastard, anyway?" said Watkins.

Calvin believed he knew, but it was not his secret; it was Summersby's. He said nothing.

"Watch it," said Watkins. "They're coming." The two men scurried behind their rampart. The five giants marched, flat-footed, down the hall, their thick arms swinging. The door opened and all of them went out. It closed behind them.

"How about that!" said Watkins exultantly, a grin on his face.

"I'll get Mrs. Full and the others," said Calvin. He felt a tingle of rising excitement. "Get up there and be ready to open it. We'll give them five minutes and then make our break."

"Right." Watkins was already clambering up the boxes and blocks.

Calvin almost ran to his wife. She was standing in front of the color organ. "Dear," he said, and halted.

"Yes, what is it, Calvin?"

"I don't know. I was going to say—"

A sluggishness was pervading his body, a terrible lassitude crept through his brain. What was it? What was happening?

"I was going to—"

He caught her as she slumped, but could not hold up her weight, and sank to the floor beside her. His eyes blinked a couple of times. Then knowledge and sensation vanished together.

VII

Tom Watkins awoke slowly. He had a cramp in one arm from sleeping on it, but otherwise he was conscious of a comfortable, healthy feeling, which told him he'd slept well and long. He stretched and brushed a few pieces of straw from his face.

Straw?

He suddenly remembered sitting down on their platform, very sleepy and worried because of the abruptness of it.

He sat up. Summersby had just stood, yawning. "Did you carry me in here?" he asked the big man.

"I was going to ask you that."

"Christ! What happened?" He was wholly awake now. "Did you drop off out in the lab?"

"Yeah."

"So'd I," said Adam. He was sitting next to the Mexican, whom he now pushed gently. "You okay, Porfirio?"

Villa erupted with a grunt. The Fulls were looking at each other owlishly.

And then it hit him. Watkins twisted, cased the floor, and saw nothing but straw and fountain and tree trunks. He was literally staggered, and nearly lost his balance.

His briefcase was gone!

He stared about wildly, panic lifting in him like a swift debilitating disease. Then he took four fast steps and grabbed Summersby by the coat. It was queer, but he didn't even think of anyone else having taken it. Summersby towered over him, but he could be brought down.

"Okay, you skyscraper," said Watkins, "where'd you put it?"

"Put what?"

"My case! Where is it?"

"I never touched your damned case."

Well, Watkins could smell honesty, and here it was. That startled amazement was genuine. He glared at Adam Pierce, Villa, the Fulls. Not that last pair, surely! As rock-ribbed and staunchly honest as their New England coasts, and about as imaginative. Not the colored boy, either, a good kid; and he didn't think it was Villa.

"We must have been carried in here by the scientists," said Adam rationally. "Maybe they left it outside."

That was logical. But he'd had a death-grip on the handle when he fell asleep, just as he always did. He looked at them all again. He went from wall to wall, kicking the straw. Then he scowled at the sand box, the only place a thing that size could be stashed away. He was suddenly on his knees, tossing sand left and right.

Avoiding certain places, he checked the pile. Nothing! Not a scrap of leather or a piece of green paper!

"If you are through," said Villa heavily, "I wish to use the box."

"Go ahead, Viva." Watkins walked across the room, groping for a cigarette, then remembering he had none left. "What happened out there?" he asked loudly. "Were we doped? Something in the chickens?"

"We were awake for a long time after we ate," said Adam. "Not even these people could make a drug act on six of us in the same minute, after that long; too many differences in metabolism. If that's the word I want."

"They weren't even in the room when we dropped off," said Mrs. Full.

*　　*　　*　　*　　*

That was a tip-off. Watkins momentarily forgot his great loss. "They left, and in a minute, we were asleep. They must have pumped some sort of gas into the lab. Sleep gas."

"Is there such a thing?" asked Cal. "An anesthetic vapor that would permeate such a large place so quickly?"

"Is there such a thing as a four dimensional maze?" asked Adam shortly.

Watkins grinned. He wasn't the only one who needed his morning coffee.

Then he thought of his briefcase again. He tried to push the moving wall to one side; no go. He got mad again. "It's no good to them," he said. "What do they want with it?"

"It couldn't have been so important that—" began Full.

"Important?" Watkins was yelling now, and although he disliked raising his voice and making scenes, he did it now, with furious pleasure. "Cal, you never saw anything more important in your life than that case, and I don't care how many blue-ribboned cows you've gaped at!"

"What was in it?" asked Villa.

"Money, goddammit, money!" It didn't matter if his secret came out now. In this insane place, God knew where, the cautious habits of half a lifetime slid away. "The best haul I'd made this year. The contents of the safe of Roscoe & Bates, that's what was in it! Better than twenty-two thousand in good, green cash!"

"The contents of a safe?" Calvin Full frowned. "You mean you were a messenger, taking it somewhere, and got on that roller coaster with—"

Adam Pierce laughed abruptly. "No, he wasn't a messenger," he said. "He wasn't any messenger. He's a safe-cracker. Mr. Watkins, what good do you think it'd do you in here?"

"We'll get back."

"You're a safe-cracker?" asked Mrs. Full, her pale face lengthening with horror, disgust, and fear. "A criminal?"

"In a manner of speaking, ma'am," said Tom Watkins, "I am."

"I'll be hanged," said Summersby. "And you accused me of stealing your loot. I ought to butter you all over the wall."

"You try it, you overgrown galoot. I didn't do a hitch in the Philippines for nothing." Watkins smoothed back his hair, which was dangling into his eyes. "Sure, I'm a safe man. Don't worry, Mrs. Full, that doesn't mean I'm a thug." She looked scared.

"That's right," said Adam, still chuckling. "This boy's the aristocracy of crime. You don't have to worry about your purse. He only plays around with big stuff."

Tom flipped him a grin. "I'll bet you even know why I was on the coaster."

"Sure. You were hiding out."

"That's it. If I kept out of sight till dark I was okay. They were out for me, because my touch is known; but who'd think of checking an amusement park?" He turned as Cal made a noise in his throat. The Vermonter was a study in outraged sensibilities.

"You—you swine," he said, a typical Victorian hero facing the mustache-twisting villain. "You stole that money—"

"My morals and your morals, Cal," said Watkins as genially as he could, "are probably divergent, but it doesn't make a whale of a difference now, does it?"

Full turned to his wife and began to mutter to her.

Villa said, "I don't like crooks, I run a respectable stand and I am an honest man," and scratching his hand where the healed burn was, he turned away likewise. Summersby was sitting on the tire, and only Adam looked sympathetic. The boy wasn't crooked, that was plain, but Watkins had the glamor that a big-time thief has for the young, the fake aura of Robin-Hoodism.

He shook his head. He'd had to spill it. For a while they'd trusted him and now he was a pariah.

The food panel opened and something plumped in. Watkins glanced at his chronograph. Ten o'clock Saturday. He went over to the food.

It was a big, glossy chocolate-brown vulture with a blue head.

"Well," said Adam. "Well, now, I don't know."

"They pulled a boner this time," said Watkins. "Unless it's part of the conditioning."

Villa picked it up. "It weighs many pounds. It's warm, just killed. I don't want any of it." He dropped it on the straw. "With my spices, perhaps; but not cooked on that grill, without sauce and spice. Aargh!"

Watkins thought, Amen to that. He rubbed the sandy bristles on his chin. No razor or soap here. It dawned on him that he was thirsty, and he went to the fountain. As it always did when he bent over to drink, the curious web of silver strands in the corner caught his eye. There were so many puzzles about this damned lab that he despaired of ever solving all of them.

After fifteen minutes, the wall opened. They went out, Villa carrying the vulture. He flung it at the feet of the chief scientist, who was there with two associates.

"No!" he bellowed up at it. "We do not eat this!" He articulated slowly, clearly, as though to a foreigner with a slim knowledge of English. It picked up the great bird and regarded it closely, then without warning threw it at one of the other giants.

The vulture caught it on the side of the head and knocked it off balance; falling to its knees, it bleated out an angry sound and dived for the boss' legs. They went down together in a gargantuan scrimmage that made the humans dance backward to avoid being smashed by the thick swinging arms.

Tom Watkins walked off, unimpeded, to look for his briefcase. It was nowhere in the lab. He cursed bitterly. Twenty-two grand, up the spout.

The head scientist, having chastised the other, left the room; Watkins had a glimpse of another fully as large, with something like a big table therein. Shortly the creature returned, carrying in one arm a load of wood chips, and in the other a bulgy, leathery thing that turned out to be a partially stunned octopus, still dripping the waters of an unknown ocean.

They killed it, rebuilt their grill (larger this time), and cut up the octopus and cooked and ate it. It wasn't as bad as Watkins had feared.

After a dragging day, they were locked into their box—no one had a chance to gimmick the wall, for the giant were watching them closely—and shortly afterward a load of raw vegetables was dumped in.

Watkins paced the floor after he had eaten, waiting for the sleep gas, determined to combat it if he could. When the drowsiness came, he walked faster. It didn't do any good. He knew he was sinking to the floor. Powerful stuff, he said to himself, very powerful st—

* * * * *

Mrs. Full kept close to Calvin all through Sunday. They had been here since Thursday, all these men without women, and she knew there were men who had to have women frequently or they became vicious and could not be stopped by any thought of consequences. The Mexican seemed all right, but you never knew with a person from a Latin country.

Another facet of the same problem was the fact that she and Calvin were supposed to be on their honeymoon. She faced it: she was frustrated. She wanted a honeymoon, no matter what sort of prison they were in. So after their first meal on Sunday, she asked Calvin to fix up a private apartment in their prison.

With various materials, plastic blocks and the different sizes of slabs, and some screens of translucent fabric she had dug up in a corner, he made a walled-off compartment just large enough for two.

Then one of the scientists looked in, saw what he was doing, and promptly knocked it down.

Adam, who had been helping in the latter stages, squinted at the ceiling of the box. "You know, Mrs. Full, I think they can see us through that. If it's opaque to us, it still might be transparent to them; like a mirror, I mean, I've seen them at home, mirror on one side, window from the other. That'd explain the light we get in here. And if they want to observe us all the time, then this private cell of yours would make 'em mad."

"But *it* had no roof," she objected.

"That's right." He shook his head. "Another theory gone poof."

"I'll build it again," said Calvin stubbornly, and did so. This time the giants left it alone. He and Adam made a screen for the sand box too, and built a permanent grill on one side of the box.

VIII

By Tuesday they were all in a state of anxiety and scarcely-contained rage. Their surveillance was casual, often non-existent, yet not once had they been able to block the wall of their prison or open the great door of the laboratory. Circumstances, chance, fate, whatever you wanted to call it, something had stopped them every time.

There were three giants in the lab today. Sometimes there would be one of them, sometimes as many as five; but always there would be the one who had first removed them from the box, who seemed to be the head scientist, giving orders, bullying the others in the queer emotional way of these creatures. Today there were three. As usual, when they had let the humans out, the lab was clean and orderly. The sloppy scientists had very efficient janitors, thought Adam. By this time the place was a shambles.

Out in the lab, there rose the honking sound of pain and anger—some of the noises they made, especially the commands, were recognizable now to the people—and a sharp slap. Then Mrs. Full hurried into the box, carrying a number of two-foot-square slabs under her arm.

"What happened, ma'am?"

"Hello, Adam. The criminal Watkins played a few bars of a real song on that device, and the brutes hit him." She laid down the slabs. "Our harmonies enrage them, I think perhaps cause them actual pain. They held the sides of their heads where ears ought to be, and shook themselves and made those hideous noises."

"They hit me when I sang the other day," said Adam, "remember?"

"That's right. Look here." She sat down, pulled one of the thick slabs onto her lap. "I found these under a shelf out there. One of the creatures knocked them off and I picked them up. I wondered why they had been up there, when so many stacks of them just sit around on the floor."

"I never saw any like these, ma'am. They have that little ridge on the edge there, and the border of different colored stuff around 'em."

"Watch what happens when I push the ridge upward, Adam. It's like an automatic button." She pressed it and the slab, at first gay orange, turned pale blue; on it appeared three lines of squiggly characters, like a cross between Arabic writing and Egyptian hieroglyphics.

"A magic slate," said Adam. "That's neat!"

"You haven't seen anything yet," she told him, and pushed the ridge again. The writing disappeared, and out of the slab leered a bull gorilla, paws on chest, eyeing Adam with beady, ridge-browed malevolence. It took a second for sanity to convince him that it was only a picture: three-dimensional, on a two-dimensional sheet of plastic, but so real he half-expected the beast to charge out at him. "What about that?" she asked.

He hit his thigh with a fist. It was a photograph, he imagined, but made by an illusory process so far ahead of anything humanity could produce that it seemed he might glimpse whatever was behind the gorilla if he put his eyes down to the side of the slate. "Gosh!" he said, feeling it a little naive but afraid to swear in front of her. "Isn't that something!"

"It's a book," she said, "an album of photographs. Look here."

The next picture was an equally miraculous one of half a dozen monkeys sitting on a tree trunk. Adam looked at it, then at the farthest trunk in their box of a room. Undeniably it was the same one.

Under the picture was a line of squiggles that probably spelled out the scientists' equivalent of "monkeys."

"They were here, in this place," said Adam. "The giants must have experimented on them too." He turned his eyes up to the woman and saw that she was white and drawn. "What happened to them?" he asked. "There aren't any monkeys here now."

"Exactly," she said. She put on the next picture, and after a moment the next.

Dogs greeted his eyes, so real he could almost hear them pant; a cow gazed stolidly at him; a cheetah sat on a mound of straw with clown's head cocked inquisitively; two cockatoos perched in rigid still life on the silver rod of the prison box.

"What happened to them?" he asked again.

"The experiments ended," she said.

Then there flashed out a thing like a blue sponge with legs, a thing which sat in the cat's-cradle they had speculated so much about. From its center two ruby eyes blazed with three-dimensional fire. *That* never came from Earth! Mars or Venus could have produced it, maybe, or a planet so far from Earth that it bore no name. He said as much, his voice quavering.

She stared at him. Moistening her lips, she said, "If that was here, in this box, then *where are we?*"

He shook his head. He could not even guess. "What's next?"

The last picture in the slate was a group portrait of himself, the Fulls, Summersby, Watkins, and Porfirio Villa.

When was that taken? They were sitting in a circle on the straw, eating something. Peering closely, he thought it must be the vegetables, for there was a small heap of round things next to Calvin Full which were probably buckeyes. Sunday night, then.

"They must have taken it through the food panel," he said. "Are there any more pictures?"

"That's all. I don't know what's in the other ones yet."

Calvin came in. She handed him the first "book" and showed him how to operate it. He flipped through it and when he came to the monstrosity in the web his eyes widened. "What is it?" he asked, in the hard twang of his region.

"A guinea pig, like all the others including us," his wife said.

"The tree trunks are explained now," said Adam, half to himself. "The sand box, too. That isn't a very scientific-looking treatise, but I guess it's more of a memento, a record of us all." He raised his brows in a facial shrug. "Us and the monkeys," he said. "Gosh!"

*   *   *   *   *

She took the next big slate on her lap. It was lavender. The first few pages to appear were covered with the curious writing, very large and only a few words to a page. Then came pictures of many things, not photographs but drawings and paintings in vivid color, and the things could in no way be linked to science. There were portraits of the tall creatures themselves, in various settings, some in labs like this one, some outdoors in a landscape that was predominantly scarlet and green; there were group scenes in which they ate odd-looking foods and walked down blue pathways and examined strange pets and familiar animals. Under each picture was a short grouping of squiggles, marks, scribbles, etc.

"Can that be a science book?" asked Cal, leaning over his wife's shoulder. The beings were pictured as simply as possible, in no minute detail whatever, and their activities were of the dullest and most prosaic sort.

This pattern was followed through page after page—a picture (some of them were of things so alien they could not be placed by either the Fulls or himself), a single character, then a short word and another, long or short as the case might be. After a dozen of them had flashed on and off Adam noticed that the large character was always repeated at the beginning of the last word.

When he realized what it meant, the whole business clicked into focus. The whole damned deal, the lab and the scientists and the experiments and the meaning of the four magic slates, and everything. There was no particular reason why this last slate should have done it, for it was no more suggestive than many other things that he had seen; it was simply the last piece of evidence, the final push that sent him headlong into terrible knowledge.

Carefully, desperately, he went over it all in his mind, while the Fulls spoke in low tones.

God, he thought, *oh, God!* He was shivering now. He was more terrified than he had ever been before. His tongue felt thick.

The punishments, the high stool and the arbitrary cuffs and swats; the gadgets, the mazes, the puzzles; were they all a part of the conditioning to neurosis of a scientific experiment? They were not.

*   *   *   *   *

Adam had found an answer, the only possible answer. The fourth slate had given it to him, although a hundred hints of it had shown up every day. His psych teacher would be ashamed of him for muddling along so many days, believing in a theory that was so plainly impossible.

He addressed Mrs. Full. She was a little sharper than her husband, and this was more in her line, too. He had to make her discover the same answer. He had to *know* it was right. And then he had to get out of that place in a hell of a hurry.

"Ma'am, you know what this is?"

"No, Adam."

"Look here. See this big letter, repeated at the first of this word?"

"Yes."

He flipped a few "pages" past. "It's the same with all of them, you see? And the middle word is always the same—four curly letters. You know what that middle word is?"

"No, Adam."

"It's 'stands for' or 'means.'" He stared at her. "Get it?"

She thought an instant. "Of course. Adam, that's very clever of you." She wasn't scared yet. She hadn't seen the implication.

"'Stands for'?" Calvin repeated.

"A stands for Apple," explained Mrs. Full. "Or A stands for Airship, or whatever it might be. It's an alphabet book, dear."

She still hadn't caught it. "Remember when Mr. Full built the cubbyhole here," Adam said, "and the giant knocked it down? Why was he angry?"

"I suppose they want to observe us without any hindrance."

"No, ma'am," he said with conviction. "That was simple frustration. They want to see everything, whether it's interesting to them or not. They aren't scientifically disappointed if they can't, they're just frustrated. Think of the punishment we get, slaps, the dunce stool."

"As though we were children," she said.

"Exactly. Now, here are these books. An alphabet book, and these others. What age would you figure them for? You taught kindergarten, you said. This is something I wouldn't know."

"I'd say they're for fairly bright children about five or six years old."

"Or for us," said her husband, "when they start to teach us their language."

"They are children's books, though, with short sentences and the gaudy pictures our own children love." Mrs. Full stared at Adam. Her brown eyes widened. "Adam," she said, "you've guessed something."

"You guess it too," he pleaded. She had to corroborate his own idea. "Think of all the things about them we haven't been able to make out."

"Nursery books...." she said slowly. "Instability to the point of insanity, if you found it in adult humans. Sloppiness and inefficiency, when these machines point to a high degree of neatness of mind. Wandering attention, inability to concentrate for long periods. Positive tantrums over nothing. Cruelty and affection mixed without rhyme or reason." She took him by the arm, her fingers strong with fear and urgency. "Tell me, Adam."

*   *   *   *   *

His breath hissed. He was filled with panic. Where there had been only anxiety for his own life and his world, there was now a fearful knowledge that he could scarcely bear without shrieking. She had it too, but she didn't dare say it. It was a horrible thing.

"These machines," he said, "aren't scientific testers at all."

"Yes?"

"They're toys."

"Yes?"

"We aren't guinea pigs. We're—we're pets. They've had other animals, from Earth and from God knows where, and now they have people."

"Yes. Go on, say it." She thrust her face fiercely up to his.

"Those twelve-foot 'scientists' are kids," he said. Then he stopped and deliberately got his cracking voice under control. She was just as frightened as he was but she wasn't yelling. "It's the only answer. Everything fits it. They're about five years old."

Calvin Full frowned. "If that's true, we're in trouble."

"You're damn right we're in trouble!" said Adam. "A kid doesn't take care of a pet like a scientist takes care of a guinea pig or a white rat. If it annoys him, he's liable to pick it up and throw it at a wall! I might get my head torn off for singing, or you could be dismembered for making a mistake with one of those toys."

"Some children tear the wings off butterflies," said Mrs. Full. She stood up. "I'll go and tell the others," she said firmly. "It doesn't seem to me that we have much time left."

"If we start to bore them—" began Adam, and shut up.

She went out. In about five minutes everyone had come into the box but Watkins, who was playing the color organ. They discussed the discovery in low voices, as though the alien children might be listening; Villa and Summersby examined the slates. After a while Watkins was pushed in, looking rather worn and frayed. Adam was standing in the far corner under the silver web. He saw the wall start to slide shut, remembered his dowel, and tried to see if it was still in place at the bottom of the wall.

He couldn't see it. Maybe it blended with the color behind it, or maybe somebody had accidentally kicked it out of place.

The wall slid shut.

IX

Summersby was losing the sense of being apart, of having no problems no matter what happened. These people had drawn him into their trouble against his will; the situation was so bad that he could no longer tell himself he didn't give a damn. So he had a bad heart! He couldn't turn his back on these poor devils because of that. It was stupid and selfish. He felt sorry for them. He was uncomfortable with them, as he always was with standard-sized people, and he would still repel any attempt on their part to get close to him; but he was a little chastened by what he had been through. He recognized that.

It was all very well to say he didn't care where he died, but it would be a hell of a lot more dignified to accomplish it as a free man, rather than as a harried rabbit. Even if he were killed trying to escape, it would be endurable. But if his heart gave out while he was, say, trundling up and down the nursery in that ridiculous little auto thing, he knew his last breath would be a bitter one.

Adam had just said, "I laid a rod across the sill there." Summersby walked to the wall, which appeared to be closed as usual. Just as he came to it, he caught the sheen of metal in a thin line up the corner, and knew that he was seeing part of one of the machines in the nursery. The dowel had held the door.

Something moved outside; he could hear the dull slap of immense flat feet. They were going to be fed. He strolled away from the corner, saying quietly, "It worked, Adam. Don't check it now, though."

The small panel opened and one of the garishly hued platters was put in, loaded with a wriggling, seething mass of grubs and half-dead locusts.

"Supper?" cried Villa. "This is supper? Do they think we are a lot of African natives?"

"Well," said Adam, "I guess they were fooled by me." It was the first time he had made any sort of joke about his color. Possibly, thought Summersby, he's becoming one of the group, as I am. God knows the kid has as much reason to be bitter about people as I have; or more reason. It's put him on the defensive.

Summersby felt more chastened than ever.

No one cared to sample the insects. They walked away from the platter and hoped aloud that their captors would see the refusal and give them something else, but nothing was pushed in. After a quarter of an hour Watkins said, "Think it's safe to have a try at the door?"

"No," said Summersby.

Watkins jumped to his feet. "Listen, I've had all I can stomach of you!" he yelled. "If you don't want to help, okay, but keep your nose—"

"I was going to say that they'll be pumping in the sleep gas pretty soon, and we don't know whether they do it from outside the nursery or outside this box."

"That's right," said Calvin Full.

Watkins eyed him a moment. "I'm sorry, Summersby," he said then. "I shot off my mouth too quick."

"They filled the nursery with it once," went on Summersby, "but it seems logical to think they could also let it into this room alone. Maybe it works on them, maybe not; if it does, then they wouldn't flood the nursery with it every night, because the adults have to come in and clean the place up."

"A clever thought, Mr. Summersby," said the woman.

"Not particularly. At any rate, I'm going to stand by the crack and try to get enough air to stay awake; then when I think the coast's clear, I'll shove the door open and scout around. If I find a way out, I'll come back and drag you into the nursery and wake you."

"Why are you doing this?" asked Villa suspiciously. "No, Mr. Big Man, I don't like you going out alone. I think you wouldn't come back. You don't like us."

Watkins, evidently on edge from his mauling by the children, whirled on the Mexican. "Oh, shut your yap! The guy's doing you a favor." Then he said to Summersby, "I'll come along."

Summersby grinned wryly.

"I'm not saying you'd run out on us, man." Watkins made the motions of going through his pockets for a cigarette, which some of them still did occasionally out of hopeful habit. "I know locks and I might be able to help if you ran into trouble."

"Come on along, then." He put an eye to the thin slit. "Here comes one of them. It's the head scientist." He grinned. "Or the kid who owns us, who lives in this house and invites his little pals in every day to play with his toys and his pets."

The monster disappeared. Presently Watkins said, "It's in. I'm sleepy."

Summersby stretched as tall as he could and put his mouth to the crack, trying to breathe only what air came through from the nursery. He saw the enormous child pass on its way to the door, and shortly the sound of its heavy feet stopped. He felt drowsy, his eyelids flickered. He beat his hands together, sucking in air from the opening. Villa started to snore.

Watkins said, "I'm about done, Summersby." He was kneeling at the crack below Summersby, and his voice was sluggish. In a few seconds he rolled over on the straw.

When did the adults come in to clean up? Summersby didn't dare wait much longer. He was fighting sleep with all his vigor. Possibly they wouldn't come till morning.

He had to chance it. He forced his fingers into the gap and heaved. The wall didn't move. Holding his breath, he propped one foot against the adjoining wall, dug his hands as far into the breach as possible, and hurled himself backward. The big door jolted an inch, hung, then slid back a couple of feet. He swung around and jammed himself through the aperture and the wall moved silently back into place; this time the dowel was not there, and when the wall stopped, there was no crack at the corner. Summersby must have kicked the dowel aside when he slid through. Watkins was inside, asleep.

He breathed deeply, and the effects of the sleep gas died, so that he was wide awake and felt very excited and eager. To analyze the reasons for his eagerness would have killed it, and besides he was in a hurry. He ran to the great door of the playroom, whose lintel towered twenty feet from the floor. Hastily he tossed apparatus, boxes, toy blocks, until he had made a pile five feet high.

Scrambling up this, the things sliding under his feet, he waved an arm above his head in the place where he believed the electric eye beam to be. Then the pile collapsed, and he fell into it, giving one knee a terrific crack and skinning his knuckles. The door glided open.

The next room was deserted, and the soft bluish light was dimmer here than in the nursery. This place was far less cluttered, containing no more than a big yellow machine, a gigantic table, and two six-legged chairs. There was a picture on the wall, the size of a barn's side, which he did not stop to look at.

The opposite door was open. The third room was a dining hall, with two tables and a number of chairs, these of metal with eight legs each. Luckily, there was no one in it.

In the next room—all four were in a straight line, and he thought, Either it's a long narrow house, or else it's as big as Rockefeller Center—there were a number of gadgets, colorful and complex like the children's toys, but of different construction. He glanced at them but did not pause until he came to the next door.

It was closed. He presumed its opener beam would be in the same place as that of the playroom, and looked around for something to stand on.

There seemed to be nothing small enough to move. He shoved at a couple of things, but they wouldn't budge. The only slim possibility was a big square brown box, set twelve feet off the floor on one of their mammoth tables. It was of a size to accommodate half a dozen cows, but looked as though it might be of flimsy enough materials, plastic probably, to push off the edge, from which it would fall exactly where he needed it.

He dragged a chair over, climbed up on its seat and then onto the table. He saw at once that the box would be immovable. There was an affair that might be a dynamotor attached to one side, various objects sticking out of the other, and four stacks of thick coils on top. He was turning away, hoping to find another door in one of the first rooms, when his eye was attracted to a square plate among the things on the right side of the box. The plate was glass, for its surface shone under the blue light, and he thought he saw the pin-point twinkling of stars in it.

On a hunch, he walked over to it. He knew quite a lot of astronomy and if this happened to be a telescope, he might be able to determine their location.

The field of the plate was full of stars, but in patterns he had never seen. He could not understand it. It was not a painting, for the stars twinkled. Where the blazes was the thing focused?

A huge dial beside the plate had a pointer and scores of notches, each labeled with a couple of squiggly characters. He turned the pointer experimentally. The screen blurred, showed a planet with rings: Saturn.

"Neat," he said to himself, and turned the pointer another notch. He got a view of a landscape, trees of olive green and crimson, seen from above. He tried other notches.

Finally, just as he had reminded himself that he had to hurry, he saw a familiar globe swim onto the glass. It was Earth, with the two Americas clearly defined.

What in hell...?

He pushed the pointer on, and was given another landscape, this time of prosaic hue, a meadow with a cow in it. He clicked the thing another notch and got a constellation pattern again. He pushed it back to the cow.

He felt his heart thudding fast, too fast; and he hoped with all his faculties that he wouldn't conk out before he had solved this riddle. There were other dials, other pointers, a little behind the first. He turned one slowly.

The cow grew larger until it almost filled the screen. Only when he could see nothing but its broad placid back did he realize that he was looking at this scene, as at the others, from *above*.

He tried a third pointer. The land whipped by beneath his gaze. He came to a city, the buildings reaching up to him in a wonderful illusion of depth.

Then it dawned on him what the machine was, and he gasped.

There was no use in looking for the outer door. He had found the answer to their last problem, and he had to get back to the box with that answer and thrash it out with all of them. There might be a salvation for them and there might not.

Leaving the screen showing the city, he jumped down off the table, raced back through the room and into the next, the dining hall. Still there were no signs of any of the giants. He had crossed the threshold of the third room when he heard a door open on his right. There was no time to gape around; he covered thirty feet in five strides, dodged under the hanging shelf of the strange yellow machine, like a low desk covered with cogwheels, and ran along beneath it till he came to the extreme end of the contrivance.

A pair of feet, either of which would have outweighed a draft horse, went past him; he dared not lean forward to see the rest of the brute, but it was undoubtedly an adult. It went into the playroom.

After twenty or twenty-five minutes, during which Summersby thought over the problem and agreed with himself that he couldn't find the solution alone, the giant came out of the playroom, crossed near his hiding place, and went out through a door beside the huge picture. It was not in a hurry, so he decided it had not noticed his absence from the box.

He dragged an easy chair over to the nursery door. It was just four times the size of Summersby's Morris chair at home, and about eight times as heavy. As he was crawling up the leg to the seat, he recalled that he had a bad heart. If he hadn't been clinging to the plastic with both arms, he would have shrugged.

He intercepted the beam and opened the door. Having no more than half a minute to get through before it shut, he had to leave the chair where it was. He hoped none of the adults would realize that its position had changed.

The playroom was clean and neat. Likely it would remain unvisited through the night. He went to the box and only then remembered it was shut tight. What did the kids do when they opened it during the day? He had seen them at it twice. They laid their hands on top of the box, there on the left.

Hauling over enough junk to make a pair of steps, he got onto the roof of the box. There was a bar, set into the coaming. He pressed it, leaned over, and saw the wall slide back. A second push returned it to its shut position. He opened it again, swung his legs over the edge, pressed the bar once more and dropped. Snatching up a green dowel from the floor, he jumped into the box as the door was closing. He had just time to lay the rod across the threshold, as Adam had done, before the wall reached it and was held.

Trying not to breathe, Summersby picked up Watkins and slung him over his shoulder. He forced his fingers into the crack and heaved. Again he threw his weight against the wall.

Then he was buckling at the knees, trying desperately to bring his mouth next to the opening, but not quite making it.

*   *   *   *   *

"Describe it again," said Watkins. "Give me all the details you can think of."

As Summersby went over what he remembered of the brown machine, Watkins tried to envisage it. A tough job, and he might not be able to handle it. To reverse a thing like that—when there'd be at least one or two principles he'd never heard of—well, that would be the job of a lifetime.

"How do you know that it's the instrument that brought us here?" he asked.

"It must be." Summersby looked intent, almost eager. "It has those dials that focus it almost pin-point on any planet they want; at least, I saw quite a few planets, from a distance and close up. I saw a cow and a city on Earth. Then there's the big brown box. It's hollow—the door was half open. If they bring things, living things, from other planets, they need a receiving station large enough to take 'em. The box. It's logical."

"It sure is." Adam whistled. "So we're on another planet. That was plain, if we'd thought about it seriously. No place on Earth could hide a race like this. Not with all the factories they must have to produce the toys and what you saw out there."

"Why couldn't we be inside the Earth?" asked Mrs. Full stridently.

Watkins said, "He looked *down* on Earth. That argues another planet."

"But how did they get us here? In two days?"

Watkins scratched his bristled chin and thought aloud. "It must have been instantaneous. Remember, we went through a quarantine and were healed of just about everything that was wrong with us. That must have taken a while."

"The octopus was still wet," said Adam, "and the grubs and locusts were still kicking. They must focus that rig on Earth and push a button and here it is, like that. Instant transmission of matter." He smiled weakly, as though he were proud of the phrase. He looked very frightened, thought Watkins, and unhappy.

Tom Watkins was scared, too, but not especially unhappy. For the first time in almost twenty years, he was free of worry about the bulls, the law. He only wished he knew what had happened to his loot.

"The planet," said Cal, "whatever its name is, must have the same gravity and atmosphere as Earth. Same water, too."

"That's right. So it's produced a race of critters with plenty of human characteristics," said Watkins.

"Have they done this before?" asked Mrs. Full. "I mean do you think we're the first to be snatched up?"

"No, I don't," said Watkins, surprised that she was talking directly to him. "People disappear all the time. Look at the famous ones: Judge Crater, Ambrose Bierce—"

"Somebody mention the *Marie Celeste*," growled Summersby.

*   *   *   *   *

The wall began to open.

"Here's the plan, quick," said Watkins. "I've got to get out and find the machine, and see if I can gimmick it so it'll work backward, send us home. The rest of you create a diversion, keep the kids' minds off me."

"What kind of a diversion?" asked Villa. His abstracted face showed plainly that he was thinking of his chili stand and what he would say to the idiot relief man about conditions he would doubtless find therein.

"If you were a kid with pets, intelligent ones, what would you watch them do for hours? Something unordinary—something you'd never imagine they'd do." He looked at his chronograph. "It's just ten. I never saw the gadget I couldn't figure out in two hours; if I'm not back by noon, you'd better come out, Summersby."

"What if it's four-dimensional?" asked Adam.

"It's possible I can cook up a way to reverse its action anyway. There are some principles of electricity and mechanics that must be universal."

"Shall we run the machines for them?" asked Mrs. Full. "To distract the children?"

"They're used to that," said Watkins. "They bore easy. Suppose you're a kid with a normal regard for pets. You've had cats and dogs and rabbits and now you have monkeys. The monkeys are a lot smarter and more versatile, but they have their limits too. You get jaded with 'em. But one day they—" he snapped his fingers—"they start playing soldiers! They drill, stage mock battles, die and come to life, scrimmage—hell, you go nuts! You can't take your eyes off 'em!"

"That's it," said Villa promptly. "The children have gorillas, cows, they have never seen anything like war."

"Maybe they don't know what war is," said Adam. "It might just look as if we were fighting. None of their toys show a sign of war being ever waged by this race, like our own kids' toys do."

"The toys of any people reflect their civilization in an unreliable and distorted way," said Cal Full rather stuffily. "A visitor from Mars in one of our playrooms would conclude that we already have spaceships and ray guns, and that our usual clothing is chaps, sombreros, and spacesuits."

"They'll get the idea," Watkins said impatiently. The giant children outside were bawling the word that meant "Come!" He was in a hurry. These fools were always arguing. "Let's go," he said. "The four of you line up over there, catch the kids' eyes, and High-pockets can boost me up to the beam. Then he'll join you."

* * * * *

Watkins grinned tightly, slapped Adam on the shoulder, poked Villa in the belly, and dived behind the nearest many-colored pile of gear the moment he saw the children weren't watching him. As he went toward the door, he heard Villa saying, "My fourth cousin Pancho was a great man for war, so I will be general. Spread out in the thin line and be ready to march when I command."

Summersby followed Watkins, and they came to the door. Watkins managed to get up on the big man's shoulders, and waved a hand above his head. Nothing happened.

"Stand on them," said Summersby.

He struggled to do so. "*Un, dos, tres*," roared the Mexican down the hall. "Begin!"

This time Watkins found the beam. The door glided aside. He dropped off Summersby's shoulders, jumped into the next room. A quick look showed him it was empty. As the door closed he heard Villa shouting hoarsely.

"Make bang noises for the guns. Fall dead, spring to life. We are mountain fighters of great skill. Climb on machines, drop off with bullets in your head, play you are—"

The door cut him off. Watkins chuckled. "What a ham," he said. He started for the opposite door.

X

It was ten minutes to twelve. Summersby was panting like a spent hound. He had not exercised in months, not since the doctors had told him his heart was just about gone, and he was surprised that he hadn't keeled over before now. Dashing around playing guerrilla like some six-year-old! It had been a damn good idea, though. The giant children—there were two of them today—were still enthralled, lying on their bellies with their furry watermelon heads propped in fantastic two-thumbed hands.

Leaning against a pink plastic maze wall, puffing, he thought, I've almost grown to like them. Why?

Because for the first time since he was sixteen, John Summersby had to bend his neck back to look up at someone. These grotesque humanoidal beings were the only living things which did not make him feel overgrown, uncouthly out of proportion, a hulking lout. If a chair was too narrow for him, it would be like the head of a pin to one of these kids: if a fork felt uncomfortably small in his own hand, it would be a minikin indeed in one of those vast paws.

In their shadows, Summersby was a very small man. It was an unwonted sensation, the most satisfying he had ever experienced.

He looked at them out there, as they lay watching Mrs. Full and Adam mowing down Cal and Villa with imaginary Brownings. He grinned, felt his lips curve in the unaccustomed grimace, and thought with no particular bitterness that he was getting mellow in his last days. "Hello, High-pockets," he said softly to the kid that owned him. "How's the weather up there?"

At five to noon the door opened. Summersby, seeing its silent motion, left off the mimic gunplay and started for the wall, where he could intercept Watkins and find out whether he'd been successful. But the safe-cracker came running down the middle of the room, yelling.

"Come on, everybody!"

"Come on?"

The two giant children were on their feet, uncertain of what was happening. Obviously they didn't realize Watkins had been out of the room at all.

"The adults spotted me!" roared the blond man, swinging his briefcase wildly; where had he found that? "They're after me!"

Summersby let out an involuntary grunt when through the twenty-foot door came an eighteen-foot creature, a thing so mind-shakingly huge that even the ranger's size complex wasn't pleased by it. This was an adult: leaner in the body, broader of hand and thicker of limb, wearing trouserlike garments and a flaring jacket of royal purple caught by a ruby bar, it advanced calmly into the hall, clumping flat-footed in three yard strides. From its heavy-lipped gash of a mouth came noises like a whole orchestra badly in need of tuning.

"Hwhrangg!" it cried, waving its hands in the air. "Breemingg!" It appeared to be soothing the children, telling them that Daddy was here.

*   *   *   *   *

Mrs. Full, on the control platform, screamed. Her husband ran to her, Summersby stepped out irresolute, Adam stood stunned. But Porfirio Villa, afire with the heady make-believe carnage of the afternoon, was as quick to act as his fourth cousin Pancho could have been. A dozen waddling leaps, a swift swing of his legs over the side, and the Mexican landed in the little red vehicle with the vast control board, the car that only he had been able to master. Pressing buttons, pulling plungers, sliding levers, he whirled it around and sent it at the towering adult.

The beast skipped out of his way, blaring anger; he came about sharply, gunned his "motor"—if it was that—and rammed the gigantean enemy on the leg. There was the clear sharp snap of bone breaking. As Villa's car overturned, the creature fell at full length, with a crash like an elephant dropping out of a tree. It contracted its body and gripped its ankle with both hands, honking dismally.

Summersby was running. He skidded up to the groveling Villa, yanked him to his feet and shoved him out of range of the injured beast. The two children had broken into the barks that were their equivalent of weeping, one drawing its goading rod. Summersby crouched, went toward it, hoping to bring it down before it stunned him. As he came within diving range, though, the orange airship streaked over his head and jammed its nose into the child's belly. It folded over with a whoosh, grabbing its middle, as the toy wobbled off in eccentric flight.

Mrs. Full, the expert at flying the miniature vessel, was hectically jamming her blocks along their metal rods; something had gone wrong with the mechanism at the crash. Her husband hauled her off the seat and rushed her toward the door.

The remaining child stood in the middle of the floor, staring at its groaning, breathless playmate and at the maimed adult, honking a little frightened song to itself. Skirting it, the humans made for the door as fast as they could go.

Summersby overtook Watkins. "I found it okay," panted the crook.

"Can you work it?" They were through the door now, the two of them in the lead, running across the first of the rooms.

"There were other adults," said Watkins. "Three or four saw me. I don't know where they went."

"*Can you work it?*"

"The matter transmitter?" He grinned briefly. "Sure. There's two principles I don't get, but—"

The doorway before them was crowded by several of the giants. They came through, not hurrying, talking rather placidly; their movements had the swiftness of the children's without their jerkiness. In their hands were green goads. They pointed and came down upon the humans.

"Scatter!" yelled Summersby, and dodged under the shelf of the machine where he had taken cover last night. He went to the end. In seconds they would be peering under the shelf, spotting him, thrusting in their shockers and laying him out. And, damn it all, he cared! He didn't want to be stopped when so much of the fight was won. His heart might stop, he couldn't help that, but till it did he wanted to go on fighting. Balling his fists, he started to leave the sanctuary. Then he heard Adam Pierce begin to sing.

He had a high tenor voice, mellow with a sweet touch of huskiness in it, and he was singing "Drink to Me Only" at the top of his lungs.

He hadn't gone crazy! Summersby remembered the punishments they had endured for making harmonious noises on the musical toy, the slap Adam got for singing, the agonies the kids had gone through at Earth-type melody. Adam had thought of the only weapon they could use—*song*.

"Or leave a kiss within the cup," roared Summersby, and without further thought walked into the room. Watkins had chimed in now, breathless but true of pitch.

Three eighteen-foot brutes were standing there. Vast hands were pressed to bulbous heads, and agonized croaks came from gaping mouths. Whatever a tune did to them, it wasn't pleasant. What weird auricular structure could cringe so from a simple song? It did, and that was enough.

Mrs. Full clutched his arm. "One of them struck Calvin with his prod," she wailed.

"Where is he?"

"Near that door."

Beginning to sing again, Summersby pelted for the prone milk inspector. He picked him up and slung him, limp as a dead doe, over his left shoulder. The others were gathering. He motioned them forward, and, as Watkins joined him, ran on.

"Where'd you find your case?"

"On a table. Hope the dough is all in there." He glanced back. "They're coming. We're racking 'em but they're game."

The woman, Adam and Villa were right behind them. As they reached the midpoint of the third room, the dining hall, one of the beings staggered through the door behind them. It had lost its goad and was flattening its hands on its skull as Adam and Mrs. Full swung into "Dixie." It came at them like a drunk, unable to navigate a straight course but determined to reach them. It'll stamp on us, thought Summersby, easing Full back a little on his arm. It only has to come down once or twice with that Cadillac-sized foot and we're squashed ants. He sang.

"To live and die in...."

The second brute appeared, lurched over and fell on the table, caught up a flat trencher and skimmed it at them. It was as big as a bathtub. "Drop!" cried Summersby, went to one knee, felt the wind of the trencher's passing ruffle his hair.

The next door was closed. Summersby slammed himself flat against the wall and Adam, cat-lithe and fast, scrambled up over him, stood on his shoulders and broke the controlling beam. The aliens came down the room like two epileptic furies. "Sing!" said Watkins. "Everybody!" The door slid aside with maddening slowness.

"Try a fast one," said Mrs. Full. "'Blow the Man Down.'" It was a funny suggestion, coming from her. Summersby actually chuckled as he started to sing.

"As I was a-walkin' down Paradise Street...."

*   *   *   *   *

The third monster entered the dining hall, caught the full blast of their five voices (Calvin Full was still out, but Villa was giving a rum-tum-tum accompaniment), and sank to its knees, shaking its head as though it had been sapped. One of the others made a desperate leap at them, landing prone within a yard of Summersby. Melodies affect its organ of equilibrium, he thought; poor thing's in agony. "I says to her, Lollie, and how d'ye do...."

They were through the doorway now. The only pursuer still on its feet was reeling after them, green rod still held in one shaking hand. Its rust-red eyes were bulging out from their deep pits, and a thin trickle of violet ichor came from its nostril. It made guttural, creaking noises.

"Down at the end," said Watkins. "The brown box."

"Did you gimmick it?" asked Summersby.

"I think so. We have to take a chance. The main idea is easy. I guessed at a few things, but I think it'll work. Unless one of our big pals checked on it and mucked up my improvements."

It was twenty yards away; but so was the last of the monsters. Summersby changed Full to his other arm and added his voice to the general clamor for a bar or so, then asked Watkins the question that had been nagging at him. "Can we all go? Or does somebody have to send the others?"

"I'll send you. I'm not too sure I can get through. The dials and focusing lenses are on the outside, you know."

"I'll work it, then." They were at the table; he dropped Full and helped Adam shove a chair to the table. The woman and Villa were singing "Quiereme Mucho" in Spanish, their voices a trifle hoarse by now.

"You will like hell. It'd take me ten minutes to teach you how to work the transmitter. Think we have ten minutes?"

The giant was standing still, weaving, pawing the air. It would not give in to its pain and dizziness. If it fell now it might hit them. It was that close.

"You've *got* to show me. I have a bad heart. I'm due to die in a month or two," said Summersby urgently.

Watkins stared at him. "Do you think you went through the past hours with a rotten ticker? Don't make me laugh."

"It's true. I'm just waiting to die. You're no more than thirty-eight or forty, and you've got twenty-two thousand dollars there," he said, gesturing at the briefcase. "I don't give a damn about the morals of the case. You're a decent fellow and you ought to have this break."

Watkins snarled, as he gave the valiantly singing Mrs. Full a hand up to the chair seat, "You think I have a martyr complex? You think I *want* to stay here? I'm elected, that's all! It's me stays or it's everybody! I haven't the time to teach you to work it!" He hit Summersby a hard blow on the chest. "Your heart's fixed up the same as Adam's eyes and Cal's sinus. These gentry could turn your lungs upside down without opening you up, they're that good. Go back to your woods. You're okay."

"No," said Summersby with stubborn rage. "I'm sick of waiting to die. That's why I took the coaster ride in the first place. That's why I wanted—"

"You're nuts. You have a heart to match your frame, Highpockets, if you'd admit it. Hand up old Cal."

The monster took two wobbling steps toward them. They were all on the chair, then clambering onto the table. Watkins swung open the door of the brown box. "Fast," he said urgently, "fast!"

Adam had Cal by the armpits; he lugged him into the dark interior. Villa jumped in, Mrs. Full following. Summersby confronted the safe-cracker.

"Show me how to work the machine. I don't believe they could mend a bad heart."

Watkins handed him the briefcase with so unexpected a motion that Summersby took it automatically. "Send it to Roscoe & Bates, if I don't turn up. I guess I can't use it here." He put a hand under his coat. "Go on, Highpockets."

"No!"

Watkins drew a gun, a small steel-blue thing that looked as wicked as a rattler. Summersby had had no idea that he was carrying it. "Hop in, tall man," said Watkins, grinning. "You're holding up the works."

Reluctantly Summersby backed away, stood in the door of the box. He could jump Watkins, but if the mechanism were so complex, he would only doom them all. "You're out of your head," he said.

"Sure."

Abruptly above the safe-cracker towered the fantastic form of their forgotten enemy, reaching for them, one hand still to its head. Summersby inflated his lungs.

"Should auld acquaintance be forgot," he roared tunefully, "and never brought to mind!"

Everyone joined him. It was a startling cataclysm of sound, even to Summersby. The alien tottered, hand outstretched; its mouth fell open, its eyes popped, the violet blood coursed from its nostril; with a shudder it clawed the air, honked grotesquely, and pitched forward, half on and half off the table, where it lay gurgling. A spot on the side of its skull, about the width of a gallon jug, on which the hair grew sparse and gray, pulsed as though there were no bone beneath the skin, as though a bellows within was puffing it in and out, in and out. Its ear, thought Summersby. Probably we've wrecked it for good. Maybe the thing will die. Then Watkins is a gone goose, if he stays. He was about to lunge at the steady gun-hand when Adam and Villa yanked him backward into the box. Adam was crying.

"Try and come too, Mr. Watkins, try and come too," he said.

Watkins laughed. "I'll make out okay, son. I like my hide pretty well." He waved with the gun. "Be seeing you." Then he tossed the dark weapon into the box and slammed the door.

XI

There was darkness, then bright sun. They stood on a street corner, and Summersby could read the signs as plainly as Watkins must have read them in the focusing lens of the matter transmitter on the unknown planet.

Broadway and 42nd Street. The five of them had clicked into being on the busiest corner of New York.

"That old crook," said Adam, gulping. "He focused us here for a gag."

"I look *awful*," gasped Mrs. Full, and Summersby, glancing at her, agreed. Like all of them, she had lost weight; her skin showed the effects of a week's washing without soap; and her skirt and blouse were mussed up, to say the least. All the men needed shaves. Calvin Full, recovering gradually from the shock of the goad, and still supported by Villa, looked like a Bowery wino.

"Is he coming?" asked Adam, addressing Summersby. "Will Watkins be along too?"

"I don't know," said Summersby. He stared up at as much of the sky as he could see beyond the block-high ads. "I hope so."

"My chili stand!" shouted Villa, suddenly awakening to the fact of New York about him. "That no-good relief man! I've got to see what he's done to it!" Pushing Calvin to Adam, who grasped him by an arm, the Mexican waved hurriedly. "Come and see me," he said to all of them. "I'll give you a bowl free." He hastened away into the crowd.

"We've got to see about our clothes at the hotel," said Mrs. Full. She sounded apologetic. "I hope we'll see you again, Adam, and Mr. Summersby."

"I doubt it," said Summersby. He looked at Full. "Coming out of it?" he asked.

"Thanks," said Cal, nodding. He took his wife's hand. "Gave you my address, didn't I?"

"I have it," said Summersby.

"Well, good-bye," said Mrs. Full.

"You did a fine job up there," said Adam Pierce. "I'm proud to have known you, ma'am."

"Thank you, Adam. Good-bye." They were gone.

"I suppose you'll be going too," said Adam, somewhat wistfully.

"I guess so. You'll go home?"

"I guess so," Adam repeated. "My folks will be sore. They'll never believe such a story. They'll think I ran wild or something."

Summersby, still looking upward, and wondering if he could be staring blindly at the planet which Watkins must be trying to leave even now, put a hand on his heart. "Was he right? They did fix up everyone else." He laughed. It was the first time he had laughed normally in seven months. "I could get into the rangers again," he said. "Adam, I've got to see a doctor. I've got to find out something."

"Yes, sir," said Adam unhappily. Summersby looked at him. "Really worried about your folks?"

"Yes, sir."

"I'll come home and tell them, if you like."

Adam said gratefully, "Mr. Summersby, you're a gentleman."

"No," said Summersby, "no."

"Yes, sir, you are. Can we wait just a minute more? Mr. Watkins might be along any minute now."

"We'll wait."

After a while Adam said, "Remember that first feed we got up there, pies and cookies and glass?"

"I remember it."

"They must have just aimed that machine at a bakery window here on Earth, and taken glass and all."

"That's it."

"Probably it was called a smash-and-grab robbery, down here." He kicked something, bent down and picked it up. It was the safe-cracker's gun. "I didn't think he'd carry one," said the boy. He looked closer at it. "God!"

"What is it?" Summersby shifted the briefcase and held out a hand. Adam laid the weapon in his big palm. "He must have won it at the park that day," Adam said. "That old crook! Old faker!"

Summersby held it up. It looked like a small automatic of blued steel, but it was plastic. He turned it over. A pencil-sharpener.

Summersby grunted. "A toy," he said, giving it back to Adam. "Nothing but a kid's toy."

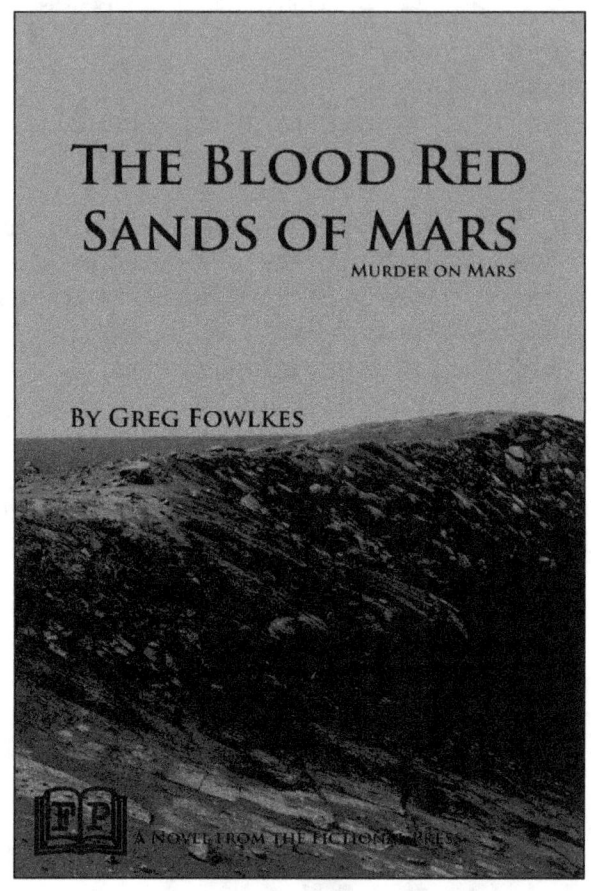

THE BLOOD RED SANDS OF MARS
MURDER ON MARS

A NOVEL BY GREG FOWLKES

THE BLOOD RED SANDS OF MARS

The wind was blowing again against the west wall of the hut. He could hear the grains of sand abrading the thin aluminum skin that protected him from the outside. Through the window, half frosted from the continuous onslaught of sand and dust, he could see clouds of dust obscuring the sky. The sky was a pastel pink, a color no sky had any right to be. The wind, despite its 120 kph. velocity, made only a thin howl as it blew over the half buried cylinder of the hut.

McKernan lay on his cot trying not to admit that he was awake. It was a losing battle. After a few minutes he surrendered and glanced over at the clock sitting on the crate next to his bed. The dim red digits of the LED display read 7:58. It was too early to get up, too late to go back to sleep. He rolled over, shivering at the cold. The temperature couldn't have been more than ten degrees Celsius inside the hut. For the twentieth time he thought to himself that he would have to fix the heater before winter—if he could get the parts. Either that, or put in more insulation—if he could find that. The cold finally forced the decision to get up.

Standing, he felt the cold plastic floor beneath his bare feet. With his foot he fished the worn and patched pants from beneath the cot and pulled them on. He dug underneath his pillow and came up with a switchblade knife that he stuck in his pocket before drawing on the turtleneck sweater that had lain next to his pants. The cold feel of the cloth did nothing to dispel the cold from his body. From the crate he picked up a shoulder holster with a small automatic pistol and put it on. McKernan drew the weapon, worked the slide once, and after examining it perfunctorily, placed it back in the holster. Satisfied, he pulled on a worn pair of leather boots and placed another knife in a sheathe between his skin and the boot top.

Dressed, he went over to the shelf that served as counter and table. He put a pan of beans onto the heating unit and got a soysteak from the small refrigerator that held up one end of the shelf. The steak went into the frying pan on the other heating element. An egg would have been nice, but at the current price of three dollars apiece it was an extravagance that he would have to put off for a while.

As the food cooked he drew a liter of water from the spigot in the corner of the hut and watered the plants in the garden under the window. The carrots and tomatoes were doing nicely. He smiled briefly because it would be good to have fresh vegetables for a change. The big, leafy oxygen plants were doing well, too. He would be able to cut down on his oxygen ration this month and save some money.

He took the beans off the heating element and replaced them with the coffee pot. The beans were still half cold, but he wasn't in the mood to hassle with them. He only had the two heating elements, and he didn't want to have to wait for his coffee. He forced down the beans and then wolfed down the steak. It almost tasted like real beef, but then maybe his memories were fading. As usual, the coffee tasted terrible and tepid, too. The air pressure in the hut was too low for water to boil properly.

He finished his meal and scraped the remnants of food into the pressure vessel that served as a compost heap. The gauge on its neighbor showed that he had almost half a tank of methane. He'd be able to sell that soon and use the money for something useful, like a still. Completing his rounds, the gauges on the life support systems showed that everything was still working at keeping him alive. He went back to the pots and scrubbed them clean with sand. That, at least, was plentiful and cheap.

He checked his watch against the clock. It was time to get going. Pulling on his jacket he went to the airlock at the corridor end of the hut. After checking the gauge to make sure that there was pressure on the other side, he undogged the latches and stepped through. Closing the door behind him, he repeated the process with the outer hatch, latching both doors behind him. The outer door he locked with a heavy padlock.

He had entered a low tubular corridor made of the same aluminum foil and plastic foam construction as the hut. The walls, however, were even thinner, and no pretense was made of heating it. He could see his breath condensing in front of him as he began to walk down its length. It was a hell of a way to live, he reflected, not for the first time. But then, it had been hell living in L.A. where he'd been born, with brown air, rats, a chronic shortage of water, and overcrowded tenements. He had made his choice, but sometimes it seemed as though life was a continual shiver.

The corridor was pierced at regular intervals by hatches identical to his own. The huts behind the hatches were identical, too, except for the modifications the owners had made to make them more livable. This part of the city was old, dating back a couple of decades to the first days of the settlement when it had been part of a scientific base. The scientists had departed, at least from that corridor, and been replaced by those who had the money to buy or rent the huts from the Trust Authority. Maintenance was pretty much left up to the residents.

Along the sides and overhead ran the pipes and conduits that pumped in the gases, liquids, and power necessary for sustaining life. The whole system looked as jury rigged and fragile as it actually was, though surprisingly few people died whenever the system failed. Martians were a cautious lot. One didn't talk much about injuries. Accidents on Mars didn't leave many.

A hundred meters down the tube he came to an airlock. Going through the same ritual that he had used on his front door, he went through to another length of corridor indistinguishable from the one he had just left. Continuing on, he passed through two more airlocks until he entered a corridor that sloped downward. The hatches were farther apart, and larger. Signs overhead indicated the businesses or functions that were carried out behind them. The air was warmer because the corridor was buried beneath the sand which provided insulation. At the end of the tunnel was a larger airlock set into a wall of fused silica bricks, the first substantial piece of construction he had met that morning.

Passing through the portal was like entering another world, which in a way he had. This was the public Mars, the planet seen by the corporation men and the officials of the Trust Authority. It was also the planet seen by tourists, the brave new colony, man's first outpost on another planet. The tourists didn't really care to see the hut town. They were part of the same world as the corporation men and the government types. It still took a great deal of money or power to reach Mars.

The difference was more than one of degree. For one thing, the temperature was a comfortable twenty. For another, the walls were flat and met the floors and ceilings at right angles, unlike the inflated skins of the huts and corridors. With a little imagination it could almost be an enclosed shopping mall on earth, though the presence of fused silica blocks was more prevalent than any architect would allow.

The most important difference, however, was the sight of people scurrying along. He hadn't met anyone in the outer corridors. People rarely lingered there because of the cold. Now, McKernan could see at least twenty people and it was still fairly early. No airlocks interrupted this corridor. Extending for two hundred meters in either direction, it was twenty meters wide and ten high, the largest enclosed volume on the planet. Arrayed along its length were the offices and store fronts of the corporations that owned Mars, as well as the more prosperous saloons and bordellos.

One day the Trust Authority promised that the whole city would be like that, with apartments and condominiums for the ordinary workers, but neither the Authority or the corporations had yet come up with the money. For the moment all that existed was the one street of a few blocks.

McKernan headed towards the Authority's offices which dominated one end of the mall, but turned aside at the last moment when he noticed that a small, dark doorway was open. He knew that he should resist the temptation, but he was not in a very disciplined mood. He went through the doorway into the darkness beyond.

Finnegan's was the only real, honest bar on Mars. There were any number of saloons and even a cocktail lounge in the Mars Sheraton, but only one quiet, dark place where a man could drink in peace. McKernan felt the need for some of that peace at the moment.

He sat down on one of the stools before the only mahogany bar on Mars. Finnegan, himself, was behind the bar, though in fact he almost always was, no matter what the hour. The bartender looked up and greeted the newcomer, "Good morning, constable. Beer or whiskey?"

"It's too early for beer. It's too early for whiskey, but give me a shot, anyway."

Finnegan poured out a shot glass of amber liquid and placed it before McKernan and then stood back polishing a glass while he studied the man opposite him.

McKernan knocked back half the glass before he spoke. When he did, there was a bitter edge to his voice. "Sometimes I wonder if it's worth it, Finnegan. I could be back on a planet fit for human life."

"Could you, now, constable?" Finnegan said, putting down the glass and picking up another in equally gleaming condition. "If mother earth was such a bed of roses, why are you here?"

He breathed on the glass and examined it against the light for a moment, then looked at McKernan with the same intentness. "You're here because you're not the sort to live off the dole or to spend your life with another man being your boss. Instead you'll spend your life trying to make this planet a fit place to live and retire in twenty years with a nice pension. Now drink up and get to work, laddy."

"Yeah, sure. Sorry to burden you with my problems. Early morning depression, I guess. See you." He finished off the shot and left five dollars in Authority script on the bar.

The bite of the whiskey so early in the morning didn't really help his disposition, but it did give him enough courage to make it to the office. The morning ritual at Finnegan's was becoming too much of a habit. His three years on Mars were beginning to show.

The jail wasn't in the brick part of the Authority building, but in the complex of pneumatic architecture that sprawled behind it. The huts were old—older than his own—but dated back to the days when governments had not begrudged a few billions for exploration, back before space had to show a profit. For that reason, they were sound and well insulated, though a bit tacky looking.

The jail consisted of two huts joined together, one for offices, the other for the two makeshift cells and storage. Ferris was the only one there when he walked in, a young kid, younger than he had been himself when he had come to Mars. He was still impressed enough with his responsibilities and had not yet been worn down by the grim realities to take his job in any way but seriously.

Ferris greeted him with a solemn, "Good morning, sir," with a stress on the sir. As a three year veteran of Mars, Ferris looked on his boss with more than a touch of awe.

"Anything exciting happen overnight?" McKernan didn't really expect much. A few fights in the saloon district, a knifing maybe if things got out of hand. Petty thievery, or perhaps not so petty. He looked at Ferris and saw a flash of excitement in his eyes that the younger man was trying hard to suppress in order to match the hard bitten image he had of his superior.

"Yes, sir. We've got a murder on our hands."

"Another knifing down at Thelma's?" he asked, naming an infamous saloon and bordello that figured in a quarter of all the police reports.

"No. A prospector was found out on his claim yesterday, over on the far side of Olympus Mons. He was shot, Inspector."

That was bad, McKernan thought. People on Mars weren't supposed to have guns. With the thin skins of most buildings and a hostile atmosphere outside that would support life exactly as long as you could hold your breath, they were dangerous, and not just to the targets. The Authority had made them illegal and the corporations had been more than willing to agree. They weren't easy to get—not something that could be picked up casually or made, like a knife. Even without the details it sounded like the work of a real criminal and not just a squabble over a claim or a woman.

"Okay. Let me have the report. I'll take a look at it."

He took the folder from Ferris who looked a bit crestfallen. He probably expects me to go rush off to the outside and track down the murderer like an Indian scout, McKernan thought. He'd learn in time. Mars was a big planet and a dangerous one, but because of its nature there were also very few places that a man could run to and none where he could hide indefinitely.

He was leafing through the report when he came to his door. For the thousandth time he read, "Inspector Erik McKernan, Chief Constable." Mother would have been proud, he thought sardonically. She had hated the L.A. cops like all the other residents of the barrio. He went through the door into the little cubicle that was his real home. There, sitting at his desk, he began to read the report, sketchy though it was, to look for some explanations.

Available now! Visit www.TheFictionalPress.com for more information, or buy it in both print and electronic format at your favorite online bookstore!

Also From Resurrected Press
SCIENCE FICTION AUTHORS RESURRECTED

FYFE RESURRECTED - THE STORIES OF H. B. FYFE
Stories from the Golden Age of Science Fiction by the author of D-99. dealing with the interaction of humans and aliens on far off worlds in ways that were as creative as they were imaginative.

SCHMITZ RESURRECTED - SELECTED STORIES OF JAMES H. SCHMITZ
Includes "An Incident on Route 12", "Watch the Sky", "The Other Likeness", "The Star Hyacinths", "Oneness", "The Winds of Time", "Ham Sandwich" and "Gone Fishing".

SHECKLY RESURRECTED - THE EARLY STORIES OF ROBERT SHECKLEY
Resurrected Press has collected some of the best of these from the 50's including "Warrior Race", "The Leech", "Watchbird", "Warm", "Diplomatic Immunity", "The Hour of Battle", "Besides Still Waters", "Keep Your Shape", "One Man's Poison", 'Ask a Foolish Question", "Cost of Living", "Death Wish Forever".

DICK RESURRECTED - THE EARLY STORIES OF PHILIP K. DICK
Early stories from the author of the novels that inspired "Blade Runner," "Total Recall," and "A Scanner Darkly".

HAMILTON RESURRECTED - CLASSIC STORIES OF EDMOND HAMILTON
Edmond Hamilton was one of the most popular writers during the 30's and 40's, the period that saw the first flowering of modern science fiction.

SMITH RESURRECTED - SELECTED STORIES OF EVELYN E. SMITH TON
During an era when women rarely appeared in science fiction magazines, Evelyn E. Smith appeared regularly in the pages of Galaxy and Fantastic Universe. Resurrected Press is proud to return these stories to print.

The Fictional Detective
by Greg Fowlkes

Who killed Ezekial O. Handler?

A beautiful dame, a hard-boiled private eye − and a dead body.

It started like any other case. When a famous writer dies in a mysterious car crash, private detective Frank Slade is called in to find answers, but all he finds is more questions. Who killed Ezekial Handler? Who is Janet Nielsen and why is she so interested in finding out? Who is leaving the neatly typed clues? And as Slade tries to find answers to these questions he starts to wonder if the ultimate answer will threaten his very existence.

Read about it in
The Fictional Detective

Visit www.thefictionaldetective.com

About Resurrected Press

This classic book was handcrafted by Resurrected Press. Resurrected Press is dedicated to bringing high quality classic books back to the readers who enjoy them. These are not scanned versions of the originals, but, rather, quality checked and edited books meant to be enjoyed!

Introducing The Fictional Press

The Fictional Press is a small, independent press specializing in the publication of fictional works by emerging authors. If you are interested in bringing your fictional works to life in print as well as electronically, contact us! We can help!